DOES
IT
HURT?

Cover Design: Emily Wittig
Formatting: Opulent Swag and Designs
First Edition: July 2022

DOES

IT

HURT?

DOES
IT
HURT?

TO BABY SHARK,
STEP ASIDE,
DADDY SHARK IS HERE NOW.

PLAYLIST

THEME SONG:
CHRIS ISAAK- WICKED GAME (JESSIE VILLA COVER)

ED SHEERAN- BAD HABITS
BILLIE EILISH- NDA
BILLIE EILISH- IDONTWANNABEYOUANYMORE
SASHA SLOAN- RUNAWAY
THE NEIGHBOURHOOD- SWEATER WEATHER
CROOSH (FEAT. IV)- LOST
SEETHER- WORDS AS WEAPONS
HEMMING- HARD ON MYSELF
ONEREPUBLIC (FEAT. TIMBALAND)- APOLOGIZE
RIGHTEOUS VENDETTA- A WAY OUT
TRANSVIOLET- UNDER
LANA DEL REY- BORN TO DIE
NOTHING,NOWHERE- REJECTER
EMAWK (FEAT. SOLACE)- PILOT
MAALA- BETTER LIFE
FRANK OCEAN- LOST
GLASS ANIMALS- HEAT WAVES
JOHNNY RAIN- HARVESTON LAKE
SEETHER (FEAT. AMY LEE)- BROKEN
KALLITECHNIS-SYNERGY

IMPORTANT NOTE

This is a dark romance that contains very triggering situations such as graphic violence and gore, graphic murder, graphic language, suicide ideation, mentions of suicide, depression and anxiety, PTSD, near-death situations, stranded in the middle of the ocean, dub/non-con, mentions of incest and pedophilia (not depicted), child abuse, mentions of rape and other forms of abuse, kidnapping, and explicit sexual situations for 18+. There are also particular kinks such as autassassinophilia (arousal by risk of being killed), breath play, degradation, and sadomasochism.

AUTHOR'S NOTE

I did work closely with someone from Italy for all aspects concerning Enzo's culture and language, but please note that some of the translations are contextual, and *not* literal. The translator did take some liberties as to portray the same meaning, even if they don't say the same thing literally. There is a glossary in the back of the book with the English text and these translations.

Enjoy!

SOME DAYS I'M THE OCEAN.

SOME DAYS I'M THE SHIP.

TONIGHT, I'M THE LIGHTHOUSE:

AT THE EDGE, ALONE, AND BURNING.

-Vasiliki

PROLOGUE

Sawyer

top staring at me, fucker.

My leg bounces profusely, and I force myself to stop for the millionth time. I'm making it obvious that I'm nervous, but how can I not be when my mother's cousin's husband's niece is staring at me?

She looks like she's seen a ghost, and I practically have been for the past six years. But if that were the case, I wouldn't need to get on this damn flight.

We're both sitting in chairs across from each other, waiting to board a plane to Indonesia. What the hell is she going there for anyway? It's nearly Christmas, for fuck's sake.

I suppose it could be a work trip considering she's wearing a skirt, a matching blazer, and Louboutin heels. Who travels in fucking Louboutin heels?

Doesn't matter. What matters is that she noticed me, and that's so not cool right now.

Sweat is pouring down my back, and I'm almost positive I have pit stains.

I'm trying to be inconspicuous, but so is she. Appearing nonchalant, yet not nonchalant *at all*, she slowly slides her phone out of her pocket.

Normally, not a red flag, but she also has pit stains, and she's glancing at me every two seconds.

Carefully, she brings the phone to her ear, attempting to hide it within her pin-straight hair. The strands are so thin, they're basically translucent—she's not hiding her phone beneath them like she thinks she is.

Bitch.

I have no idea how I'm supposed to escape with her watching, but I don't have a choice. It's either I leave, or they find me.

Fuck being inconspicuous, my life is on the line. I grab my carry-on bag, stand, and attempt to calmly walk away.

"Hey!" she calls, but fuck that and fuck her. I slip through the crowd, on the verge of tears. I've put off leaving the country for so long, convinced I'd be caught, and that's precisely what might happen.

Heart racing, I head directly to the gift shop, purchase a zip-up hoodie, along with sweats and a ball cap, then find a bathroom to change in, all the while checking over my shoulder.

Even the restroom is crowded, so I keep my head down and quickly duck into a stall. Hands shaking, I wind my hair into a low bun, shove the hat over the top, and then slip on the jacket, flipping the hood over my head to cover the rest of my hair. Lastly, I pull the sweats on over my shorts, already sweating from the layers and adrenaline.

Then, I wash my hands and rush to the ticket counter, out of breath and practically panting in the agent's face. She looks up at me, startled by my sudden presence.

"May I hel—"

"I need a ticket to the next flight out," I interrupt, nearly tripping over my words.

She blinks at me, then focuses on her computer screen, clicking around with her mouse and tapping a few keys.

"A flight to Indone—"

"Not that one," I cut in again. "A different one."

She shoots me a glare. I'm pissing her off, but I'm sure a big glass of red wine will soothe her woes, whereas I will definitely be meeting my maker if I'm caught.

"A flight to Australia is departing in forty minutes."

"Sold," I say, slapping a wad of cash and my ID on the counter. Giving me an unimpressed look, she processes the ticket and counts through the money. Albeit very fucking slowly.

"You're $8.09 short," she clips.

I'm not usually a snappy person with customer service. They deal with enough shit. That being said, if I get caught over $8.09, I'm pointing directly at her and screaming *she did it* before bolting.

Muttering beneath my breath, I fish out a ten-dollar bill from my pocket and slap it on the counter.

Giving me the evil eye, she takes the bill and continues.

I'm constantly checking over my shoulder, but thankfully, the airport is crowded, and I don't see any angry faces wearing a uniform and a gun headed my way yet.

"Do you have any luggage?"

"No, just my carry-on," I reply.

After a few more minutes, she finally slides the ticket to me, along with my change and ID.

"Gate 102. Terminal B."

I snatch them from the counter, clip out a quick *thank you*, and take off toward the shuttle, my duffel bag slapping against my legs.

My heart is beating nearly out of my damn mouth by the time I make it through TSA, off the shuttle that takes me to the terminal, and ultimately reach the gate. It took fucking forever, and they've already called my name over the speaker. I'm panicking that I won't make it, and they're literally about to close the door when I finally arrive at the gate.

"Wait!" I shout.

The employee sees me coming, and I swear to God, he deserves a blowjob for kindly stepping aside and allowing me through. Even as I run down the hallway to get to the plane, I'm checking over my shoulder.

My heart refuses to return to its designated area until the plane takes off.

Even then, I'm waiting for air traffic control to stop the plane and tell them a fugitive is on board.

CHAPTER 1

Sawyer

Cancer tastes like shit.

I suck in deeply, menthol gliding past my tongue and filling my lungs with manufactured chemicals. How many of these do I have to smoke before cancer invades my cells, metastasizing until I'm ridden with disease?

My throat tightens and revolts against the tobacco, forcing out a harsh cough. I pull the cigarette away and stare at it, my face twisted in disgust as smoke filters out of my nose and mouth. I rock my hand, viewing it from different angles.

A bright orange glow radiates from the tip, gray ash eating at the paper.

Fire is on the tip, flaring as if to entice me to wrap my lips back around it.

Nope.

Still isn't appealing.

A tanned hand reaches out, nabbing the cigarette before I can stub it on the sand.

"Give me that before you waste it."

I frown. How flammable is sand? I bet not at all. It's too dense—nothing to feed the oxygen. Not unless I pour gasoline all over it. I bet it'd make the beach prettier, though.

Fire on the shoreline of a vast, blue ocean? Who wouldn't want to see that? The salty sea breeze blows softly, coercing the blonde, curly tendrils around my face into a sensual dance. I tuck the locks behind my ear, too tired to pull them back into the loose knot tied low on my head.

I look over to the guy sitting next to me. His overgrown sandy hair curls against the nape of his neck and the dagger tattoo behind his ear is alluring against his sun-kissed skin. All of his tattoos are—he's covered in them.

I still don't know his name, but his cock is nice, and that's all that really matters. Well, that, and his murderous nicotine. He's not the type I usually go for, but I was feeling lonely and entertained the first guy who didn't make me nauseous.

"What kind of cancer do you think you'll get from that?" I ask, nodding toward the cigarette in his hand.

He quirks a thick brow, his pretty blue eyes sparkling in the morning glow. "I dunno. Lung cancer is too typical. Throat?"

"Do you think you'll die?"

He barks out a short laugh. "I fucking hope so."

I nod, reaching out my hand for him to give it back to me. He looks at me like I'm strange, a beat passing before he does as I ask.

Another inhale, and it tastes a little better with the reminder that I'm ingesting death into my lungs.

Yeah, that tastes *much* better.

Loud waves crash up the shore, rolling up and reaching toward my chipped baby blue painted toes with outstretched claws, before sinking back down and dragging sand with them.

The ocean is beautiful. But it's also unforgivable. Within seconds, it can turn against you. Drag you down so violently, you don't know which way is up, and feed you into its cavernous mouth until you drown or end up between the teeth of something much scarier.

I inhale again deeply, closing my eyes as I feel the smoke fill my lungs and stick inside of them.

Cigarettes are also unforgivable, with the way they eat at you from the inside out. Kill you slowly, and then all at once.

I decide I like the ocean, and I like cigarettes.

Because I... I am also unforgivable.

"That will be $68.10," the cashier says pleasantly, a smile on his face.

"For a pregnancy test and a pack of cigarettes?" I ask incredulously.

The guy chuckles. "'Fraid so."

"That's literally robbery," I mutter, but I'm not sure if he heard me because he's still smiling.

I'd love to siphon some of that happiness for myself, but after three weeks in Port Valen, Australia, I don't feel any safer than I did in America.

After landing, I checked the news online, and authorities were informed that I was possibly sighted at the airport and presumed to have escaped on a plane. The lady at the ticket counter may or may not be able to identify me and confirm my flight to Australia, regardless of using a different name. At the very least, she could say I was acting suspicious and give them a reason to look.

I'm not safe in this country—they'd turn me in to U.S. authorities if caught—but it's too risky to fly to a country that'd grant me mercy. So, I've resigned myself to the fact that I'm staying here for a while yet, and that it's time to take on the life of someone else again.

There are worse places to be, I suppose.

Port Valen is a beautiful seaside town on the east coast, surrounded by a bright aqua blue ocean and crowded with tourists looking to shark dive or explore the coral reefs. Outside of the beach, it's rich with massive waterfalls and diving holes surrounded by wildlife and miles of bright forests, attracting hikers from around the world.

It's also expensive as hell here.

I dig through my ratty coin purse, strings frayed at the edges and getting caught in the zipper. I count out the bills and coins, berating myself for winding up in this situation. Precious money down the drain because I can hardly stand to be alone, plus the extra cost since now I feel the need to get a buzz just to take the edge off.

Problem is, that edge is sharp and jagged, and there's not a drug in this world that will prevent it from cutting me.

"Here ya go," I tell him, forcing a smile on my numb face. Feels like when Mom used to take me to the dentist, and I walked out with lidocaine injected in my mouth and no control over my facial muscles. I always used to giggle at the odd feeling, but I don't feel much like laughing now.

He hands me the change and my purchases, another smile on his face. Now it's almost annoying how happy he is.

"Have a good day," he chirps.

"Thanks," I murmur.

I snatch the sack and rush toward the exit of the grocery store, my bright orange flip-flops clacking against the dirty white tile.

This stupid fucking pregnancy test really cut into the little allowance I give myself. Still, I'd rather know if a little alien is invading my body than live in fear, obsessively checking my stomach on any reflective surface I come by just to see if it grew an inch.

I live with enough fear, I don't need any more.

They can't find you, Sawyer. You're safe.

I shake my head, persistent on staying in the cold, lonely place where the terror resides. *Am I safe?*

If my insides are being invaded by an alien, that will make my life that much harder. I can't take care of a child *and* provide for myself. I'm barely doing that as it is, and my means for doing so are... God, they're awful.

My thoughts spiral, picturing a little blonde baby in my arms, screaming at the top of its lungs because they're hungry and suffering from diaper rash or something. I'd have to give the baby up for adoption, no question.

But it'd break my fucking heart. Or whatever is left of it.

My breathing is starting to escalate, and I work to control it, fighting to fill my tightening lungs. Bright sunlight warms my cheeks as I storm out of the automatic doors, run out of the parking lot, and onto the sidewalk, my dollar store flip-flops threatening to snap from my speed.

I inhale deeply, desperately sucking in oxygen, but it's clogging my throat.

My period is a week late, though I've been stressed. Really stressed. I've never prayed so much—hovering over a toilet with my thumbs hooked in my shorts, begging the gods to give me a reason to use the tampon in my hand.

I think Heaven has me on their shitlist.

Which is such bullshit, even though I can't blame the angels for rebuking me in the name of the Lord.

The taste of the salty ocean lingers in the air, coating my tongue as I continue to suck in deep breaths and feel my tightened chest loosen just a bit. Something about the smell of the sea always soothes my tortured lungs, whether it's because I'm abusing them with a panic attack or cigarette smoke.

It's something I'll mourn when I eventually move on to the next destination.

For now, I appreciate the beauty of Port Valen while I can. Greenery surrounds the streets, along with bright pops of pink, orange, and purples from flowers. Massive cliffs are far behind me, and though miles away, their imposing structures are not to be ignored.

A group of women pass by in their thong bikinis and tops, and I can't help but fall in love with how laid-back this town is.

Even more dangerous, I'm falling in love with Port Valen as a whole, despite the man-eating spiders that inhabit this country.

I speed walk toward the bus stop and plop on the bench with a shaky exhale, the plastic bag dangling between my spread legs. There's a magpie circling overhead, setting me further on edge. I've learned the hard way that the demon birds like to swoop down and attack unprovoked. I'm still traumatized from the last one and pray the bus gets here quicker than scheduled.

I could've driven Senile Suzy, the van I bought last week. It's an old, buttery-yellow Volkswagen—the ones you'd see hippies back in the 70s driving around. Living out of a van is more ideal than a hotel, and I got incredibly lucky to find one for much cheaper than it's worth. He claimed it was his daughter's who had passed away, and he just wanted it gone.

I don't have my license here anyway, and I'm not confident enough to drive on the opposite side of the road. I'm convinced I'll perish from a car wreck or get pulled over and caught driving without a license.

On cue, the magpie squawks as if to warn me that taking my chances with Senile Suzy might be safer, but thankfully, it flies elsewhere.

Hands shaking from the residual anxiety, I dig through the bag and pluck out the pack of cigarettes. I shouldn't be smoking these in my possible predicament, yet the thought of death is too enticing, and I'm too scared to do anything else.

I'm ashamed of myself, but I don't think I know what it's like to feel anything else.

Don't make it a habit, Sawyer. You have enough of those.

Just as I slide one out and stick it in my mouth, I realize two things. I forgot to buy a lighter, and there's somebody sitting next to me, the weight of their stare hardening on my face like dried clay.

I turn to find an older man with deep brown skin holding out an orange lighter as bright as my flip-flops, his thumb poised on the striker and ready to ignite it for me. He's wearing an old white shirt and an aged khaki-colored ball cap on his head. Sweat gleams down the side of his face, but he smells like Old Spice and salt.

Smiling, I lean forward, and he flicks it. I'm just as mesmerized by the fire as I am by watching it eat at the flimsy paper. Smoke coils from the stick into the salty air, burning my eyes as it wafts into my face.

"Thank you," I say, waving away the smoke. "Do you want one?"

"Sure," he says. I hand him a cigarette and watch him closely as he lights his own, an orange glow blaring as he inhales.

"Been trying to cut back on smoking but can never seem to let 'em go for good," he muses conversationally.

A terrible problem to have, and one I shouldn't inflict on myself, but then a wave of euphoria washes over me, and I suppose it's not so bad. It won't last more than a minute, however it makes the sharp edge bearable, and that's all I need right now. That, and good company.

"When have we ever been able to let go of the things that hurt us most?" I mutter.

"Well, you got me there."

I grin. "What's your name?" I ask, attempting to blow out a smoky O but failing miserably.

He chuckles, the sound husky. "Can't remember the last time a pretty young lady asked me my name. Name's Simon."

Normally, an old, strange man calling me pretty would have me getting up and walking away without a backward glance, but the way he says it doesn't make me uncomfortable. In fact, it makes me feel a little like what a home is supposed to feel like. Warm and welcoming. Safe.

That sense of comfort lulls me into doing something I rarely do. Something I *never* do. I give him my real name.

"Sawyer. Thanks for keeping me company, Simon."

A beat of silence passes, and then, "Want to see my new tattoo?"

Surprise has me pausing for a brief second, the cigarette suspended halfway to my mouth before I shoot out a quick, "I'd love to," and then trap the filter in the corner of my lips.

He rolls up his cargo shorts and shows me his new ink. Black, uneven lines make up the words "Fuck You" stacked in the middle of his thigh, still puffy and irritated. This time, I genuinely am caught off guard.

Astonished laughter bursts from my throat, and I almost lose my cigarette in the process, but I wouldn't have cared if I did.

"Oh my God, I love that. Probably more than my favorite toe. Did that hurt?" I ask, leaning closer to inspect the ink. It's obviously not professionally done—in fact, it's a pretty shit job—but I think that's what I like most about it.

"Nah," he says, waving a hand. "It's therapeutic. Not sure what you mean by a favorite toe, though."

I hold up my left foot and point to it. "My pinkie toe is really cute, don't you think?"

He leans over and inspects it closely. "You're right. I like that toe, too."

Smiling, I drop my foot and stare down at the misshapen words. I'm in love with it. I could always use a little therapy in the form of a reckless—and slightly manic—decision.

I suck in another mouthful of smoke and blow it out, trying to fight the impulse rising inside of me.

"Where did you get that?"

He shrugs. "I did it myself. Ever heard of *tebori*?"

I shake my head, so he digs in his pocket and pulls out a vial of black ink and a handful of sealed needles.

I raise my brows, wondering why he would carry this stuff with him, but glad that he's at least using unused needles.

"It's a traditional Japanese method. People call 'em stick and poke tattoos," he explains.

"How does it work?"

He explains the process to me, which sounds pretty simple. So simple, that I consider doing one myself. I don't have any tattoos nor the luxury of going to a shop and paying for one.

Just as I open my mouth to ask where he got the supplies from, he cuts in, "You want me to do one for you?"

I cock my head at him, a grin clawing its way up my cheeks.

"Yeah," I say, nodding my head, deciding the idea of a stranger giving me a tattoo at a bus stop is too good to pass up. It's the perfect kind of spontaneity I need. "What do you want for it?"

He nods toward my plastic bag. "That pack of cigs will be enough."

The look he casts me gives me the distinct feeling that he's more interested in keeping me from smoking them rather than smoking them himself. I wonder if he noticed what else was in the bag.

I smile. "Deal. I want one just like yours. Same place, too. We can match."

I like the idea of having a matching tattoo with Simon. I guess it makes me feel like I've found a friend in my lonely little world and will have someone to remember when I eventually leave.

More importantly, I like the message. Because really, those exact words cross my mind every day. What better phrase to get tattooed than my daily mantra?

He grins, showcasing slightly crooked teeth, and motions for me to turn my thigh toward him. Cutoff shorts are my everyday attire here, so he'll be able to put one in the same place as his easily.

The bus is approaching, so we'll miss our ride, but another bus will show up in thirty minutes—plenty of time to get my first tattoo.

He uncaps the vial and pours out a tiny bit of inky black liquid into the lid, and then tears open the package with a new needle.

"Octopus ink," he tells me. "Best ink you can get."

I nod, though I don't necessarily care. Everything about this is unsanitary anyway. If my body rejects it, it will make a pretty cool scar. Though I've always really liked octopi, so I guess it'll be nice to have a part of them injected into me.

They can disappear so easily, camouflage themselves to blend in with their surroundings, and that's all I've really wanted in life. Maybe with this new tattoo, I can pretend that its ink corroded everything that makes me human and will allow me to disappear just like them.

I frown, knowing it's never like the movies where a lonely kid gains an incredible superpower. I think I resent octopi a little, too.

My new friend leans down close to my thigh, his brown eyes never straying from his task as his surprisingly steady hand meticulously pokes ink into my skin. The sharp pinpricks release all kinds of endorphins into my system, and I decide here, and now, that I'm addicted to tattoos.

This is better than cigarettes, though since they're his now, he does allow me to smoke one more during the process. To take the edge off, he says.

A few more people join us, and it makes me laugh when none of them look the least bit surprised to see a girl getting a *tebori* tattoo while waiting for the bus, as if this is a common occurrence in Port Valen. One guy even comes over and asks for one of his own, but Simon tells him to find him another day.

The whole experience is odd, but it's brought me happiness, and that foreign feeling is better than sex. I experience so little joy, and too often, strange men crowd over me and invade my body.

Most importantly, it's made me forget.

Twenty-five minutes later, Simon straightens up, his face contorting in pain and his back cracking from being locked in an uncomfortable position for so long.

I feel bad for the pain I caused him, and he must note the expression on my face because he shoots me a stern look, much like how a father would when scolding their child. "Don't you feel bad for me, young lady. It's a blessing to be old, and every blessing is a little bittersweet."

I still feel bad, but I nod and lean down to examine my tattoo. My thigh is bright red and irritated, amplifying the harsh lines.

Fuck You, in bold black letters, though mine looks a little neater than his. Regardless, they're still uneven and wobbly, and I'm relieved about it. That's why I love it so much.

"It's perfect."

"Imperfect," he corrects, eyeing his work.

"Perfectly imperfect," I compromise, smiling big at him. My cheeks hurt from how widely they're being stretched, but just like every time that needle poked through my skin, the pain feels good. "All the best things are."

He lights another cig and leans back like he doesn't have a care in the world. Simon looks like he's lived his life very thoroughly, and I want to know what led him to this bus stop, giving a strange girl a tattoo on a Tuesday afternoon.

"You're right," he concedes. "You're also very strange." I grin wider when he echoes my exact thoughts.

"So are you, Simon. So are you." The look we share speaks volumes—we're both content with being strange.

Right then, the bus pulls up, the engine rumbling loudly. When the doors hiss and then glide open, I stand up and offer my elbow to him, as if I'm escorting him to a ball.

He waves his hand, shooing me on.

"I prefer to walk. My old bones need the movement, or else they'll lock up forever."

My brows draw in. "Then why were you sitting at the bus stop?"

He shrugs. "I was passing by, and you looked like you needed a friend."

Dropping my elbow, a weird piercing feeling stabs me in the chest. Disappointment.

I wanted to talk to Simon more. Ask him questions and learn more about the man behind the worn clothes and octopus ink.

He's observant, too, once more noting the expression on my face. Or maybe I just wear my feelings on my sleeve too much.

"We'll cross paths again, Sawyer. Life has a funny way of throwing people into your path when you're meant to collide. It's up to you to choose to make it permanent."

"Permanence," I mutter, tasting the foreign word on my tongue. "You're already permanent, Simon, just as much as this tattoo."

He smiles at me, a knowing twinkle in his eye.

"Then I'll see you soon, won't I?"

Feeling a tad better, I pick up my plastic bag, and the rustle of its contents reminds me of what else is in it. The small grin on my face slips. Simon will no longer distract me from my impending situation, and suddenly, I'm really dreading this ride alone.

"I hope so. Nice meeting you, Simon."

And then I turn, my thigh burning as I make my way onto the bus. I put my coins in the slot and find a seat far in the back. The faux leather is hot and sticky against the backs of my thighs, but I hardly notice.

I face the window, getting one last glimpse of Simon waving at me before the bus takes off.

At least I didn't have to go to a shop and use a credit card or take out any more money. I'm only giving myself a couple more days before it's time to grab a drink.

Then, I'll start over as someone else.

Not Sawyer Bennett, but someone who wishes they never met her.

CHAPTER 2

Sawyer

*J*amie Harris.

I stare at the ID for a brief second before sliding it over to the bartender. He glances at the card, back to me, and then at the card again.

"You're American," he notes.

"Unfortunately," is my answer.

"You don't look twenty-nine," he comments, before returning the card. That's insulting because I'm only a year younger than what the ID says.

I force a smile. "I'm terribly sorry for not passing your standards on what a woman of twenty-nine years should look like. Thank my skincare routine. Can I have my drink now?"

The bartender rolls his eyes before moving away to make said drink. The second he steps away, I deflate. My chest is tight with anxiety, but I don't dare let that show.

That's my face on the ID, but not my name.

Jamie Harris is a successful business owner in Los Angeles, California, has a stellar credit score, and a credit card limit of a whopping fifty-thousand dollars.

He's also a man and doing quite well for himself.

Well, I suppose it's *me* that's doing well for myself now.

However, I have no plans to spend all that money—not more than absolutely necessary. Before flying here, I took out enough cash to last me a while.

All of my victims are men, and most of them have unisex names, making it easier for me to impersonate them. I've also slept with almost every one of them. Some... I didn't really want to, and my skin crawled with every touch. But it was necessary to take what I needed.

I don't have the skills to do it online, so the good old-fashioned way is my only method. And in order to get close enough to obtain their private information—they have to take me home.

I could get a job, but that would mean either stealing the identity of a dead person that no one knows is dead or using my real name, and both make me want to fucking vomit. If I'm being honest, stealing other people's lives, to begin with, makes me want to die.

I'm a shit person, no doubt about that. But I'm not a sociopath, either. I don't lack empathy, and I'm not guilt-free.

Nevertheless, no one can know where I am. *Who* I am.

So *no*, I can't sleep at night, nor do I look myself in the mirror.

But I'm doing what I can—the only thing I know how to do to survive.

The bartender comes back with my vodka and Sprite and slides it over, shooting me a disgruntled look.

"What's your name?" I ask, sipping on my drink and instantly smiling. For someone who doesn't seem to believe me, he made the drink awfully strong.

Which I'm glad for, considering this is the only drink I plan on buying. I can't risk getting drunk. Not when I'm working tonight and need to have all my wits.

Though I didn't come here only to work, but to celebrate as well. The pregnancy test came back negative. After that scare, I immediately got an

IUD. It cost me money that I didn't want to spend, but it's a hell of a lot cheaper than a child. No babies or periods for the foreseeable future, and that's something to definitely fucking celebrate.

The nurse at the clinic confirmed that my period is most likely late due to stress and also pointed out a few other health concerns. Apparently, I'm underweight, and hardly being able to eat certainly doesn't help.

While Jamie's credit limit would allow me to buy a brand-new car if I wanted, I can't bring myself to buy more than the bare minimum. Once I leave a place, I never use their card again in case they figure out who I am and get the police to track me down. Don't know if that's possible or not, but my paranoia won't allow it otherwise.

"I have a busy bar to run," is his answer. I glance both ways down said bar, spotting not a single soul. It's one o'clock in the afternoon on a Thursday. This bar is shit, and apparently, the bartender's attitude isn't any better than the outdated décor.

"You really don't like me. Why?"

"You give me a feral dog vibe."

My mouth parts, before a bout of shocked laughter bursts from my throat. "A feral dog?" I repeat incredulously. It's so true that I can't even be offended. I rest my chin on my hand, a grin on my face. "Do tell."

He rests both arms on the bar and leans down. "You're destructive and uncontrollable."

"You must be a psychologist," I return dryly.

"I just know trouble when I see it."

I tighten my lips and then shrug, taking another sip instead of giving him a verbal answer. Still not wrong.

He eyes me, waiting for a response. When I only take another sip, looking him straight in the eye as I do, he nods as if confirming something to himself.

"You're scared. That makes you dangerous," he finishes. My expression drops, and with that validation, he clicks his tongue, slowly sliding his arms from the bar and walking away.

To tend to the ghosts, I suppose, since there's still nobody fucking here.

Or at least I thought so.

"Didn't you know? A drink comes with free therapy these days."

The deep, accented voice from behind me is startling, though it's not the familiar Australian accent I'm used to hearing. I jump, twist in the barstool, and take one look, then immediately turn back around.

"Nope. I could get pregnant just looking at you. Go away."

He grunts. "Isn't that a rite of passage to manhood? Knock a girl up and leave?"

I snort. "That's what they seem to think."

The man takes a seat next to me, enveloping me in the smell of the ocean and a hint of sandalwood. He's wearing board shorts and a black tank top— and what man wears a tank top and gets away with it? Maybe because he possesses the most delicious arms I've ever seen.

He's exactly the type of guy that I stay away from. I prefer to go for the men who are dressed in suits and ties and wear mortgages on their wrists. The type that is so overworked and stressed they pass out after fifteen seconds of... well, whatever *they* consider sex.

This man next to me? I'd have to work hard to tire him out, and by the time I accomplish that, then *I'd* be too fucking tired to do anything else.

He's dangerous.

I lean into him, nearly pressing my nose to his muscular bicep, and inhale deeply, rolling my eyes to the back of my head.

"You smell good, too," I groan. "Get away."

I angrily snatch my drink, seriously mad about how tempting he is. I peek at him, enraptured as he shakes his head, clearly annoyed. Yet, he doesn't move away.

"Don't sniff me."

I raise my brows. I've never been able to arch just one, and I always wished

I could. It'd make my next response extra flavorful. "Then leave."

The bartender said I was dangerous, but this man embodies danger. His hair is buzzed close to the scalp—short little spikes that would probably feel incredible against my hands—hazel eyes with a dark splotch on the right one, and deeply tanned skin. A light dusting of hair is scattered across his sharp jawline, accentuating the near-criminal look he's got going on.

Body of a Greek god? Check.

Could ruin my life with just the tip? Check.

Has a permanent scowl and carries himself like he hates the world? Just fuck me already.

"Make me," he retorts, tipping his chin at the bartender. The direct challenge in his tone causes shivers to run down my spine, even if it does sound condescending. Doesn't stop me from needing to clench my thighs.

Clearing my throat, I say, "I'd rather not embarrass you in front of company."

His gaze slowly slides to mine, a stoic expression on his stupidly handsome face. "Do I look like I have anything to be embarrassed about?"

Before I can reply, the bartender approaches, his demeanor much less feral, while the asshole next to me orders his drink. He doesn't even get carded.

I scoff. *Men.* They all suck.

I lean toward the bartender. "'Scuse me. This man—" I pause and look to the side. "What's your name?"

"Enzo," he supplies readily, as if I'm not about to tattle on him. I scowl. He has a ridiculously sexy name.

"*Enzo* is bothering me," I say, looking back to the bartender and nodding my head toward the culprit. "I'm scared for my life."

I swiftly turn to Enzo and add in a quick, "My name's Jamie, by the way, thanks for asking," before facing the bartender again, giving him an expectant look.

All I get is an eye roll from him before he walks away. I slump, and my new companion chuckles deeply from beside me.

"He really doesn't like you."

"I know!" I say, throwing up my hands. "Never hurt a fly."

I nearly choke on the blatant lie, and my mood plummets with the reminder that I only hurt people for a living.

Seeming to notice the sudden change in my demeanor, he flicks his gaze at me. I'm not too fond of the way he's observing me. I shift in my seat, my thighs sticking to the cheap leather.

"I'm going to move away now," I warn him.

He stares at me, and I glare at my empty drink. I don't move. Not even an inch. And he just lets me get swept away in the tornado in my brain.

"How does another drink sound instead?"

"So, you're telling me that you swim with *sharks*? As in the big scary monsters in the ocean that eat people?"

He shoots me a droll look, unimpressed with my assessment.

"They don't *eat* people. You're more likely to get in a car accident than get bit by a shark."

"Really, that lame ol' statistic? They say that with everything." I deepen my voice mockingly and say, "You're more likely to get in a car accident than a plane crash. Why don't you make it more interesting and say you're more likely to get killed by a falling coconut?"

He shakes his head, though there's a glimmer in his eye while the corner of his mouth turns up ever so slightly, and in that moment, my soul leaves my body.

He has dimples.

Fuck me. Not cool.

It's also the first time I got him to smile. Or at least, that's what I'm telling myself. I'd barely call it amusement any other time.

Enzo may act annoyed with me, but he secretly enjoys my company. A man like him wouldn't force himself to stay if he didn't want to. In fact, I think he'd find enjoyment out of telling me to fuck off.

"It's true," he shrugs. "Sharks are very misunderstood, and the media portrays them as man-eating beasts, but that's not the case at all. They're curious animals that commonly mistake humans for seals. Sharks don't enjoy the taste of us."

"So, you're saying that if I got in the water with a shark, it wouldn't go *Jaws* on me?"

He hoods his eyes, and I know he doesn't mean for it to appear seductive, but it's the most heart-turning look I've ever had aimed my way.

My thighs have long since started to ache from constantly keeping them clenched in the past two hours Enzo and I have been talking. But it also goes beyond physical. Something about him draws me in, has me hanging on his every word, and makes it impossible to look away.

Maybe it's the alcohol. Or maybe it's not.

He stares deeply into my eyes when I speak; I've never felt so heard. The best part—he doesn't offer unsolicited advice or lackluster comfort. He just... listens, and attentively at that. Like the next thing out of my mouth just might be the cure for cancer. Too bad I *am* the fucking cancer.

We're both slightly buzzed now, and while he's not exactly the nicest, he's easy to talk to.

I like that he speaks as if he's dying and doesn't have time to be pleasant when he has no fucking interest in doing so. He doesn't waste time on false narratives and assurances. He's the type that will sit next to you because he wants to and stays in a conversation because he cares enough to know what you're going to say next.

He's intentional.

And somehow, it's made for a very intriguing conversation.

"It wouldn't put a personal hit out on you. But at the end of the day, they're wild animals and need to be respected. They can be temperamental and territorial and will attack if you agitate them or if they mistake you for food." He shrugs. "But more often than not, they'll just keep on swimming."

I rest my chin on my hand, enraptured by how he talks. He's passionate about his job. His hazel eyes are sparkling with excitement, he talks with his hands when he gets really fired up, and there's always a trace of a dimple on his right side when he speaks about his profession, as if he knows something the rest of the world doesn't.

I guess, in a way, he does. He knows what it's like to swim alongside one of the world's oldest and most feared predators, and not many could say the same.

He may not have the best of manners, but I can admire his passion. The only thing I've ever been passionate about is surviving, and even then, I feel like giving up most days.

"Have you ever been bitten?"

"Not by a shark," he drawls. I do a double take, sensing the innuendo within his words.

"You say that like you enjoy being bitten by not-sharks."

He arches a brow, a slight grin pushing that dimple deeper into his cheek. He can arch one brow. Suppose it's no surprise. God has always played favorites.

"Is there a reason not to?"

I sigh loudly. "Stop trying to knock me up, Enzo. We're not even friends." I pick up my drink and finish it off just to distract myself from testing his theory.

"I'll try my best," he states dryly.

"And I will accept nothing less. The only type of daddy I'm interested in is the sugary ones."

"Would you like to go write your number on the bathroom wall?" he proposes. "Don't think whoever calls would be the type to take home to your parents, though."

His words are innocent, but they create a stabbing pain in my chest anyway. Sharp enough to cause me to set my glass down a little too roughly.

Noticing the shift in my mood, he sets his drink down and looks at me. Just... looks at me. Waiting without asking.

I force a smile and shrug easily. "Don't have those."

"No family?"

"Just me."

Again, he waits quietly while I fiddle with the wet napkin soaking up the perspiration from the ice in my cup.

"I had them until me and my brother, Kevin, were eighteen. They were driving home drunk and fighting like they always did. Probably because Dad got too handsy with another woman again. They went off a bridge and didn't come back up until the next day. Found scratch marks all over Dad's face from her nails, and both of their alcohol levels were high."

He nods slowly, then asks, "Twins?"

"Yeah," I confirm quietly. "Kev and I were twins. But now it's just me." I finish the statement with a broad smile, signaling the end of that depressing conversation.

He casts an indecipherable look my way but ultimately says, "Come on, I want to show you something." He nods his head toward the exit. "I don't want to spend my entire fucking day in this shitty bar."

Valid. So, I pick up his drink and finish it off.

Whiskey. Gross.

"You're really rude," Enzo observes, standing up and looking down at me with an unimpressed quirk to his brow.

He's so fucking tall. Like, he has a solid foot on me.

"And you're a mammoth," I retort.

The bartender—who finally relented and told me his name is Austin—

snatches the glasses while passing by without a glance, even as Enzo fishes out his wallet to slip out some bills and slap them down on the bar to cover our tab.

"You're annoying."

Not the first time I've heard that one.

"Does that mean you're canceling our date?" I ask, a hint of hope in my tone. As much as I *need* Enzo to take me home—I always hate what comes after.

"It's not a date. But, no, if you want out, then leave by yourself like a big girl."

God, he's mean. Why do I like it?

"Whatever. Let me just get the money for—"

"You put any money out and I'll shove it down your throat," he warns, his voice deepening dangerously.

My eyes snap to him, round with shock.

"Jesus, if you want to be a gentleman, just say that. Weirdo."

He ignores me, and brushes past, heading toward the exit without a backward glance. The dickhead just assumes that I'll follow him.

Well.

He's right.

I've never been one to possess self-control. I hop off the barstool and hurry after him, my flip-flops clacking against the sticky floor as I work to catch up to him.

"I appreciate your unreasonably fast pace," I pant as we emerge into the hot Australian sun. I squint, the blaring light stabbing at my sensitive eyes. "Doesn't waste any time. I like that. I'm a busy woman, you know?"

I'm already sweating, his long legs eating up an ungodly amount of space far quicker than my little legs can handle.

"Somehow, I doubt that."

CHAPTER 3

Sawyer

"Why do people say the universe makes them feel small but never say that about waterfalls?"

"Probably because they feel waterfalls can be conquered. But no one will ever conquer the universe."

I jut out my bottom lip, considering his response. "The ocean hasn't been conquered. People don't say that about them, either."

He scoffs. "Those people have never been in the middle of the ocean then."

Fishing out his wallet, Enzo tosses it on the ground before reaching behind his head, grabbing the back of his shirt and pulling it off. My mouth dries as he drops the material to the wet rock, wondering how he can make it so a stone retains moisture better than me.

He's only wearing black swim shorts, leaving far too many inches of skin exposed. Every muscle that shouldn't be physically possible to exist... well, exists. My knees are seconds away from crashing to the rock.

"Please put your shirt back on," I beg.

He brushes past me without listening to my very reasonable request and dives headfirst into the massive diving hole before us. His skin barely touched mine, yet it still feels like electricity is dancing across my body.

If I jump in now, I'll die via electrocution.

"You could've hit your head!" I shout above the thundering rush of water as soon as his head pops up from the aqua surface. He ignores me and swims toward the waterfall, his tanned back glistening beneath the sunlight.

Really, I'm not even sure why he invited me.

But I'm glad for it, because now that his muscles are no longer visible, I can properly appreciate the view.

It's breathtaking. A small alcove surrounded by cliffs and bright green plant life that bleed into the sparkling blue depths. Straight ahead is a massive waterfall, the force of it vibrating my bones. Vines crawl up hundreds of feet of rock, and I'm deeply considering grabbing onto one and testing my *Tarzan* skills. I've always wanted to swing from a vine and jump into water. Be one with nature and shit.

Enzo turns to look at me, and my heart stops for a very brief moment.

"You coming in?"

"Only if you promise not to touch me," I call back.

"I promise not to do anything you don't beg me for."

Then, he turns around and dips under the water, disappearing under the falls.

I groan aloud, kicking my head back. I'm equal parts relieved and pissed that he couldn't just make the promise. He's sending me some seriously mixed signals.

Sighing in resignation, I slide my tank top over my head, unbutton my jean shorts, and let them drop. Thankfully, I've learned not to go anywhere without wearing my bathing suit.

I slide my fingers over the fresh tattoo on my thigh. It's only been a couple of days, and I'm risking infection by getting in the water. But *not* getting in it and never finding out what will happen behind the waterfall feels worse.

I think the only wise decision I'll make today is not swinging from a vine.

I won't show up the king of the jungle today, although I wish Enzo didn't disappear so I can ask him if it's safe to cannonball into the spring. He may have dived, but I also get the feeling he could dive in four feet of water and not even scratch his nose.

Deciding to go for it, I do a running jump, curl into a ball, and slam into the water like a true imbecile. Most girls would probably sashay into the water like they're in a photo shoot, but my life is too uncertain not to do the things I truly want to do.

Like, seduce the hottest man I've ever seen behind a waterfall. I groan again, this time at myself. It took two seconds to talk myself into it, though I already knew I wasn't going to say no.

I like to lie to myself.

I come up for air long enough to breathe in one big gulp and then dive back under, cutting beneath the waterfall.

It's so warm in here; it feels like being wrapped in a heated blanket on a cold day. So comforting that it gives you goosebumps.

When I re-emerge, Enzo is sitting on the rock floor at the edge of the pool, one knee kicked up and supporting his arm, and the other still dipped in the water while he waits for me. His body glistens, and one droplet in particular snags my attention, trailing down his defined stomach and toward the waistband of his shorts.

Swallowing, I meet his stare, staying in the water where it's safe. I can't decipher any of the emotions in his eyes. He has them on lockdown, and not knowing how he's feeling or what he's thinking—it's disconcerting.

"Are you going to murder me now?" I ask, my voice scarcely above the thunderous sound from the falls. It would be incredibly easy for my screams to be washed away.

"Would anyone be looking for you?" he retorts.

I smile sardonically. "Yes. I have people looking for me right now." He'll never understand the truth of that statement. Not until it's too late, at least.

"This waterfall isn't well known," he responds, dragging his gaze down the column of my neck before returning to my eyes. "It'd take a while to find you."

Despite the fact that I'm sweating from the temperature, his answer—no, his *voice*—sends shivers down my spine.

I shrug. "I never want to be found."

"Then I suppose I have you right where I want you," he drawls lazily.

I'm in trouble, but it's the type of danger that makes you smile uncontrollably as you ride the line between life and death. The kind of danger that gives you a thrill, makes you feel alive, and then leaves you bereft and empty when it's over.

"Want to know what I thought of you when we were in the bar?" I quiz.

"That I could get you pregnant with one look," he reiterates dryly. Liquid heat pools low in my stomach from his words. I don't even want kids, so it's shameful to admit that I'm incredibly turned on.

It's like your celebrity crush talking about knocking you up. Doesn't matter if you want kids or not, your panties immediately melt at the thought.

I shake my head, breathing in deep, hoping I inhale oxygen that will cleanse the delirium from my mind.

"That you could ruin me with just the tip," I admit, grinning when he looks a little taken aback.

"What makes you think I'd fuck you?"

Ouch.

I shrug, ignoring the embarrassment beginning to creep up my cheeks.

"Are you saying you wouldn't?"

He stares at me for a moment, his eyes assessing. It feels like he has a lockpick and is poking through my brain, trying to unravel all my secrets.

But I'll never tell.

Finally, he slowly shakes his head, his tongue swiping across his bottom lip. I zero in on the act, my mouth both parting and salivating.

He drops his knee, both legs now submerged in the water, and leans forward. I bristle under the intensity of his stare, unsure if his eyes are blazing because he's attracted to me, too, or if he's tired of my questions.

"You're going to ruin me, too. But unfortunately for you, that's where I feel most at home."

I gather enough courage to tread closer to him, but not close enough for him to grab for me. I'm not that brave yet.

I've never been brave at all.

"What does that mean?" I ask, getting distracted by another droplet trailing down his chest.

"It means that if anything happens, tonight is it. One night."

I look up at him through my lashes, and I feel a bead of water drip from my eyebrow and trail down my cheek. It feels symbolic.

"Deal," I say, my voice hoarse with desire. "Then we never see each other again."

Before he can answer, I dip below the surface and swim until I'm right at his feet. I pop up, swiping my hands back through my blonde strands, and nearly choke from the fire in his hazel eyes.

Heart pounding, I brace my hands on each of his knees and lift myself up until we're eye to eye. He tenses beneath me but doesn't move away. Up close, I can see just how extraordinary his eyes are. Swirls of golden brown and green mix together, rimmed by a dark ring. And on his right eye is that dark spot, like someone accidentally dropped a bead of ink.

"But I need to make sure of one thing first," I tell him, darting my tongue out to wet my lips. His eyes drift down, watching my tongue disappear before traveling farther south, lingering on my breasts that are pushed together and the water trailing over my curves. Slowly, he lifts his stare, and by the time our eyes reconnect, I'm nearly panting. Now, I can see raw emotion reflected back at me. Near-feral desire, and it's fucking invigorating.

His fists clench and my breathing stutters as I watch a man possessed with need hold himself perfectly still, not even a breath expanding his chest.

Forging on, I whisper, "I'm tired of men who don't know what they're doing. So, kiss me first. If you don't know how to fuck me with your mouth, then you won't know how to use your dick, either."

He chuckles, the sound low and deep. Humorless, like I've just told him that I'm not scared of him while he's holding a knife to my jugular.

Even though his smirk is cruel, it does things to my insides anyway. Twists them up like a rag drenched in gasoline before lighting a match to it. I just know I'll never be the same again after tonight.

A dimple appears in his right cheek as those white teeth sink into his bottom lip, as if he's holding in cynical laughter.

"You want me to fuck you with my mouth? I can do that, baby. But it will be your pussy I'm fucking."

He lifts a hand, trailing his fingers up my cheek and into my hair. I tremble beneath his fiery touch, my bones turning to jelly just from a single brush of his skin.

His grip turns rough, jerking me forward and wringing a gasp from my throat, nearly causing my hands to slip.

"But I promised I wouldn't do anything you didn't beg me for," he reminds me, a vicious challenge in his tone.

I've never begged for dick in my life. Never had to, when men are so fucking simple. Though, I guess that's actually not true. There were a few occasions when they accidentally stumbled upon my G-spot, and I pleaded with them to stay right there.

They never did.

"Please," I croak.

He only shakes his head, and I try not to feel rejected. Cocking my head at him, I scan my eyes down his physique, questioning if he's even worth begging for.

Noting the look on my face, he reaches between my thighs and presses firmly down on my clit, causing me to jolt beneath his touch.

"I'm not the type of man you want to doubt," he says, his voice deepening. He can locate the clit. Good enough for me.

Biting my lip, I lean forward until my lips brush against his jaw, delighting in the way he stills.

"Please, Enzo. I need you," I whisper, ensuring he can hear every note of desperation.

A deep growl rumbles in the base of his throat as I drift my mouth toward his, coming so close before he pulls back.

Denying me his lips, he grabs my waist and lifts me up, relieving my trembling arms from supporting my weight. Spinning me around, he sets me down on the slick rock and slips back into the water.

Our positions now reversed, he weaves his arms under my knees, grabs my hips, and roughly tugs me toward him. The unforgiving surface grates against my flesh, but it only serves to sharpen the desire cutting through my nerve endings.

Steam billows around us from the hot springs and the rushing waterfall fifteen feet away. It coats my skin, leaving me flushed and panting. Or maybe it's the way Enzo leans forward, staring up at me through heavily arched brows and thick lashes, that is setting me aflame.

His finger teases the edge of my bathing suit at the apex of my thighs, creating a full-body shiver strong enough to make my teeth chatter. Then, his gaze drops as he slowly slides my bottoms to the side, baring me completely.

He hisses between his teeth, and all I can do is thank God that I shaved today.

"So fucking pretty," he murmurs before placing a slow, soft kiss directly on my clit, glancing up at me as he does. I inhale sharply, disappointed when he retreats.

"Is that the type of kiss you wanted?" he taunts, sparing me another glance before his eyes gravitate back down like he can't stand to look away.

"No," I whimper. "You can do better than that."

"Can I?" he muses. "How would I do that? Use my tongue?" Right as the last word leaves said tongue, it darts out, lashing at my clit before disappearing between his teeth.

I groan, my hips involuntarily rolling toward his mouth, desperately seeking what he's so cruelly depriving me of.

"Yes, like that," I mewl, my legs beginning to tremble. Arousal is gathering low in my stomach, and my pussy throbs from how potent it is.

"Like that," he echoes, licking my clit again. Though this time is slower, causing me to shudder from how fucking good it feels.

"Don't stop," I gasp, my head falling back and my legs widening. Another moan bounces off the stone walls when he heeds my request, sensually curling his tongue as he would if it were in my mouth waging war against my own.

I find myself desperate to experience that, too, because he *can* kiss. And without a shadow of a doubt, I know this man can fuck just as well.

He groans against me. "You taste better than the sweetest wine, and I could fucking drink you forever."

My heart stutters, and my hips swivel, grinding against his mouth as he tastes me, drinking from me like a sorrowful man desperate to escape through a bottle. The stubble on his jaw only serves to heighten the pleasure, making me grind harder against him.

He sucks on my clit, earning a sharp moan followed by his name, and it's like watching a flower blossom with the way he comes alive.

The veins threading throughout his arms swell, and I can see the tension gather in his shoulders as he brings me closer, the entirety of his mouth covering me like he can't get enough—*eat* enough—of me.

"Open wider, *bella,* I need more of you."

bella - *beautiful*

I do as he says, hiking my knees as far up as I can. His tongue explores every inch of me, plunging inside my pussy and gathering my arousal on the tip before dipping even lower and laving at my tight entrance. Something I'd normally shy away from, but with Enzo, my body only seems to beg for more.

It's when his mouth closes over my clit again, sucking in deeply while lashing it with ferocity, that my knees snap inward, nearly crushing his skull between my thighs. My eyes roll to the back of my head, and my surroundings dissipate, all of my senses honing in on the sensations radiating from beneath his persistent mouth.

My legs squeeze tighter, but I don't relent—can't relent—too lost in the never-ending pleasure to give a fuck. Breathless screams are pouring from my throat, and my nails score across his scalp. The orgasm building low in my stomach is reaching a sharpened peak, and my desperation to reach it is ruthless.

He pries my thighs apart, holding one down with his arm while his other hand swipes up my slit, the only warning he grants me before two of his fingers sink inside me, drawing out a high-pitched moan while he curls them up and fucks me with them.

It feels like I'm on the verge of losing control of my bladder, yet it mingles with the acute need to come. Then, he hits a spot that makes me go blind, and oh my God, he doesn't stop or move even a centimeter.

I lose all function.

I can only choke on the euphoria, all sounds ceasing while I fight for oxygen. My mouth opens on a silent scream, incapable of giving anything else when my body has lost control.

My eyes roll, and I feel something just... snap. Every one of my vital organs has been overpowered by the orgasm crashing through me, and it feels like I'm quite literally exploding. It isn't until I'm on the verge of blacking out that my lungs finally open, allowing me to let out a sharp cry.

"*Fuck*," he curses against me, continuing his assault with his fingers. Vaguely, I glimpse a pool of liquid in his hand, but I'm too delirious to care as long as he keeps doing... oh God, *that.*

"Oh my God, *Enzo*," I sob, my body convulsing while his is tense, battling to keep me still. His fingers withdraw, replaced by his tongue, and he greedily drinks from me.

Just when it becomes too much, he retreats, and I feel my soul slump inside me, spent from the most world-bending orgasm I've ever experienced.

"That," I gasp, out of breath, "was *not* normal."

My legs are shaking, and aftershocks ravage my being as he lifts himself out of the water and crawls over me.

It takes effort to get my bleary eyes to focus, and when they do, I immediately flush from the sight. His face is... soaked, and his eyes are blazing hot.

"Did I...?" I trail off, too embarrassed to even say it aloud. I've never squirted before, and the experience was as otherworldly as others have claimed.

"You did," he confirms, his voice deepening with unrestrained desire. "And now I want to see you come like that all over my cock." He leans down, sending chills skating across my flesh as he whispers, "I won't stop until you do."

Oh, fuck. I'm dead, aren't I? Suffered a heart attack of some sort. Surely, a man determined to make a girl come more than once doesn't actually exist, right?

He tugs at the strings around my neck, the buttery-yellow bathing suit top slipping from my breasts as the knot releases.

A deep rumble builds in his chest as his hands sweep up and cup them in his large palms, swiping his thumbs across my pebbled nipples and wringing a whimper from my throat.

"Beautiful," he murmurs.

I bite my lip, peeking up at him through my lashes. He looks at me as if I'm a masterpiece, a shrine to worship, and I can't deny how invigorating that feels.

I wet my lips and then croak out a weak, "Thank you. I grew them myself."

He pays me no mind, instead swooping down and capturing a nipple between his teeth. Inhaling sharply, I arch into his hot mouth, eyes rolling in sync with his tongue.

He groans deeply before switching to the other. His grip turns punishing, and I revel in the feel of his hands marking me. I want to be covered in bruises by morning. It'll be the last time he'll ever touch me, and I want something good to remember him by before I ruin it.

He pulls away with a plop and then curses. "Goddamn it."

"What, what's wrong?" I ask, looking around to find the source of the problem. Did he lose his boner? Christ, that'd be my luck. Find a guy that can fuck like a god, but only when he can get it up.

"No condom," he chokes. He starts to pull away, but I stop him.

"Uhm, not to be weird because we're strangers, but I'm clean and on birth control."

His brow pinches, a frown pulling down his lips.

"I don't fuck without condoms."

"Then why did you bring me *here*? Why not, like, your house or a hotel?"

"Because you looked like you needed an escape. I wasn't planning on fucking you."

"Oh," I say, clearing my throat awkwardly. "Well... uh, you provided an escape all right."

There's a hint of his dimples, and once again, I'm overcome with the need to bring them out.

Slowly, his eyes track down my curves, and for the first time, I feel a sense of insecurity. Inadequacy. Like he can see the sins that cover my body like oil.

"Maybe just this once," he murmurs, seemingly to himself. I roll my lips together, impatiently waiting for him to decide. When his hazel eyes lift, it nearly stops my heart in my chest. He's just so goddamn... intense.

"You're going to ruin me," he reiterates.

I will.

"I won't."

At least not like he thinks.

"You're lying."

I am.

"You won't be the only one that will be ruined, remember?" I settle on, deciding to go with the truth.

I absolutely will destroy him, and later, I'll hate myself for it more than I already do.

CHAPTER 4

Sawyer

"I'm clean, too," he says gruffly. "Now, take them off," he demands, nodding at his shorts.

My limbs are buzzing with relief, making them feel numb as I hook my thumbs into his waistband and pull them down as far as I can reach. He kicks them the rest of the way off, and my eyes widen when he sits up on his knees.

He's not just long but incredibly thick, with veins threading throughout the length.

"Absolutely not," I say, shaking my head. "No. No way. I change my fucking mind." I point at it. "That will puncture a lung."

He raises his eyebrows, a hint of amusement mixing with the lust in his hazel orbs.

"Just the tip, remember?" he reminds darkly, mirth in his eyes. He's not amused enough to free his dimples, but it sends my heart scattering anyway.

I eye him, radiating nervous energy as he plucks at the two bows on either side of my bottoms, freeing me completely. Then, he grips me by the waist and pulls me against his chest. I curl my weak legs around him and loop my arms around his neck, inhaling sharply when I feel his cock brush against me.

Sliding a hand between the valley of my breasts and up my throat, he grips the underside of my jaw and swipes a thumb across my bottom lip.

"I can't wait to prove you right," he rasps, sending another tidal wave of shivers skittering throughout my body.

But I'm having trouble processing his words through the thick cloud of lust. "What...?" I breathe, the word ending on a whimper when he nips that sensitive spot right below my ear.

"Just the tip. That's all you get."

I bite my lip, both excited and disappointed. I don't need to take this any further to know I'm going to crave all of him, and even then, I'm not sure it'll be enough.

"You're going to make me beg again, aren't you?" I ask. He pulls back just enough to ensnare my eyes with his own, desire swirling in them like a pit of snakes.

"No, *bella*, I'm going to make you take it from me. If you want a predator to submit to you, then you need to be stronger."

He leans forward, brushing his lips along the column of my neck, eliciting sparks of electricity. "So, if you want every inch of my cock filling up your sweet, little pussy, then you better make sure you can handle me."

In lieu of an answer, I reach between us, my hand circling around his dick. His teeth clench, the muscle thrumming in his jaw. It looks on the verge of bursting, and the moment I feel the head slide along my slit, I know I'm not far behind.

His hands are on my hips and jerking me down, brimming with impatience and hunger. I gasp, shuddering as the tip of his cock fills me, though it's not nearly enough. He stops me there, and when I try to seat myself further, he resists, his grip turning punishing on my hips.

"That's all you get," he reminds me in a hushed voice, a mocking lilt to his tone.

Fine. If he wants to play this game, then I'll fucking play.

I lean forward, prepared to brush my lips against his, but he turns his head.

"You don't get to kiss me," he warns.

Cheater.

The rejection stings, but I don't let it deter me. So I slide my lips against his jawline and trail my hands down his chest, reveling in the feel of his tense muscles. His body is something to be worshiped, and it's torture knowing I only get one night.

"It seems you have forgotten that you need more of me to come, but I don't need you," I say in a hushed tone.

Then, I'm gripping him by the throat and shoving him down until his back lies flat on the stone, dislodging his firm hold on my waist. His head hangs over the edge of the pool, and he stares up at me with utter astonishment, but I'm already straightening my spine.

My hands rove down my body, slowly and sensually, ensnaring his wild gaze like a magnet snapping to its counterpart.

So easy.

When my fingers brush over my sensitive clit, I moan and tilt my head back slightly, showing him just how good *I* feel.

A growl forms deep in his chest, but he doesn't scare me. Strength doesn't only reside in our muscles but in our minds, too. And men—theirs are so easy to bend.

I circle my hips, reminding him of what he's missing, rubbing my clit harder. My other hand ascends back up to my breast, squeezing tightly as I work to get myself off.

"Fuck," he curses breathlessly. Once more, his hands are on my hips, gradually tightening.

"*Oh,* Enzo," I moan, and his grip loosens, whether in surprise or because he went slack from lust, doesn't matter. I seat myself entirely onto his cock, biting back a yelp of pain.

His outburst brings a slight grin to my face, the sound a mixture of a roar and a groan. I pant, my face twisting while my body adjusts to his size. Despite how wet and turned on I am, it doesn't abate the burn.

"Does it hurt, *bella*?"

"You're so big," I choke. Thunder reverberates through his chest, and I think he's becoming unhinged.

"And you're going to fucking take it," he snarls.

Trapping my bottom lip between my teeth, I readjust my position. I plant my feet on the stone and spread my legs wide, as if I'm crouching over him. His eyes glaze over while I balance myself on his rigid stomach.

With this new angle, he will see just how well I can take him.

Then, I rise up to the tip and slam back down on him, causing his head to drop back, the water grazing his hair. A cry leaves my throat, only this time, it doesn't hurt.

"*Yes*," he encourages, lifting his head once more. "Fuck me just like that, good girl."

My eyes threaten to find a new home in the back of my skull when I repeat the movement, finding a steady pace that sends trembles rolling down my spine. If this man were my kingdom, I'd sit on this throne for fucking eternity.

Gnashing his teeth, he rises to lean on one elbow while his other hand grips the back of my neck and pulls me into him. It creates the perfect amount of friction between his pelvis and my clit, and a gargled moan leaves my lips in response.

"That's it," he purrs. "Just like that, *bella. Cazzo, quanto mi fai godere.*"

I've no idea what that means, but *Jesus*, the way he speaks should be illegal—it's fucking heart-attack-inducing. I draw up and slam down again, over and over, until a cyclone is forming in the pit of my stomach.

Cazzo, quanto mi fai godere - *Fuck, you feel so good*

42

It doesn't take long before he's pumping his hips and meeting my thrusts in earnest. His mouth hangs open, with his brows pinched and eyes locked between our thighs. It's the most erotic sight I've ever seen, and I'll be fucking sad to see it go.

"Come here," he rasps. Hand still gripping my nape, he pulls me down until I'm lying flat on his chest, and my knees are tucked into his sides.

He bends his legs and plants his feet on the stone. For a moment, he pauses. My mouth is suspended over his, still being held hostage from the hand on my neck as he peers up at me with a devilish glint in his eyes.

"Are you ready?"

No. "Yes," I whisper.

There's a slight knowing curl to his lips, and before I can find any victory in bringing out a half-ass smile, he's grabbing my hips and burying himself inside of me.

My eyes pop open, a gasp leaving my lips from the new angle, any victory quickly forgotten.

Of course, he gives me no reprieve. Instead, he anchors my hips down as he fucks me. My hand slaps on the wet rock to brace myself, a staccato cry bouncing off the hollow cave walls.

Hot breath fans across the shell of my ear as his lips tease the sensitive skin. "Still think you can handle me?" he asks, voice tight and uneven from exertion and pleasure.

God, no.

Except I can't get a word out edgewise, the orgasm churning low in my stomach growing more demanding.

"You know what I think? You take me so fucking good. But I want to see how good you take me after you've been coming around my cock for hours."

I wouldn't survive that.

My moans slowly bleed into screams, and the rock floor is beginning to tear into my knees, but the pain only intensifies the pleasure.

One of his hands dives into my hair, fisting my curls tightly and forcing my head back. His teeth clamp down on my neck a moment later, wringing another cry from my lips.

Stars form in my vision, and I'm so fucking close to exploding all over again.

"Enzo," I plead.

"Lift up," he orders. I listen, straightening my spine and seeking balance on his abs once more.

"Touch yourself, *bella*. Rub your clit and let me feel how tight your pussy gets when you come."

He continues to pump inside me while my hand drifts to the apex of my thighs, finding my clit and rubbing firmly. My head kicks back, his name falling from my lips as if he's the one touching me.

Just when I think it can't get any better, he flattens one of his palms on my pelvis and applies firm pressure. My spine nearly collapses again, unprepared for the onslaught of sensation. I can feel him so much more intensely, and once more, it creates that feeling of needing to release my bladder.

"Oh my God, Enzo, I'm going to come again," I pant.

A growl rumbles in the depths of his chest, sending shivers rolling down my spine from its carnality.

"My name and God's don't belong in the same sentence, *bella*," he rasps, his voice as rough as the rock below us. "One is holy, and the other is depraved."

He curls his fingers past my lips with his free hand and hooks them around my bottom teeth, pulling my unfocused stare to his, a snarl on his face.

"Guess which one I am?"

A strangled cry is my only response as the orgasm slams through me. I erupt, my teeth biting into his flesh and my vision blackening from the powerful waves rolling inside me. He lifts me off him long enough to relieve the pressure, liquid pouring onto his stomach as I convulse.

It would be embarrassing if I had the capacity to feel anything past the euphoria.

Then, with his free hand, he guides me back down, driving inside of me and reigniting the bliss to almost painful levels while keeping his fingers firmly crooked over my teeth.

My body trembles as his thrusts quicken, feeling him swell inside me. Then, his head tips back, his strong throat working a groan out of his mouth as he explodes alongside me. He stills, the veins roping throughout his hands, arms, and neck thicken as he vibrates beneath me.

Still riding out the waves, I grind against him, pulling out another savage growl and causing him to lift his eyes back to me, an inferno blazing within.

"*Fuck*, keep milking every last drop. You can have it all, baby. You only have to take it."

He pulls me toward him further by my jaw, like reeling in a fish on a hook. I'm drooling around him, but it only seems to throw fuel on the fire raging in his eyes. I rest my hands on his broad shoulders, both hating and loving how tiny my hands look compared to him.

His eyes drift to my mouth for a brief moment, almost as if he's contemplating kissing me.

But he doesn't. He only stares into my eyes as we come down from our high, creating one of the most intense experiences of my life. I've never had a man stare at me the way Enzo does. It feels like he's throwing me onto a table, taking a scalpel to my flesh, and slicing me open to see my blackened soul bared for him.

Finally, he releases me, and I just barely clamp my mouth shut in time, catching the drool before it drips onto his face. I bite my lip, relishing in the way his nostrils flare as he watches me.

He doesn't shy away from my gaze, although I can't say the same for myself. It feels too intimate—too probing. Like maybe if he stares long enough, he'll see that I'm the worst person he could've given himself to.

I look away, curling my lips into a lighthearted grin.

"That was..."

"Don't insult me by condensing what that was down into a single word," he cuts in, his deep voice hoarse.

"Okay," I say simply, rolling off him and shuddering from the feel of his cum coating the inside of my thighs. Another thing that feels too intimate. "I won't then."

"Good."

He's still staring at me, and my flight instincts are beginning to kick in.

"Come home with me," he says as if sensing that.

Normally, I feel relieved when I'm invited into their house, but this time, I feel nothing but sadness. The worst part is—it's not enough to stop me. It's not enough to override my desperation to survive.

"I'd be happy to."

CHAPTER 5

Sawyer

The morning rays peek through Enzo's curtains, which feels like a punishment. Maybe because my mood is the exact opposite of sunshine and rainbows.

Heart pounding, I carefully sit up and swing my legs over the edge of the bed. Enzo softly snores beside me, his arm tossed over his head and the sheets down to his waist.

It's hard to swallow. A defined body with muscles, grooves, and divots that made my mouth water several times last night is on full display. And that perfect V that points directly to the weapon between his thighs.

We only fell asleep a couple of hours ago, and every time I shift, my body aches. My *core* aches.

The man was relentless and insatiable. His fingers and tongue were in places that had never been touched before, and even thinking about it now has my face burning hot.

I'm going to miss you.

But I need to survive more.

Steeling my spine, I gently slip out of bed, quickly gather my clothes, and yank them on.

Casting another glance at Enzo, I pick up his discarded shorts and rifle through them until my fingers close around his wallet. Smooth, black leather encasing his identity.

Enzo Vitale. Thirty-four years old. Born November 12th—Scorpio; Lord, help me. Six-four—so he *is* a foot taller. Hazel eyes. He's as delicious on paper as he is in the flesh.

I never physically steal anything. It's too noticeable. So, I snap a quick photo of it, then replace the wallet in his shorts. Before slipping out of the room, I give him one last glance-over, every beat of my heart ringing hollow. I hate that I'm doing this to him, but then I hate that I do this to anyone at all.

Softly closing the door behind me, I walk out into his living room and kitchen area.

He lives in a beautiful home—lots of white with brown wooden beams lining up the walls and across the ceiling. I was surprised to find that Enzo has good taste and interior design skills. Almost as surprised as he was when he discovered my lack of a gag reflex.

Tiptoeing through the space, I open random doors until I find my gold mine. His office. A simple wooden desk, black leather chair, and several diagrams of sharks hanging on the walls. Bookshelves line the wall behind his desk, full of textbooks that are most likely for smart people.

Adrenaline is racing through my system as I approach the desk and start rifling through the drawers. Nothing of value in any of them—until I tug on the bottom one, finding it locked.

What I need is definitely in there. There's a small bobby pin hooked around the string of my bathing suit top. I always have one there. Always.

Slipping it off, I straighten it out and insert it into the lock. I've gotten pretty good at this, so within a minute, I'm carefully sliding the drawer open.

Pausing intermittently to listen for sounds, I dig through the contents, my heart spiking when I find a card that says *Repubblica Italiana* written across the top, with a bunch of numbers and letters below. I slip my phone from my back pocket and do a quick Google search, matching it to what's called a *tessera sanitaria*. I'm not sure how to interpret what it says, but I can make out his first and last name, birthdate, and place of birth. I'm almost positive it's the equivalent of a social security card in America and precisely what I need.

I also uncover an official document naming Enzo as the owner of a corporation labeled V.O.R.S., along with a business address.

Guilt tugs at my heartstrings as I quickly snap photos of them, close the drawer, and sidle out of the room.

God, I hope he thinks he just forgot to lock it, but I know better, which is why I will do everything in my power to never see Enzo Vitale again.

The loud banging on a door from somewhere nearby has my heart nearly bursting from my chest. I'm in the midst of bleaching my roots, so I toss the brush into the bowl and grab for my gun lying in the sink, adrenaline causing my vision to sharpen.

Breath short, I stare out past the entryway to the bathroom and at the door to my hotel room straight ahead, waiting for someone to bust through and take me away in handcuffs. Time ticks by, only nothing happens, yet there's no calming the thundering in my chest.

Inhaling deeply, I face the mirror, averting my eyes as I set the gun back into the sink.

My very illegal gun, but I couldn't resist. In the U.S., I had bought one from some shady dude for protection, but I had to leave it behind in order to travel. Here, gun laws are extremely strict, and obtaining one is nearly impossible in my predicament.

I had been walking past a shooting range when I got the stupid idea. A man had just finished up and put his handgun into a padlocked case in the trunk of his car and his ammo in a second locked case next to it. I hid behind a tree on the sidewalk while he ran back into the building, muttering to himself about having to pee. He didn't even bother locking his car, too distracted by nature's call.

I didn't think at that moment, I just acted. I tiptoed to his car, opened the trunk, and stole both cases. Thankfully, my hotel was only a few blocks away, but my heart was nearly beating out of my chest the entire way back.

After, I was forced to find a hardware store to break into the damn things, though once I had the weapon in my hands, I felt like I could breathe again.

Blowing out a slow breath, I grab my brush from the bowl, then resume lathering the chemicals onto my roots, hands shaking. My natural brown has been coming through, and about once every couple of months, I make it my life's mission to expunge it from existence.

I hate this shit, but I think my abused scalp is used to it by now.

When I'm finished, I toss the brush and the now empty bowl into the trash. The hotel room I'm staying in reeks of the bleach, but it also stinks of other things that are probably better suited in a lab.

Then, I pick up my burning cigarette that's been resting in an ashtray on top of the toilet and inhale, still avoiding my reflection.

During the twenty minutes it takes for the chemicals to do their magic, I go through another cigarette and swallow down a quarter of a bottle of vodka. I really shouldn't be drinking, but a deep impenetrable sadness has a tight hold on me, and alcohol is the only thing that drowns it.

Then, I strip off my clothes and get in the cruddy shower to wash out the bleach. My body feels sluggish and heavy as I rinse, and I can't tell if it's from the vodka or because life feels so fucking abysmal.

Halfway through, the alcohol hits and my surroundings begin to swirl around me. It feels like I got trapped in a rocket and it's blasting off.

"Fuck," I mutter, slapping my hand on the wall in an attempt to stabilize myself.

I crank off the water and stumble out of the shower, snatching a towel on the way out. I wrap it around me, the material nice and scratchy. So much better than the fluffy soft shit.

Cold droplets from my drenched hair trail down my body and cause goosebumps to rise. I tug on a white tank and sleep shorts, water from my half-dried body soaking into my clothes.

The stall is directly in front of the sink, so the moment I look up into the mirror, Kev is already staring back at me.

The only things he and I share are our blue eyes and broad smiles. He always favored our father, with stick-straight hair, round eyes, and a strong nose, while I favored our mother, with the wild curly hair and more elfish-like features.

Doesn't matter, anyway. The eyes were always the worst part. I can't see my own without seeing his, too.

"Fuck you," I snarl at my—his—reflection. He grins, and that only serves to amplify my fury.

The half-empty bottle of vodka sits on the sink edge, and I swipe it off by the neck, taking a generous swig. The burn feels like acid going down my throat, but it forces back the vomit trying to climb up it.

"You know, sometimes I wish that when we were in Mom's stomach, I would've eaten you," I say, then take another gulp.

I chuckle because that's also kind of gross.

But that stupid fucking grin is echoing my own, enough to make me snap.

Snarling, I grab the gun from the sink again, except this time, I point it directly at Kev. Tears well in my eyes, and his smile widens. He's still taunting me. I have no idea where he's gone, but he's always been good at tormenting me even when I'm alone.

"You don't get to do that," I choke. "You don't get to win. *I* win. Not you."

My hand trembles violently as I glower at him, a tear slipping free and trailing down my cheek. He always got angry when I cried. Could never understand why he made me so sad.

Don't you love me, pipsqueak?

"No," I sneer. "I *hate* you."

You don't mean that.

"I HATE YOU!" I scream with all my might, feeling my face rush with blood and my chest crack open. I smash the gun's tip into the glass, right where his head is.

You only hate me because you're just like me. We're the same, pip. And the only one who will love you for you is me.

I'm shaking my head as the phantom in the mirror continues torturing me.

"You'll never let me go, will you?" I cry, my voice breaking from anguish and defeat.

I'm not considering my actions when I turn the gun on myself, the cold press of the barrel sinking into my temple. Kev's face contorts in rage, but I can't hear him anymore. The only thing I can hear is the loud ringing in my ears as my fingers dance over the trigger.

Would it be so bad if I was gone?

Who would even notice?

No one would care. I'm a small blip that will blink out almost as quickly as it appeared.

So, what am I even fighting for? If I'm not fighting to stay alive for someone else, what's the point in staying alive for myself when I don't even want to be here?

A high-pitched laugh trickles out of my throat while Kevin continues to rage. He's not real, but at this moment, I've never felt closer to him.

"Weren't expecting that, were you?" I point at him in a *gotcha* moment with the hand still holding the bottle, causing the liquid to slosh over the rim and onto the floor.

"You don't want me to kill myself because you've always wanted to be the one to do it," I tell him.

Tears stream down my cheeks, and his image blurs from the flood.

"But I can't do it, either," I cry. "Because if I do, it would still be because of you."

My stomach churns, but I'm incapable of looking away as he slowly fades away. I still end up hearing the last thing he says, anyway.

We've been together from the very beginning, pipsqueak. I'll never let you get away from me.

I'm dying.

Sweat glides down my forehead as I flip my most recent crime through my fingers, with "Swimming in the Moonlight" by Bad Suns playing softly on the radio.

A gold plastic rectangle with Enzo's name on it is glaring back at me. It took a week and a half, but my new credit card has been approved. This is supposed to save me, yet all I can feel is sick. Coupled with the fact that Senile Suzy's AC is broken, and it's hotter than the pit of a volcano in here.

Alas, it's my home, and I've already spent the past several days in a hotel waiting for the card to come in the mail. I had just enough money left to put down a deposit for my stay, and I think I broke out in hives when I paid the bill after getting it in the mail.

Blowing out a slow breath, I wipe away a bead of perspiration that's gearing up to drip right into my eyeball and burn the shit out of it when my phone dings; the chime letting me know an email just came through.

My heart drops, already knowing who it's from without having to see it. Despite my brain screaming at me to just ignore it. *They can't find you.* I grab the device and click on it anyway.

Come on, pipsqueak, stop lying to yourself and the rest of the world about what happened. You're spending all this time running when you could have already faced what you've done to the one person who loved you most in the world.

Just... do it for Kevin.

You owe him that much.

Garret

Fucker. Growling beneath my breath, I punch my thumb into the delete button, then sit up and turn off the van.

I'm out in the scorching sun seconds later, slamming the door shut behind me and stomping through the trees until I come out on a dirt road that'll lead me into town.

I met Garrett after Kev joined the police academy, when we were twenty. He adopted Kevin's nickname for me, and every time I see it, I want to claw out my eyeballs. Since I ran off, he's been sending me emails, pleading with me to come back and *'face what I've done.'* He's just another cop who believed my brother over me.

And why wouldn't he? They'll always believe a cop over a civilian. Even if I'm their twin sister.

I'm trudging to the bus stop in a sour mood when I spot Simon. I hadn't even realized I was walking over here. It's as if a switch was flipped in my body and it went on autopilot, gravitating toward my only friend in this town.

There's no one else to go to. No one else to talk to.

Instantly, a spark ignites in my chest, and I'm rushing toward him.

"Simon!" I call out, waving my hand excitedly. He waves back, a small smile tipping on his face when he spots me.

"Well, hello there, pretty lady."

"I've missed you. You've been gone," I tell him, taking a seat next to him. "Why?"

He chortles, the sound shaking his entire body. Simon doesn't laugh with his mouth; he laughs with his chest.

"My ex-wife told me the same thing our whole marriage. Probably why she divorced my ass. Can't seem to keep me in one place for very long."

I twist my lips. "I feel you, Simon, I feel you. But I think maybe your wife should've just gone with you."

He waves a hand. "Meh, the fast life ain't for everyone. You're just like me, kiddo, I can tell—always on the move."

I smile and nod. "Can't hold me down, either."

He studies me for a second, then reaches into his pocket and pulls out a cigarette from a pack.

"You know, we're also different. I've always been running to something—always searching for something that I could never find. But I suspect you're the opposite. You're running *from* something."

My smile slips, and I reach my hand out. "Gimme that."

He chuckles again and hands the cigarette over. I curl it between my lips and lean over, allowing Simon to light it for me.

After inhaling deeply, I ask, "How can you tell?"

He doesn't answer until his own is lit and he's taken a few puffs.

"You got that cornered animal look to you. Jumpy. Haunted. Like you're gonna bite and run any second, without warning."

I frown. Austin, the bartender, also compared me to an animal.

"Apparently, I'm not as mysterious as I thought," I mumble, taking another drag.

"Sweetheart, you carry your baggage like it's the only belongings you got."

"Ouch," I mutter, though a grin tips up my lips. "Maybe that's my appeal then. Everyone wants to fix the broken, right?"

"Nah," he says. "People don't actually care about fixing you. They just want to shape your broken pieces until they fit their standards. Smooth 'em out, make 'em less sharp, so they don't cut so deep when they collect 'em. But you ain't any less broken."

"He's a wise one," I announce loudly, earning a few side-eye glances. "If I'm a feral dog, you're an owl."

Another body-shaking laugh and I feel my soul ease just a little. Simon has no interest in fixing my broken pieces, but he also smooths them out without even trying. Just a little.

"Tattoo healin' nicely?"

My grin widens, and I show him my leg. "It's perfect. I want another."

"We can do another, but let's wait until it's the right time, yeah?"

Another frown. "How will I know it's the right time?"

He pats my leg as the bus hurtles down the road, coming to a screeching halt in front of us. Neither of us gets up to leave.

"You'll know."

CHAPTER 6

Ladra.

My hand lays flat against the rough texture of the great white beneath me. She glides through the water smoothly, her body wiggling back and forth as she swims.

She's a serene one. Hasn't minded me one bit hanging onto her fin.

There's a plastic six-pack ring caught on one of her teeth, but I've been letting her get used to my presence first before I extract it. Something that should never be in any fucking animal's mouth.

I wouldn't mind if it were wrapped around the neck of someone else, though.

Fucking. Thief.

It's all I can think—a constant loop in my head, reminding me how easily I got played. And the only one stupid enough to let her in was me.

Doubt I'm the only one to fall victim to those big, sad eyes, though.

When I awoke the morning after I fucked her, my heart was already pumping adrenaline into my system. I just *knew* she did something to fuck me over. And when I found her gone, my fear was cemented.

It took me the rest of the day to figure out what she did. Nothing was missing from my wallet, and my safe went untouched. It wasn't until I went into my office and found the bottom desk drawer unlocked that I knew she had pulled something.

Nothing was missing, and I couldn't figure out what she was up to for several days. That is, until I looked at my credit report and discovered I had a new credit card on it. One that I didn't fucking open.

The bitch stole my goddamn identity.

It's been a few weeks since that happened, and since then, I've been calling to see the charges on my account. She hasn't blown through the money as I expected, but there's still time. For the life of me, I can't figure out what her angle is.

Can't figure out my own either, considering I haven't brought myself to freeze the account and call the authorities.

Yet.

The anger coursing through my system is fucking astounding. If I didn't possess control over my emotions, it would've been dangerous for me to get in the water today.

Sharks can feel when we're anything but relaxed. An elevated heart rate would be the equivalent to strapping seal guts to my body and going for a swim.

I'm furious enough to take on a two-ton animal, and though I can't promise myself I'd win, I'd put up a really good fucking fight. Problem is, I don't *want* to fight a shark.

What I want to do is throttle the little siren that tricked me.

Christ, and to think for one fucking second, I thought I might actually want to see her again.

I force her from my mind, for now, focusing on the beauty before me. She darts to the left, thrashing her tail a little and throwing me a tad off-balance.

Down here, it's where I feel most calm—swimming alongside Mother Nature's fiercest creation.

I run my hand alongside her fin, coaxing her back into a relaxed state.

Slowly, I slide up the side of her body and toward her mouth, continuing to pet her as I do. She's a fourteen-footer and bulky, too. Covered in mating scars, which gives me hope for research. It's not very often we find females mature enough to give birth.

Keeping a close eye on her body language, I snag the plastic and slowly slide it off her tooth. Then I release her fin, letting her swim out of my hold while I aim for the ladder to the enclosure ten feet away. The second my head pops out of the water, I find my research partner, Troy, crouching down at the ladder, waiting for me.

"You good, Zo?"

I hate when he calls me that.

His red, curly hair is piled into a bun today, the freckles smattered across every inch of his face, prominent beneath the blue light.

"Stop calling me that, asshole," is my response.

"Well, you've been stomping around the place all day. Surprised she didn't take a bite out of you. I was expecting to have to get the net and fish out your limbs today."

"Watch me throw you in so I can fish out yours instead," I retort, pulling myself out of the water while ensuring to splatter Troy as I do. He only chuckles, used to my attitude by now.

"She good to go yet?" Troy asks, referring to the shark circling in the massive enclosure.

A few years ago, I built this research center from the ground up—Vitale Oceanic Research for Selachians. It's my life's work and something I've been privileged to do since I got the funding for it from the government.

It's a massive lab built a few hundred miles off the shoreline. The only way to get here is by boat or helicopter—one of my favorite things about being out here. It's an oasis.

The surface is made up of mostly all boardwalks surrounding the four enclosures where we bring the sharks into. There's a platform for helicopters to land—sometimes other scientists travel here to learn about what we've gathered—and a dock for the boats. Below the surface is where the research is conducted.

Not much is known about mating rituals for great whites, and I've spent my entire career trying to learn as much as possible about it. We bring them in every so often to conduct our research and then immediately release them with tags attached to their fins so we can hopefully gain insight into something humans know very little about.

"Yup," I say.

"You're a sourpuss today—more than usual. What stingray barb got lodged up your ass?"

My eye twitches with irritation at his shitty joke. Then again, his jokes are always shitty.

Troy has been with me since the beginning. We went to college together, and despite how much of a pain in the ass he is, he's a damn good marine biologist and just as passionate about what we do as I am.

"Got my identity stolen," I answer shortly, not really wanting to get into it but too furious to contain it.

Troy's eyes widen, making him look like a cartoon character. He follows me as I make my way down the metal walkway. The sun is beaming down on my skin, and more than anything, I wish I was back down in the water. Where it's cool and fucking *silent*.

"No shit? You fall for one of those phishing emails, you old fart?"

I sigh. I'm only a year older than him, but he loves to treat me like I'm ancient.

"No," I bark, leaving it at that. I'm having trouble forcing myself to admit aloud that a girl swindled me. Troy would never let me live it down, and then I'd have to attach cinderblocks to his ankles and throw him in the ocean to find peace again.

Right alongside Jamie—or whoever she is. I'd bet my last dollar that's not even her real name. Was the real Jamie another unsuspecting victim?

Jesus.

I rub my hand roughly over my hair, the short spikes soothing my frayed nerves. Hatred is churning deep in my stomach and polluting anything good I had thought about her previously.

I want to fucking *hurt* her. Even worse, I want to fuck her again while I do it. Her body was addicting that night—so addicting that I couldn't leave her alone until the early hours of the morning. And it makes me sick that the craving hasn't dissipated in the slightest.

"You'll get it back, man," Troy assures quietly, sensing my turmoil. He knows better than to push me. I'm already on the verge of snapping, and the last thing I want to do is take it out on the wrong people.

Nodding my head, I head into the small cement cabin, V.O.R.S. painted across it in bold black letters. There's only an elevator within, and it'll take me down a couple of hundred feet below sea level to my lab. Then, I will spend the rest of the day watching a camera feed of the female shark gliding throughout the vast blue ocean.

"Yeah, you're right. I'll get it back. Go tag her and then release her from the enclosure," I order, pointing toward the female shark I was swimming with. "We got a lot of screen time ahead of us."

Troy offers me a smart-ass salute, then turns to do as I say while I smash my finger in the button to open the elevator doors.

I will absolutely get my identity back. However, I'm not waiting on the legal process to accomplish that for me.

I'm going to fucking find her first.

The sand compresses beneath my feet as I walk the beach for the fifth fucking time today. If I ever get my hands around her throat, there will be no disputing that it was premeditated.

It's been a little over three weeks since I fucked her, but I've been looking for her for only two days. There's a sinking feeling that she could be out of town already, but I refuse to give up just yet.

Port Valen is a small beach town, and Jamie had mentioned in a passing comment that she's still getting used to the ocean, so it's the only place I can think to look, aside from the bar I had met her in.

A woman in a royal blue string bikini starts heading my way, a bright white smile on display beneath her obnoxious sunhat.

"No," I clip. She stops in her tracks, the smile melting off her face as if it were a scoop of ice cream. In a matter of seconds, her lips twist into a scowl.

Except my attention is already drawn away from her, now locked on the source of all my anger.

Ecco la mia piccola ladra.

She's walking the beach now, wearing a neon green bathing suit bikini, and tiny denim shorts, the matching bottoms to her top peeking through the unfastened jeans. Her lithe, tanned body is on full display, which only serves to brighten the hair curling down past her shoulders. The blonde is radiant beneath the sunlight, a soft breeze blowing the tendrils around her face.

She looks tired—sad—but I'm not falling for that bullshit again.

It was one of the reasons I had bothered with her in the first place. She had a sense of humor and a perpetual grin, but nothing about her seemed happy or carefree. Which is exactly why I liked her. My darkness was attracted to hers, and it seems I learned the hard way just how dangerous it is.

The second I spot her, I gun it straight for her. Instead of storming up to her and grabbing her by the throat like I'd prefer, I keep my pace casual and relaxed.

Ecco la mia piccola ladra. - *There's my little thief*

Moments later, our eyes clash, and hers round at the corners. She bristles, and I can see that alarm system blaring in her head, banging the gong like a madman, and screaming at her to turn around and run away. If she does, I'll fucking tackle her ass, uncaring of who sees.

She forces herself to keep walking, probably hoping I hadn't noticed her little crime. Which is precisely what I plan to make her think.

"Thought you didn't want to see me again," I say casually when she's close enough.

She forces a grin, light-years away from reaching her eyes. Her nervousness is palpable; just like the sharks lurking in the ocean, I can smell her fear.

"Just couldn't stay away, I guess," she says, ending it with an awkward laugh. "This doesn't have to be weird. We saw each other naked. It wasn't anything special for either of us. I'm okay with us keepin' it moving."

Now that's a fucking lie.

I raise a brow. Normally, I'd enjoy the way it makes her swallow nervously, but that comment is enough to infuriate me. I don't need her to stroke my ego, but the fact that even now, she still fucking lies.

I don't get the fucking point of it.

That was the best fuck of her life, and she doesn't even need to open her mouth and tell me so to know that. My soaked bed sheets and her red, shell-shocked face were a clear indication.

"Wasn't anything special?" I reiterate.

Another awkward laugh. "Don't make this weird, Enzo."

"Okay," I tell her. "I won't remind you of the best night of your life. But I am curious if you want to experience the best day of your life now."

Her brows pinch, and she stares at me like she's waiting for the punchline. She even glances around as if a film crew is going to pop out and tell her she's being punked.

Patiently, I wait for her to make up her mind.

"I don't think that's a good—"

"It's not sex, Jamie. I won't even ask you about yourself."

It'd all be a lie anyway.

She blinks. "What exactly is going to give me the best day of my life then?"

"A shark."

"Oh, you're fucking cracked," she tells me with an incredulous laugh, and for a second, it almost seems genuine. It makes her look... innocent.

Yet another lie.

"Scared?"

"Uhm, who wouldn't be?"

"Me."

She frowns. "Okay, well you got me there."

"I'll keep you safe," I assure her. And it's the truth. I will keep her safe from the sharks. Just not from *me*.

CHAPTER 7

Sawyer

This is a mistake.

Yet, here I am, following Enzo as he leads me toward a massive boat on the harbor, a credit card with his name on it burning in my back pocket.

The only voice I can hear right now is Kev's. He berated me often, especially after our parents died. I can only imagine what he'd say now, watching me get on a boat with a man I hardly know. The worst part is *I'm* the criminal and allowing Enzo to take me out after what I've done... It's too far, even for me.

Yet, I'm too fucking selfish to walk away.

We stop at the end of the dock, and he turns to look at me, watching me take in the boat before me.

She's a beauty—gleaming white with the name *Johanna* on the side in big, blue letters. Windows line either side of it, and I'm pretty sure that thing could fit a bedroom or two in it comfortably, but what's most notable is the cage attached to the back. A shark cage, to be exact.

"You expect me to get in that?" I ask, pointing to the mini prison.

"If you're feeling brave enough," he challenges, his deep voice quiet yet wicked. There's a spark in his eye, though I can't decipher what the fuck it means.

I was expecting an immediate confrontation when he saw me. Denial was poised on the tip of my tongue, but he's acting oblivious to his stolen identity.

Most people aren't aware their identity has been stolen until it's too late. He has no reason to suspect me yet. Nothing was missing from his house, and despite his bottom drawer being unlocked, who would stop to consider identity theft?

Relax, Sawyer. He doesn't even look angry.

Well, okay, that's not entirely true. Enzo wears a perpetual scowl on his face like it's an oxygen mask and has string beans for his lungs. According to him, it's what keeps people far, far away and allows him to live his life in peace.

Regardless, allowing him to take me in the middle of the ocean where I quite literally can't run isn't one of my brighter ideas. In fact, it's honestly fucking stupid.

That reminder settles in deep, and I'm beginning to feel all kinds of wrong again. I don't necessarily feel like I need to fear for my life with Enzo, but I still feel on edge.

I take a step away. "I don't know about this," I hesitate.

He stares down at me, silent, but I feel his disappointment anyway. And like a typical adult who grew up deprived of praise and attention from their parents, I'm now seeking those things from a man.

Fuck.

"I'll give you a kiss as a reward," he murmurs, his voice deep and seductive.

I put my hands on my hips, hating how alluring that sounds.

"That's pretty special," I retort. "You never told me why you won't kiss me."

His hazel eyes dance down my profile, wetting his lips before returning to my own. "I don't kiss anyone. I've never met a woman who deserves that intimacy from me."

I raise my brows. He definitely has mommy issues. But then, I can't disagree with his logic, either. I've always hated kissing my flings for that exact reason. It was just something that always seemed like the natural thing to do when getting a dick rammed inside you. I guess on the bright side, it allowed me to find more interesting ways to utilize Enzo's mouth.

"Until now," I tack on. "You're saying you'll kiss me if I get on that boat?"

He pauses, then says, "*Si.*"

"You're lying," I respond, narrowing my eyes. Another indecipherable emotion flashes in his irises, gone before it can settle.

"Only one way to find out," he says dryly.

"You think a kiss from you equals getting in a shark cage?" I question with a scoff.

"*Si,*" he responds readily. Confidently.

I can't help but laugh, and it actually feels a little nice. His stare locks onto my mouth, zeroing in on it like it's a fortune ball revealing his future.

"This is something very few people experience, Jamie."

The smile on my face is uncontrollable. "Kissing you is that special, huh?"

He gives me a dry look. "Getting in a shark cage," he clarifies, though we both knew that already.

I twist my lips and rock on my toes, contemplating his offer. My muscles are lined with tension, and there's a deep, uneasy feeling in the pit of my stomach.

I recognize it as guilt. He doesn't know what I've done yet, and this may be the last time I'll ever see him. And as much as I hate to admit it, I want to spend one more day with him before he hates me forever.

Indecision traps me in a vicious cycle of talking myself out of it, only to convince myself to try it. 'Round and 'round, until I finally settle on an answer.

"Fine. But if I die, make sure it's *before* a shark eats me."

Stoically, he rakes his gaze down my figure, then turns without a word, which feels entirely ominous. He steps on the boat and holds his hand out for mine, a hint of fire in his stare.

I take it.

I've never been good at making the right decision.

Salty ocean air whips through my tangled hair as Enzo speeds us through the vast, blue ocean. Anxiety is swirling in my stomach, and it doesn't matter how many times I wipe my hands on my shorts, they're still clammy.

I'm not sure how much time has passed, but Port Valen has become a speck. With each passing second, I feel more and more isolated, and my body still can't figure out who is the one in danger.

After what feels like forever, the boat finally slows to a crawl. I had opted to feel the wind lashing at my face instead of staying in the closed-in area where he drives.

Right behind me is an open area where several oxygen tanks and scuba gear line the walls, along with a couple of benches to sit on while getting dressed.

"Nervous?" he asks, stepping down onto the deck.

"We're in the middle of a big bowl of monster soup. I'm pretty sure I should've brought diapers." I'm not even embarrassed by that. Enzo claims he gave me the best fuck of my life—and he's not wrong—but I'd wager that I did the same for him. So, who cares if I need a diaper when I am to be facing a massive beast soon?

He may be incredible in bed, but I guarantee these monsters are far scarier than the one between his legs.

He shakes his head and stalks toward the side where there's a massive anchor. He begins to lower it while I turn to stare out at the horizon. It's so easy to feel like you're alone out here. Yet, I'm surrounded by life. So much life.

Enzo was right—being in the middle of the ocean absolutely does make you feel tiny. It stretches as far as my eyes can see no matter which direction I turn, and I don't even want to see what's below the surface.

When I manage to drag my eyes away from the glittering water, I find Enzo prowling toward me, and my body tightens with anticipation. For a brief second, my heart suspends in my chest, convinced he's about to throw me overboard, but instead, he grabs a gray bucket by my feet.

He's so intense, he would have a slug stiffening when he comes near.

I'm confused about what he's doing until he opens the container. My cheeks blow wide, vomit rising up my throat. The bucket is full of... guts. Bloody chunks of entrails.

Lifting the bucket, he proceeds to dump it in the ocean, the crimson immediately clouding the water.

"How... how long does it take them to get here?"

He shrugs. "Shouldn't be too long. Sharks have an incredible sense of smell."

Rubbing my lips together, I nod my head, feeling all sorts of out of place.

The cage is suspended on a crane on the back of the boat, but he doesn't lower it yet. I'm sure he's going to walk me through how to get in the scuba gear and the oxygen tank first.

"Are you going to swim with them outside of the cage?" I ask.

"No. I only swim with them when they're in my research center—and I don't do it just for fun. You should never touch wildlife in the ocean."

I'm definitely okay with never touching them, as long as they don't touch me, either.

"They won't, like, eat the boat, right?"

"Why eat the boat when they can eat you instead?"

My eyes round, and I stare at him, waiting for him to smile. He doesn't— of course, he doesn't—but there is mirth swirling in his eyes.

"You're joking," I state.

"I've already said they don't like the taste of us," he reminds me.

"Sure, they'll take a little nibble, say *blech*, and swim away. Meanwhile, they have my leg caught in their teeth, and I'll live the rest of my life as a half-cyborg."

He shrugs. "There are worse things in life than being a half-cyborg," he says, grabbing another bucket and dumping it in the ocean.

He would know, he practically is one.

"If it's not so bad, get in the cage and stick your toes out. Let me know how dandy it is when it's bashing you on either side of the cage while it slowly tears your leg off."

He grunts. "It wouldn't be slow. Your leg would be gone before you could blink. They have incredibly powerful bites."

So maybe he knows what he's talking about, but I can't get that image out of my head anyway.

"Maybe I shouldn't go. I wouldn't want to lose my favorite toe."

His brow furrows. "Do I even want to know?"

I point to my pinkie toe. "It's cute. Sharks like cute things. They eat seals. Seals are cute."

He looks to where I'm pointing, then shakes his head at me. "I don't think they care much about how it looks. More like how it tastes."

"I'm talking myself out of this," I declare, anxiety starting to make me feel a little nauseous.

"So, stop doing it."

I purse my lips. "Yeah, you're right. I'm going to do this. For sure."

I'm lying again, and we both know it.

"*Vieni qui*," he demands roughly, his hazel eyes searing as he reaches out his hand and motions for me to come to him.

I shiver, the beautiful lilt of his voice and its roughness gliding across my nerves.

Vieni qui - *Come here*

Swallowing, I approach him and let him grab ahold of me, immediately shivering from the feel of his rough skin on mine. He directs me toward the back of the boat, where it's an open flat ledge.

Somehow that's even more terrifying.

"Kneel," he whispers, his voice dipping low and reaching into the pit of my stomach where arousal is blooming.

I'm ready to question him, but then he starts to lower as well, so my body follows along without further question.

"Put your hand in the water," he directs.

"Fuck no."

"Nothing is going to come up and bite you. Just feel it."

Exhaling a shuddering breath, I lean forward and brush my fingertips through the cold water.

"You're touching an entire universe right now. A microscopic portion of a universe. It's an ecosystem full of millions of species, some of them you couldn't even imagine."

His hands drift to my hips, cupping them in his large palms and squeezing, sending delicious tremors down my spine. "What you're touching right now is sacred. It's to be respected."

Hot breath fans across the shell of my ear, followed by his wicked voice, "It's to be feared."

I swallow, my eyes fluttering when his fingers brush up my stomach, eliciting goosebumps.

A sharp gasp leaves my lips when I see something massive and gray swim beneath the surface. I jump back, bumping into Enzo, but he's solid stone and doesn't allow me to get very far.

"Oh my God," I breathe when a great white shark breaks the surface only mere feet away, swallowing a large chunk of chum in the water.

"There's another!" I squeal, noticing another great white about ten feet away.

"Mmhm," he hums deeply, his hands wandering down to the button of my shorts. I can't decide which to focus on—the terrifying beasts that are several feet away or what Enzo is doing.

Deftly, his fingers slip past my unbuttoned jeans and slide along the waistband of my bottoms, snagging my attention completely. Fuck the sharks, I'm more concerned about the one behind me.

"What are you doing?" I whisper, though I'm not sure if I really care.

In lieu of a response, his thumbs hook into the waistband of my shorts and bathing suit bottoms and he pulls them down as far as they'll go.

"Take them off," he orders, voice deeper than the ocean we're treading on, sending another shiver rolling down my spine.

"I thought this wasn't sex," I say shakily.

"Do you want me to stop?"

"God, no," I choke out, removing the bottoms the rest of the way and tossing them to the side.

"Good girl," he purrs, sliding down his own shorts. I feel his length brush across my backside, and my body immediately tightens with visceral need.

Why can't he be like the other men?

Mediocre, at best—if I'm lucky. They were so much easier to let go of. To forget about, until someone called me by their name.

"Can you take me, *bella ladra*?"

I don't know what *bella ladra* means, but I'm too lost in the feel of him dragging his fingers through my pussy to care.

"Yes," I moan, trembling when I feel the tip of his cock replacing his fingers.

My teeth clamp down on my bottom lip as he slowly pushes inside me, stretching me until the burn is as cathartic as the bruising grip around my hips.

He gives me barely any time to truly adjust and sets a quick, steady pace, pumping inside me until my eyes are crossing.

bella ladra - *beautiful thief*

"I needed one more time with you," he rasps. *"Ancora una volta."*

Heart in my throat, a choked moan slips past. Adrenaline ignites when one of the sharks splash right in front of the boat, causing my muscles to tighten. Enzo groans in response, feeling my body clench around him.

He drives into me harder and reaches around to slip his fingers between my thighs, circling them over my clit. My head kicks back, and the world around me fades, monsters be damned.

"Do they scare you?" he murmurs.

"Mmm?" I mumble, an orgasm forming in the pit of my stomach. All my focus is on that tightening knot, so desperate for it to snap, yet never wanting it to end.

"Goddamn, you're gripping me so fucking tight. Move up," he demands, grabbing my hips and nudging me forward. I try to resist, but he easily overpowers me. My breath stalls as he coerces me to the very edge of the boat, where two massive sharks swim beneath.

"Enzo," I breathe, fear filling my bloodstream, yet it only serves to heighten the pleasure streaming throughout my body as he rolls his hips.

My head tips back, a moan working its way out of my throat. I'm so close, and my lungs are depleting of oxygen as he drives me to that edge. I need to breathe desperately, and I won't be able to as long as he's inside me. I reach down between my legs to circle my clit, but he stops me.

"Did I say you could come?" he asks darkly.

"Please, I need it," I plead, my brows pinching.

"*Cazzo*, I don't know how you do it," he groans.

A gasp leaves my lips when his hand reaches around and seizes me by the throat, pulling me into him until my back is molded to his chest.

Ancora una volta. - *Just one more*
Cazzo - *Fuck*

"Tell me how," he murmurs in my ear, his voice hardening. Even with an orgasm on the horizon, an alarm starts ringing in the back of my head when his hand tightens.

"How what?" I choke out, his thrusts becoming more savage.

"Tell me how you can fuck me so easily knowing that you've stolen from me."

My eyes widen, and though my body turns solid stone, he doesn't stop rolling his hips.

He knows. He's known this whole time. And I walked right into his trap like an idiot.

"It's like you're fucking begging for me to break you."

A whimper breaks through the constrictive barrier his hand is creating around my windpipe, and my hands fly to his, clawing at them to release me. He doesn't stop thrusting, and despite the terror beginning to take over, I'm still on the precipice of coming.

"You want to draw blood, baby?" he breathes, forcing my head back until his lips are poised over mine.

"I can do worse," he whispers, rolling his hips again, his cock hitting a spot that has my eyes threatening to roll. I force them ahead, desperately trying to bring myself away from oblivion, but he's making it impossible when he hits... *fuck,* when he hits that spot there.

"Let me go," I wheeze, scraping my nails harder.

"I said I'd give you a kiss for coming with me, didn't I? Unlike you, I'm not a fucking liar."

And just as the last word slips from his mouth, his teeth clamp onto my bottom lip and bite. *Hard.*

I squeal, thrashing against him as copper fills my mouth. This isn't a fucking *kiss.* It feels like he's trying to sever my goddamn lip from my face. He rips himself away, breathing heavily, my blood smeared across his chin.

I'm gasping for breath, terror constricting my chest from the feral look on his face. He's fucking scaring me, and as his eyes zero in on my bleeding lip, I have a sick feeling he hasn't even begun to truly scare me yet.

"Such a pretty sight, to see you bleed for me," he rasps. "I don't think I'm the only thing that'll love it, though."

Before his words can be processed, he's forcing my head down. Immediately, his intentions become clear. My eyes widen as a horror unlike anything I've ever felt grabs ahold of me. Of my heart, my lungs, my entire fucking being.

"No, no, *no, NO...*" I scream, fighting like my life depends on it because my life *does* depend on it.

"You wanted to be a shark expert, baby girl? You wanted to take that from me? Then you gotta learn how to fucking swim with them."

My pleas are cut off as he finally pushes my head into the water. My eyes open, immediately burning from the salt, but I hardly notice. Not when I see the blood from my lip swirling within the seawater.

The water where two massive great white sharks are lurking.

I desperately thrash against him, feeling like the predator in the water is going to come up any second and bite me. Meanwhile, Enzo continues to move inside me, his other hand bruising on my hip.

Just when my vision begins to blacken, he's lifting my head up, and I suck in a harsh breath, my eyes wide with hysteria. Still, he roughly fucks me while I heave in precious oxygen.

"The taste of you is fucking addicting, I must admit," he purrs in my ear. "Let them taste you, too, baby."

"Wait," I choke, the word overpowered by a wet cough. My nails score into his thighs, but I can feel him beginning to push my head back down. "Wait!"

All I can manage is another scream before he's shoving my head back underwater.

My heart is beating erratically, and I thrash in his hold again but only achieve drowning myself faster. Water fills my lungs, and *oh God*, I feel the pulse of water moving. Like something massive is heading right toward me— and fast, too.

For the second time, he's pulling me out of the water, and I'm immediately heaving in air, choking on it, and hacking up water.

A sob bursts from my throat, tears streaming down my cheeks and mixing with the water pouring down my face from my drenched hair.

"Enzo! P-please, don't let them—"

"Don't worry, baby, they're not the ones you should be afraid of."

Before I can get another word out, he's forcing me back down again. My eyes snap open, and this time I *do* see something move beneath the surface. It's blurry, but it's fast. And it's shooting up from the depths of the ocean, aiming straight for me.

Enzo moves inside me quicker and then suddenly pulls out. Just barely do I feel something wet splash onto my back, but I'm far more concerned about the predator seconds away from taking me under.

Just as I'm convinced that I'm going to be eaten alive, he yanks my head out of the water again. Once more, I'm heaving in air, choking on it, and coughing as my eyes bug from my head.

Seconds later, the shark bursts through the surface right where my head had been, bashing into the boat, its mouth open as it searches for its prey.

I scream, scrambling back into Enzo as the boat rocks violently. He gets to his feet, dragging me backward, then drops me, leaving me hyperventilating. I'm still drowning, but only in absolute terror.

I cough up more water and pitifully crawl away. There's nowhere for me to go, but I'm moving on autopilot, and the only thing I'm desperate for more than oxygen is to get the fuck away from the edge of the boat.

The vessel rocks from when the shark bashed into it, but it barely registers. Tears are spilling from my eyes, I'm still naked from the waist down, and I'm pretty sure he came all over my back. I feel... I don't know, but I do know that nothing has ever made me feel worse.

Nothing.

Enzo is leaning against the glass wall that leads to the scuba gear, dressed once more, with his arms and legs crossed and tongue in his cheek as he stares at me stoically. As if he didn't just get off while he held me underwater.

Avoiding his eyes, my bottom lip violently trembles as I grab my bathing suit bottoms and slip them back on, at a loss for words.

Maybe I deserved that. Maybe I deserve worse.

I've stolen from so many people—fucked with so many lives, and caused a lot of grief. I know that.

So, I keep my mouth shut, grab my jean shorts, and wipe my back down as best I can before slipping them on. I'm berating myself for leaving my phone in my van, even if it's completely useless right now. His credit card is still in the back pocket, the outline of it searing against the fabric as he watches me clean off his release. I'd rather my clothes be covered in him than my skin.

Then, I huddle in the corner, praying he'll just take me back. I don't really have a home, but right now, anything but here will suffice.

"Why'd you do it?" he asks finally, devoid of emotion. I shiver, the ice in his voice colder than the water he drowned me in.

I glance at him, my eyes on fire from the salt.

"I'll pay you back," I croak. My throat is also on fire, and my words come out broken and hoarse.

His brow furrows. "You can't stop lying, can you?"

Red crawls up my cheeks, embarrassed because he›s right. I would run before I ever did the right thing. "How much did you charge on the credit card?"

My shoulders hike to my ears, ashamed. "Less than a grand, I think."

His lips flatten. "Ever heard of getting—"

"A job? Yes, I have. I may live out of a van, but I don't live under a rock," I snap, growing tired of his questions. I may owe him money, an apology, and maybe even a couple of years in jail—but I *don't* owe him an explanation.

Or maybe I do, but that's the one thing I won't give him.

"I could have you arrested."

I shrug and mutter, "I guess then maybe I can stop running."

He narrows his eyes, once more staring at me as he contemplates something.

"You're wanted for your crimes, aren't you? That's why you can't get a real job."

I tighten my lips and say, "Yep."

I've worked under-the-table jobs before, but most places require socials, IDs, and conduct background checks. I'm not stupid enough to use another person's name, and I sure as hell can't use my own.

He scoffs, shaking his head. "Why not just get a job at sixteen like a normal fucking person? Why even dig yourself in a hole like that to begin with?"

I glare at him and conjure the energy to stand. Oxygen flows through my lungs like they were never full of water, but I'm still shaking like a leaf.

"You know nothing about me. If you want to think I'm a petty criminal who only does it for the thrill, fine. But don't insult us both by making ignorant assumptions about me."

He snarls, and my stomach tightens with fear. The sharks seemed to have grown bored and are wandering off, but that doesn't mean he still can't throw me overboard and let them find me again.

Glowering, he runs a hand through his hair, visibly frustrated.

"Was I calling you by another man's name this entire time? When I fucked you?"

Again, my stomach tightens, only for different reasons. Namely, because any reminder of him inside me has my face burning, and I hate that because of what he just did to me. And how badly I still feel humiliated.

I look down, and that's answer enough.

"What's your real name?" he demands.

I don't want to tell him. There's a chance I can escape once we get on land.

Make a run for it and somehow slip from his fingers. I can find somewhere else to hide in Australia until I'm ready to risk flying again.

There's still a chance of survival, and if he wants to figure out my name *after* I'm well and gone, all the power to him. I'm sure there are plenty of articles about me, though he won't find many truths in those, either.

When I continue to hesitate, he stalks toward me, causing my muscles to stiffen and my throat to thicken.

I stumble away from him, but I'm already backed into the corner, leaning against the side of the boat. He advances until he's pressed into me, his arms trapping me against his heated body.

"*Guardami*," he orders sharply.

I shake my head, not understanding him but knowing that whatever it is, I don't want to do it. I suck my bottom lip between my teeth in an effort to hide how it quivers.

Enzo reaches up and grips my jaw, forcing my eyes to him. Snarling, I still try to put distance between us, but his strength prevails over my weak attempt.

"I want to know the name I *should've* been moaning that night."

Tears are rising again. Not because he's hurting me, but because I see my chances of getting away slipping through my fingers like water in my palms.

Screwing my eyes shut, a tear slips through, but they quickly pop open when he leans forward and gently kisses the tear. Pulling away, he licks the droplet off his lips.

"Those tears—they're mine now. And I'll pull plenty more out of you if you don't tell me what I want to know."

Jesus. Fucking psychopath.

Guardami - *Look at me*

"Candace," I bark out.

"Last name?"

I stutter, unable to think of anything quick enough.

His lips slide along my cheek, whispering, "I'm getting impatient, baby."

Tears swim in my eyes, and as badly as I want to give him another false name, all I can think is that lying about my name isn't worth getting eaten alive over.

"Sawyer," I rush out finally, followed by another useless attempt to pull my face out of his grip.

"Sawyer," he repeats slowly, my name sounding like roses and chocolate on his tongue. "Is that another lie, *bella ladra*?"

"No," I snap.

"Last name?"

"Bennett," I mutter.

He hums, something poised on the tip of his tongue, but then his eyes are snapping above my head.

"Fuck," he curses, ripping himself away from me and hurrying toward where he dropped the anchor.

Confused, I turn around, wondering what the hell could make him react like that—and then immediately wish I hadn't.

The horizon is nearly black. Storm clouds are coming in fast, and from here, I can see the waves growing choppier and bigger. The water beneath us has already become more turbulent, though I'm sure this is mild compared to what's ahead.

"Enzo?" I call out, concerned and wary. My poor heart can't take all this stress. I still haven't recovered from nearly getting my head bitten off by a shark, and now this.

"Let me concentrate," he snaps, working on pulling up the anchor. Just as he says that, a strike of lightning appears in the quickly approaching storm, yanking a gasp from my throat.

Despite our very concerning situation, I want to fucking laugh. So badly, I want to laugh.

A smile cracks on my face when he throws the heavy metal on the boat and rushes toward the wheel. He catches sight of my face but doesn't let up on his mission.

"Something funny, Sawyer?" he asks, ensuring to use my name. I don't know if it's to reassert power, or what, but it has the smile slipping from my face like melted wax.

"You brought me out here to make me think I'm going to die. And now look, we're *both* going to die."

CHAPTER 8

Enzo

The boat groans and the wheel in my hand slips as a powerful wave rocks into us, salty water pouring over into the hull. The cage on the back swings, the heavy weight working against us as we sway dangerously side to side. Sweat gathers along my hairline as I fight to keep us from going under.

Cazzo, cazzo, cazzo!

Seeing Sawyer on the beach fucked with my head more than I expected it to. I had a mouthful of shit I planned to say to her, but the only thing at the forefront of my mind was to teach her a lesson. Taking her out on the boat wasn't planned. Fucking her again definitely wasn't planned. And now, I regret all of it.

I know better than to go out on the water without checking the goddamn weather, but today... God fucking dammit.

It's my own fault, yet I still want to kill the little blonde thief for it anyway.

It was never my intention to kill her, and my stomach is twisted with the knowledge that I might have anyway.

"Enzo!" she screams, snagging my attention. I turn to find a massive wave building up over the boat, like Poseidon himself is reaching up from the depths of the ocean and preparing to grab onto the vessel and pull it under.

Time slows, and my heart drops. And I know... I just know that this one is going to send us over.

"Sawyer! Get up here!" I shout, but she's already clambering to the helm, eyes wide with panic.

Just as she slams into my chest, the wave breaks, and I grab her face, forcing her wild gaze to mine.

"Deep breath, baby."

Seconds later, the wave is crashing down upon us. A loud scream rings in my ears, but only the echo of it remains. My vision is snuffed out, and freezing water encapsulates me. I'm swept up in a powerful riptide, and the only thing I can do is succumb to nature's will.

I feel myself spinning as I'm ripped away from Sawyer and dragged down into the deep ocean, nothing but blackness surrounding me.

Instinctively, I kick my legs, forcing my eyes open to find my bearings. The salt stings, but my adrenaline supersedes the pain. Above me, the *Johanna* is belly-up and quickly nose-diving toward me.

My chest burns with the need for oxygen, but I can only think of one thing. *Where is she?*

Swimming with all my might, I search for Sawyer but see nothing except pieces of broken wood drifting by.

I breach the surface and immediately suck in a lungful of air, only to choke on it. Taking another deep breath, I bellow, "SAWYER!"

But the sea is unforgiving, and I'm swept up by another wave, sending me spiraling once more. I'm growing tired already, so I force myself to relax until the tide releases me. Only for me to kick toward the surface once more.

Her name is the first thing out of my mouth the second I break the surface, but it's no use. My voice is only swallowed by the thunder, and I'm being dragged under again.

I can't let this be it. I can't let it end this way.

But then I'm slamming into something hard, and everything goes black.

Enzo.

Wake up, please.

Please, please, wake up.

Even in death, her voice haunts me. It's tragic that I can't escape her—my own undoing. But then something is tugging me out of the bottomless pit of darkness I've settled into. I'm comfortable here. Content. Something I only feel when I'm swimming along with a great white.

"Enzo."

Her voice sharpens, becoming louder and harsher to my ears.

Slowly, the feel of gritty sand digging into my cheek registers, and then the lapping of water periodically splashing against my face.

It's hard to breathe. My lungs produce a loud wheeze, and after a moment, a fist lands painfully on my back. Liquid rushes up my throat, forcing me fully awake and plunging me deep into a coughing fit, water pouring from my mouth.

Jesus, fuck, she should've just let me drown in it.

"Oh, thank God," her sweet voice filters in, saturated with relief.

Pushing myself to my hands and knees, I work to catch my breath while cracking open my eyes. Squinting against the burn in them, my vision filters in. I'm staring down at sand that's clustered with gray rocks. It's dark outside now, but the moonlight and stars are bright out here.

Sawyer kneels before me, her hands resting on her knees as she stares at me. Lifting my gaze to her, I find her cutting a look over my form, likely checking for injury. Then, her blue irises meet mine again.

She doesn't look much better off than I feel. Curly hair a tangled mess, jean shorts tattered, and her exposed skin is covered in dirt and scratches, dried blood crusting over them.

I'm almost angry at how relieved I am that she's alive.

I don't want her death on my conscience, I tell myself. But that sounds hollow even in my own goddamn head.

Fuck.

How long has it been? How long have we been here? Wherever here is.

"Your head is bleeding," she informs me. "Doesn't look too terrible, though."

I sit back on my heels and brush my hands over my temple, hissing when it stings. The wound is clotted, and I can feel the blood crusted down the side of my face, though infection is still a possibility.

"How long have you been awake?" I ask, pulling my stare away from her and looking up to find a massive, imposing lighthouse.

It's decrepit, the red and white stripes ringed around the building chipped and blackening. It sits upon a treacherous rock cliff, and the sight of it has dread's sharp claws sinking into my skin. It appears like it came out of a horror movie. Of course, this is our only option for refuge.

It's too dark to see exactly how big the island is, but it doesn't seem to span more than a few miles. From what I can tell, the land is mostly barren, save for what looks like more rock cliffs.

Cazzo.

"A few minutes," she answers, turning to look at the lighthouse over her shoulder.

We're stranded out here but not out of luck yet.

Hopefully, we can find an old radio inside that might have some juice left or turn on the beacon until someone notices us. If it still even fucking works. This place looks ancient, but there has to be something we can use.

I sigh and drop my head low between my shoulders, angry and frustrated that I'm here. With her.

"Glad to see you're alive," I rasp out. It wasn't intended to sound sarcastic, yet it did anyway. And I don't bother correcting it.

I may not want her dead, but that doesn't make her any less dead to me.

"Yeah," she whispers. "Me too."

When I raise my head, she looks forlorn, her brow pinched as she chews on her swollen, bruised lip. I did that, and I'm having a hard time feeling an ounce of guilt.

With the rise of the moon comes a deep chill in the air. My damp clothes are freezing, the cold settling deep in my bones.

"*Andiamo*," I say simply, nodding toward the lighthouse. "We need to get warm and see if there are any radios in there."

She sniffs and nods. Aches come alive the moment I stand, screaming at me as I trudge behind Sawyer.

As we make our way toward the cliff, I notice the sand is littered with sharp rocks. Somehow, my shoes managed to survive the storm, and I'm glad for it.

Within minutes, though, I notice Sawyer's stride grows choppy. The rocks are beginning to cut into her feet. She wore flip-flops onto the boat, so those are long gone.

Good.

Her body is bowed with exhaustion, and truthfully, it's a miracle she's alive. I still have no idea how we both managed to get here, but I'm quickly distracted from asking when I see a flash from one of the windows above. It happened too quickly to see what it was.

Probably just my mind playing tricks on me, but I stay on guard anyway.

Andiamo - *Let's go*

We come up to a set of stone steps, and as we climb toward the crumbling structure, the dreaded feeling in the pit of my stomach grows.

"Someone still lives here," she tells me. "I think I saw the beacon earlier."

I pause, prompting her to stop and face me while I stare up at the top of the lighthouse. It doesn't look like it's been used in years, but for probably the first time, I believe she's telling the truth. If that's the case, then we have a good chance of getting out of here.

"We'll stay cautious," I assure her, motioning for her to keep going.

"Or do you think it's haunted?" Sawyer bursts out, as if physically incapable of keeping the question in any longer. "Maybe I hallucinated it. Or a ghost turned it on."

"I think ghosts are the least of our worries," I answer. "Starvation and dehydration are a little more fucking concerning."

"Well, which is worse? Dying of hunger or dying of scary ghosts?" she volleys back.

"Which is quicker?"

She nods. "Okay, you got me there. May the bean gods bless us then."

"The what?" I snap, my annoyance deepening. Even shipwrecked, she can't stop fucking talking.

"The bean gods," she repeats, reaching the last step and coming up to a cement pathway. "Canned beans survive the apocalypse. They're always the number one thing left in cabinets after the world ends. So, I imagine they'll be in this abandoned lighthouse that potentially hasn't seen life since the dinosaurs."

"There is so much wrong with what you just said."

Ignoring me, she shoots me a look over her shoulder.

"Be careful, though. The beans will give you flatulence."

"Sawyer, stop fucking talking."

"It's helping with my anxiety."

"Yeah, well, it's not helping with my headache. Now get behind me. I want to make sure it's safe first," I snap, grabbing her arm and physically dragging her back when she nearly steps on a piece of glass.

"Chill," she huffs, ripping herself out of my grip.

"You were about to step on glass. You almost hurt yourself. Walk where I walk."

"My hero," she grumbles, venom in her tone. But I ignore her, approaching a dirty and splintering wooden door. That ominous feeling deepens, and I'm starting to wonder if I should just take my chances with the ocean.

Stopping before the door, I knock on it a few times, waiting for several long moments. Silence.

Slowly, I turn the rusty knob, finding it unlocked. The door creaks open, and I'm immediately overwhelmed by the smell of mildew and stale air.

We come directly into a small living area. There's a blue couch to the right with a little end table next to it, and a lamp on top with junk scattered around it. A crease forms between my brows when I spot bullets and what looks like an antique key. The crease deepens when I note a portable fireplace in front of the couch, sitting next to a tiny box television on a stand. There's ash piled inside the fireplace. Placing a hand to the black metal, my chest clenches when I feel how warm it is.

My eyes skip around the room, my muscles tensing with wariness. The far left wall is covered in bookcases, filled with cracked spines and what looks like children's books. There is a thin layer of dust on the end table and only a few cobwebs draping along the peeling floral wallpaper. This place should be covered in grime, and though it's no five-star hotel, it certainly looks lived in.

Straight ahead is a doorway that leads into a large kitchen and dining room area, my stomach twisting as I walk farther in. The white cabinetry is sagging and rotting, and one of the doors is slightly ajar. A big wooden table is off to the left, a ratty, dirty rug beneath it. To the right is a spiral staircase, rust corroding the black metal.

"Is that a dirty dish in the sink?" Sawyer asks in a hushed tone.

Obviously, it's a dish.

But how could someone possibly survive out here by themselves?

Just as I'm ready to turn toward the staircase, a hand is gripping my arm, fear imprinting into my skin beneath her sharp nails.

There's an obnoxious noise as someone comes down the steps, but I'm quickly distracted when I realize I'm staring down the barrel of a shotgun. Behind it is a short, old man with a beard down to his waistline and a stormy expression beneath his worn red hat.

"Wanna tell me why you're in my home?" he asks slowly, his voice creaking worse than the wooden floors.

Slowly, I lift my hands, and Sawyer presses into my side, tucking herself behind me. I'm tempted to push her the fuck away, but her clinging to me is the least of my worries right now.

"We got caught in that storm and shipwrecked. We knocked, but no one answered," I explain evenly.

"We're sorry to intrude, sir," Sawyer rushes out. "We don't really have anywhere else to go right now."

The old man looks at Sawyer, and I can visibly see his eyes softening. Gun or not, I'm seconds away from shoving her farther behind me and telling the fucker to find something else to moon over. She may be a siren, but she's mine to hurt just as much as she's mine to protect.

After several long seconds, he lowers his gun, casting a suspicious look my way.

"The storm could be seen from a mile away," he grumbles.

I grind my teeth, the muscle in my jaw pulsing, but I abstain from snapping at him. He's right, anyway.

"But ah'ight," he continues. "I'll let ya stay here. The more, the merrier, I s'pose."

He waddles over toward the kitchen, and it's then that I notice that his right leg is a wooden peg. His gait is uneven, the ancient prosthetic too short, even for his stunted stature.

I furrow my brow. How long has this man been here for?

"Name's Sylvester," he introduces, shooting a glance over his shoulder.

"Do you have a radio here?" I ask. Don't care to know who he is, just how the fuck we can get off this forgotten island.

He grunts, opens a cabinet to pull out two mugs, and then slams it shut, seemingly bothered by my manners.

I just stare, waiting for an answer.

"'Fraid not," he finally responds, cutting me another unimpressed look before turning to slide out a pot of coffee from the machine.

"Coffee is from this mornin', so it's cold," he warns. "But I'll warm it up for ya first."

Sawyer nudges my arm from behind and whispers, "See, the bean gods did bless us. With coffee beans."

My eye twitches.

"Would like to know yer names, if ya don't mind," he says, turning to stick the two mugs in the microwave.

I mind.

"Sawyer," the little thief supplies hurriedly.

I grind my teeth harder. Apparently, she doesn't feel the need to lie to *him* about her name, and something about that annoys the fuck out of me. Then again, there are very few things in this world that don't.

"His name is Enzo. Sorry for his manners. He got bullied in school and hasn't seen a therapist yet. We really appreciate your kindness."

Anger spikes in my chest, and slowly, I turn to glower at her. The microwave beeps loudly, and the old man turns to grab the cups, unaware of how close I am to wrapping my hands around her throat. She spares me a glance before turning her attention back to Sylvester, who is now carrying over two steaming cups of coffee toward us.

Here, she's not so scared of me. She thinks an old man with a wooden leg will save her.

Ignoring my glare, she smiles wide at Sylvester, accepting the mug with a warmth in her entirely fabricated expression. Just like everything else about her.

It's not hard to see she's as broken as they come—the only thing warm about her is her pussy.

Still, she radiates sunshine, and all it makes me want to do is wipe it clean from her face. She's the light that blinds you right before lightning strikes.

Silently, I accept the mug from Sylvester, dipping my chin an increment. Sawyer's right—I don't have manners. But I also know better than to bite the hand that feeds you.

"You both go on over to the couch and relax. I'll start a fire and get ya warmed up," he directs, grunting as he hobbles to the kitchen sink.

"Thank you, Syl," Sawyer says warmly. She pivots and heads toward the couch while I stand firm.

Syl? She's nicknaming the fucker already?

I snarl at her as she passes by, and she puts an extra pep in her step to get away.

My mood souring by the second, I turn to the caretaker, his back to me as he rinses off the dish in the sink.

"So, how do you get all these supplies?" I question. Sylvester stills. "If you have no radios and such," I tack on, my tone dripping with doubt.

I don't like liars.

"My radio stopped working a week ago. Dead batteries and got no replacements. A cargo ship comes 'round here about once a month, and I buy everything I need from 'em."

"Buy? You're still working?"

He shoots me a glare. "I'm retired. And being retired pays well. My money ain't no concern of yours."

It isn't, but his story adding up is.

Finishing at the sink, he hobbles toward a woodpile stacked against the far left wall, and I narrow my eyes.

"When did the last cargo ship come by?"

Another grunt as he starts piling wood into his arms.

"Three days ago," he answers. "I told 'em about it, and they didn't have any with them, so they promised to bring me replacements next month."

I just barely manage to suppress a scowl as he turns around and hobbles toward me. Fury is bubbling in my chest, threatening to spew out of my mouth.

What he's not saying is, we're stuck here for a fucking month. A month with an old, strange man and a girl who nearly stole my entire fucking life from me.

"I'm sure we can shine the beacon and wait for someone to come by."

He scoffs. "Ain't no ships come around here if they can help it. These waters are dangerous, as you've come to learn yerself. That's why my supplier only comes by once a month."

I grind my teeth. Sawyer may have made a fool out of me, but I know deep in my bones that he's hiding something.

"I'd like to see the radio."

"Be my guest, boy," he chortles condescendingly, digging in his pocket, pulling it out, and then tossing it at me. I catch it in my hand, shooting him a glare.

"You carry dead radios in your pocket often?" I challenge, quirking a brow.

He grunts. "Habit."

It's a black compact device and completely dead. The switch is already in the ON position. Unconvinced, I slide off the back cover. The batteries are hot to the touch, which immediately invokes suspicion, but I can't prove he did anything yet. So, I stay silent as he makes his way into the little living room and starts piling the wood inside of the fireplace.

"Coffee okay?" Sylvester asks Sawyer. "Go 'head and put your feet up."

"Coffee is great," she chirps, lifting her feet to the fireplace. The bottoms are cut up and bleeding, but she doesn't complain.

"Got a first aid kit?" I ask.

Sylvester looks to me and then slides his gaze toward Sawyer's feet when he notices where I'm staring.

"My golly, young lady!" he exclaims. "Yer gonna get yerself an infection. Let me grab the kit."

As if I don't have dried blood on the side of my face, but what-the-fuck-ever.

Sawyer opens her mouth, guilt etched into her face and gearing up to likely tell him not to worry, so I snap, "Let him."

She glances at me, now clenching her jaw with irritation. Must've lost all my fucks to give in the ocean.

"He has trouble getting around," she mutters once Sylvester leaves, making his way slowly up the spiral steps.

"They'll get infected, and then *you'll* have trouble getting around. You want wooden pegs just like him?"

She rolls her eyes. "I would never use wood. I'd be cursed with splinters for the rest of my life. I'd much prefer to be a cyborg."

My frustration mounts. Everything is a fucking joke with her.

Right as I open my mouth, Sylvester is clanging loudly down the stairs and calling out, "I got plenty of stuff in here! Must admit, I don't find much reason to hurt muh-self these days, so use whatever ya need."

Grinding my teeth, I meet him halfway and grab the first aid kit, sweat gleaming along his red face.

"Thank you, son. Most days, I use my crutches to get around. This leg ain't so agreeable with me. I don't have much as far as clothing, but I got ya both some dry t-shirts and some sweats fer now."

He hands over the clothing, the small pile smelling musty. Again, I keep silent as I sit next to Sawyer and hand her the kit after grabbing my own alcohol pad.

She can clean her own damn wounds. As long as they heal and can carry her happy ass onto a boat, then into a police station when we get back to Port Valen, I'm satisfied.

Muttering a *thank you*, she gets to work while I clean up the cut on my temple. My head feels like it's splitting open, and it's possible I may have a concussion, but I'm not anticipating sleeping much tonight anyway.

"How is it you still have electricity?" I question, glancing at Sawyer. Her tongue is sticking out as she swipes at the bottom of her foot.

"Got me some solar panels out back and a nice generator. Them things cost me a fortune, but suppose it was necessary."

"How long have you been here?" Sawyer asks, finishing her sentence with a hiss.

"Since 1978," he declares proudly. "I've been takin' care of Raven Isle since it was built. Been out of commission for about twelve years or so, but I couldn't let 'er go."

"Raven Isle," Sawyer repeats, glancing at Sylvester. "That's the name of the island?"

"Sure is. Named 'er myself."

"It's pretty," she replies, though she's distracted. She keeps trying to turn her foot at an angle that's not physically possible so she can reach a cut.

"Your foot doesn't bend that way," I tell her, since apparently, she needs to be reminded.

"It would if I was a cyborg," is her rebuttal.

I'm going to kill her.

Even still, she tries to twist it in a different direction, but that fails, too.

"Jesus Christ, let me see it. You're going to fucking break it."

Shooting me a glare, she sticks her foot right in my face. I angrily snatch her ankle and push it down to my lap, returning her glare tenfold.

"Lover's quarrel. Been too long since I've had one of them," Sylvester cuts in.

I turn my glare to him for a brief moment before focusing on her shredded skin.

"He's not my lover," Sawyer says. "Just an asshole who got us in this situation in the first place."

My hand flexes around her ankle until she squeaks. It takes effort to relent on my grip. I'd love nothing more than to crush it and watch her suffer.

"Ah," the old man says, clearly uncomfortable with our arguing. Couldn't give a shit less, so I keep quiet and start cleaning her cuts.

As tempted as I was to leave her to her own devices, she was annoying the shit out of me, and I really didn't need the extra trouble of her injuries.

She hisses when I wipe at a wound unkindly, dried blood crusted over it.

Only then, do I feel a little better. It's not the worst pain I'll cause her, but it'll suffice for now.

CHAPTER 9

Sawyer

I hate him.

I *loathe* him.

If I could physically rip out every word that defines him as an asshole from the dictionary and shove it down his throat, I would.

But I'm also scared.

I'm trapped in a creepy lighthouse with a strange caretaker and a man who looks at me as if he'd prefer to see me between a shark's teeth.

There's no escaping this place—no escaping *him*. I've always been able to run. It's what I've done my entire life. And now that I can't, it feels like my body has been invaded by tiny needle-like parasites. I'm tempted to put my nails to my own flesh and start clawing my way out, but it wouldn't get me any farther away from this place.

It's late at night, and there's as little artificial light as there is natural.

Shadows dance across Enzo's and Sylvester's faces, their features only visible beneath the orange glow emanating from the fireplace. There's a lamp on the end table, but Sylvester doesn't seem inclined to flip it on.

I yelp when Enzo suddenly grabs my other foot. He gives me a look, probably because I hurt his precious ears, then continues with cleaning my injuries, reigniting the flares of pain.

I'd rather stick my foot in the ocean and call it a day, but going outside in the dark sounds even more terrifying than the prospect of Enzo taking care of me. Just barely, though.

"When yer done with 'er, I'll show you two to yer room," Sylvester announces. My heart drops, the implication in his words sending ants crawling down my spine.

"We'll have our own rooms, right?" I ask. Enzo stops cleaning, looking up at the old man, also waiting for a response.

"'Fraid not. Only one other room here."

Oh, no. This day couldn't have gotten any worse, yet somehow, it did.

"I can sleep on the couch," Enzo offers.

"That ain't gonna work for me, son. This is my home, and I don't like nobody sleepin' in my living space. Sometimes I like to stay up late and watch some television." His tone is stern and brokering no room for argument.

"There's only one bed?" I ask sullenly, already knowing the answer and hating it.

"That's right," he affirms. I must've been clinging onto some shred of hope because my heart withers into dust right then and there.

Either I'll have to share a bed with a man who hates me, or one of us will sleep on the floor with the bugs.

I work to swallow. Knowing him, Enzo will force me to sleep on the floor while he takes the bed. He's no gentleman, that's for damn sure.

Enzo pushes my feet off his lap angrily and stands. The tension in the air thickens, and unsurprisingly, Sylvester doesn't shy away from his glare. Awkwardly, I shuffle to my feet, the pain flaring in them again while I clear my throat.

"We'll make it work, Syl. Thank you."

Enzo turns his eyes to me, but I'm not as brave. Not that I ever plan to let the asshole know that. So despite the need for my spine to bend, I force it straight. It's ingrained into the very marrow of my bones to shrink beneath the weight of a stare. If I allow them to look too long, they might see beneath the brittle mirage I've built around myself. They'll see the cracks and the imperfections, and with one poke, they'll find that it was nothing more than a clever illusion.

The man before me has already seen the ugly beneath the glimmering rainbow. Turns out, he was only looking into his own reflection.

I may carry ugliness inside of me, but he's no fucking beauty queen, either.

Sylvester waves us toward the spiral staircase.

"I'd like fer you two to be in your room by nine o'clock every night, if ya don't mind," Sylvester says as he leads us toward the metal steps. "It's about ten o'clock now, so I'll get ya settled in quick."

My brows plunge. I can't remember the last time I've been given a bedtime. Certainly never when I was a grown adult. But despite Sylvester posing the request as polite, it goes without saying he wouldn't care even if I did mind. Which I do.

Clearing my throat, I say, "Okay."

I suppose a bedtime isn't the worst thing to be bestowed upon me in the last twenty-four hours. I'm just grateful that I'm no longer submerged in the middle of the ocean, where ninety-five percent of it is left undiscovered— something I learned after my night with Enzo. That's all I could think of as the wave wiped us out. It's all that ran through my brain as the riptide sucked me under and then spat me out like spoiled food.

What's lurking beneath the surface? Will it swallow me whole or eat me slowly?

I don't know why the unknown creatures were haunting my thoughts more than the fact that I was surely going to drown before whatever creature could sink its teeth into me anyway. But then, somehow, my legs were kicking me toward the surface, and it was all I could do but hang onto a piece of driftwood from the boat. It said '*ana*' on it; the rest of the name lost at sea.

Sylvester's wooden leg clangs loudly as we ascend the stairs. The metal groans beneath our combined weight, and suddenly my fear morphs from strange sea creatures to being impaled by twisted metal once it finally gives.

We come up to a skinny, short hallway. At the end is a small staircase consisting of only a few steps that lead to a door. There are two more doors, one on either side of the hallway.

"The room up the steps is mine. Yours is on the left."

"What about the one on the right?" I ask.

"That would be the toilet, but I don't like anyone creepin' around my hallways at night, so there's a bucket in the room if nature calls."

I stop short, causing Enzo to collide into me.

He growls, but I'm too stunned to hardly care.

"I'm sorry, we can't use the restroom?"

"Well, of course, ya can!" Sylvester bursts, his loud voice booming as he chortles at me. "Just not after nine o'clock," he finishes as if what he's saying is even remotely reasonable.

My mouth opens then closes, but Enzo's frustration overturns my shock. He pushes me forward and spits, "*Cammina.*"

I glance over my shoulder at him, surprised that he has nothing to say about our restrictions. But then I snap it shut once again when I note his thunderous expression. Enzo may not be vocalizing the words, but his seething glare says it all. He's not any happier about being confined to the room so strictly than I am.

Swallowing, I glue my teeth shut as Sylvester opens the door, walks in, flips on a small sconce hanging over the head of the bed, and presents the room to us. It's barren, save for a rickety circular table and two chairs to our right, the wood weathered and splintering. The walls are all gray stone with a single bed shoved sideways in the left corner. A small square window is above it opposite the sconce, the beautiful night sky in perfect view.

Cammina - *Walk*

Sylvester points toward the right corner of the room. "Right there is yer bucket. You can empty it in the morning," he instructs, pointing to a white bin that looks like it's been used before without being properly cleaned.

It takes effort to keep my cheeks from blowing out. There is no fucking way I'm using that. I'd sooner pry that window open, stick my ass out of it, and let nature take over.

Enzo and I keep silent, and the stagnancy in conversation grows awkward. Does he expect us to thank him for the lovely accommodations?

"Breakfast is at seven in the mornin'. You can come down then. After that, I'm sure we can find something to keep ya occupied."

"Okay," I say softly.

"You two have yerselves a good night."

With that, he turns and hobbles out of the room, gently shutting the door behind him.

Right when I go to open my mouth, curious how he'd even know if we use the bathroom, I hear a soft click.

My teeth snap shut, and mine and Enzo's gazes collide, both full of surprise.

"Did he...?"

Enzo is already charging toward the door and turning the doorknob. But it sticks.

"He fucking locked us in here," he spits, jiggling the knob again with no luck. "*Stronzo.*"

A slimy feeling crawls down my spine and wraps around each bone until I'm encased in a deep, insidious feeling.

"Why does it feel like being imprisoned?" I ask aloud, mumbling the words as I wrap my arms tightly around myself.

"Because it fucking is," he snarls, his accent strengthening with his anger. He slams his hand against the door before storming toward the bed.

His expression is enraged yet calculating as he sits on the edge of the bed, elbows on his spread knees and fingers linked. He stares at the wooden door, likely deciding when the best time would be to bust it open.

"Don't do anything crazy," I tell him. "We literally have nowhere else to go."

He turns his blazing eyes to me, but again, I refuse to crumble beneath his fire.

"You're right, we don't have anywhere else to go. But I'm not the weaker man out of the two of us."

My eyes bug from my head. "You have the audacity to punish me for my crimes, and here you are, planning to rob an old man of his home."

The muscle in his jaw pulses, and he only glares as a response.

"Obviously, this situation is really fucked up, but it is *your* fault we got caught up in that storm to begin with. Don't punish everyone else for your fucking mistake, Enzo."

He stands abruptly and charges toward me. I blanch, stumbling back until I'm flattened against the door. His palms slam against the wood on either side of my head, consuming me in a raging storm as violent as the one that brought us to this place.

"You can steal an entire identity, but breaking out of a room is too far for you, baby? Are there any other unforgivable morals you want to share, or is it only okay when you're the one ruining lives?"

Ouch.

"Be better than me, Enzo," I bite out.

He chuckles without humor. "Not very difficult to do."

I frown, his words like a sharp hook digging into my chest.

"You can hate me, but don't put us in an even worse situation than you already have," I respond finally, my voice hushed yet firm. "He's opening his home to us, so it's only fair we respect him."

There's only a minuscule amount of space between us, and it's filled with crackling tension. He clenches his jaw but turns away, and it feels like he's ripped himself out of a force field, blanketing us.

I inhale deeply, finally able to breathe, like my body had powered down and the on switch has been flipped again.

He prowls the room like a caged animal, his shoulders nearly hiked up to his ears.

Limbs shaking, I take the opportunity to switch out of my sandy clothes while he's distracted.

Picking up the questionably clean clothes Sylvester gave me, I wrinkle my nose at the stale, musty smell emanating from the t-shirt and sweats, but it's better than sleeping in salt-dried clothes covered in sand.

I switch out my attire with his, and the entire time, I attempt to keep myself covered as much as possible as if Enzo hasn't seen me naked and spread open in ways that Jesus will surely crucify me for later. Though he's now staring out the window, arms crossed, and brooding.

When I'm finished, I make sure to tuck my belongings in a small pile, already planning on washing them tomorrow. Surprisingly, his credit card survived the storm and is still lodged in the back pocket of my cutoff shorts. I plan to hide it under the mattress later when he's not looking, but for now, I keep it rolled up between my clothing.

My selfish side and my moralistic side are clashing, both relieved and disappointed. Worse yet, I'm partly disappointed because the ocean didn't take matters out of my hands and rid me of it, granting me an easy break from it.

"I'm taking the bed," I announce after I'm done, forcing a grin and pouncing on the lumpy mattress.

"Absolutely not," he snaps, his head whipping toward me.

"I am *not* sleeping on the floor," I argue.

He thins his eyes. "You think I will?"

I cross my arms. "You're seriously not going to be a gentleman?"

"That would imply there's a lady in the room, and all I see is a fucking leech."

My mouth falls, and it feels like he just drop-kicked me in the gut. That hurt, so I get angry.

"Fuck you," I spit.

I fucking *hate* him.

"Already did, and it was the worst mistake of my life," he retorts.

He gives me his back, undressing completely, and showing me his bare ass like he didn't just stick a hot poker in my chest. It's a great ass, but even that can't distract me from the pain radiating beneath my rib cage.

The clothes are just as ill-fitting on him, and it's safe to say we'll both be reverting to our own as soon as they're clean.

I'm surprised when he gets in the bed beside me. I didn't exactly expect him to be virtuous, but I also didn't expect him to willingly sleep next to me, either. But I'm stubborn and refuse to sleep on a dusty wooden floor that will give me arthritis within a single night.

Swallowing, I make another weak attempt, "I kick in my sleep. My foot might accidentally lodge itself up your ass."

He arches a brow. "And if that happens, I will do so much worse, *bella ladra.*"

Tension simmers in the air between us, and if it weren't for the lack of smoke, I'd think this place was on fire. It's hot, and I can't fucking breathe with him next to me.

"What does that even mean?" When he doesn't immediately answer, I clarify, "*Bella ladra*. What does that mean?"

Bella is familiar, and I'm almost positive it means beautiful. And that alone is like sticking a blender in my already twisted headspace. But I don't know what *ladra* means, or if it means something different with those two words together.

"It doesn't matter. I'm tired. It's been a long day, so either move to the floor or go to fucking sleep."

Furrowing my brow, I plaster myself against the wall and tuck my legs under the threadbare navy-blue blanket.

I really don't want to sleep next to him. Still, my stubbornness persists. And apparently, so does his.

Bastard.

He gets under the blanket and immediately rolls away, giving me his back again. Even though I have no interest in him pointing his face in my direction, his iciness accompanies the tension, turning my muscles into blocks of ice.

Whatever.

Getting comfortable—or attempting to—I close my eyes, praying that when I awake, I'll be anywhere but here.

Something heavy smacks into the side of my head, knocking me out of the nightmare I was having and thrusting me into another.

I'm instantly reminded that I'm trapped on a near-abandoned island with two strangers. One of them hates me, and is currently deep in the clutches of a brain demon. That's what my mom used to call nightmares when I was young, and I haven't been able to think of them any other way.

I sit up, trying to figure out the best way to wake him, when a disturbing noise distracts me.

There's something right outside our door.

An eerie feeling cascades over me when the sound becomes more apparent. Chains. The clanging of metal chains, and them dragging slowly across the wooden floor. It reminds me of the sound of a dangerous prison inmate pacing back and forth.

My brow pinches, and uneasiness soaks the stale air. Whatever is outside feels sinister, its malevolence bleeding through the cracks in the door and reaching toward me, daring me to take its hand.

I inhale sharply, holding my breath as the dragging chains slowly fade. Just as I begin to relax, another heavy limb whips in my direction.

I yelp, just barely dodging the blow. From the flying limbs to the terrifying sound, my heart is pounding against my chest.

A low moan is building in the base of Enzo's throat. It's hard to see much, but the moonlight cutting through the window accentuates the pained look on his face.

"Enzo," I call. My voice wobbles, still shaken by the creepy prisoner in the hallway.

He groans again, but I don't dare touch him. I know enough about nightmares to know how easy it is to go into attack mode when you're convinced that you're still in the middle of it.

He thrashes his head to the side, imprisoned by his own mind.

"Enzo," I call again, louder this time. When he still doesn't wake, I gather enough bravery to nudge him.

I don't remember him having nightmares the night I stayed with him, but to be fair, by the time we actually went to bed, we were both exhausted and knocked out cold. Even my demons remained in the darkness.

Still, his dreams keep him trapped. Instead of risking getting clobbered, I slip my hand into his and thread our fingers together.

I don't know what I'm doing or why I'm doing it, but I can't seem to convince myself to let go. Especially as his pumping chest slowly calms and his twisted features begin to gradually relax.

As his anxiety eases, mine heightens. The reality of my situation is sinking in now that I'm left alone with my thoughts.

Up until this moment, I was able to distract myself from what was happening, never allowing myself to dwell on the storm and how fucking traumatizing it was. How disorienting it was to wake in the middle of the ocean, the sun quickly setting, and Enzo floating nearby, head bleeding and knocked unconscious. I hadn't let myself think about how he had just taunted sharks with my bloody lip, and seeing his injuries sent me into a tailspin, convinced the sharks were going to come back, intent on getting the meal they were previously denied.

He doesn't know the terror that was coursing through my system as I swam *to* him instead of away from him, scared for my own life yet only thinking of his.

I'll never tell him how relieved I was when I checked his pulse and felt how strong it was. Or how I immediately burst into tears when I saw a bright light in the distance, nor about how I swam the both of us there, only a piece of wood to keep us afloat. How exhausting it was. How many times I almost gave up, his weight too much for me, but my determination heavier. How much I cried. And how I refused to let him go.

How my heart cracked when he woke and looked so disappointed that I was alive.

Tears well in my eyes, and my chest tightens. The cracks yawn until a crater forms. A sob escapes, and I slap my free hand over my mouth, quickly looking to Enzo to make sure he's still asleep. But once my stare lands on him, I can't take my eyes away. His image blurs as rivers continue to fall down my cheeks.

For the first time in six years, I have nowhere to run. I'm well and truly trapped. The more this new reality sets in, the more the panic begins to take over.

God, what would Kev say now?

You're smarter than this, pipsqueak, and now look at what you've done. I told you men were bad for you. That's why you only need me.

I squeeze Enzo's hand harder, now seeking comfort from the man with a frosted heart rather than giving it. He's the last person I should be seeking anything from. But as much as I hate him for getting us into this situation—something that could've been avoided if he had only looked at the forecast—I hate myself more. Because at the end of the day, none of this would've happened if I wasn't such a shit person and left him alone.

We're in a terrible situation, but even though Sylvester makes my skin crawl, it's better than being out in that cold, lonely ocean. It's better than being dead.

At least, I think it is.

Enzo's hand flexes, so I quickly pull from his grip before he catches me. Frantically wiping the tears from my cheeks, I manage to gather myself right as his eyes open.

"What are you doing?" he asks, voice raspy and causing my lower stomach to clench. Even half asleep, his tone is cold and hard, yet the most enticing sound I've ever heard.

Clearing my throat, I clip, "Couldn't sleep."

"You're crying," he observes.

"I'm not," I lie.

He's quiet for a beat, the silence arctic.

"I'm sure you've never had to be strong before, Sawyer, but now is the time to learn."

Then, he turns over, and I close my eyes, gathering the strength I so greatly lack and holding the tears in while the cracks in my chest deepen.

CHAPTER 10

Enzo

The last time I went fishing was in college. Calling it fishing is being generous, though. Really, it was four dudes going out on a boat and drinking too much beer because we were too fucking exhausted to do anything else. Exams were kicking our asses, and I had more interest in going overboard and swimming with the fish than I did bringing them *on to* board.

My shoddy experience is now biting me in the ass.

"You're a fish expert, but you don't know how to catch them? Isn't that, like, a part of Fish School 101?"

Whoever said that breathing exercises help manage anger is a fucking con artist. I've tried a million of them since we've been out here, and I still want to choke her.

Biggest problem with that is every time I entertain that fantasy, I'm also fucking her.

Fuck.

"I don't *fish*, Sawyer. It is killing the ecosystem, which goes against everything I've literally dedicated my entire career to. I'm more interested in saving the ocean."

She purses her lips and nods thoughtfully.

"Well, I appreciate your gallant heroism. I'll make it my life's mission to have them write a book about you once we get off this island. Until then, we need to eat. Sylvester has made it clear he doesn't have enough food for us."

"Yes, I'm very aware of that. Hence, the attempt at fishing," I bite out, waving a hand at our failure of a trap. We've been out here for hours and haven't even caught plankton.

We both slept all of yesterday, and aside from occasionally getting up to pee before nine o'clock, we didn't leave the room. Both of us are still holding out on using that bucket.

Now it's the following day, and I'm no less exhausted and sore from the shipwreck. And the little witch tromping in the water isn't fucking helping.

Today is Monday, and I'm confident Troy will call the police when I don't show up at the research center. In the years we've known each other, he's never seen me miss work.

"What if we try spearfishing?" Sawyer suggests, utterly oblivious to my annoyance with her. That, or she doesn't care, and if that's the case, I have no issue making her care.

"How do you plan on making a spear?"

In lieu of a verbal response, she rushes toward the lighthouse, skipping over the sharp rocks with ease, despite her feet still being injured. At least she wrapped them this time.

Ten minutes later, she's rejoining me with a long, gnarled wooden cane, a butcher knife, and duct tape.

When I just stare, she gives me a wide grin.

"He let me use his old cane if I promised not to break it."

"Pretty sure you break everything you touch," I comment. Her smile drops, but she immediately forces it back into place. However, any light that was previously in her eyes has dissipated, and now *I* feel like the thief.

An apology is on the tip of my tongue, but I bite it back. I fell for her tricks and took pity on her before; I refuse to fall for it again.

Instead of responding, she quietly gets to work on constructing her spear. I cross my arms, unable to pull my gaze away from her, no matter how hard I try.

There's an entire ocean before me that deserves my reverence, yet all I want to do is give it to her.

And nothing... nothing has made me angrier.

She snaps me out of my turmoil when she thrusts the spear into the air with a triumphant *aha!*

"I am a master inventor, and now I will be a master spearfisher," she declares with a grin.

I really want to do something to her right now, but she's got me too fucked up to figure out what.

Keeping my expression blank, I watch her waddle back into the water, her tanned skin stark against the murky blue surface.

"Now to find the fish," she murmurs to herself, a determined pinch between her brows as she chews her bottom lip.

Her eyes widening is my only warning before she sends the pointed end of the spear into the water, a battle cry echoing across the waves.

"Oh, I so fucking got you."

Her shoulders droop when she lifts the spear and finds that she did not, in fact, get the fish.

I can't control a fraction of a smile from emerging, delighting in how her stare darkens when she glimpses it and sees how cruel it is.

She turns away, her muscles tense as she searches for a new victim.

I want to make her feel worse.

"You're going to stab your own foot before you catch a fish."

"I've been doubted my entire life, dude. I'm capable of more than you think."

I hum, slowly approaching her, intoxicated by the way her muscles ripple.

She knows who the real predator is, and it's not the one clutching a weapon for dear life.

I press into her back, and she stiffens further. Brushing my mouth over the shell of her ear, I whisper, "I know exactly what you're capable of. But you haven't managed to escape me yet, *bella ladra*. You're not as good at running as you think."

She lifts her head, her blonde curls brushing against my nose. She smells of the ocean, and I fucking hate it. It's my favorite scent, and she doesn't deserve to wear it.

"You're not as good at many things as you think you are."

The implication is loud, and I'm happy to let her make assumptions. Truthfully, Sawyer could make me come with a single look.

Even still, I'm being honest. She's a fucking godsend when it comes to sucking my cock, but she can't lie to save her life. Now that I can look beyond the cloud of lust, I see everything she doesn't say. She thinks she's good at what she does, but really, she's only made it this far by dumb luck. And based on her circumstances, that shit has run dry.

"I will stab you. Get away from me," she bites out, her tone colored with hurt.

"No."

She hisses between her teeth, only I continue before she tries to prove a point that she'd really regret.

"There's something right at your feet. Let's see if you can do one thing right, aside from ruining lives."

A strong gust of wind whips through her hair, sending the tangled curls over her face. My fist tightens, ignoring the urge to gather it in my hand and use it to hold her still while I fuck her mouth.

Whether it's because she's rising to my challenge or simply trying to ignore me, Sawyer slowly lifts the spear, immovable as she tracks the dark shadow swimming around her legs. Part of me is surprised by her ease in the ocean. There could be anything lurking beneath the surface, but she doesn't shy away as it nears.

I hope it's a jellyfish.

One moment, she's frozen. The next, she's plunging the tip of the knife into the water. And then she straightens. I can feel the victory rolling off her in waves.

Peeking over her shoulder, she cuts me a look, staring up at me beneath thick lashes, a smirk tugging up the corner of her lips.

Without looking away, she lifts the weapon, a kingfish stuck on the tip.

Dragging my gaze back to hers feels like two cars colliding head-on. The air between us thickens, and lightning races down my spine when her eyelids droop and her blue eyes heat.

"I win."

Then, she turns and goes to walk past me, gearing up to shoulder-check me, but I'm stopping her before she even makes it an inch. My hand snaps out to the side, wrapping around her throat and causing her to stiffen once more.

"*Bravissima.* Now do it again."

"Excuse you? Get your own," she chokes out, her tone dripping with malice.

Her hand grabs my wrist, nails digging into my skin as she tries to free herself of me, but it only invigorates me. Before she can blink, I release her and pluck the dead fish off the makeshift spear.

I finally give in and fist her hair with my other hand, bringing her in close.

"We're a team now, baby. Do what you do best and kill anything unfortunate enough to come near you." By the time I finish my sentence, my hand has moved to her jaw, my thumb swiping along her puffy bottom lip, a cut on it from when I bit her.

Bravissima - *Impressive, well done.*

Instead of her face flushing like I had expected, she pales, her eyes dimming like when the sun dips beneath the horizon.

Carefully, she raises her trembling hand and removes my hand from her face. Then, she turns and wades farther into the water wordlessly, resuming her search for another fish.

I can only stand there, both confused and suspicious over what the fuck that was about.

Ultimately, I walk away, deciding that I don't really care.

Sawyer doesn't bring back just one kingfish, but three.

I cock a brow, in the process of gutting the first one she caught when she tosses a bundled t-shirt onto the counter.

She reaches over and unravels the fabric, proudly displaying the dead fish within. The sight disgusts me. Fucking humans and their greed. They've overfished so much that even three kingfish being killed damages the ecosystem.

"Wow!" Sylvester exclaims, in the process of trudging down the stairs, when he catches sight of the fish. "How'd ya manage that?"

Sawyer shrugs, an effortless smile gracing her lips, back to her old self as if she didn't completely shut down only an hour ago.

"A spear."

Sylvester scoffs, impressed. "So that's what ya needed the cane for? Usually, I just shoot 'em with my gun. Took me a lot of years and wasted bullets to get my aim that precise. Seems you're just a natural."

"Apparently a hidden talent of mine," she answers breezily. I arch a brow. Not even going to touch on that statement.

With her t-shirt now being used as a net, Sawyer is left in only her jean shorts and bikini top. Something she seems to be regretting now that Sylvester's stare is boring into her. Twin bright spots form on her cheeks, and her shoulders curl inward. *Che stronzo.* I clench the knife handle, preparing to gut him instead.

He must sense my furious glare and the threat on the tip of my tongue because he quickly turns his beady eyes to me. It's not enough to abate the need to spoon them out from his skull anyway.

"Is cooking yer hidden talent?" Sylvester asks.

I narrow my eyes, reluctantly swallowing down the warning.

"I've always known my way around a kitchen, though I don't eat fish, so we'll see how this turns out," I answer, my tone cold.

"Ah," he says. "Never known a man to turn down good meat."

I assume the ensuing silence is awkward based on how Sawyer looks like she'd rather be the kingfish beneath my knife, though I don't feel any of it. His implication that I'm not a real man is obvious, but him being sorely mistaken is also fucking obvious.

Sawyer glances at me. "Enzo is a shark expert. He likes to swim with fish. Not eat them."

I meet her gaze for a moment before focusing back on my task. Not sure why she's defending me to an old crook who undoubtedly has an outdated view of what it means to be a man. I'm not even sure why she's defending me at all.

I'm not so threatened by Sylvester that I lack confidence in my manhood. He can think what he wants, it doesn't make him any better than me.

"Shark expert, huh? I s'pose you got to have a pair to get in the water with one o'them. You'll like it here then. We get sharks on this beach all the time."

I pause, looking at him and echoing, "We?"

"Sorry?" he asks, unsure of my point.

"You said *we* get sharks," I clarify, grabbing another fish. "Is there anyone else here?"

"Well, you two are, ain't ya?" he grunts. "This'll be yer home for the next month or so."

"Enzo is also a dick," Sawyer cuts in.

I keep quiet, debating on if I should push. Normally, I'd chalk it up to a figure of speech, but not after hearing what I did last night.

"Thought I heard someone walking around last night," I say finally.

Sawyer's eyes snap to me, but I avoid her gaze. After she had laid down again, I couldn't fall back asleep, bothered by her crying, and pissed at myself because I couldn't fathom why.

I wasn't sure how long I had been lying there for when I heard footsteps from above us, along with the sound of dragging metal.

A booming laugh bursts from Sylvester's throat, startling Sawyer.

"Was wonderin' how long it'd take 'em."

"Take *who*? And to do what?" Sawyer asks.

"When this place first opened, lots of freight ships were passin' by in these waters. Then, the biggest storm I ever seen hit in 1985. A huge ship got caught up in it. Didn't know it at first, but it was carrying about eighty criminals. They were being transferred to a different prison when the boat capsized.

"I had my beacon on and waited up all night to see if anyone would make it."

"Did they?"

Sylvester grunts. "They sure did. Four of 'em. Used some of the wood from the boat to keep afloat and kick their way here. Was on edge, let me tell ya. These was some dangerous men. Convicted of murder and rape. I couldn't just leave them to die, but I wasn't stupid enough to invite them in. As far as they were concerned, it was their lucky day."

"So, what did you do?"

I continue to cook while Sylvester goes on with his story.

"I gave 'em some tents, a first aid kit, and some food and water. Storm was sticking around for a while yet, which means I was all alone until help arrived. Wasn't letting 'em in for nothin', and they wasn't too happy about it.

Later that night, two of 'em decided to break down my door. Course I saw it coming and was forced to shoot 'em dead. They died with those chains around their ankles."

Sawyer gasps, her blue eyes rounding in shock.

"The other two learned their lesson and stayed outside."

"Then what?" she asks, riveted by the story. I'm still waiting to hear how this has anything to do with what I heard last night.

"Only one of them survived. The other came down with a fever and eventually kicked the bucket. I did let him in when it got bad enough, and tried my best to nurse him back to good health, but he didn't pull through. Eventually, help arrived, and they took the remaining prisoner. Out of eighty men, he was the only survivor."

"Wow," Sawyer breathes.

"Those two I shot decided to stick around. Been creepin' in these halls ever since. Those damn chains dragging across the floor. Used to it by now, but I'll admit it took a few years to stop sleepin' with my shotgun in hand."

I sigh, place a cast-iron skillet on his stove, and drop a fish into it, glowering at the pan while the oil crackles.

"So, you're telling me this place is haunted," I deadpan.

"Sure is."

Bullshit.

"Interesting," is my only response.

I've always been a skeptic of ghosts, though I wouldn't consider myself a disbeliever, despite being raised Catholic. But I am a disbeliever in Sylvester and everything that comes out of his mouth.

The old caretaker chuckles. "I know what yer thinking. Truth be told, I'd think the same thing if I wasn't living with these sons of bitches the last thirty years or so. That's ah'ight. I respect a skeptic. 'Fraid that's the only explanation I got fer the weird noises at night, though."

Sawyer's still wide eyes turn to me. Clearly, she believes him.

And I'm not sure if that's a good thing or not yet. Either she's going to sleep better at night, or worse.

"Do they, like, touch you and shit?" she asks, turning her alarmed stare back to him.

"Nah, they just get a little restless at night, that's all. No reason to worry. They're harmless."

I spare her a glance before concentrating on the sizzling fish.

They may be harmless, but I'm not.

And something tells me Sylvester isn't, either.

CHAPTER 11

Sawyer

"I don't fucking trust him," Enzo grunts, storming down the hallway to our room.

I roll my eyes. "You realize that's the equivalent of saying that you have a stick up your ass. Or that in another life, you were a fire-breathing dragon and destroyed an entire village in a single breath?"

He stops walking and turns to look at me, an incredulous look on his face and his hazel eyes alight with distaste.

I hate how fascinating he looks, even when he's staring at me like I've snorted marijuana. He's far from pretty, yet his face is constructed of fine brush strokes, heavy shading, and sharp lines that create an exceptional masterpiece.

Too bad the inside of him is crusted with off-brand paint, frayed brushes, and muddy colors.

"What the actual fuck are you even saying?"

I sigh. "My point is—that's not surprising. You don't look like you'd trust a nun."

The crease between his brows deepens.

"Nuns are, like, super trustworthy. Not priests, though. Stay away from them."

He shakes his head and stalks into our room, taking a seat on the edge of the bed and putting his chin in his hand as he contemplates the meaning of life and why the sky is blue.

It's only just after one in the afternoon, and there's not shit to do around here. We had the fish I caught for lunch—which was admittedly really good for someone who doesn't eat fish—and Sylvester promised us steaks tonight. With nothing else to do but force a conversation while Enzo glares at him with suspicion, we decided to retire to our room for a little while.

I'm half-tempted to leave Enzo to his drama queen moment and go scrub some of these floors, but then he's standing in front of me.

"I'm going to check out his room. See if I can find anything."

My mouth pops open. "Why must you harass the old man? He's just out here living his life, and you're questioning the direction he pees in."

He blinks. "What?"

"Maybe his penis curves to the side." I throw my hands out in exasperation. When his face twists with anger, I cut in before he can bark something rude. "Look, the point is, you don't know his life, and he hasn't given you a real reason for you to question every single thing about him."

He crosses his arms. "You believe the ghost story?"

"What else am I supposed to believe, Enzo? I'm trying really hard not to gaslight you right now, but other than giving us a bedtime, he hasn't done anything. Sometimes people are just weird and have odd quirks."

He shrugs a shoulder, a glimmer in his eye. "And I'm going to go find out just how weird."

He breezes past me, and I tip my head back in frustration, sighing loudly.

I don't entirely disagree that there's something off about Sylvester, but I also stand by the fact that he's probably just a harmless kook. He's lived here by himself for decades, completely removed from society. It's only obvious he will lack social skills and have pet peeves when two random strangers come in and disrupt his life.

And after his story with the prisoners and how they attempted to break in and possibly kill him, it's no wonder he has trust issues.

We don't know him, and he doesn't know us, either. Locking us in our room at night probably makes him feel safe, and I can't fault him for that.

By the time I make it to the doorway, Enzo is already climbing the steps toward Sylvester's room.

"Oh my God, you're unhinged. No more fish for you. Clearly, it messed with your critical thinking skills."

His chin tips over his shoulder. "As pretty as that mouth is, I'm going to need you to fucking shut it."

I open said mouth, ready to tell him how pretty a black eye would look on *him*, but before I can, he growls, halting the words in my throat. "Don't make me do it for you."

I feel my face flush hot, his accent making those words sound more delectable than they should, causing my stomach to tighten as his cruel words elicit the exact opposite reaction of what they're meant to.

Without waiting for my response, he turns the knob and slowly opens Sylvester's door, the hinges creaking loudly.

My eyes bug from my head, and I'm whipping around, expecting to see—or hear—Sylvester making his way up the steps to catch us red-handed.

But after a full minute of listening, I hear nothing. Turning back toward Enzo, I roll my eyes when I find that he didn't even bother to stick around and make sure he wasn't in danger of being caught.

Self-assured dickhead.

I waffle between not wanting to get involved and putting my nose where it doesn't belong in case Sylvester *does* have something to hide.

Biting my lip, I shut our door behind me and slink toward the three steps leading up to the room.

Try as I might to deny it, I have an attraction to doing the wrong thing.

I creep up the stairs and into the room, finding Enzo pulling open the top drawer in a lopsided dresser. Pictures of sailboats and lighthouses adorning the stone walls, dust covering the frames.

His bed is neatly made, and something about that eases my mind. As if it confirms my theory that Sylvester is just a meticulous person, and that perfectly explains why he locks our door at night and forces us to pee in a bucket—not that either of us has done so yet.

Adrenaline pumping through my system, I softly close the door behind me.

Next to a tall dresser is a big closet with sliding shuttered doors that draws my attention. With Enzo right beside it, I decide to head for the nightstand next to the bed instead. Anything to avoid being close to that barbarian.

He ignores me anyway, but I'm sure he'll find a time to insult me for going along with his plan later.

I slide open the top drawer and am immediately disturbed when there's a full set of dentures right there, the teeth dirty. This is going swell already.

There's loose change, a tarnished gold watch, a box of bullets, and a few Polaroid photographs.

Sparing a glance at Enzo, I pick them up and flip through them.

The first is a photograph of a younger version of Sylvester smiling down at a blonde baby girl in his arms. He looks to be in his thirties or forties. Beside him is a blonde woman, staring at the duo with a grin. Though, when I get a better look, I see that the man is gripping the woman's wrist with his other hand, his fingers visibly digging into her skin tightly. Studying her face closer, I notice now that her smile is strained, and her shoulders are curled in.

Flipping it over, messy feminine handwriting is scrawled on the back.

Sylvester, Raven, and Trinity, 1994.

Raven? Sylvester mentioned he named the island himself. He must've named it after his wife.

So, what happened to her?

The next photo is of the same blonde baby, though a few years older, sitting next to Raven, who is swollen with another child. The girl—Trinity, I assume—is sitting on the floor with a miniature wooden horse between her legs. Her hair is disheveled, and her pants are stained. None of which is out of the ordinary for a toddler. I'm barely put together as an adult. I flip the image over.

Raven, Trinity, baby Kacey, 1996

In both photos, they're in the lighthouse, with the same bookshelves. I guess this explains the children's books on the shelves. At some point, Sylvester had a family.

I move on to the last one. This one is of a sunset on the beach. It's dark and grainy and hard to see, but with closer inspection, it appears there's someone standing in the water.

I squint, straining to figure out exactly what I'm staring at.

A young woman. She's facing the camera, and it looks like she's naked, an arm crossed over her chest to cover herself. For a moment, I'm still confused, until I realize her palm is raised, hiding her face.

My stomach drops and my heart picks up speed for a reason I can't place.

Unsettled, I place the photos back in the drawer and shut it quietly.

"Find anything?"

"Sylvester had a wife and children..." I trail off, unsure how to explain how sinister those photos felt. Part of me doesn't want to validate Enzo's concerns, but I've been in enough dangerous situations to know better than to hide that.

Before I can continue, a thud sounds from down the hallway.

My eyes widen, and panic ensues as I pivot toward Enzo.

His stare locked on the door, he slowly shuts the dresser drawer while simultaneously reaching for the closet door.

The rhythmic thudding continues down the hallway, heading directly toward us. It's the sound of Sylvester's wooden leg.

Clenching his jaw, he cracks open the metal closet door just enough for him to slip through.

Enzo finally meets my stare, and something flashes across his eyes. I know exactly what he's thinking—leave me out here by myself.

But if I'm caught, he knows I wouldn't go down alone. So, he slides to the side and waves me in.

Sylvester opens the bedroom door just as we get the closet shut. My breath is short and chest tight as we peer through the shutters. I'm beginning to shake from the adrenaline.

Worse yet, we're trapped in a confined space. Though wide enough to fit us side by side, we're cramped against flannel shirts and musty coats. My vision tunnels and it feels like the walls are closing in around me.

I don't like small spaces. I don't like feeling trapped with no way out.

Desperately, I glance around, but there's nowhere for me to go, and the panic only worsens.

Enzo stands still next to me, appearing unaffected by our situation, while Sylvester sits on his bed, the springs protesting beneath his weight. He grunts as he works the wooden peg off, letting it drop heavily to the floor.

Oh, God.

He's not leaving.

Eyes wide, I watch him swing his legs onto the bed and shift to get comfortable.

Fuck me. The old-ass geezer is taking a goddamn nap.

I can't stay in here forever. I'm already hanging on by a thread and am contemplating busting out of the door, consequences be damned. How angry would he be if he knew we were in here?

He'll kill you, pipsqueak.

Kevin's voice has my heart stopping in my chest. My breath shortens further, and my lungs are reduced to noodles.

If we're caught, he will either pull his gun on us or kick us out. We'll be forced to weather the elements with virtually nothing to protect us. It's possible to survive, but suddenly that bed and bucket seem so inviting.

But that's only if he chooses to act rationally.

Slowly, I turn to look at Enzo, feeling unhinged, cramped, and so angry with him. I know I followed him in here on my own, but goddammit, this is all his fucking fault.

Though dark, the air crackles when he meets my stare. I don't know what he sees, but whatever it is, it prompts him to raise his hand and put his finger to his lips. His hazel eyes cut through me with a warning, but I can't draw in a deep enough breath to let him know I won't say anything.

I can't decipher the emotion that shadows his irises, but before I can figure it out, a loud snore startles me, and a quiet yelp escapes me. I slap a hand over my mouth, my heart beating out of my chest.

Trembling, I'm relieved to see that Sylvester hasn't moved. He's on his side, beard splayed across his tattered red blanket as he snoozes.

When I look back to Enzo, he seems frustrated. Jaw is clenched, and one of his hands runs through his short strands.

My throat is closing, and I can't help but look around again, taking in how little space is in here.

I shake my head, trying to express something, but I'm not even sure what.

Flicking a glance to Sylvester, Enzo grabs my arm and pulls me into him. I stiffen, resisting him.

First off, I don't want him touching me.

Secondly, he's giving me *less* room. How the fuck does he think that's supposed to help?

But he just tugs me harder until my back is pressed against his chest. Hot breath fans across the shell of my ear a moment before his whisper penetrates the screeching in my brain.

"Quiet, *bella ladra.*"

I *am* being quiet. Or at least I think I am. I'm not so sure anymore, but I'm pretty confident the asshole is just mansplaining how to hide properly.

I open my mouth, ready to tell him in a very quiet but firm whisper to suck my favorite toe, but the only thing I manage is a squeak.

His hand curls around my hip, and I jump in response. My eyes dart to where he's touching me, his palm flattening against my stomach as he glides it along the edge of my jean shorts.

I fixate on his hand as he pops open the button of my cutoffs and slowly slides down the zipper.

I don't want this. At least that's what I chant to myself.

So why can't I stop him?

"What are you doing?" I whisper.

"Shh," he hushes. "I don't want to hear your words."

"Then what do you want to hear?"

His tongue darts out, licking along the side of my ear and eliciting a bone-deep chill down my spine.

"I want to hear what it sounds like when you're breaking and can't scream." Just as the last word falls from his tongue, his hand slips into my bottoms, and his finger presses firmly against my clit.

My knees buckle, so his other arm bands across my abdomen, keeping me still as he slowly begins to circle it.

My vision is still tunneled, but now that little pinprick of light is focused entirely on what he's doing to me.

Mouth open on a silent moan, I exhale heavily when he travels farther down, giving me little warning before his middle finger plunges inside me.

Again, I jump, but the pleasure radiating from my thighs has me pressing deeper into his chest.

"Do you think it's hard to breathe because you can't escape or because I'm inside you?" he croons in a hushed tone, his voice barely loud enough to hear through the waves roaring in my head.

As if to remind me where I am, another loud snore breaks through the silence. My stomach tightens as my attention begins to divide. But then he adds another finger and slowly begins to fuck me with them, bridging the divide and forcing my focus back onto him.

Only him.

I lose myself, my arousal embarrassingly audible as he pumps in and out. My breathing grows heavier, and I'm on the verge of no longer being quiet.

The arm holding me against him moves, his palm moving to my face, covering both my mouth and my nose as he attempts to keep me silent.

It takes only seconds for my brain to register that he's cutting off my air supply. But he doesn't stop finger-fucking me. Even goes as far as pressing the heel of his palm against my clit and rubbing firmly.

My eyes roll, and I feel the blood rushing to my face.

"Does it hurt, baby?" he asks quietly. "Not being able to scream for me like you want to."

I pinch my eyes shut, an orgasm forming deep in the pit of my stomach. It feels like standing at the beach and watching the water retreat hundreds of feet. That looming unease plaguing you, knowing that when the water returns, it'll come back with a vengeance.

This does hurt. Because I know when it's over, I'll be a fucking wreck.

"This little cunt is so fucking wet," he continues, his accent deepening with desire. With my breathing silenced, the only thing that can be heard above the rough timbre of his voice is his fingers pumping into my soaking pussy. "Do you hear how pretty it sings for me? Why don't you sing me a lullaby, *bella*? Let me hear it."

He quickens his pace, continuing to rub against my clit. My chest pumps wildly, and I can feel my heartbeat in every inch of my body.

I'm torn between needing him to stop so I can breathe and praying to whomever will listen that it never ends.

"That's it," he encourages, sensing how close I am by the way I start bucking against him. "I want you to come on my fingers now, *bella*."

Fuck him. I won't come on demand. He doesn't get to control my body like that.

But then he leans down and clamps his teeth right below my ear, sucking harshly as he curls his fingers just right.

My knees collapse as the orgasm tears through me without permission, seizing my body in a cyclone that's just as devastating as I feared.

He moves his hand down just enough to uncover my nose, and I instinctively suck in a deep breath, the rush of air heightening my delirium.

I convulse against him, and he's forced to slide his hand from my shorts and wrap himself around me, attempting to keep me both still and silent.

If Sylvester wakes, I wouldn't know it. Don't know if I'd care, either.

I'm too wrapped up in the stars, and up here, I'm fearless.

Eventually, I come down, my head fuzzy and legs weak.

"You're so easy to break," he murmurs darkly.

Immediately, what just happened smacks me upside the head.

I go to step away, feeling ashamed for reasons I can't name, but he's gripping my bicep tightly, pulling me back into him. I cringe when I feel how wet my arm is.

Because his fucking hand is soaked, and he hasn't bothered to wipe it clean.

"Did your lullaby rock him to sleep, baby?"

"Shut *up*," I hiss, my cheeks burning hot, jabbing my elbow into his rock-hard stomach before reaching for the door again.

"Where do you think you're going?" he growls.

"Are you planning on staying in here forever?" I snap back.

If he thinks I'm going to stick around after that, then he really can suck my toe. I can deduce that he was distracting me from my very apparent panic attack, but now I feel cheap and regret it already.

Now, he's just being cruel.

Tension rolls off him in waves, so I rip my arm from his grip.

Sylvester is still snoring away while I carefully slide open the closet door, so desperate to get away that my hands shake.

Slowly, I slip out from the little black hole Enzo sucked me into and hurriedly tiptoe toward the bedroom door. Enzo follows close behind, ensuring to shut the closet before slipping out of the room behind me.

Instead of heading toward our room, I beeline down the hallway. I need to get away from him before I do something stupid and try to earn his forgiveness.

He may not have deserved what I did to him, but that doesn't mean he deserves my body.

Now, if only I could just stop fucking giving it to him.

CHAPTER 12

Sawyer

Do you think anyone is ever going to love you, pipsqueak? I'm the only one that does.

But not if you're going to be a whore. No one can love a whore.

I squeeze my eyes shut, then proceed to trip over a rock.

"Fuck!" I shout. It's stupid to come out here barefoot on injured feet, but I don't care right now. I just need to get the fuck away.

I want to hear what it sounds like when you're breaking and can't scream.

"Shut up," I mutter through gritted teeth. "Both of you, shut *up*."

You're so easy to break.

Blood is pooling in my head from shame and embarrassment, and beneath the hot sun, I'm confident a plane could see my tomato-red face clear as day from ten thousand feet above.

Who needs a goddamn radio when my hatred for men could signal an alien race from an entire galaxy away?

I'm storming from the lighthouse, perspiration forming along my hairline and the back of my neck. I've no idea where I'm going, but I don't care as long as it's far from that place—far from *him*. Yet, I'm never left alone anyway. I've been running for six years, and I've never been able to escape Kev.

There's no hope of escaping Enzo, either. His cruel words, his wicked tongue, and his sinister intentions.

And I have a terrible feeling that even when I do slip between his fingers, he'll follow me wherever I go. Just like Kev, he'll fucking plague me and won't stop until I'm exactly where he wants me.

I climb over a few rocks, growling more insults toward both men, when I find a massive stone mound, my words trailing off. Something about it seems a little peculiar to be more than just a cliff, so I deftly amble toward it, attempting to be cautious of the sharp rocks.

As I get closer, I notice an opening in the boulder, a black abyss beyond it. It's a cave.

My heart thunders, but I'm not sure if it's from exertion, excitement, or trepidation. Hesitantly, I approach the mouth of the cave, straining my ears to listen for wild creatures.

This doesn't seem like the type of place for any kind of animal to thrive. But I've seen one too many B-rated horror flicks with monsters that do just fine in these conditions.

Yet, it feels like a rope is tied around my waist, and something is pulling me in, whether I want to go or not.

Chewing my lip, I turn to stare at the looming lighthouse behind me. It takes only a few seconds to decide that I'd rather be in a cave than in there.

But I need to get a light first.

Excitement takes over as I hurriedly make my way back to the lighthouse, flying through the front door and finding Sylvester sitting at the dining room table, cleaning his shotgun.

He's already awake from his nap. At this moment, I'm glad my face is already red, because the sight of him has all kinds of reminders rushing back in.

He looks up at me, seemingly shocked by my sudden entry.

"Well, hiya there. You all right?"

He seems oblivious to what happened in his closet. Good.

"Can I borrow a flashlight, please?" I ask, breathless and sweaty.

His bushy brows furrow. "Whatever for?"

"I'm just exploring the island," I say, not wanting to tell him about the cave. I'm not entirely sure why. It could be because I don't want him to tell Enzo, but really, I like the idea of having a place to escape where no one can find me.

Frowning, he gets to his feet and opens a drawer in the kitchen island.

"Just make sure ya bring it back, ah'ight? These ain't cheap," he instructs, holding out a small black flashlight.

"Yes, sir," I say, thanking him with a wide smile as I grab it from him. Just as I go to rush back out, he stops me.

"Lemme get ya some shoes first before ya hurt yerself more. I think I still have some left over from when my daughter lived here."

I remember the old photos in his drawer and my curiosity about where his family went is burning. It's the first time he's mentioned having a daughter, and it seemed like he didn't even realize it. But I don't have the time to pry now, so I let him hobble up the steps to get the shoes.

I shift on my feet impatiently, praying that in the time it takes Sylvester to return, Enzo doesn't walk out of his portal from Hell and terrorize me some more.

Thankfully, only Sylvester comes down, holding a pair of blue water shoes. I grin, grabbing them from him and chirping out another *thank you*, barely stopping to put them on before I'm out of the house again.

When I reach the cave, I switch on the flashlight and scamper in. Almost immediately, I'm going down a steep decline, and I'm forced to nearly get on my butt in order to keep my balance.

The air grows colder as I descend, but what's more disconcerting is an aqua blue glow dancing across the cave walls. I'm in a tunnel of sorts, and it curves gradually to the left, the color growing brighter as I approach.

Confused, I round the bend and then freeze in my tracks. I'm absolutely paralyzed as I take in the sight.

Before me is a massive open area filled with glittering rocks that appear like black diamonds. Every surface is glinting, and it's almost as mesmerizing as the ceiling of the cave.

Strange blue dots shine across every inch of the surface. It's like staring up into space with how bright they are. There's an entire universe in here, and just like outer space, I'm bereft of oxygen.

My mouth drops open, taking in the extraordinary sight and then gasping when I notice a massive pool in the middle of the cave, the surface as blue as the ceiling.

"Oh my fuck," I mutter, stepping farther into the vast space, taking it all in slowly and all at once.

It's fucking mesmerizing, and I've never seen anything like it.

For reasons I can't explain, tears rush to my eyes.

Maybe it's because it's just so damn beautiful here. Or maybe it's because, amongst the darkness, I've found a safe haven.

The prisoners are restless again.

And so is Enzo.

"If you're going to keep rolling every five seconds, can you do that on the floor?" I grouse, my irritation spiking when he shakes the bed for the millionth goddamn time.

"If you're so bothered, then leave," he responds, his voice low and deep with unrequited sleep.

He's as cold as ever, and for the first time, I'm glad for it. His fire is exhausting, and as much as that exhaustion would serve me in getting a good night's sleep, it's not worth it when he's keeping me awake.

I spent hours in that cave today. Lying on the rock and staring up at the mysterious little lights, wondering how nature could produce something so beautiful in such an ugly world.

When I returned to the lighthouse, Enzo was fixing a pipe under the sink while Sylvester stood over him, telling him how to fix something he could never accomplish himself.

Enzo snapped at him, and we spent dinner in awkward silence.

Even now, he's acting like I don't exist. Or at least he's trying to.

And I still haven't figured out if it bothers me. The pit in my stomach would be a great indicator, but clearly, my body can't be trusted around him.

He shifts again, and my anger mounts. I turn to face him and shove him. His head whips toward me, and though immediate fear races through my bloodstream, it's no match for my sleep deprivation.

"Get *out*," I bite out through gritted teeth, shoving at him again.

His hands close around my wrists harshly, and it feels like they're on the verge of snapping like twigs.

And then I'm flipping over his body, off the edge of the bed, and onto the hard ground. I land with a *thunk*, a puff of breath forced out of my throat.

For a moment, all I can do is gape at him, in utter shock that he just tossed me off the bed like a hot potato.

"*Merda*," he curses, swiping a hand over his head in frustration, then he stands from the bed and scoops me up. It's enough to reset my brain and send me spiraling back into my fury.

Merda - *Shit*

"Oh, fuck you," I spit, bucking out of his hold until he's forced to set me down. Then I'm full-out tackling him. Fuck self-preservation, I'm too furious.

Furious at him for throwing me off the bed, then acting guilty like he didn't fucking mean to. For going into Sylvester's room and getting us trapped in that closet. For touching me and making me feel things I shouldn't feel—that I *can't* feel.

For messing with my fucking head.

I slap at him wildly, slipping out of his attempts to grab my wrists again a few times before he succeeds, catching hold of them in a bruising grip. Then, I'm being pitched back over the bed, but I quickly grab onto him, taking the asshole with me.

Though, I instantly regret it when he lands on me, another harsh breath being forced from my lungs.

"Goddammit, Sawyer," he groans. "The fuck is wrong with you?"

"*You!*" I shout, slapping at him again. "Get off of me, you fucking mammoth."

"Stop hitting me," he growls, adjusting until he's sitting atop me, pinning my hands to the floor, and getting in my face. "You're acting like a fucking cu—"

"Don't you *dare* finish that sentence or so help me God, I will drown you in that ocean when you're least expecting it," I threaten, panting. It's hard to breathe, but only because his proximity is so damn suffocating.

"Do you honestly think you scare me? A shrimp is more intimidating than you."

I gasp. "That is so fucking rude."

He leans in closer, and it's a regretful discovery to find that I can't move through solid objects. I try to lean away, but there's nowhere to go, the floor refusing to become penetrable no matter how hard I press the back of my head into it.

"You want to hear rude, Sawyer? How about the fact that it's hard to sleep next to a fucking soul-sucking demon? And you being so close makes me sick to my stomach."

I bristle, a stone forming in the base of my throat. I had thought it was hard to breathe before, but now it feels like I'm chained to the bottom of the ocean. Not only is there no oxygen down here, but there's so much pressure on top of me, making it impossible to even suck in a breath.

"What's worse? I can *still* smell you on my fingers, despite washing you clean of me. Now tell me how the hell you expect me to find peace when you're invading every one of my goddamn senses?"

The ice chips in his eyes are melting, slowly replaced by a fire so strong, it's radiating from him in waves, burning me up from the inside out and turning the air dense.

He's hurting me, the ache in my wrists spreading down, down, down, until I'm clenching my thighs beneath him.

I'll never understand why I want him when he's so fucking cruel.

"You're so fucking hot and cold," I bite.

"Good," he barks. "Because there's not a damn second that goes by where you're not fucking with my head. You're the worst thing to ever happen to me. Every day, I regret walking into that bar. I hate myself for falling for your lies and believing you were nothing more than a sad girl. I hate that I allowed myself to be seduced by you. And I hate that I can't stop, even now."

I fight against his hold, his harsh words needling beneath my skin and hooking into the sinew. They hurt, but only because I can't blame him.

"Get off of me," I hiss, bucking my hips, but only accomplishing in straining my back. He's so fucking heavy. "Better stop touching me, Enzo, or else you might accidentally be seduced."

He bares his teeth. "Everything you do is calculated. Were you even truly panicking when we were in that closet or was that another one of your schemes?"

I gape at him. "I didn't ask you to touch me, you dickhead! How could I have possibly known what you were going to do?"

"You were doing it to gain sympathy," he accuses.

I'm so fucking baffled, I'm speechless.

Arguing with him is pointless, though, so I buck my hips again.

"Get off of me!" I bark, that feeling of being trapped trickling into my system. My thrashing becomes more desperate, yet his lips only tip up cruelly.

Far from a smile but amused all the same.

"You gonna panic again, *bella ladra*? Hoping for my cock this time?"

"You're sick," I spit. "I don't want that thing anywhere near me."

He tilts his head to the side. "No?"

That's a challenge, and it only stirs the panic. He rolls his hips, his hard length pressing firmly against my clit.

"Enzo," I snap, but it comes out breathy.

His lips lightly skim across the shell of my ear. "Would you scream this time?" he questions darkly. "You always do when you create your own little ocean all over me."

"Fuck you," I breathe, accompanied by a full body shudder when he rolls his hips again.

"I won't. I've already conquered your ocean, *amore mio*. You have nothing left to give that I want."

Finally, he releases me, standing above me with his legs on either side. I slide out from beneath him, pressing myself into the stone wall and panting heavily.

"You're a liar. Even now."

Colorful words build on my tongue, and I open my mouth to let them spew, hoping they're sharp enough to cut past his thick skin, but before I can get a syllable out, his head is snapping to the side.

His eyes are caught on something outside the window. Whatever he sees causes him to stiffen, his spine snapping straight as he rushes toward it.

Amore mio - *My love*

"What? What is it?" I ask breathlessly, climbing to my feet to stand next to him.

My eyes widen, a gasp on my lips when it registers what's outside.

It's a girl. She's standing in the ocean, about knee-deep, black water licking at her legs. Only a thin white dress covers her rail-thin body, the collar hanging over one shoulder and exposing moon-white skin

"Oh my God," I mutter, rushing on to the bed and reaching for the lock on the window, but there are gnarled nails pinning it down, keeping it permanently closed.

"What the fuck?" I mumble, but my attention is diverted again when the girl walks deeper into the ocean, causing my heart rate to skyrocket.

"Hey!" I scream out, slapping the palm of my hand on the glass, but I'm sure the sound is being swallowed by the howling wind. The girl stills, so I shout some more, hoping she'll turn around. But she only stands there, frozen as the waves batter into her.

"Sylvester is coming," Enzo warns, his voice low as he steps away from me.

Loud footsteps are stomping down the hallway, but they're not coming from his room. He's coming from the staircase.

I turn around and scramble off the bed, the door handle jiggling as he unlocks it. Already, I can feel his anger seeping through the door.

When he gets it open, he busts in, stomping his wooden peg on the floor.

"What in tarnation is going on in here?" he barks. His eyes find mine and then slide to the window behind me.

"What in the hell do you think yer doing, young lady?"

"There's a girl out there," I explain, hiking my thumb over my shoulder. "She was standing in the ocean."

"A gir—now, what are you going on about?" he grumbles, hobbling toward us to look out through the glass.

"There ain't no girl out there," he booms.

"What?" I squeak, peeking around him. But he's right.

There's no one out there.

Mouth open with bewilderment, I turn toward Enzo to find him staring out the window, too. Quiet and face smooth, but his eyes are shadowed with suspicion.

Facing Sylvester again, I insist, "There was a girl out there. We both saw it."

Sylvester leans over the bed to get a better look.

"Ain't no one out there," he grunts finally. "You're seeing things."

I clench my jaw in frustration, knowing damn well we both saw her.

Training my gaze on Enzo, I watch him stare Sylvester down, his suspicion as evident as the old caretaker's missing leg.

Enzo shrugs casually, a glint in his eye. "Must've just been another ghost."

CHAPTER 13

"Where the hell are you going?"

The question is out of my mouth before I can think it through. Seems there's very fucking little I think through when it comes to her.

It's been a week since we got stuck in the closet, and every day since then, she disappears somewhere for most of the day. Leaving after breakfast and not returning until the evening. She acts normal enough, joking with Sylvester but then ignoring my existence at night, keeping her back turned to me even in sleep.

She doesn't talk about where she goes, and as each day passes, my curiosity burns hotter.

Maybe it's because I don't like being here alone with Sylvester all damn day, though I've found plenty to fix around this place to keep me occupied. Or maybe it's because I don't like that she's found an escape.

Slowly, Sawyer turns to face me, halfway out the door with a stony look painted on her face.

Her skin is beginning to pale, indicating she's not spending as much time in the sun. This island is nothing but rocks. There's nowhere to go but *up*.

"None of your business," she snips, shutting the door behind her before I can respond.

A booming laugh needles into my skin, filling my muscles with tension and my body with anger. Clenching my jaw, I turn my head to stare at Sylvester, who is leaning against the counter drinking coffee.

"Something funny, *stronzo*?" I ask. He frowns, not understanding what I called him, and I have no inclination to clue him in.

We don't get along, though neither of us has outright spoken of our distaste for each other. He doesn't like that I show him little respect, and I just don't like him.

"Girl's gotta mouth on her. Haven't been around people much the past several decades, but it's always interestin' to see how feisty women are these days when I do come across 'em. Met a few women on deck when the cargo ships come 'round, and boy, they give those men a run for their money."

He's trying to have a conversation.

I turn my glare back to the door.

I don't like having conversations. Least of all with him.

Standing, I toss over my shoulder, "I'll be back later."

Sylvester just grumbles, clearly displeased with my manners. He's not a meek man, but it's become increasingly evident over the past week that he keeps the peace with me for Sawyer's sake.

He likes her. And I don't fucking like that about him, either.

By the time I get outside, she's nowhere in sight. Even after walking for several minutes, I don't see her climbing on any of the cliffs or sprawled across the jagged rocks like I'd half expect. Nothing about her screams graceful.

By the time I circle the entire island and still can't find her, there's a seed of concern sprouting in the pit of my stomach, slowly taking root as the minutes pass by.

Where the fuck could she have gone?

This island isn't that big. There are only so many places to hide. We had to have somehow missed each other, and she's already made her way back to the lighthouse.

Just as I'm about to give up and head back, I catch sight of a big hole smack in the center of a cliff.

And suddenly, it dawns on me why she's been getting paler, how she has seemed to have disappeared without a trace.

It's a goddamn cave.

Something about her keeping that from me pisses me off.

Then again, everything about her accomplishes that without even trying.

Lord knows how big it is, and she could've easily gotten hurt and would've had no way to let me know. As the scenarios play out of all the ways she could've gotten herself in some type of trouble, my fury only heightens while I make my way into the cave. I can't see shit, but I'm conscious of each step as I descend. I reach flat ground and charge through a tunnel, a bright blue glow emitting from beyond.

I'm annoyed enough that the beauty of the cave hardly registers once I emerge on the other side. My only focus is finding Sawyer, ensuring she's not hurt, and then leaving again.

Curiosity satisfied.

Sounds pointless even in my own fucking head.

I stalk through the cave, stopping briefly to note the blue pool of water, before continuing to search for the constant thorn in my side.

"What are you doing down here?" a quiet voice asks from behind me. I turn around, finding Sawyer standing there, her wild curls around her face.

"This is where you've been going?"

"You know the song "Obsessed" by Mariah Carey? I think she knew what she was doing when she wrote it," she says in place of an answer.

My brow furrows. "What?"

She walks past me and heads toward the pool, humming the tune to the song. "I'm just saying, obsession comes with some serious side effects. Might want to keep that in check before you turn into a murderous psycho."

I'm silent for a beat before asking, "Who says I'm not already?"

She seems to freeze for several seconds before she aimlessly kicks her foot against the rock floor.

"You could be. Are you here to murder me, Enzo? Is it because I don't return your affections?"

"Baby, if anyone were to become obsessed with you, it would only be for what's between your thighs, not because you have anything else to offer."

She doesn't respond.

She always has something to say until she's faced with the truth of her character and actions.

"Why are you here, Enzo? This is my safe space, and you're... making it unsafe."

Instead of answering, I finally take in her *safe space*. It would be pitch black in here if it weren't for the luminous ceiling and glowing pool in the middle.

È davvero bellissima. I can appreciate anything that is not of the human or man-made variety.

Tourists pay hundreds of dollars to visit caves like this. The chances of having one on this tiny, abandoned island are incredible.

"Do you know what's hanging above your head?" I ask.

She turns her head, giving me her side profile. It's enough to tell me she's interested, and still, I'm not sure why the fuck I'm here, either.

"Glowworms."

Her mouth drops a moment before her gaze shoots up, head now tilted back as she stares at the deceitful little creatures.

È davvero bellissima - *It is beautiful*

I expected her to squeal, be grossed out, but Sawyer always does the opposite of what I expect. Without looking away, she stands as if trying to get closer to them.

"Might want to close that before one drops in."

Her mouth snaps shut, the click of her teeth audible from several feet away.

"Why do they glow like that?" she asks with wonder.

"It's a secretion to attract prey."

She gasps, and I continue, "These caves are in New Zealand, too. They're actually silk strings that come from egg larvae. They regurgitate mucus onto them and turn them into strings of watery, reflective droplets. Then, they light them up with their tails and attract mayflies. Thinner than a strand of hair, and they can break, so watch your mouth."

Once more, it closes. I don't think she even realized her mouth had fallen open again. Can't help but admit that seeing one land in the cavernous space that produces all her lies would feel like a form of justice.

On cue, her lips slowly begin to part again.

Casting a glance in my direction, she asks, "How do you know all of this? Are you a walking encyclopedia?"

I shrug. "I studied a lot of things when I was getting my degree."

She hums distractedly. "Who knew worm secretion could be so pretty?"

I approach her, enjoying the way her body senses mine. The cords of muscle swelling with tension along her dainty shoulders and the way her bones seem to stiffen.

I like that she feels me. Fears me.

Stealing from me is the worst she'll ever do to me, but I will do so much worse to her.

She backs away from the pool as I near, dropping her head to watch me.

I like that, too. Making her so nervous, that she can't take her eyes off me whenever I come close to her.

Only makes me want to get closer so I can hear her breath quicken and see those baby blues darken.

I'll admit—I was wrong earlier. Her sweet pussy isn't the only thing that is addicting. Not when her fear is just as appetizing.

"Have you ever been to New Zealand?" she asks in a hushed tone, a useless attempt to distract herself.

"No."

"Why not?"

"Never had a reason to."

"Not even for the glowworms?"

"No."

She quietens, the air growing dense with tension so thick, I can feel every shift of her body within my own.

I hear her swallow. "Are you going to hurt me?"

"*Si*," I say, my cock growing hard from just the thought of it.

"What... what are you going to do?" Her voice wobbles, the words pitching and sinking with fear.

A corner of my lips curls up. "Now, why would I tell you that?"

She turns away, and I study the way she stares straight ahead, beyond the pool and into her own mind, likely imagining all the ways I could hurt her.

A shot of excitement leaks down through my chest as I circle behind her and press into her back. She sucks in a sharp breath, feeling my cock resting against the swell of her ass. She's solid stone as I lean down and brush my mouth across her ear.

"That's what makes it so fun," I murmur, lingering for a beat so I can memorize the way her lip trembles.

"Are you going to try to fuck me?" she spits.

"No, *bella ladra*. I'll never fuck you again, not even when you beg me to."

She scoffs, her upper lip curling with disgust. "I would never."

Reaching around her, I grab her jaw and force her head to the side, her glassy blue eyes catching hold of mine.

Not good enough. I want those tears spilling over.

I squeeze tighter, and utter bliss releases in my bloodstream when a tear wiggles lose.

Now, that's a sight that can make any man come undone.

I lean closer, my lips a mere inch from hers.

"You're already so close, *bugiarda*. All I would need to do is kiss these pretty lips, and the words would be slipping off your tongue before you could stop it." Releasing her jaw, I grab her hand and force it between her thighs. "Feel," I order.

"No," she bites out, anger boiling in her glare.

"I wasn't asking," I snarl, my voice dropping lower with warning. "Feel for yourself, or I will."

Swallowing, she tucks her fingers into the side of her shorts for half a second and then quickly slips them out. She resists as I grab her hand and raise it high for both of us to see, the evidence of her arousal reflecting the luminosity from above on her fingertips, turning them bright aqua.

"Look at that. You can glow, too."

Then, I step away, saying nothing else as I make my way out of the cave and toward the lighthouse. She'll stay behind, embarrassed and ashamed, and won't dare show her face for a while.

Plenty of time to make myself come to the image of that tear falling past her eyes.

CHAPTER 14

Sawyer

I fucking hate him.

I'm still seething by the time I step back into the lighthouse.

Closing the door behind me, I begin to charge toward the staircase, and pray to God that Enzo isn't in there. It would be a form of justice if he slipped and hit his head on a rock.

Natural selection, bitch.

I'm stopped in my tracks when a booming voice pipes up to my right, causing me to jump, a high-pitched yelp slipping free.

"My, my, you look mighty angry. 'Magine you'd give that storm that took ya'll out a run for its money."

Shut up, you crinkly dinosaur.

Forcing a smile to my face, I say, "I'm fine. Just didn't catch any fish today."

He waves a hand in dismissal. "You'll have your days, sweetie. Come sit, I'll make ya feel better."

An uneasy feeling washes over me as he pats the cushion on the couch beside him, giving me a crooked grin. His teeth are beginning to blacken—

something I hadn't really noticed until now.

He's been asking me to sit next to him a lot these past few days. It's weird, but I've continuously brushed it off, considering Enzo hasn't seemed to think anything of it.

You're looking for something that isn't there.

Right. He's just being friendly.

All men want you for one thing, pipsqueak. I'm the only one who actually loves you.

Tightening my lips into a strained smile, I sit down, coercing my stiff muscles into relaxing. Not that it's working.

His rough, calloused hand lands on my shoulder, sending a riptide of goosebumps across my body. He squeezes it playfully and chuckles. "Yer so tensed up! Fish got you that much in a tizzy?"

I shrug, hoping to dislodge his hand, but it's unsuccessful. I've never been good at confrontation. Throwing up the peace sign and moonwalking out of the vicinity is my go-to response.

But before I can do anything, Enzo is walking into the living room, his eyes immediately finding mine. Instantly, Sylvester's hand tightens on my shoulder, and while my confrontation skills are lacking, my intuition skills are not.

It feels like he's trying to claim me.

Enzo's gaze sharpens as it zeroes in on where Sylvester is touching me.

"What are you doing?"

"We were havin' a conversation, boy. What else?" Sylvester answers, his tone disgruntled and slightly defensive

"Then why are you touching her?" he snaps, voice hard and unyielding.

My mouth pops open, ready to make peace, but Enzo's eyes cut to me in warning. I tighten my lips and keep quiet for now. Mainly because Sylvester's hand has only grown heavier on my shoulder, as if asserting dominance, and by the darkening look on Enzo's face, he's about to hike his leg.

"You got a problem with it? Don't see yer name written anywhere on her," Sylvester retorts.

"I won't just write it, I'll carve it. Take your hand off her, or I will do it for you."

Abruptly, I stand, dislodging Sylvester's grip and attracting both of their attention.

"Let's not fight, okay? And while I appreciate both of your concerns, please don't use me as a tool in your pissing contest."

Sylvester opens his mouth, but I rush out of the room before he can get a word out.

I run. Because that's what I do best.

I'm sitting on the bed reading through an old book about lighthouses when a knock rumbles against the door. Sylvester opens it and steps through a moment later, not even giving me time to let him know it's okay to come in.

I sigh.

He has no concept of privacy except when it comes to his own. I could have been changing, though I only have a few spare t-shirts and one pair of shorts anyways. My bathing suit is my only source of undergarments, and I only take them off long enough to wash them before slipping them right back on.

"I owe ya an apology for earlier," Sylvester says, appearing contrite.

It's been a few hours since I escaped from the dick-measuring showdown, but I haven't seen Enzo since.

The bastard probably went to my cave, and I'm fully prepared to fight him over it. I found that damn cave, so I reserve the right to control who has custody of it and when.

I shrug. "It's cool. Testosterone gets the best of us," I say mildly.

"Meh, well, I don't think it gets the best of you, but I hear what yer saying. That boy doesn't got no manners, and my pride got in the way there. I'm sorry if I made ya uncomfortable."

"Sure. I think as long as everyone keeps their hands to themselves from now on, there shouldn't be any more issues like that."

His bottom lip juts out as he nods, and for a moment, he almost looks displeased by my answer. It seems as if he was expecting me to say his touching me didn't make me uncomfortable, but well... it *did*.

And I may be a liar, but I'm not about to invite this old man to put his hands on me whenever he pleases.

I'll go live with the fucking glowworms before that happens.

"That include yer friend, too?" he asks finally, keeping his stare pinned to the wooden floor.

I frown, my brow furrowing.

"What do you mean?"

Sylvester shrugs, feigning nonchalance. "I imagine any man would have a hard time keeping their hands to themselves when you look like ya do and are dressed how ya are. Can't exactly blame 'em, can ya?"

I blink. "Sounds like you're talking about little boys. A man wouldn't touch a woman without their consent," I volley back. "Plus, a bathing suit isn't an invitation to be violated."

Sure it is, pipsqueak. You're practically crying for fucking attention.

He chuckles deep in his throat, the rough sound lacking humor.

"It's been a rough day. Bedtime is at seven PM tonight, ah'ight?"

"What? Why?"

He grumbles something, waddling his way over to the door.

"We'll all start fresh tomorrow mornin'," is all he says.

Just as he steps out, Enzo appears, his face immediately cast in suspicion. He's shirtless, and it's almost enough to distract me from the caretaker's odd behavior.

Sylvester keeps silent and just waits for Enzo to enter the room, the pair watching each other closely.

"You two have a good night," the old man calls before firmly closing the door behind him.

I stand, having no idea what the hell to say but prepared to say *something*, until I hear an audible click.

"Did you just lock us in here?" I shout, rushing to the door and jiggling the doorknob.

"Sleep tight," he calls back, before hobbling down the hallway.

"The fuck? He seriously locked us in?" Enzo barks, pushing me aside to try the door handle for himself.

Enzo slams a hand on the wood. "Hey! It's fucking seven o'clock, man. Let us out."

However, Sylvester is already gone, on his way down the metal steps, if the metallic ringing sound is any indication.

"What the hell happened?" he snaps, turning his glare to me accusingly.

"I didn't do anything!" I shout defensively. "Where were you anyway?"

"I've been downstairs fixing a few things so I could focus on something else other than throttling him. I just went to take a shower ten minutes ago and came out to this," he explains, frustration evident in his tone.

It's only now that I realize that water droplets are clinging to the fine dusting of hair on his chest, dripping down the contours of his abs. His hair and beard are growing out, yet it doesn't make him look any less devastating. Coupled with the fierce expression on his face, my organs are currently on fire, and my blood is the gasoline.

"So, what happened?" he repeats, his brow furrowed with anger.

Clearing my throat, I will myself to refocus on the issue at hand.

"He came in here to apologize and then ended up saying if a man touches me, I asked for it because I'm wearing a bikini and shorts."

He takes a menacing step toward me, a black shadow blanketing him. "Did he touch you again?" He doesn't wait for an answer, turning to glower at the door. "*Lo uccido,*" he spits, deathly calm.

"What does that mean?"

He turns to me, searing me beneath his blazing stare. "It means I'm going to fucking kill him, Sawyer."

I scoff, baffled at why the hell he's acting like he gives a shit.

"Whatever. You don't have much room to talk anyway."

He turns that glower to me, and I shift. He's seriously scary.

"Come again?" he challenges.

"Well, did you not fuck me while actively drowning me? You're going to act like there isn't something wrong with that?"

A dimple begins to appear in his cheek, and I swear to *God,* if the fucker actually smiles right now, *I'm* going to kill *him.*

"You're right," he concedes, pausing a beat before saying, "and I'd do it again. I'm the only one allowed to touch you, *bella ladra,* and I'm the only one who will cause you pain. *Capito?*"

My eyes widen in shock, and for a few seconds, the only thing I'm capable of is sputtering at him.

"What are you—a barbarian? Did cavemen raise you?"

"I wouldn't call nuns cavemen," he responds casually. I just stare at him, and he calmly walks to the bed, picking up the book and studying it. I get the feeling he's just trying to distract himself from me, and for some reason, that pisses me off more.

"You were not raised by nuns."

"Where did you get this?" he asks, wiggling the book and ignoring me.

Lo uccido - *I'm going to kill him*
Capito - *Understood?*

"The bookshelf. It's a shelf that you put books on," I clip. "Where did you get your audacity?"

He continues to ignore me as he flips through the book, refusing to offer me a real response.

My hands ball into tight fists, a cocktail of emotions churning in my stomach. From his threats in the cave to Sylvester's strange attitude, and now this... I'm overflowing with frustration from the entire male species.

I'm pretty sure women can live just fine without them, yet here they are, still plaguing Earth like cockroaches. A definite hiccup in evolution.

"Learn anything valuable about lighthouses? Anything that might actually help us?"

Us. There is no *us.* There's only him and me. No we. No unit or team. No partners or even someone to trust. We only became one person for a night. Now it's he and I. That's it.

I cross my arms. "If I did, I wouldn't tell you."

He hums deep in his chest. It might as well be a tornado alarm.

"Is that because you want to get off this island alone?" he questions lightly, though there's a hint of darkness in his tone that's unmistakable.

I turn away from him, fully prepared to put myself in timeout and stick my nose in the corner just so I don't have to look at him anymore.

Kevin used to get me in trouble all the time, and that was always my mother's solution. Nose in the corner. I was tired of looking at cracked white paint, so one day, I decided to stick my nose between the walls so hard I nearly broke it. I told my mother it had attacked me and that timeouts were too dangerous. So her solution was to make me stand outside on the front porch, facing the little playground set they bought for Kev. She said now the walls couldn't hurt me anymore.

Just the sight of watching my brother play without me. Free of sin.

Or at least that's what he claimed.

And what Mom always believed because I accepted punishments for *his* wrongdoings in silence.

So, why stay quiet now?

"I don't care what happens to you," I mutter beneath my breath.

I only manage one more step when suddenly a hand is roughly gripping my curls and spinning me back around. A gasp leaves my tongue, and my heart bottoms out when I come face-to-face with two fierce hazel eyes. That dark spot in his right iris is sprouting, turning it nearly black.

He steps into my personal space and bares his teeth, tightening his grip on my hair until my skull is laced with pain.

"You've made that clear, baby, and it's so fucking unfortunate for you that I care about what happens to you."

I push against his chest, but he doesn't budge, and I'm breathless as I bite out, "Why the fuck would you care?"

He leans in impossibly closer, a cyclone of electricity forming in the room. Every time his skin slides against mine, a storm cloud swells, and lightning strikes somewhere around the world.

How many others have shipwrecked because he can't stop touching me?

"Because I want to see you suffer. And I will do everything in my power to make sure that happens. If that means keeping you alive just so I can tear you down, so be it."

Then, he harshly pushes me away, causing me to stumble and land right on my ass, a harsh breath forced from my lungs.

"Asshole," I wheeze, tears stinging the backs of my eyes while a shooting pain races up my spine.

God, I can't fucking stand him.

Once again, he ignores me. Instead, returning to sit on the bed, leaning back against the stone wall with his feet crossed, skimming over the lighthouse book as if he doesn't have a care in the fucking world.

But last time I checked, I've been ruining lives far longer than him.

CHAPTER 15

Sawyer

"What are you doing?"

The screech that leaves my mouth sounds like it came straight out of *Godzilla*. I'd be embarrassed if it wasn't for the fact that I'm too busy trying to claw my heart back down from my throat.

"Oh, my God," is all I manage.

I've been knocking lightly on the walls in the hallway outside our room for the past few minutes, searching for a hollow point. I'm hoping there's a hidden entrance to a staircase somewhere.

Enzo stares at me, an unimpressed quirk to his thick brow. I grab my chest, sucking in a deep breath to calm my erratic heart rate.

"What are *you* doing?" I ask breathlessly. He holds up the lighthouse book.

"Looking for the beacon?"

I scoff, "No. Why would you think that?"

"You dog-eared the page."

"Oh. Did I?" I mumble. I couldn't sleep last night, so I stayed up late with the book shoved against the window, trying to read as best I could with the webs of moonlight highlighting only a few words at a time.

The book is about Raven's Isle and its history, published in 2008. It has a record of what seems like every important event. Sylvester is even mentioned in it, named the official lighthouse keeper since 1978.

Over the years, he's assisted with hundreds of vessels. These waters around Raven Isle are perilous and rocky and are known for sending ships down under. Lighthouses can have several meanings, and this one was meant to both warn and to offer a safe haven if it was already too late.

There are dozens upon dozens of recounts of ships wrecking and Sylvester guiding them to his island. Every one of them lists the vessel, what it was transporting and where to, and even the names of known survivors and deaths.

Except there is no record of the prisoners. Nothing about a transport ship capsizing or any of the survivors washing up on Raven Isle. It doesn't mean it didn't happen, but it only makes me wonder why it wasn't documented like the others.

"Why are you looking for the beacon?"

In the book, there was a brief mention of how Sylvester would guide the sea captains here while manning the beacon. Which means that he had to have some type of way to communicate while up there.

There obviously must be another set of stairs somewhere leading to it, and I was curious as to where. There could be another radio up there. Maybe a way to send out some type of distress signal and prompt a ship to come to rescue us.

Or just me.

It would be nearly impossible to hide a boat from Enzo. Then again, I could always lie and say he's dangerous...

I shrug, attempting nonchalance. "I wanted to go stare into the light."

Enzo crosses his arms, waiting for an honest response.

The fucker can keep waiting.

Turning back around, I place my hands on the wall and start lightly knocking again, resuming my search for a hollow point.

"Sawyer," he growls, the rough timbre of his voice deepening his accent and sending shivers down my spine. I never actually got to hear him moan my real name, and I think I'm glad for it. If I had, I don't think I would've ever left that man's bed, and while maybe that would have prevented this entire mess, it wouldn't have prevented me from falling for him.

And that is by far more dangerous than shipwrecking in the middle of the ocean during a storm. Ask anybody.

"What?" I snap, embarrassed by the flush slowly crawling up my throat and the fact that I need to clench my thighs just to abate the throb between them.

"Why are you looking for the beacon?" he repeats, his voice closer than it was a minute ago. "I think it's best you don't lie to me this time."

"I wasn't lying. I was diverting. There's a difference," I defend lightly.

When I feel his presence close in on me, I yelp, twisting around and pressing myself into the wall.

"Don't come a step closer, or I'll scream," I threaten, pointing a finger at him.

One of us is a lion and the other is a rabbit. And it's not hard to guess which one is scared and which one looks hungry.

"Stop looking at me like that," I demand.

Fuck. Didn't work. He's still looking at me like that.

"Answer my question. I'm not going to ask it again," he orders, taking another step closer, his searing gaze locked onto mine.

The entire expanse of my body is flattened against the wall, and once more, I'm faced with the unbending fact that I can't walk through solid objects.

He's always using his body against me. Using it to intimidate me, to distract me, to get what he wants.

Flip the script, dumbass.

Right. Easier said than done when there might as well be a Minotaur in my face, huffing down at me.

Working to swallow, I force my shoulders to relax, and then slowly, every other muscle in my body follows suit.

I cast my gaze to the floor long enough to gather courage that is entirely fabricated, then lift my eyes back to him, allowing myself to feel the throb radiating between my thighs and the way his proximity makes my nipples tighten painfully.

While my bravery is forced, the way my body reacts to him is anything but. There's a constant battle of fighting my attraction to him and convincing myself that any man could make my knees weaken with a single look. And ridding myself of that internal war feels like wearing a tight costume for too long and finally taking it off to breathe. There are no pretenses, no denying the way my clit pulses beneath his stare, and the wetness that coats my inner thighs when he gets close enough.

There are no shutters over my eyes, hiding the truth from him as often as I hide it from myself.

Though he wasn't moving, Enzo's body seems to still. Like hitting pause on a movie. Except I double-clicked the button, and just as quickly as he stopped, he's striking, wrapping a hand around my throat, and lifting until only my toes touch the ground. His form is pressing into mine so deeply, our lungs just might entwine.

How am I supposed to breathe if all my oxygen is going to him instead?

"I know what you're doing," he snarls. The heat radiating from his body threatens to burn me alive, the outline of my body forever charred into the stone wall behind me.

"I'm not lying to you," I whisper, whimpering when he squeezes my throat tighter. His eyes dilate when the helpless sound reaches his ears.

Enzo hates me. But he also wants me. And I have no intention of letting him stop when it's the only thing keeping me alive.

Slowly, I drag my leg up around his hip, inviting him deeper between my thighs. A low growl rumbles deep in his chest, yet he presses the hard ridge of his cock against my pussy, eliciting another cry from my constricted throat. A shudder works through my body from how good it feels, and it takes little effort to roll against his length, seeking something from him that I shouldn't be.

"No, you're not," he agrees before leaning closer, his lips whispering across my jaw. "You know what else you're not doing?"

"Hmm?" I'm distracted by the way he's begun to rotate his hips, drawing out a breathless moan. A knot is forming in the trenches of my stomach, tightening each time his cock slides against my clit.

"You're not begging, *bella ladra*," he murmurs.

Then, he pulls away just an inch, enough for me to lose the sweet pressure he was creating between my thighs. In place, there's a chill forming between us.

I can feel him distancing himself, and I'm latching on harder, desperate and needy. Any coherent thought has long fled from my brain, determined to escape the collapsing tomb of senselessness. Reason and logic don't belong in there. Not when all it cares about is how to convince him to make me come.

Enzo and I stand in the eye of a hurricane, a perfect storm of lust and hate.

"Please," I whisper, uncaring of how pathetic I've become. Reduced to thoughtlessness and single-mindedness with a simple thrust of his hips.

He makes a dissatisfied noise in the depths of his throat.

"Didn't I say I wouldn't fuck you even when you begged me to? Tell me why you think that is."

His voice is so cold. So, so fucking cold.

I shake my head, feeling the heavy weight of denial soaking through my bones. Not just denial—but shame, too. I didn't mean to beg for him. Didn't *want* to. But the word slipped out as readily as my self-preservation did.

"It's because it's not good enough, Sawyer. *You're* not good enough."

There are tears welling in my eyes before I can stop them.

"You know why else?" he bites out through gritted teeth, anger beginning to glow in his eyes.

"Because I fucking *hate* you," he spits, shaking me to punctuate his words. I claw at his hand, breaking the skin and leaving bloody trails in its wake, but the sting doesn't faze him.

I hate him, too—*God*, do I hate him, too. I hate everything he is. His fucking arrogance. His holier-than-thou attitude. Everything. Fucking *everything* about him.

So badly, I want to shout these words in his face, but I can hardly draw in a breath, let alone utter a syllable of my wrath. Before I can do anything, there's a long dragging noise coming from above us.

The colorful words poised on the tip of my tongue dissipate like smoke, and the blazing fire shining in Enzo's eyes quickly freezes into ice picks.

Both of our heads shoot up, paralyzed by the sound of chains dragging against the ceiling.

Slowly, Enzo releases me, stepping away as his eyes track the footsteps.

"Hello?" he calls out, keeping the volume of his voice controlled, assumingly, so Sylvester doesn't hear.

The footsteps don't falter, and it's only when my chest begins to ache that I notice how hard my heart is beating.

Enzo drops his chin and scrutinizes me, asking in a low voice, "*Perché*, Sawyer? Tell me why."

I blink, taken aback that even now, he's asking why I'm looking for the light. "Are you asking because you think I'm, what—conspiring with the ghosts? Because if I'm being perfectly honest, I have no fucking interest in going up there now."

"*Sawyer.*"

Perché - *Why?*

"Oh my God, because I thought maybe there would be an extra radio up there," I whisper-shout, fed up with him invading every aspect of my privacy. It's bad enough being forced to share a goddamn room with him, but him trying to get inside my head is just too far.

There's a small thump from above, causing me to jump and snap my gaze up. After a moment of silence, the dragging sound continues.

Aside from the prisoner above us, there's an eerie silence pressing in around us. Glancing around nervously, I note how dark this hallway is, with no source to allow the early morning sunlight to pierce through.

Just a dark hallway with an imprisoned spirit pacing above.

"Hello?" Enzo calls again, this time a tad louder. And this time, the footfalls do stop.

Holding my breath, an ominous silence descends. So quiet, it makes my ears ring while an impenetrable cold closes in around me. There's no noise from Sylvester below, even. For the first time, it seems like we're completely alone on this island, save for the souls who haunt it.

I'm not entirely sure I like it.

Heart racing, I attempt to force my shoulders back down again with the spirit now gone. Until something bangs against the ceiling loudly, causing a startled yelp to rip from my throat.

Enzo stands firm and silent as another loud bang ripples across the wood. I, on the other hand, am nearly shitting my pants. It feels as if my ribs are cracking from how hard my heart thrashes against it.

It sounds like someone is stomping or slamming their fist into the floor above us. Hard enough that I can feel it tremble the ground beneath my feet.

"Enzo," I breathe, my chest tight and a dangerous cocktail of terror and adrenaline mixing in my bloodstream.

"Let's go outside," he says quietly, but the end of his sentence is cut off by another booming thud.

There is one last pause, and then two limbs are pounding against the ceiling in quick succession, growing louder and more frantic.

The panic becomes too sharp, and I'm screaming and bolting toward the spiral steps, sightless in my desperation to get away. I lose my footing and pitch forward. Another scream is torn from my throat as I go down face-first.

Suddenly, Enzo's hand is gripping my arm a moment later, hauling me up before my nose can connect with the metal stairs.

"Fucking hell, Sawyer," he growls, nearly dragging me the rest of the way down and out of the lighthouse.

The burst of sunlight is startling and blinding as he nearly drags me down the steps and onto the beach. I cover my face, reeling from the last twenty seconds that for sure removed twenty years off my life.

"What's goin' on?" Sylvester shouts from a little way down the shoreline, but my nerves are too fried, and I hardly hear him at all.

"Something was pounding against the ceiling," Enzo answers, his tone hard as Sylvester approaches, struggling as his peg sinks in the sand.

Knees weak, I crouch down and drop my head low, sucking in a deep breath and working on getting my pounding heart under control.

"I... heart attack," I gasp.

"You're not having a heart attack," Enzo responds dryly.

"Dying," I wheeze. "Need the water police. Call 911."

I'm only met with silence, but I would hardly be able to hear them past the thumping in my ears anyway.

Then, "Did she just say water police?"

"Ignore her," Enzo grumbles. "911 isn't even the right number to call."

"Well, did she hit 'er head or somethin'?"

Enzo sighs. "I wish I could say yes. But that's just Sawyer."

CHAPTER 16

Sawyer

"*Let me taste you, bella.*"

I moan, spreading my legs just as Enzo crawls up my legs, placing soft kisses along my thigh as he goes.

"*Please,*" *I whisper.*

A flailing hand whacking me in the head brings me out of my dream, startling me awake.

I growl, sitting up and glaring at Enzo. He's sucked into another nightmare. Whatever brain demon is plaguing him is causing me bodily harm now, and with the fact that I was in the midst of a sex dream and now feel like I have blue balls, I'm beyond frustrated.

All day, we've been on edge after that thing scared us out of the lighthouse. I was damn excited to pass out and hopefully escape into some place better. I had achieved that, too.

I don't even care that the dream was about him. I can't blame my subconscious for wanting to relive the best sex I've ever had. Nonetheless, I am mad that the real-life thing fucking *ruined* it.

"Enzo," I snarl, pushing his arm roughly. Fuck not waking him. If I have to be wet and miserable, then he gets to be angry and awake.

He doesn't wake up, so I ball my fist and send it flying into his shoulder.

One second, he's thrashing his head, the next, his hand is wrapping around my wrist, and he's rolling on top of me while his other hand is around my throat, squeezing tightly.

I yelp, my brain having trouble catching up to the sudden change.

"Enzo," I squeak, the pressure around my wrist and throat becoming too much. "Enzo!" I shout, my voice barely making it through.

Then, his spine is snapping straight, releasing me with a gasp.

"*Che cazzo succede?*" he barks. I can't see his eyes, but oh, can I feel them. The heat from the fire spouting from them is giving me a sunburn.

I choke out a cough. Now that I'm no longer dying, the anger comes right back.

"You dickhead!" I shout, pushing at his chest, but he's an immovable beast. He snatches my wrists, forcing them above my head, the both of us panting heavily.

"The fuck is your problem? I could've fucking killed you."

"Oh, I don't know. I was having a really fucking nice dream, and your stupid-ass hand smacking me in the head ruined it."

"*That's* why you woke me? Over a fucking dream?" he asks incredulously.

"It was a nice one," I say petulantly. "And it seem I did you a favor anyway."

He's silent, and I huff out angry breaths.

"What was the dream?"

I blink several times, wondering why the hell he cares, and especially why he's still on top of me.

Che cazzo succede? - What the fuck?

"What? Why does that matter?"

"Apparently, a lot, if it's making you hit me."

"You hit me first."

That was childish, but I'm regretting mentioning the dream. I refuse to admit that it was about him, and I am absolutely adamant he never finds out that he was about to fuck me in it.

"What was the dream, *bella*?" he asks again, his tone dropping wickedly. And just like a goddamn wizard, I'm opening my mouth to tell him exactly that.

"You know what? Whatever. When a man and a woman are attracted to each other, they have coitus. That was *about* to take place in my dream, and you fucking ruined it. Happy? Get off me now."

It was my intention to make it sound as unsexy as possible—a fantastic distraction technique—yet his weight seems to have only grown heavier as he leans in more.

"It was about me," he states plainly. I open my mouth to deny it, but it feels like my lungs have been incinerated. The air between us is smoldering, and even if I did have lungs to speak of, I wouldn't be able to breathe through the tension.

Arousal is rebuilding between my thighs, and I'm transported back to that place of needing something that I should never have had to begin with. I never should've touched Enzo Vitale.

"What was I doing to you?"

"N-nothing," I stutter. "You woke me up, remember?"

"That's another lie, Sawyer. I can smell your pussy from here. That's not nothing."

A whimper whittles out of my throat, despite my desperate attempts to swallow it down.

I don't know what to say to that. It's much easier to just spread my legs and let him have his way.

The sound of the chains begins, starting from the metal steps, up to the hallway, and down toward Sylvester's room.

I hold my breath, waiting for Enzo to roll off me and let the sounds of a lost prisoner take over.

Except he doesn't. Instead, he draws my wrists together, holding them in place in one hand while his other slowly trails down my arm, leaving a trail of goosebumps. I shiver as his fingers catch the collar of my t-shirt, brushing across my skin, then moving down again.

"What was I doing?" he asks again, quieter this time.

I have a mouth full of sand, unable to formulate a coherent thought beyond his touch.

Hours ago, he spat in my face about how much he hates me. He also swore that he wouldn't fuck me even if I begged him to.

What good is that promise now while he plays with the edges of my shirt, as if my body is a composition where his fingers engrave each note of intention within?

He's no better than me—throwing away his integrity for selfish needs.

"You were going to fuck me," I tell him. "You were going to do exactly what you said you would never do again."

He's quiet for a beat, and part of me wishes I just kept my mouth shut and let him fuck me. Wait to remind him how much of a liar he is after he's come inside me.

"What's one more nightmare to live with?" he whispers.

It's a punch to the chest, enough to bring tears to my eyes.

Normally, I'd thrash to get him off me and refuse him, but a different type of anger courses through me. If he thinks I'm a nightmare, I'll be the worst one he's ever had. I'll be the one keeping him up at night for the rest of his life, waking without me there but always yearning for me.

I'll let him have me one more time, only because he'll regret losing me after.

"What's one more," I echo forlornly.

Tonight, he's determined to do this, and I wonder if it's only to escape his own mind. More than anything, I want him to tell me what plagues his dreams at night, but the lingering sting of his words and the hard press of his cock on my lower stomach keep me silent.

"Were you naked?" he prompts.

"Yes," I whisper.

He hums, then grabs the end of my t-shirt and pulls it up, releasing my arms to remove the fabric altogether.

My nipples harden as the chilly air settles on my flushed skin, coercing goosebumps to the surface. I shiver, despite how I'm burning up inside.

Next, he slides my bathing suit bottoms off, then spreads my legs so he can settle between them.

My cheeks burn when I feel just how slick my inner thighs are. My brain is split into two sides of the same coin. I want him to feel how badly I need to be touched, but I don't want him to know it's only for him.

Gathering my wrists back in one hand, he once more pins them above my head, hovering above me. Hot breath fans across my sensitive flesh and I can't help but squeeze my thighs around his hips.

"Where did I touch you?" he questions, keeping his free hand safely on my outer thigh. His palm burns against my skin, but his mere presence radiates heat.

"My nipples," I confess hoarsely. "With your mouth."

He hums, the deep sound crawling along each nerve in my body. I inhale sharply when he leans down and captures my right nipple between his teeth, drawing the peak into his hot mouth and sucking sharply.

My back is bowing off the bed, tremors racking my body as a moan rolls off my tongue.

"Yes," I whisper, grinding my pussy against him, disappointed when I feel the material of his shorts instead of his bare cock.

I should've said *he* was naked first, purely for my own self-gratification.

He delivers a sharp bite before releasing my nipple, tipping his chin up just enough for the moonlight to catch the severe planes of his face and reveal his darkened eyes.

It's paralyzing—the way he hates to want me. It's empowering.

"You were kissing up my thighs," I tell him, holding his stare. "You were begging to lick me."

A divot appears in his right cheek, a slightly crooked curl to his lips. Those dimples give him away, otherwise, his amusement could only be detected in his eyes.

"You said *let me taste you, bella.* My pussy was dripping wet just as it is now, and you were nearly drooling just to get a taste."

A growl forms deep in his chest, and he sits up, releasing his grip on my wrists.

"Keep your hands above your head, Sawyer. If you want to touch me, you'll be held to the same rules and you will beg for it."

Shouldn't be an issue.

Except the moment he slides down my form, settling his shoulders between my legs, I'm bursting with the need to run my hands through his hair.

I resist while he brings my sweet dreams to life and places soft kisses up my thigh, maintaining eye contact as he does. The shadows are deeper now that he's no longer directly in the moonlight, but I can still see his eyes just enough to feel the intensity behind them.

Right when he reaches my pussy, he pauses, his breath fanning across the sensitive area.

"Let me taste you, *bella,*" he whispers devilishly, that accent making the words sound so much more delicious than in my dream.

My heart flies into my throat, nearly preventing the desperate *yes* from escaping.

The dimple reappears, but he denies me the sight, dipping his chin down and gliding his tongue in one long sweep up my slit.

Again, my back is arching off the bed, and I'm curling my hands into tight fists to abate the need to touch him.

"Oh, fuck," I moan, panting when the pointed end of his tongue swipes back and forth across my clit, igniting every single nerve within.

How does he manage to hit every one of them?

My hips buck, and my eyes roll. Already, I'm nearing an orgasm. That dream pushed me toward the edge, and Enzo bringing it to life is transcendent.

My hands grip the pillow above me, curling into it fiercely. He diverts his attention down, plunging inside my pussy with fervor, licking me so thoroughly that I'm convinced there isn't an inch of me he hasn't feasted on.

He hums against me before growling, "How does it feel to be eaten alive?"

"It's not enough," I mewl breathlessly. "I'd rather you fuck me to death."

He rises to his knees and tugs his shirt over his head by the back of his collar. My mouth waters at the sight of moonlight and shadows engaging in a war across every ridge and curve on his physique.

I'm on the verge of sitting up and licking his abs. However, he's already pulling down his shorts, revealing something much more tantalizing. His cock juts straight out, curving upward just the slightest bit. That's the secret to him hitting all those perfect spots inside me.

"Why did you get to be God's favorite?"

He stares down at me with a savage expression.

"You can ask him yourself when I take you to see him."

I bite my lip, but a gasp breaks through when he grabs my hips, lifting them to the height of his own, and then lines his cock to my entrance with only my upper back on the bed.

He keeps me there suspended, so close to feeling complete again.

"Let me take you to him, *bella*."

"Fuck, yes, fill me up—"

He drives inside before I can finish, a sharp cry replacing my plea. He pauses, giving me time to adjust to his size. It's unnatural, the way he fills me so completely.

"Shh, the caretaker will hear you," he murmurs.

On cue, there's a creak outside our door, racketing up my heart rate to catastrophic levels. I curl my lips together, attempting to keep quiet while Enzo withdraws, then slams inside me again.

"Enzo, let me touch you," I beg.

Uncaring of his response, I grab onto his forearms before he can answer, feeling the thick protruding veins threaded throughout them. He picks up a steady pace, his grip on my hips becoming bruising.

My mouth opens on a silent scream, my back bowing until I'm practically balancing on my head as he fucks me.

I'm clawing at his arms while the sharp sound of skin slapping arises.

"Oh God," I cry, trying to keep my voice down but failing miserably.

"Can you see him, baby? Ask him for forgiveness."

"Why?" I pant, another high-pitched moan nearly swallowing the word.

"Because you worship me now."

He ends his promise with a sharp thrust, this one angled differently to hit that spot inside me that has electricity racing down my spine.

God, how could I not worship him? Sex with him is the only time I've ever prayed.

I bite my lip hard, the orgasm deep in my stomach building rapidly. I'm trying to slow it down—to savor this—but my body has taken on a mind of its own. My hand darts to my center, and I'm circling my clit firmly, amping the pleasure up to dizzying heights.

"Enzo, I need to come," I rush out, my tone hushed but high-pitched.

"You come when I tell you to," he growls.

One hand releases my hip, moving to where he drives inside me. I feel pressure, and then his finger is slipping inside my pussy above his cock, stretching me further.

An unnatural sound leaks from my throat, the foreign sensation shocking. I've never in my life had a man fuck me with his dick and finger at the same time.

His digit curls, hitting my G-spot so precisely, it's almost too intense.

"Oh my God, that—wait, fuck, Enzo," I stutter, the entirety of my body beginning to vibrate.

My bladder feels like it's on the verge of releasing, and though I know exactly what he's going to make me do, I feel out of control over my bodily functions.

"You're going to come for me, *bella*, and you're going to fucking paint me in it. If I'm not covered, then I will make you do it again until there's nothing left of you."

Once again, he's curling his finger, massaging the area with savage persistence. It only takes seconds before I'm erupting.

I have enough forethought to slap my free hand over my mouth in an attempt to disguise the scream tearing out of my throat.

After that, I lose all cognitive function. My soul is ripped from its vessel, no longer sustainable when it's been completely decimated in this moment.

I'm consumed by the euphoria transporting me back into the middle of that ocean, where a much greater force seized control over me.

This time, I don't know if I'll ever resurface. I don't know if I want to.

Distantly, I feel Enzo pull out of me and deliver sharp slaps directly on my pussy, heightening the pleasure. I'm exploding, but I'm too far gone to process what's happening around me. All I know is that my eyes are rolled far back into my head, and my body is seizing.

Then he's driving inside me again, resuming his position with both hands gripping my hips while he savagely rolls his own into mine. It doesn't take long before he's lost right alongside me; my name growled so deeply, that I feel it along the surface of my skin.

Reality eventually takes over, pulling me from the sea of bliss. Slowly, my senses come hurtling back in, and I'm thrown back into my body.

I'm flat on my back with Enzo hovering above me, still inside me but no longer moving. His head is bowed, and he's trembling and silent.

"Enzo?" I croak, growing concerned. There's an innate fear that he's already regretting what we just did.

He straightens, and my eyes widen. Just as he demanded, his chest and abs are dripping with my release, droplets trailing down the contours of his body.

"Oh," I breathe, at a loss for words. I grab for my discarded t-shirt on the bed and sit up. "Let me clean that off."

His hand snaps around my wrist just as I lift the shirt to him. "Don't."

Awkwardly, I retract my hand and scoot over to huddle against the wall. The bed is soaked, and I'm glad it's on his side.

"Was that the nightmare you were hoping for?" I mutter, feeling the tension thickening between us.

He glances at me. "No. It was worse."

I swallow the hurt, not even sure how to interpret that. I can't tell if it's a play on words or if he truly thought the sex was awful.

It doesn't matter anyway.

We're back to hating each other.

The silence is suffocating as I slip under the covers and turn away from him.

On our first night together, we either talked or basked quietly in the aftermath of a good fuck. Now, all I feel is cold while I listen to the low creak outside our door, followed by the sound of chains dragging along the floor.

CHAPTER 17

Enzo

"How often is this island surrounded by sharks?" I ask, staring hard at the two fins that pop up every now and again. I think there's a third out there, but I can't be sure.

Sylvester comes up beside me, panting a little as he leans on his good leg.

"All the time," he responds. "One of the things that make this island treacherous. We get seals out here, so they tend to stick around."

I nod, crossing my arms and wishing more than anything I could be out there with them, holding on to their fins and feeling them move beneath my hand as they glide through the water. It's a feeling unlike anything else and only serves to remind me how fucking stuck I am.

"You, uh, like them, right?" he asks awkwardly. It's been awkward all morning. I'm almost positive he heard us last night, and I'm not the least bit ashamed of it. However, he's the type to usually say something if he feels disrespected, which tells me he enjoyed it, too.

Sick fucker.

We still don't care for each other, but for the sake of not making things more tense than they already are, I answer, "Yeah. They're incredible creatures."

"Ever been in the water with one?"

"All the time," I say.

He guffaws, shaking his head, seemingly to have trouble imagining it.

"Outside a cage, too?"

"Absolutely. If I'm out in the ocean, I don't touch them—I respect their space. I own a research center in Port Valen, Australia, and there's an enclosure to bring them in when we need to conduct certain testing. I will usually get in the water with them then."

"You keep 'em?"

"No, never. They're not meant to be imprisoned."

He nods, an awkward silence descending. I pay him no mind, my attention zeroed in on the shark. Restlessness is gathered in my bones, and I'm almost stupid enough to consider swimming out of here. But despite my experience with them, it's too dangerous, especially if this is a hunting ground for them.

"I'm uh, sorry about the little scare ya'll had yesterday," he apologizes. "I ain't ever had that happen, but I imagine it made you two very uncomfortable."

Dragging my gaze away from the water, I eye him closely. He's staring down at the sand, watching how the rolling waves wash up to the wooden leg that's slowly creating a hole within the grains. He's tense, and I can't tell if it's because of what he's saying or because he just doesn't like being in my presence.

"Guess the ghosts just don't like us. Odd, when we're not the ones who killed them."

He chortles, but the sound comes out forced. "Maybe they was just askin' fer you to help them, then. Can't say I like their company, either."

"Why don't you leave?" I question, turning my gaze back to the water. Though, I keep him in my peripheral, trusting him as much as I would if he claimed his wooden leg was real.

"It's what I know best. Been out here since I was eighteen, and by the time the lighthouse shut down in 2010, I'd been here for thirty-two years. S'pose it's a lot like getting out of prison. Don't know how to adjust to the real world."

"Sawyer mentioned you having a daughter," I probe.

"Had a whole family once upon a time," he answers, though his tone is hardening. "I've tried to make this place a home. Sometimes people just ain't willin'. But doesn't stop me from tryin.'"

I glance at him. "Must've been hard to let them go."

Instead of answering, he turns to me and points over his shoulder. "There's a storm comin' in tonight. I'd be inside within the hour. They can come on fast, and the waves get big. But I'm sure you know that now."

My fists clench when he slaps the back of my shoulder a couple of times before heading off. I tuck them deeper into my armpits, refraining from sending one of them flying into the back of his head.

"Hey, Sylvester?" I call, keeping my back to him. He doesn't verbally respond, but I know he's stopped walking, his uneven gait no longer audible. "Don't touch me again. And don't touch Sawyer, either."

The silence turns murderous. It feels like having a serial killer breathing down your neck, their intent to kill you as potent as the salt is in the air.

I don't think I'd mind him trying.

But after a moment, his gait resumes, and he walks away without a word.

"You probably just shouldn't have said anything," a soft voice says from behind me. This time, I do turn, finding Sawyer walking toward me, her demeanor unsure.

"Are you expecting me to let him belittle and lay hands on me just to avoid discomfort?"

She tightens her lips and nods. "Good point. I'm sorry."

I shake my head and face the water again. How is it that my hatred for how she makes me feel is somehow shifting, and now I'm hating the way *I* make *her* feel?

"I don't want your apologies. It's men that made you feel and think that way. They should be apologizing to you."

"Are *you* going to apologize? You're one of those men."

"If I ever feel sorry about it," I murmur. She's right, I should be apologizing. But I also don't lie, and while there is guilt needling its way into my system, I'm not ready to give in to it yet, either.

"It was wrong. Fucked up."

"It was," I agree. "But you're not upset because I fucked you. You're upset because I scared you."

She's quiet for a beat. "You're right. I've been scared my entire life, and I've been touched my entire life. It'll never hurt when you touch me, but it hurt that you were no longer safe."

Fury explodes in my chest, and I'm whipping toward her, putting my face in hers.

"So, I made you feel what you made me feel? I won't deny that I'm the villain in your story, baby, but please don't insult me by acting like you didn't hurt me first."

She bites her bottom lip to hide the tremble. I tsk, raising my hand to her face and using my thumb to pull her lip out from between her teeth. She still smells of the ocean, and she's so fucking beautiful—that's what hurts.

"Don't hide your tears, *bella*. You're so pretty when you cry."

"I'm so—"

"I said I wouldn't apologize until I meant it. I suggest you do the same," I tell her, turning away. I thought I'd be able to breathe easier when I did, but she's still taking up too much space in my chest.

I haven't been able to get last night off my mind, replaying it over and over in my head. I said I'd never fuck her again, but in my weakest moment, I gave in. The nightmare of my mother abandoning me on those damn steps, laughing as she drove away from me, was fresh in my mind.

I needed to escape it, and seeing the evidence of Sawyer's unbending need for me was too good to resist. Because right before me was someone who couldn't let me go even when she wanted nothing more than that, and all I wanted to do was make sure she *couldn't* let me go.

Despite how cruel I can be, she comes undone for me so fucking easily. As if she was made just for me.

Suor Caterina used to tell me that we were all God's creations, but I never bought into that shit. But if it were true, then fuck Him for making her the bane of my goddamn existence.

And fuck Him for making her the one thing I want most.

Was that the nightmare you were hoping for?

No, it was worse.

And it was. It's like I've scribbled all my resistance into a charcoal ball deep into the paper, and she took a fucking eraser to it until there was nothing left but the faded remnants of when I hated her.

"I *am* sorry. And maybe you are, too. Isn't that why you told Sylvester not to touch me again?" she insists. "Because you don't want any more men hurting me?"

I shrug. "If he does, I'll just do what I said I'd do."

The thought of carving my name into her soft skin has my cock thickening. She makes it so hard to feel sorry when hurting her is so fucking intoxicating.

Suor Caterina - *Sister Caterina. Literal meaning: nun, used in lieu of Sister.*

She comes to stand before me, her shorter stature forcing me to look down. Her face is twisted into a snarl, and she's glaring at me. How cute.

"That defeats the purpose of not hurting me."

"I never said I didn't want to hurt you."

"You're not carving your name into my skin, you freak."

I cock a brow. "Watch me, *bella ladra*."

She snarls. "You like to fuck me when you hurt me, Enzo. And you said you wouldn't unless I begged, which I will never do."

"You are as unreliable as I am when it comes to fucking each other, and last night was a clear indication of that. This may come as a surprise to you, baby, but I don't believe a goddamn word you say anyway."

Dropping my arms, I spare one last glance at the darkening ocean, the waves becoming ferocious as the storm nears. Even the ones licking at our legs are becoming angrier. Then, I turn and head toward the lighthouse, dreading another night trapped in a dark room, left with nothing but my own thoughts and a girl I want nothing more than to get away from, but can never seem to. Even when she's not around.

"You know, not everything I say is a lie," she calls, stumbling over a rock as she chases after me. I shake my head in disbelief that she doesn't have a chipped front tooth or a crooked nose with how much she trips over herself. She's almost bashed her face in as many times as Sylvester wheezes whenever he moves a muscle.

"And how would I know that?" I retort. "You lied about your entire identity."

"I lied about my *name*, Enzo. Not who I am as a person."

The anger constantly boiling beneath the surface bubbles up again, like a pot of water left on the burner for too long. For the second time, I'm pivoting and getting in her face. It catches her off guard, causing her to stumble back and almost land on her ass again.

Blue eyes wide, she stares up at me in shock as I spit, "There you go lying again. You did lie about who you are as a person, Sawyer. You *did*. Because the girl I took home was not the same person as the one who stole my life from me. I don't care who you say you are because I *see* it. *Vuoi sapere cosa vedo?* I see nothing more than a lying thief who only cares about herself."

Her eyes fill with tears halfway through my tangent, and fuck if it doesn't make me want to both throttle her and take back everything I said. She's got me so twisted, I can't get my head straight.

How is it that I want to hurt her, yet protect her from my own damn self?

She looks so fucking sad, but part of me is still convinced it's a façade. A pretty, little costume she dresses up in to make people feel sympathy for her.

Growling, I turn away, but she's grabbing my arm and stopping me. I'm not entirely sure what she sees when I look back at her, but it's enough to make her release me like she was holding on to a hot poker.

"I didn't want to steal it, Enzo," she insists. "I... I didn't have a choice, okay?"

The wind is picking up, howling as it rips through her hair and our clothing, strong enough that I steel my spine.

"You always have a choice. You could've chosen to do anything else with your life than steal from people."

"I couldn't!" she shouts, her voice cracking. She's shaking, but I can't tell if it's from the influx of emotion bubbling within her or because of the intensifying wind. Tears spill over, tracking down her cheeks as she stares up at me with sorrowful eyes.

And I hate her even more in this moment. Because the longer I stare at her, the harder it is to fucking breathe. It's enraging that she has that control over me—that she holds so much power, she can suck the oxygen from my body like it's hers to wield.

Vuoi sapere cosa vedo? - *You want to know what I see?*

"Why, Sawyer?" I shout back, throwing my arms out, actively fighting against the powerful wind. We need to get inside, but I need to know why she would do something so fucking horrible.

Her bottom lip trembles and she glances away.

I drop my arms, straightening my spine, her answer written all over that deceptively beautiful face.

"You're not going to tell me," I conclude.

She shakes her head, several tears spilling over. Her mouth opens and closes, fighting for words.

But I've already lost interest.

This time when I turn away, she doesn't stop me. By the time we make it into the lighthouse, the quiet compared to the outside is almost deafening. Sylvester is setting down three glasses of whiskey on the table. In the middle are several lit candles.

"Lights will go out any minute," he says, glancing up at us knowingly. I don't know if he heard us, but frankly, I don't give a fuck.

"I think I'm going to—" Sawyer starts, but Sylvester waves a hand.

"C'mon, don't leave an old man to drink alone. Ya'll can stay out late tonight, too. I tend to dislike when we get storms."

Clearing her throat, she nods, giving him a strained smile. "Sure."

Sparing me a glance, she sidles past me and sits down at the table, making a point to take a seat next to Sylvester instead.

For reasons I'm not ready to name yet, that pisses me off, and the bitterness toward her only deepens. Everything she does just... pisses me off.

Silently, I take a seat across from them, leaning back in the rickety, wooden chair and snagging the glass of whiskey. I stare at them as I take a slow sip, watching Sawyer bend beneath the weight of my stare while Sylvester meets it head-on. The taste of spiced bourbon blooms across my tongue, scorching my throat on the way down.

Just the way I like it.

"Why don't we get to know each other tonight, yeah? Instead of livin' like strangers like we have been."

Sawyer gulps down her bourbon in one swallow, hissing as it goes down while slamming the glass on the table.

"Let's! How about we start with you, Sylvester? Tell me about yourself." The enthusiasm injected into her voice is forced, and the control over her emotions is brittle as fuck. "How'd ya lose your leg?"

Noticing the tension still between us, Sylvester clears his throat. Her question was rude, but I've never been kind a day in my life, so I keep my mouth shut.

"Stonefish. Got stung after my second daughter, Kacey, was born. Nearly killed me. It was almost too late by the time help arrived. They life-flighted me to the nearest hospital and saved me, but my leg had necrosis, so it had to go."

Sawyer frowns. "That sucks," she says shortly. I shake my head. Her social skills are almost worse than mine sometimes.

Sylvester doesn't say anything, and it grows awkward, so she pushes for another question.

"You said you had a family?" she asks. "Tell me about them."

"Yep," he says shortly. "Was married to Raven for about thirty years, but she didn't like livin' out here. Named the place after her and e'rything. And what does she do? Takes off without sayin' goodbye. That was a couple o'months before the place shut down. Been alone ever since."

She hums, not sounding all that interested in Sylvester's woes. "That's not very nice."

Then, she turns her gaze to me, little knives shooting from them. "What about you, oh perfect one? Tell me about your perfect life and how you've lived it just so. Fucking. Perfectly."

I narrow my gaze, purposely taking another slow sip of my drink just to piss her off. She seethes but keeps quiet.

"What would you like to know, Sawyer? About my perfect childhood first? Let's see, that's probably where my hatred for liars began, funnily enough. My perfect mother was the one to teach me that lesson." Her face smooths out, but I find no victory in my own tragedy. "My favorite place to get *maritozzo* was at *Regoli* in Rome. We were extremely poor, and Ma had to do questionable things for the money we did have, so when we went, it was special. I didn't think it was going to be any different on my ninth birthday. Instead, she dropped me off at *Basilica di San Giovanni* and swore she would be right back. You want to know how long I waited?"

She swallows and sits up, looking away instead of giving me an answer. One side of my lips tilts up the slightest bit, but there's nothing funny about a mother abandoning her child.

"That's the thing. I'm *still waiting*," I finish, never lifting my searing gaze from her.

If she thinks she's the only one who's suffered in life, then I'd love to introduce her to the little boy still sitting on those steps, convinced his mother is going to show up any minute.

Sylvester stares hard at me for a moment before turning his gaze to her. For a second, I had forgotten he was here.

"Well, young lady. What about you?"

She sniffs, leans forward, and grabs the bottle of bourbon, filling up her glass halfway before taking a large sip.

"Careful there. Your tiny body can't handle all that at once."

"My tiny body can handle a lot," she retorts, and her words are like throwing lighter fluid on a fire, the flames bursting in my chest as she stares at me pointedly.

Maritozzo - *Italian raised dough, sweet filled with whipped cream*

The air around us thickens, and a low vibration buzzes beneath my skin. The beginnings of an earthquake are forming, and if she's not careful, I won't stop myself from proving just how little she can take of me.

If she thinks she has no control over her life and the decisions she makes, I'll show her what it looks like to be truly uncontrollable. And if she thinks she's broken now, I'd like to see how well she can walk after I'm done.

I cock a brow and take another swallow, keeping my gaze locked on hers.

"I didn't have the worst parents," she announces. "Mom and Dad loved Kev more, though." She pauses and glances at Sylvester. "Kev is my twin brother. Betcha didn't think there was double the trouble, huh?"

She doesn't let him answer, though, and turns back to me with a vicious smile on her face. "Grew up with all the nice things. Full playground in our big backyard. Trampoline, too. Always had all the neighbor kids over to play. We were just living the fucking life, right?"

She quiets, the tension thickening while she waits for a response.

Sylvester grunts. "Right."

"Wrong," she exclaims, slamming her glass down on the table loudly, liquid sloshing over. Sylvester opens his mouth, preparing to berate her most likely, but she cuts him off. "You want to know the funny thing about having a pretty-looking life? No one would ever suspect that it's actually pretty fucking ugly. Especially not your own damn parents, who had the *perfect* fucking son that could do no wrong."

She picks up her glass and chugs the rest of it, and now the flames in my chest are darkening, a terrible feeling polluting it like when plastic is thrown in a fire, creating a cloud of dense, black smoke.

Sawyer sets the empty glass on the table and pushes it away from herself, staring at the cup like it's replaying every nightmare she's ever lived.

On cue, the lights flicker and then extinguish, leaving us in near-complete darkness save for the candles between us. The orange glow illuminates her face, but it's not enough to hide the pain within the shadows. A loud boom of thunder shatters the silence, followed by the sound of a wave crashing into the cliffside.

"Kev became a cop," she says quietly, and my chest clenches. "Cops have friends. And their friends tend to have the same morals as they do."

"What did he do?" I ask, though my voice doesn't sound much different than a growling dog.

"Fill me up, Syl," she says instead. Sylvester leans forward and pours her two fingers.

"You don't need any more," I warn.

"Do you want your question answered or not?" she snaps, grabbing the glass and taking a swig.

I clench my teeth, prepared to tell her that her secrets aren't worth the cost of her getting sick over, but she's already speaking.

"Kev and I used to have a lot of friends in school. We were both popular, but as we got older, he didn't like the attention I was getting. It was a gradual progression of him isolating me. In middle school, he started nasty rumors that turned my friends into my bullies. That made for a lot of lonely nights stuck in the house. Oftentimes, our parents would go out and leave us with a nanny, and while she wasn't mean, she was far more interested in talking on the phone with her boyfriend."

She shrugs, as if telling whatever thought is in her head that it's not a big deal. "That also means the nanny didn't notice when Kev wanted to... play."

"God fucking dammit," I mutter beneath my breath, rage now seeping out of my pores. I'm growing restless again, though this time, it's with the need to find her brother and fucking murder him.

Losing whatever courage she found, she shrugs again and finishes off her third glass, tipping her head back as the liquid pours down her throat. When her chin dips and her eyes meet mine again, they're no longer clear and full of pain. They're glazed over and lost.

I may hold on to stones from my past—keepsakes that I'm not ready to let go of—but the stones Sawyer carries are too heavy, and she doesn't think she's strong enough to throw them away.

After the shipwreck, I had told her that she was weak. But I realize now that I was wrong. Being scared and weak aren't synonymous. It takes strength to keep getting back up after constantly being knocked down.

"Sounds like he's a real piece of work," Sylvester says, resting his palm on hers. The muscle in my jaw pops, and the only thing that saves me from shattering this glass and reaching over to stab his fucking hand with a shard is Sawyer sliding her hand out from beneath his.

"He was, Syl, he was. Him and his cop friends. S'kay, though, they can't find me."

Sylvester shifts his body toward hers. "Stay here then, sweetheart. You're more than welcome to stay here with me."

"Absolutely not," I bark. My bones are ready to take on a life of their own, and I'm not sure what will happen first—taking Sawyer out of here or wrapping my hand around the old man's throat.

"Can't say anyone would find me then," she agrees. She pats Sylvester's hand, still resting in the same spot where she abandoned it. "I'll think on it. But the room is spinning, and I can't see my thoughts right now."

Sylvester keeps quiet as Sawyer stands, wobbling and seeking balance from the table. I immediately get to my feet and round to her side, grabbing her arms and pulling her into my chest. There's a slimy feeling crawling down my spine. Definitely from Sawyer's story. But also from the way Sylvester stares at her.

As if he's already decided she's staying, and now he only needs to make sure it happens.

CHAPTER 18

Sawyer

The entire world is submerged underwater, and I'm swimming through it. I'm convinced the storm got so bad that it drowned us out, and my vision just hasn't caught up yet.

Or maybe that's not true. My eyeballs are definitely swimming.

Enzo carries me into the room—or rather, drags me—and those revolting feelings in my stomach churn like it always does when I think of Kev.

Miss me, pipsqueak? I've missed you...

"Does touching me make you feel even more disturbed than usual?" I ask, bitterness staining my words. "Now that you know my brother liked to touch me, too?"

"Sawyer," he snaps, spinning me around to face him. But my vision also spins, and all he accomplishes is sending me teetering on two left feet. I think I feel sick, too. My entire body is full of alcohol, and everything inside me is sloshing around in it like they don't have assigned seating.

I giggle, imagining myself telling all my organs to go back to their seats or else extra homework for them.

Then I frown, my brows knitting. Maybe they need the extra homework. It's going to be a lot of work to get them functioning correctly again.

"Look at me," he demands, but it's dark in here. Only the moonlight cutting through the dirty glass allows me to see the outline of his face and shadowed eyes.

Even then, the torrential downpour is skewing most of the light.

"I can't," I tell him. Hot breath fans across my lips as he brings me in closer.

"Don't ever think of yourself that way. And don't ever think that I will, too. You're so much more than the people who have hurt you."

My face twists, not believing that for a second.

"I will make you see that," he vows. "What happened to you does not define you. It only forged a new path that will take you to a different version of yourself. But no one can force you to walk that road; only you can determine who you will be once you get there. It's your choice who you become, Sawyer."

I think there are tears in my eyes, and I'm blanketed by that familiar sadness. Even the alcohol can't dilute it.

For so long, I had convinced myself that it was clinging to me, despite my desperate attempts to escape it. But now I realize it's me that's been holding on, like a child with their favorite teddy bear.

"No more running, baby. I want him to come looking for you just so I can have the privilege of ending his life for touching what's mine."

My stomach clenches, and as much as I'd like to say it's the effect of the alcohol, I know better.

"I wasn't yours then. You didn't even know me."

The pad of his thumb brushes across my cheek, but it's far from loving. It feels like the placating touch of a killer right before he ends your life.

"You were always destined to be mine," he says.

His words make no sense. So hot and cold... and as much as I want what he's saying to be true, it could never happen.

"It doesn't matter if he's dead or alive, he'll always haunt me," I rasp, sadness ringing from the truth.

"Then I will haunt you worse."

Just when it seems like he's going to kiss me, he pulls away.

"Let's get you to bed."

A crack of lightning pierces the air, causing me to jolt in his arms and send my heart skyrocketing. Right when I turn toward the window, another strike hits the water, washing the world in a bright glow long enough to see a massive wave hurdling straight toward us.

"Oh my God," I gasp, stumbling back into Enzo's chest as it crashes into the side of the lighthouse.

Even as the water drowns out the glass for several seconds, the building holds firm. It doesn't even creak beneath the power of the wave.

"That... That is a strong window," I breathe, heart still thundering. Another wave is already swelling, the massive shadow prevalent in the darkness.

"Lighthouses are built for situations like this. Get in bed," he orders. If I'm not mistaken, his tone isn't as harsh as it usually is. But I also could just be drunk.

"Hey, Enzo?" I call as he helps me into bed.

"Hmm?" he hums.

"Try to hide the judgment, okay? Kev always used to tell me that no one would believe me, and well... he was right. No one ever did. And I think I prefer that now. It's better if you think I'm a liar."

"I won't judge you," he says softly.

"That's good," I nod, flopping into the bed ungracefully. The room is spinning, and I would like it to stop now.

"Maybe I will stay here forever," I sigh whimsically. "Live on in the cave with the glowworms and Sylvester as my neighbor. At least then I won't have to hurt people anymore."

Whatever Enzo says—if he says anything at all—is lost to me. Darkness already has a hold of my brain, and I'm more than happy to let it take over.

Someone is crying.

My brows pinch, the odd noise filtering past the fog in my ears and the dream that clutches onto my subconscious like a frightened cat.

I stir, my body jerking, finally plunging me back into reality. The muffled crying becomes clearer, though I can't place where it's coming from exactly.

"Do you hear that?" Enzo asks quietly.

Turns out, my world is still spinning on its axis just as much as it was when I passed out. I'm not sure I slept off even half of the alcohol.

"What is that?" I mutter, sitting upright and attempting to gain clarity over my surroundings.

Almost as if they could hear my question, the sobbing quietens, and the silence that ensues is loud.

"*Non lo so,*" he mutters.

"Another ghost?"

Enzo doesn't answer, prompting me to turn and look at him. The moonlight spears through the glass at a sharp enough angle to highlight his face. He's staring straight up at the ceiling, the muscle in his jaw pulsing.

I don't know what possesses me—maybe the ghosts in this place—but I reach out and poke his forehead.

Non lo so - *I don't know*

He blinks rapidly at me for a moment, turning his stunned gaze to me.

"Are you noticing similarities between the wood on the ceiling and the stick up your ass? I'm sure they have comparable textures."

"What is wrong with you?" he mutters, turning his glare back to said wood.

I shrug, then flop back down on the mattress, rolling to the side and facing the window. It's still storming, the rain pattering against the glass. "You now have extensive knowledge of that question, I believe." That reminder positively causes the toxic chemicals in my stomach to churn. "Anyway, whatever it was, it's gone now, and I have a lot more alcohol to sleep off."

"Then shut up and go back to bed," he says stiffly.

I'm too drunk to let his attitude bother me at this very moment. Tomorrow, I'll be contrite again.

But when I lay back down and close my eyes, sleep doesn't come for me. I beg and plea with it to take me away to some neverland, even if it's riddled with fairytale monsters, but it persists in its absence.

"Enzo?" I ask.

He's quiet for so long I've convinced myself he's fallen asleep. But then he sighs, "What, Sawyer?"

"Did you ever see your mom again?"

Again, with the weighted silence.

"No."

"Did you ever look for her?" I ask, feeling the thickening tension radiating off him.

"Why are you asking?" he deflects.

I struggle for words, feeling the familiar tide of fear rise up my throat anytime I think of my dearest twin brother. Rolling toward Enzo, I tuck my hands under my head. He's still staring up at the ceiling.

"I guess I just want to know if it's possible to let someone go that doesn't want to be found."

He sighs again and trains his gaze on me.

"I'm capable of deducing, and I get that you do what you do so he can't find you," he says slowly, as if offering his understanding and empathy to someone is new, uncharted territory.

"Have you tried—"

"Yes," I cut him off. "I've gone to my parents, and I've gone to the authorities when we were sixteen. Kev was always really good at manipulating people. So charming and charismatic, he would give you the shirt off his back without having to ask type. They just said, *I know Kevin Bennett. He would never do such a thing.* But he did."

I hadn't realized I started crying until a hot tear was burning a vengeful path across the bridge of my nose and onto the bed sheets. Thankfully, Enzo won't look at me long enough to notice.

"You went to the authorities, and they still allowed him to be a cop?"

I shrug pitifully. "It's not like they let me file a report. There was no record of my accusation."

There's something insidious mixing with the tension seeping into the air around us. Something dark and violent. It takes a moment to realize that Enzo is angry.

Which isn't anything out of the ordinary by any means, but this time is different. He's angry on *my* behalf.

"Lead him to me," he says, his voice hushed and deep with malice. The request is similar to his declaration earlier, and even in my drunk-addled mind, I remember him claiming me as his. My heart stops, then restarts, stuttering and tripping over itself in a syncopated rhythm. Butterflies sprout in my stomach, and I decide they're fucking drunk, too.

"Why would you want to hurt him?"

He faces me and lightly brushes his fingers through my curls, eliciting a shiver that racks through my entire body. The feel of his skin brushing against my temple has my lashes fluttering, a blaze of fire left in his wake. It's anything but a sweet and tender moment, though. Rather, it feels like a predator playing with its food before taking a massive bite out of it.

"He's forced you to strip people of their identities, so I will do the same to him," he murmurs darkly. I swallow, the saliva lodging in my throat as his implication settles.

Enzo wouldn't be stealing the identity of a cop. He'd be snuffing it instead.

And God help me, but the thought impels a deep throb between my legs. I clench my thighs tight in an effort to abate the need, but it's hopeless when his fingers trail into my hair again, getting lost in the waves as his precious boat did. And for a moment, I wonder if someone a hundred years from now will happen across his vessel, deeming it another tragedy that succumbed to nature's most unforgiving creation.

"Why would you do that for me?" I whisper, suppressing another shudder when his hand tightens, fisting my hair until the strands hold taut. I hiss between my teeth as sharp pinpricks bloom across my scalp.

He lifts up, resting on his forearm as he crowds over me, the heat of his body pressing into my front. I struggle to hold on to a coherent thought while my heart rate elevates dangerously.

His breath fans across the shell of my ear, and I both want to shrink away from him and notch my jaw up toward him, daring him to come closer.

"Because I want to be the only thing that keeps you up at night, *bella ladra*," he growls. "And if anyone is going to hurt you, it's going to be me."

I shake my head, uncaring of the way it tugs painfully at my hair.

More than anything, I want him to. And that scares me. Enzo can't save me from my fate, and I will never ask him to. Whatever this is, it will never work. We've caused each other too much pain, and even still, I know he's struggling to forgive me. Another thing I could never ask of him.

The familiar bone-deep urge to run arises. I have nowhere to go, so the only thing I can think to do is make *him* go.

"I will survive you, Enzo, just as I have survived him. And I will do no different than I've done before." He's silent as I exhale slowly, then whisper,

"I will do what I must."

He releases me but doesn't retreat. Ice so cold descends over us, and I know I've accomplished what I set out to do.

And that's just heartbreaking.

"I never found my mother," he tells me quietly. "I did search for her, but I didn't search for long. You know why?"

There's a foreboding feeling replacing the electricity crackling in the air.

"Why?" I ask, though I don't think I want to know.

"Because she let her sadness transform her into a miserable human being, capable of hurting others just to save herself. She wasn't worthy of my forgiveness."

Just like you.

He doesn't say it, but the words slither over my skin and needle beneath like tiny little parasites. I bite my tongue while he pulls away.

I asked for that, but it doesn't make it any easier to swallow.

"Bring him to me, Sawyer. I'll take care of him. I won't let you get away as she did."

I shake my head, frustrated that this man can't let me go.

"She was lucky then," I whisper, hoping my words were as sharp as his. He doesn't deign to give me a response, but he does turn away, and I know they were. I can feel it.

Did that hurt, baby?

CHAPTER 19

Sawyer

There's a boat outside.

It emerged from the dense fog surrounding the island as if it came from an entirely different dimension.

I stare out at the large ship, slowly drifting by, a longing feeling that sorrowfully bleeds into hopelessness.

They'll never see us from there. Not with this fog that seems to drench this tiny little pocket of earth floating in the middle of the Pacific Ocean.

Sylvester says there's going to be another storm tonight, and according to the radar, it could be worse than the one last week.

I swallow, my heart withering as it passes the island. Maybe if I could get to the light, I would've been able to figure out a way to turn it on and beckon the ship to us. I'm not entirely sure it would've cut through the fog, but it's better than standing outside my cave, watching it drift by.

What-the-fuck-ever. We've been on the island for nineteen days now, but Sylvester had said the ship came by a few days before we wrecked. That leaves about eight before it comes by again, and we can get the hell off.

Do you even want to?

I bite my lip, turning away from the fucking tease that just passed by. Do I?

Is it really feasible to stay here with Sylvester? The man truly gives me the creeps, but I hardly see him as long as I make myself scarce.

Or are you just trading one prison for another?

I'm trapped in other people's lives. Tangled in the web of names carefully selected by loving mothers and fathers. Or maybe they weren't loved at all. Maybe they weren't even wanted.

Just like Enzo.

I sniff, still put off from last week. I feel like my insides have been scraped raw, and every time I feel an emotion swelling, it rubs painfully against the open wound. I drank too much. Shared too much. Then caused more pain. And now I'm left with the tattered remains.

Enzo and I have barely spoken, and much to my dismay, Sylvester has used that opportunity to get me to spend time with him instead. But I tolerate it anyway because bad company is still better than being left alone with Kev in my head.

I don't like attachments, but I cling to those who offer something meaningless.

Until Enzo, at least.

Last night, the mounting tension finally broke me. So I whittled some vodka in a water bottle and stayed up all night sucking it down while Enzo slept beside me.

I came so close to reaching out to him, getting down on my knees, and begging for his forgiveness. I don't know why or how, but I fucking miss him.

I prefer his fire over ice, his anger over silence, and his hate over indifference.

I would take the worst of him if it meant I never had to go without him.

Sighing, I stand and amble down into the cave, tripping over a loose rock that crumbles beneath my unstable feet. I'm still feeling the ramifications of that vodka, and every breath stokes the urge to empty the contents of my stomach onto the floor.

Never. Again.

Fuck alcohol. It never gets me anywhere good. It got me caught up in Enzo's arms, to begin with, and seems to keep bringing me back—and every time, it's a colossal mistake.

I stumble again, tripping over my toe and just scarcely catching myself. Jesus, I need a fucking walker. I'm pretty sure I'm still a little drunk.

When I heard the snick of the door unlocking this morning, I was out of the lighthouse within a few minutes, which means it's just after seven AM now. My sleep was fitful and entirely frustrating. Even in a catatonic state, the tension is impenetrable and refuses to budge.

I couldn't stand it any longer. I jumped out of the warm blankets, threw on my only pair of shorts and a random t-shirt I found on the ground, and hightailed it out of there. I felt his eyes on me the entire time, but I refused to meet them.

I'm angry, and I'm not even sure why anymore. I shouldn't give him the power to hurt me, but I've always been malleable to him. He draws me in, uses my body against me, and then shuts me down seconds later, leaving me bereft and feeling colder than before.

He's just... he's just a fucking *asshole*.

My skin glows an aqua hue as I emerge into the cave, the glowworms wriggling above me. I've come here every day since I discovered this place, and it still takes my fucking breath away.

"Hi there, friends," I call out gently, even going as far as to wriggle a finger at them affectionately. I only sweet-talk them because I don't want one of them to drop in my mouth unexpectedly.

Though I suspect if I do take refuge here, I'll grow so lonely that I'll make them talk back.

I'll cross that bridge when I get there, I guess.

Instead of resting by the water and dipping my toes in like I usually do, I bypass the pool and head toward the back end of the cave. For the past couple of days, I've been pushing to see how far I can go. The uncertainty clings because I'm still convinced there's a chance some otherworldly creature will crawl out from the depths and slaughter me, but if this place can foster glowworms and an underground pool, then I'm curious if there's more to discover.

I stumble again but manage to right myself easier this time. The dizziness is beginning to recede, though nausea lingers. I'm hoping to sweat the rest of the toxins out, walk back into that lighthouse later, look Enzo in the eye, and not feel like hurling.

I trek through the opening until I reach an uneven path. At the end, it drops down about ten feet into a cavern. That's where it gets rocky. Literally and figuratively.

Nevertheless, once I reach the bottom, it'll flatten out and lead into another tunnel. I've gotten as far down to the mouth of it but haven't ventured past that. Before, I chalked it up to not having proper lighting, but this time I brought the pocket-sized flashlight Sylvester had let me use previously.

It won't offer a substantial amount of visibility, but I think it'll take me as far as my courage reaches, which won't be very far. I'll also need to build that up slowly and find a bigger flashlight. But I have over a week to accomplish that, and even longer if I decide to stay.

I sit on the edge of the hole and point my toe toward the nearest rock. Slowly, I make my way down, eventually sliding out the flashlight as I descend deeper into the cavern, the air growing icier.

My breath clouds around me as I reach the bottom with a satisfied grin. That wasn't so bad.

Kev and I grew up in the mountains in Nevada, so I've always loved hiking, but I was never stupid enough to do it hungover.

I frown, then shrug my shoulders. If I die, I die.

I clamber into the tunnel, wiping sweat from my brow as I dart the light around, feeling a little creeped out. This is where the intrusive thoughts come in.

What if they're flesh-eating vampires? What if we've been invaded by aliens, and this is their home base? What if there are mutated glowworms in here that grew ten feet tall and have a taste for blonde girls?

I shudder, pushing those thoughts away, delighted when the tunnel ends, and I come out to another open area. No creatures to speak of, but there are glowworms down here, too. I grin, craning my neck and walking aimlessly as I stare up at the tiny little things.

What I would give to be one.

The position causes my equilibrium to teeter, and I'm swaying heavily to one side. I snap my head down, attempting to right myself, but my foot catches on a divot in the rock, twisting my ankle and knocking me completely off-balance. My vision spins and I land flat on my back, my head smacking off the rock a moment later. Within seconds, everything goes dark.

CHAPTER 20

Enzo

For the millionth time this morning, Sylvester shifts, casting a nervous glance toward the front door. I have already asked what his problem is, but of course, he just waved a hand and insisted he was fine.

Not caring how rude it was, I walked up to the front door and swung it open, convinced something was happening. All I could see was dense fog, and after standing there for a few minutes, I sat back down. Ever since, I've been staring at the old, lying fuck, hoping I'm making him more uncomfortable.

"Sounded like someone was crying last night," I say casually. He pauses, then turns to look at me. "Were there any women that died here, too?"

Sylvester stares down at his coffee, as if the black sludge he drinks is going to provide him with a suitable lie.

I haven't forgotten about the woman standing in the ocean soon after we arrived. She disappeared without a trace, but she lingers in the back of my mind.

It doesn't help that things have been going missing. Yesterday, I had been reading *Wuthering Heights* and left it on the end table. When I came down this morning, it was gone, and I haven't been able to locate it since. Not under or between the cushions and not on the bookshelf. Sylvester seemed clueless as to where it went, deepening my suspicions.

Seems like he's been hoarding more restless spirits than he lets on.

"My daughter did. Trinity."

My brows shoot up my forehead.

Okay, I wasn't expecting that one.

"One of the reasons why my wife left me. The grief was too much for her, and she blamed me for Trinity's death."

I nod slowly, studying him closely. It's not that I don't necessarily believe him, but there's just something about Sylvester that makes me question every single word out of his mouth.

"How did it happen?"

He sniffs, glancing at me. "S'pose it's only fair since ya'll shared so much with me last week," he mutters.

I just manage to bite my tongue. That wasn't a sweet moment where we all had a heart-to-heart and made fucking friendship bracelets.

"Trinity wasn't happy here. Wanted to leave, but we was tryin' to make it work as a family. I knew it would happen eventually. She was a teenage girl and felt like she was missin' out on life. My wife and I were worried, but I was still working at the time and couldn't just up and leave. Raven wanted to take her somewhere else, but Trin was only sixteen and couldn't stay anywhere by herself, so that meant they would all be leavin' me. Kacey was fourteen and didn't want to stay here with 'er old man, either."

He ambles toward the island and leans against it heavily, staring off into space and reliving the memory.

"We was fightin' a lot. I didn't want them to go. Trin decided to take matters into her own hands and hung herself outside the window."

I turn to stare out the windows on either side of the front door, imagining what it must've been like to look over and see your daughter's feet dangling right outside, swinging back and forth. It's morbid as fuck, and I feel a pinch of sympathy for the old man.

"Raven left with Kacey two days later. Couple of months after that, the lighthouse shut down due to a newer and more advanced structure being built. Been alone ever since."

"Why didn't you go to be with them once it shut down?"

He's agitated, his lips twitching and his fingers stroking his beard.

"They hated me, and I loved being here. I knew that if I left, ain't none of us would've been happy with my being there."

Maybe his wife and daughter would've forgiven him had he only made an effort and prioritized them, but it doesn't matter now. And I'm not interested in therapizing the old man.

Sylvester meets my stare, guilt swirling in his eyes.

"She cried a lot."

Then, he drops his gaze and ambles toward the stairs. I stare off into space as the clink of metal groans beneath his weight, slowly fading away.

My gaze cuts to the window again, and instead of looking from the inside out, I'm standing right outside the front door, a girl dangling from a rope. Then, the faceless girl fades into the image of Sawyer, her body swaying in the air. Another sad soul that found a different way out.

My throat closes, and it feels like a punch to the chest. I shake my head, pinching my eyes shut and rubbing them harshly with my finger and thumb to banish the fucked-up thought from my brain.

I'm not ready to admit why it's so fucking hard to breathe.

The witch has done enough damage; the last thing I need is her needling her way into my head like a worm in an apple, eating at my common sense and self-preservation.

È una maledetta bugiarda, and I can't look at her without being teleported back to that damn step outside the church, a priest at my side, consoling me because my mother lied to me, too. They both stole so much of my life from me and left without a backward glance. Without remorse.

Yet, the urge to go find her and fight with her again is almost unbearable. Growling in frustration, I swipe my hands over my hair, the strands longer than I'm used to. Seeing her is a bad idea. I still want to fucking throttle her, but fuck if I don't want to kiss her, too. Even worse, I want to protect her while also wanting to protect myself from her.

After admitting what her brother did to her and seeing the raw pain in her eyes—the terror that one day he is going to catch up to her—the sadness that clings to her like a second skin makes so much more sense now.

She's a wild animal that has entered survival mode and doesn't know how to live any other way. And it's driving *me* fucking wild. *Mi sta facendo uscire pazzo, porca miseria.*

The rage I felt in that moment of her confession was blinding, and not for a single fucking second has it let up since. All I can think about is how to make her pain go away. The near-obsessive need to search down the fucker and bash his head in until there's nothing left is all-consuming.

He's still haunting her, and all I can feel is rage because *she's fucking mine.*

But that's the goddamn problem, isn't it? She's made it more than clear she doesn't actually want that. She will always bite the hand that feeds her because she's more comfortable being starved when it's all she's ever known.

I'm charging toward the front door, swinging it open, and storming toward the cave before I process what I'm doing and why. I just... need to talk to her. I've had enough of the fucking silence.

È una maledetta bugiarda - *She's a goddamn liar*
Mi sta facendo uscire pazzo, porca miseria. - *She's driving me insane, dammit*

I'm so lost in my head that I don't even remember walking to the cave or getting down into it. But I draw short, confused when I realize she's not in here.

"Sawyer?" I call, my voice bouncing off the stone walls and echoing.

She doesn't answer. Instantly, all my furious thoughts come to a screeching halt, and my mind goes deadly silent. Something is wrong.

I call her name again, louder and more urgently, except she still doesn't answer. My eyes frantically search around the cave, my head swiveling in every direction.

My eyes bypass a tunnel far in the back of the cave and then quickly snap back to it. I beeline for it, continuing to call for her. It's darker back here and curses spill from my mouth because I don't have a goddamn flashlight to see properly.

"I swear to fucking God, you better be alive," I spit, coming up to a cavern that drops down several feet.

I can't see anything from here, but I don't have any choice but to feel my way down. I take it as slow as I'm physically capable of, which isn't very slow when there's a little siren who could possibly be hurt.

"Sawyer!" I call again, just as I reach the bottom. No answer.

Sweat beads along my hairline, despite how much cooler it is down here. I plant my hands along the cave wall and feel my way through. A blue hue begins to form, making it easier to see. I come out to another opening, glowworms scattered across the ceiling.

There.

My gaze instantly finds her, laid out on the floor and unconscious.

My heart drops. "Mother*fucker.*"

I rush to her, feeling like my chest is caved in as I crouch down and gently lift her head, blood instantly coating my hand. Head wounds can bleed profusely regardless of the severity, but I need to get her to the lighthouse and assess the damage properly.

"*Cazzo, che cazzo hai fatto?*" I ramble, immediately feeling for a pulse. It's strong, and she's breathing, but I have no idea how long she's been out for.

"Wake up, *bella*. Let me see those eyes."

She doesn't move, and my panic deepens.

There's a flashlight next to her fingertips, so I quickly grab it and switch it on.

"Sawyer, I need you to wake up," I say, opening one of her eyelids and shining the light directly into it.

A groan filters from her mouth, and a moment later, she's twisting her head out of my hold.

"Jesus fucking Christ," I mutter, relief overcoming me when she mumbles, "What happened?"

"You fell. I need you to sit up so I can get us out of here," I tell her, urging her up. She groans again but sits up.

"Come here, baby," I whisper, gathering her tiny body against my chest. "I need you to hold on to me very tightly. Don't let go."

"Goddamn, I'm still not dead yet?" she whines, and Christ, I'm going to fucking spank her the second she recovers. "It feels like my head is splitting in half. Maybe I need to give it a few more seconds before the Lord takes me."

Groaning, she slings her arms around my neck while I arrange her onto my back, her thighs coiled around my hips. She tightens them, crossing her feet while I stand.

Sweat coats my body like oil, dripping into my eyes and stinging them while I make my way back through the tunnel. I shine the light up toward the opening of the hole, mapping the best route to climb up with her on my back.

"Hold tight, baby."

Cazzo, che cazzo hai fatto? - *Fuck, what the fuck did you do?*

She attempts to tighten her arms, but her hold is weak as I ascend the rock wall. Sawyer's head rests on my shoulder, flopping around as I jostle her, worrying me further. It couldn't have taken more than thirty seconds to reach the top, but every second felt like too many.

Carrying her through the cave and out of the entrance is a blur. The cool air is a balm to my flushed skin, though the bright light pierces my eyes and forces me to stop until I can focus properly.

"Oh no, Enzo, I'm looking into the light," she mutters, a teasing lilt to her tone.

"You're not funny," I snap, squinting against the harsh sun as I carefully make my way across the uneven terrain and get us onto the sand.

"I'll get you to smile one of these days," she murmurs. "Maybe you should do it one time before I die."

"You're not dying."

"You sure? I think I hear Jesus talking to me."

"Then you're definitely not dying. Jesus would never talk to you."

She snorts, then groans. "You're right. Maybe it's just your voice I'm hearing, and that's my sign I'm going to Hell. You are the devil, after all."

If I'm the devil, she's fucking Lilith.

Finally, I reach the lighthouse, getting the door open and rushing her to the couch. Setting her down gently, I take off to find the first aid kit.

"You're weirding me out," she says when I return. I pause long enough to pin her with a glare.

"Didn't I say you can't get away from me? That means in death, too, *bella*."

She crosses her arms, keeping silent as I get to work cleaning her wound. There's a minor laceration across the back of her head, but it doesn't appear to be too deep.

"What's the diagnosis, doc?"

"You'll be fine. Doesn't need stitches, but you probably have a concussion."

She sighs, opening her mouth to respond, but the creak of the metal steps cuts her off. Sylvester reaches the bottom floor, hobbles through the kitchen toward us until we come into view, stops to take one look at us, and then rushes over as quickly as his wooden peg will carry him.

"What happened to 'er?" he asks, crowding over her to inspect her injury.

"Give her some space," I snap. Sylvester huffs but backs away.

"I fell," Sawyer explains sheepishly, shrugging her shoulder. "'Tis nothing but a flesh wound."

I cast a look to Sylvester. "I'm taking her upstairs. She has a concussion and needs to relax."

"Well, all right then," he agrees easily, stepping farther away.

Sawyer goes to stand, but I swoop her in my arms before she can take a step. A little gasp slips from her pink lips, and once more, that desire to taste them arises.

"I can walk."

"You've proven you can fall, too."

Her face twists into a snarl, aiming a glare my way. She looks like an angry kitten. This close, I can see how bright her eyes are, with a darker navy-blue outer ring.

A buzz forms beneath my skin, and now that I'm no longer distracted by her wound, having her this close is dangerous. It feels too fucking good, and rather than my typical anger, it terrifies me. I've faced far worse, yet a five-foot-nothing nymph is what brings me to my knees. I want her out of my fucking head, but she's in too deep.

I feel Sylvester's eyes burning into my back as I carry her up the stairs and into our room. When I set her down this time, it's less gentle. I'm still angry she nearly killed herself, and the prospect of that is debilitating.

A puff of breath shoots from her lungs, and another glare is burning into my face.

"Thanks," she mutters. "Call us even, I guess."

I arch a brow. "Call us even for what?"

Her eyes swirl with an emotion I can't put a name to.

"I saved your life, you saved mine."

I frown. What the fuck is she talking about?

"Is this another one of your lies?"

Her features twist, and in a matter of seconds, the cute angry kitty grows into a fierce lioness.

"No," she bites out. "Do you think you washed up on this shore by luck?"

I stare at her, processing her implication.

"You were knocked out cold, and I swam us here."

What... the fuck.

I clench my jaw. I don't know what the fuck I'm feeling, but whatever it is has my knees threatening to crash to the ground with reverence.

Tightening her lips, she turns her head away, and my eyes latch onto how her blonde curls have turned bright red on the back.

"You need to shower," I say. She flicks her gaze at me, appearing affronted that I changed the subject.

I have plenty to say, and I will make sure she hears it, but only when I feel like I can speak without wanting to simultaneously stick my tongue down her throat.

Clearing her throat, she stands and begins to brush past me, but my hand lands on the flat planes of her stomach, stopping her in place.

I turn my head, a fire rising in my chest when I hear the little pants coming from her mouth and the goosebumps prickling her flesh.

"Let me help you with that, *bella ladra*."

CHAPTER 21

Sawyer

What a little shithead. I *did* die, and he's just trying to convince me Heaven is real before he pulls back the veil and reveals a hellfire that will burn me alive.

There's a flutter deep in the pit of my stomach, steadily growing stronger until the flap of wings has morphed into the breath of a dragon. I'm already burning alive, and only his hand has touched me.

I wet my dry lips, my tongue darting out for no more than a second, but his eyes have latched onto my mouth, the blaze within them powerful. It's then I realize *he* is the hellfire.

His hand slides away, and with only a moment of hesitation, I walk past him. I feel him fall in step behind me, scorching a hole into my back.

I coerce my muscles to relax as I walk straight across the hall and into the tiny bathroom. It's barely big enough to fit a stand-in shower on the right side and the sink and toilet on the left.

Swallowing nervously, he brushes past me to turn the nozzle, the spray stuttering before the stream evens out. The water pressure is awful, which usually calls for long showers.

I don't know if that's a good thing or not yet.

He turns to me, leaning against the wall next to the stall, and crosses his arms. Flicking his sharp gaze down my body, he commands, "Undress."

Oh, shit.

This got intense way too fast, and it's almost instinct to heed his demand. *No, Sawyer. Bad girl. He's mean. He's terrible to you and thinks he has a claim on you. So what if he saved you? You probably would've woken up eventually anyway. It's not like you were on the brink of death—he's just dramatic as hell.*

My subconscious is screaming at me nearly as loud as the pounding headache, but it all fades away as his eyes heat, searing into my flesh while he watches my hand drift to my t-shirt, moving without my consent.

Goddammit. It's my pussy in control, not my head. Not even my heart.

This is the first time Enzo and I have truly spoken since the storm, and the fact that I'm already undressing for him is almost pathetic. Though completely unsurprising. Getting naked for him is as natural as it is for myself.

I bite my lip as I pull it over my head, cautious of my injury. Next, I shimmy out of my jean shorts, left in my green bathing suit.

I feel the touch of his gaze as intimately as if he were caressing my body with his fingers.

"Those, too," he says, voice deeper and huskier.

"These can get wet," I argue weakly. "They are designed for that."

He meets my stare, the muscle in his jaw pulsating. The moment he does, a deep throb pulses between my thighs. My pussy *aches* from a single look, and if that isn't giving someone too much power, I don't know what is.

"Take them off. Now, *bella*."

The pulse intensifies, and he doesn't miss the way my thighs clench, though I try to distract him by untying the strings around my neck and letting the top fall.

It reminds me of when we first met, and he took me behind the waterfall.

It feels like ages since that day. Like we've lived entire lives.

I look away, focusing on a corroded spot in the cheap vinyl on the floor, but I can still feel him staring. Quickly, I untie the knot around my back and then let my bottoms drop, too.

Before I lose my nerve, I quickly step in the shower, though I'm forced to step within a foot of him to do so. Those twelve inches didn't spare me from his heat any more than if I were standing twelve inches from the sun. What do those measly inches matter when I'm still being charred to ashes?

The hot spray immediately causes goosebumps to rise on my skin. I peek over my shoulder at him, finding him in the same spot, though his head is turned, and his eyes are locked onto my ass.

Thank God it's not flat. It's not big by any means, but plenty plump and round to attract the male gaze. Though these days, that's not entirely hard to do anyway.

Just as he goes to meet my stare once more, I turn away, too chickenshit to face him. I grab for the shampoo, readying to squirt a dollop into my hand before he snatches the bottle.

"You can't get soap in your wound. I'll do it."

"You don't hav—"

"Did you think I came in here to merely watch?"

"I—well, I don't know. I wouldn't put it past you to be a creeper."

"I wouldn't put it past me, either," he retorts, squeezing out the shampoo into his palm. "Maybe that's why I need to touch you so badly."

I inhale sharply, shocked by his admission. His fingers sliding into my wet hair distracts me quickly enough, and I shudder as he gently massages soap into the red strands. Pink water floods beneath my feet, swirling down the drain as he meticulously works around the cut.

"Tell me about the shipwreck," he says.

Instantly, I'm transported back into that cold ocean, disoriented and deprived of oxygen as powerful waves commanded my body.

"It's all kind of a blur. I remember the terror the most and feeling so disoriented. But I saw you there floating, and I tried calling your name, but you wouldn't answer. I swam to you and saw that you were unconscious and bleeding. All I could think about was the sharks."

A shudder rolls through me, and I'm convinced it's by pure divine intervention that one of them didn't show up. Especially since this island tends to be a feeding ground for them, and they're constantly nearby.

"I didn't know what to do other than keep trying to wake you. I'm not sure how much time passed. I think I might've passed out for a moment, too, but I just recall seeing a bright light in the distance. It was just... there. So, I grabbed onto you, pulled you onto a broken piece of wood, and swam us toward it. Eventually, I saw the lighthouse, and it was the only thing that kept me going."

He's quiet for a beat. "How long did you swim?"

Fifty-eight minutes and ten seconds.

I needed something to focus on other than the burning pain in my muscles and the pure horror that anything could come up and eat me alive any minute. So, I counted every fucking second, muttering the numbers aloud as if, at any moment, I would wake up from the nightmare I was lost in.

"A while," I tell him. "It felt like forever. But I got us there eventually, dragged us both onto the beach, and then passed out again. I woke up only minutes before you."

He grows quiet again for a moment.

"You could've left me and saved yourself."

I shrug. "It didn't cross my mind. But I don't know if it's because I'm all that virtuous. I would've rather struggled with you than be alone."

His hands are unmoving for a beat, then resume.

"I called you weak," he states. "Why didn't you correct me?"

"Because I am—"

"You're not," he interjects, voice hard and unyielding. "You're not weak,

Sawyer. You're exceptional. And I'm sorry I ever validated that misconception."

My mouth moves, but I'm incapable of uttering a sound.

"You did something admirable. Imagine what you could do if you only believed in yourself."

I have nothing to say, and I don't think Enzo is interested anyway. Instead, I mull that over while he meticulously cleans my hair.

Kev backed me into a corner, and it feels like I've been snapping and growling at anything that has come close since. I've been so scared that I've forgotten that I've been fighting, too. I've been fighting to survive, to live, to have freedom. Just like I fought each and every wave that threatened to drag me under.

What would I be capable of if I just stopped running? If I lived my life as Sawyer Bennett. What would it feel like to walk in my own shoes and live without reservation?

But that could never happen. Kev's influence is too powerful and follows me no matter how far I run. Those are dangerous dreams, and they could get me in serious trouble.

Lost in thought, it snaps me back to reality when Enzo hits a sore spot, and I can't hold back the hiss.

"*Scusa, bella,*" he murmurs quietly.

I lick my lips again, my heart doing odd twists and turns from the husky candor of his voice, and how intimate it sounds when he slips into Italian. All of this is intimate, and it's almost too much to process.

"*Bella* means beautiful, right?" I ask.

"*Sì,*" he confirms.

Shit, that shouldn't make me happy. Even with his hatred toward me, he still calls me beautiful.

"And *ladra*?"

He's quiet as he continues to massage the soap into my hair.

"You asked me for the truth, and I gave it," I whisper. "Tell me one of your truths."

After a pause, he says, "It means thief."

My heart withers, though it's only true.

"You ensnare men with your beauty, spin them into your web, and then steal from them. You're a beautiful thief."

"I guess I can't really argue with that," I mumble, feeling like my insides are crumbling to ash. That's what happens when you stand too close to the sun.

"Turn your head," he directs, his fingers reaching forward to grab either side of my jaw and twist my head toward the spray.

It smarts, the water deepening in color until eventually, it runs clear again. Even still, he doesn't retreat.

"I think I got it from here," I say, glancing at him over my shoulder. "Thank you for helping."

"It's going to continue bleeding a little until it clots," he tells me, ignoring my request. "Keep your hair parted, and I'll patch it up the best I can when you're done."

"Okay," I whisper.

Our eyes meet, and the fire-breathing dragon in my stomach grows angrier.

"Okay," he parrots.

Slowly, as if he wants me to make sure I'm watching every move, he leans back against the wall, crossing his arms again and getting comfortable. Water is splattered all over the front of his shirt, and the floor is soaked. Yet, he doesn't seem to notice anything outside of me standing beneath the stream staring at him with a puzzled expression.

A bead of water catches his attention, and I'm not sure which it is of the hundreds, but I know it's trailing between my breasts and down the planes of my stomach. His tongue slides along his bottom lip, slowly and sensually, as if he's imagining lapping it up.

Without looking away, I blindly reach for the body wash and squeeze that on my hand next. We've been using our own rags, but my hand will be so much more interesting.

Beneath his penetrating stare, I rub the soap between my palms, then cup my breasts, spreading the suds across them. The heat in his eyes deepens, and his nostrils flare. I can see the outline of his hard cock in his shorts. At some point, he must've readjusted, so it's tucked in the band, and I'm disappointed by that.

"*Concentrati,* Sawyer," he demands, his voice laden with desire. *Concentrate.* I can interpret that command.

Biting my bottom lip, I move my hands down my stomach, across my hips, and over my ass cheeks. He tracks every move religiously, as if the secrets to the universe will appear within the suds coating my skin.

Holding my breath, I watch him closely as I glide a hand toward my pussy. The muscle in his jaw pops, his teeth clenched tightly together. I brush my pointer finger across my clit, a tiny moan slipping free. His eyes rocket to mine.

"*Attenta, bella.* You shouldn't strain yourself with a head injury."

"It doesn't take much to make myself come," I say. "It's you who has to work for it."

A thick brow rises, the challenge sparking his hazel pools.

"Is that so?" he croons. "Let's see it then."

I hesitate, uncertainty beginning to taint the desire.

Enzo has probably seen me from every angle possible, yet all I can feel is an utter embarrassment at the thought of doing something so intimate. Maybe because the relationship between us has been built on cruelty from both sides, and so easily, he could use this as another opportunity to hurt me.

"My head is really hurting, I'm not in the mood," I lie, turning away. My head *does* hurt, but I'm definitely in the mood. Or at least I was until I ruined it.

"Is that a lie, Sawyer?"

Attenta - *Careful*

Shit. I don't know why I thought I could get away with that. Maybe because most people would take my word for it, considering I just suffered a head injury.

"Finish up," he snaps, pushing off the wall and storming out of the room. I close my eyes in defeat, angry with myself for defaulting to the one thing he despises most. It's a habit. One I haven't figured out how to break yet.

Feeling dejected, I finish washing the rest of my body, then wrap myself in the tiniest towel I've ever seen. It might as well be a goddamn hand towel. My hair is still dripping wet, too sore to do much more than squeeze the excess water out as best I can.

When I enter the room, I find Enzo sitting on the edge of the bed, facing me with his elbows on his spread knees, fingers linked, and head bowed.

Hearing my arrival, he lifts his head, and I'm a little stunned to find his stare no less intense than it was in the bathroom. If anything, it's only strengthened.

I stop short, nearly wheezing from the sight. It feels as if I can hardly expand my lungs past the size of a strand of hair. His mouth is pulled into a slight frown, and his thick brows are low over his eyes. He appears angry, sure, but when doesn't he? He's looked this way every time he's been inside me, and this time... this time is no different.

"Do you think you'd still lie to me if I knew that you were?" he asks quietly, his tone inquisitive but lethal. Like a hitman asking if you're ready to die now.

I roll my lips, contemplating how I'm supposed to answer that. I don't always *want* to lie, it just comes easiest. It's a better alternative than confrontation.

"What do you mean?" I ask finally.

His eyes trace the top of the towel where I clutch it tightly against my chest, down the middle, and to the bottom where it barely covers me. The towel doesn't even fall past my ass entirely, but I guess I can't be surprised Sylvester doesn't own Egyptian cotton extra-large towels.

Shivering beneath his probing stare, I clench my thighs tighter, hoping to conceal myself further and abate the incessant need pulsating in my clit.

It only draws his attention.

"I mean," he starts slowly. "If I knew exactly when you were lying every time you did it, do you think you would continue to do it?"

I shrug, but I instantly regret it. It only served to lift the baby napkin around my body higher. Again, his attention is ensnared on my clenched thighs.

"I'm not very brave," I confess, and with great hesitation, he lifts his eyes to mine once more.

"I'm a coward," I tell him, my chest tightening from the truth of it. "Running and hiding is easier. Sometimes, I will say and do anything to get someone to turn their attention away from me. It feels safer that way. Confrontation... it's never led to anything good."

He doesn't respond, but he does seem to be listening.

"Shut the door, and come here," he says finally. And just like any other time he orders me around like a warlord, my body listens despite my head screaming otherwise.

The door creaks shut, the click feeling like a bomb. Then, I approach him as one would a sleeping bear, my knees trembling as I near. When I'm only a foot away, I stop, attempting to keep my breathing even but failing miserably. My chest is moving too fast to be natural, but fuck, I can't breathe.

I open my mouth, attempting to ask what he wants with me, but I can't get the damn words out. Keeping silent, he lifts one hand and gently brushes his fingers along my outer thigh as if curious about how smooth it is. Admittedly, I could've cried when I found a pack of disposable razors stuffed in the back of the sink cupboard a few days ago, and I've been treating them like rare jewels ever since.

My skin tingles beneath his touch, and my flight instincts are kicking in.

"Tell me a lie," he says quietly.

"You're the kindest man I've ever encountered," I respond automatically. His fingers pause, and he glances up at me beneath impossibly long lashes. That look is like a snake bite directly to the heart, the venom paralyzing the muscle and rendering it entirely useless.

"Now tell me a truth," he directs. I don't understand what he's doing, but I'm not entirely sure I like it. This feels more intimate than sex.

"What a fun game this is," I deflect.

"Sawyer," he prompts sternly, voice as sharp as a whip. I jump, startled by the severity of his tone.

Jesus.

"I want to run," I say unevenly, a slight tremor to my words.

"*Brava ragazza*," he whispers, his accent deepening while he drops his gaze, resuming to draw little circles on my skin. Goosebumps break out across my entire body, and that's honestly embarrassing.

"What does that mean?" I whisper.

His eyes flit to mine, and that brief moment is heart-stopping.

"Good girl," he translates, causing a shiver to roll down my spine. I shift on my feet, the need to run deepening until it's all I can think about.

"Another lie?"

"Huh?" I mumble, peeking over my shoulder to gauge the distance between myself and the door. It's only when his touch drifts toward the apex of my thighs that my attention snaps back to him, a rock forming in my throat.

"A lie," he prompts, lifting his stare again. "Tell me another."

"Uh," I breathe shakily. "I'm very calm."

I swear to God, the corner of his lip twitches, hinting at a dimple. Zeroing in on his mouth, I hardly notice how he's picking apart my face. Which also makes me wholly unprepared when he suddenly grabs my hips, pulls me forward, and twists us while I fall back onto the bed, air knocked from my lungs as he crawls over me.

Brava ragazza, - *Good girl*

The towel falls apart, and I freeze as he positions himself between my legs, his eyes eating up every inch of exposed skin. My nipples tighten painfully, and those hazel ice chips in his skull liquefy, turning into a pool of golden brown and green with that odd splotch of black in his right eye.

The way he's looking at me now, there's no stone fortress built around him. He's entirely exposed, and it's one of the most heart-wrenching sights I've ever seen.

"A truth," he demands again.

"I don't want to run anymore," I murmur, feeling my face flush hot. If he asked me to ride him like a cowgirl, I'd have no issue pushing him down and showing him exactly what a wild animal looks like. But asking me to be vulnerable quite literally feels like pulling teeth.

"Do you want me to touch you?" he questions.

"Yes," I admit.

He nods his head slowly. "I'm not going to."

My mouth parts with shock, and I blink at him.

"I want you to show me how you like to be touched. Show me how you make your pussy feel good."

My eyes widen, and I begin to shake my head.

"Are you afraid?"

"No."

Oh, fuck. He's grinning. Just the slightest, but it's entirely sinister. Nothing about the way he's looking at me makes me feel warm and fluffy inside.

"That was a lie, *bella ladra.*"

It totally was.

He sits up, resting his ass on his heels, his knees spread, and my thighs curled around his hips. He grabs my waist and pulls me closer until his hard cock is pressed against my core. The few millimeters of fabric separating his flesh from mine is too thick. I need to feel him.

As if sensing my thoughts, he asks, "Would you like me to show you, too?"

217

"Yes." The answer is out before he can finish, and that grin deepens, displaying the dimples on either side of his cheeks.

No, no. Go back to frowning. That smile is far more dangerous.

Enzo lifts on his knees just enough to slip the shorts down his ass, maneuvering until they fall away completely. The second his cock is freed, I can't look away.

So fucking beautiful. So fucking lethal.

Long and thick, with veins roping throughout the hardened flesh. Flashbacks of that first night we spent together bombard me, and even now, I can remember the feel of him driving inside me. How he used his dick and fingers with so much precision that he made me physically squirt too many times to count. Something I've *never* been able to make myself do. Yet, I implied I could touch myself better. When, in reality, no one has ever touched me the way Enzo does.

He wraps his hand around his cock, and if I were standing, my knees would collapse from the sight. My mouth waters as he pumps himself once, twice, three times, and his head kicks back, his Adam's apple bobbing as he groans.

Dropping his chin, he gives me a look full of both warning and challenge. "Now, Sawyer. Show me how to touch yourself like I will show you. And when we're both done, we will see who lied better."

He knows that I don't need to demonstrate how to make myself come any more than he needs to. Enzo and I—we're not very compatible, I think. We speak different languages most days, and it's a constant battle of figuring each other out. But when we're stripped of our clothes and our bodies are doing the talking, we understand each other as if God was never angry with humans and separated us by the way we move our tongues. When we're like this, the way we move them is the only thing that makes sense.

I slide my hand down my stomach and in between my thighs, biting my lip when he follows my movements raptly. My eyelids flutter when I brush my finger across my clit, teasing myself for a few seconds before dropping lower and dipping my middle finger inside me. I'm dripping wet, and the noises my body makes are vulgar, but I'm past caring when it pulls a groan from deep in his chest.

He fists his cock tighter, as if overcome with the sight, and begins to slowly pump himself, his mouth falling open.

I move my fingers back up to my clit and circle it firmly, unable to contain a husky moan. My entire body is on fire, and the pleasure radiating from my pussy has my eyes rolling.

Normally, I'd close them and pretend someone else was touching me instead. But with Enzo crowding over me, pleasuring himself as he watches me, it would kill my building orgasm if I dared look away.

"Tell me a truth," he rasps, his hips jerking as he strokes himself faster.

My legs quake, a coil forming deep in my stomach and stealing my breath from the intensity of it. This feels too good, and thinking of something to say is challenging. He might as well be asking me to sprint through quicksand.

"I... I still feel dirty," I profess, and I have no idea why the fuck I just said that, but it's enough to send liquid heat straight up to my cheeks. I can feel how hot my face burns from the confession, but I only rub my clit faster. Determined to run away from what I said and hide from the way he seems to stare right through me.

"T-tell me a truth," I stutter, hoping he'll relieve me from that painful confession.

"I lie to myself every day. I tell myself that I'm so fucking addicted to you because of how sweet your pussy tastes or how it cries so easily for me. But I know it's only because of you."

I bite my lip, my face crumpling from how raw and exposed I feel, and for the first time, I don't feel like running. I feel like staying and letting him watch me unravel.

"Now tell me a lie," he demands, his voice gravelly, deepening his accent just the slightest.

I shake my head, my brow pinching with concentration as the coil tightens.

"I hate you," I whisper, spreading my legs wider so the pleasure sharpens.

Enzo's face contorts, and once more, he appears angry as he stares down at me. Despite the severity of his features, he groans, stroking himself faster and tugging harder.

"Fuck, I hate you, too, baby."

My hips jerk while my heart seizes, a maelstrom of pain and pleasure circulating throughout my body. I gasp as the coil tightens, then snaps, my orgasm ripping through me and tearing me to shreds.

"Yes, yes, that's so good," I chant breathlessly, bucking uncontrollably against my hand.

Enzo follows a moment later, streams of cum jetting from his cock and leaking down his hand. Every vein in his body is strung tight, pulsing against his flesh as he seems to come and come, curses spilling from his mouth.

"*Fuck,* Sawyer," he groans, and hearing my name—my *real* name—fall from his tongue is my undoing.

"Oh my God, Enzo," I cry, my orgasm spiking to an almost violent level before finally waning.

While I work to catch my breath, Enzo rips his t-shirt over his head and cleans himself up, the silence pressing in.

My head is fucking pounding, and I'm pretty sure there's some rule that says you shouldn't orgasm with a concussion, but the only thing I can focus on is what he said.

I hate you, too, baby.

He asked me for a lie. But I never asked him for one.

"Was... was that a truth or a lie?" I ask quietly, my voice still hoarse.

He glances at me, tossing his t-shirt to the side and standing. Still, he stays quiet as he pulls his shorts back on, prompting me to now suddenly feel exposed. I wrap the towel back around me while he straightens.

"Enzo?" I push.

When his eyes meet mine, my chest caves. There's no emotion on his face, as if what we just did meant nothing.

It didn't mean anything.

With one last lingering look, he turns away, walking out of the room without a word and shutting the door softly behind him.

My lip trembles, but I clamp it between my teeth, refusing to cry over him.

We built our tower to Heaven, but God is angry again, and once more, we're speaking different languages.

CHAPTER 22

Sawyer

Nothing makes you feel more alive than being imprisoned within the ocean's cold embrace.

My teeth chatter as I sit on the sandy bottom floor, tipping my chin up to the moon and allowing the ends of my hair to be tossed in the waves.

"What are you doing?" a deep, stern voice says from behind me.

I jump, not expecting him. After him leaving me naked on the bed last night, we've been avoiding one another since we awoke this morning. Or rather, I've been avoiding him. Every time we're in the same room, he stares at me openly, but I've been too chickenshit to speak to him.

I'm still hurt, and I don't even have the right to be. Enzo *should* hate me. I just don't want him to.

"Having an existential crisis," I answer mildly.

The sun has set, and we only have a couple of hours left before Sylvester locks us in the room. I needed to take advantage of my time left while I can. I walked to the opposite end of the island to get away, but I still didn't feel any closer to freedom.

I stare up at the big ball in the sky that controls the body of water I'm treading in.

Screw Poseidon. I think there's a lunar goddess above that deserves our worship and respect instead.

"Do you believe in aliens?" I ask.

"If you've seen some of the creatures that live in the ocean, it's not much of a stretch to believe they exist elsewhere too."

I smile. "Do you think I'd be happier if I lived in another world?"

His response isn't immediate, but it stops my heart anyway. "Maybe. But I wouldn't be."

A soft breeze brushes across my chilled skin, eliciting another shiver to rack my body.

"Get out of the water, Sawyer," he demands.

I turn to peek over my shoulder, noticing my green bathing suit top dangling in his hand. I'm still wearing my bottoms, but I wanted to feel the water across my skin.

"What will take me first? A sea creature or hypothermia?"

"You'd run from a sea creature," he states dryly.

I chuckle, turning back to the moon. "You're right. Hypothermia it is."

"That won't happen, either. I don't think you're ready to die."

I shake my head. He's wrong. I've been ready. I've just been too stubborn to give up doing the hardest thing I've ever had to do. Live.

"I've never feared death, Enzo. I'm only afraid to live and it all be for nothing." A tear slips from my eye, despite my attempts to hold it back. "I've spent so much time running that I don't remember why I'm living."

Again, I turn my head over my shoulder to look at him. His jaw is shadowed with a beard, aging him just as deliciously as whiskey.

"Do you remember why you're living?"

It takes him several moments to answer. "Even as a kid, I was angry at the world, and I was always told that I'd waste my life away if I settled into that anger. Of course, I didn't care. And until recently, I stayed firm in that way of thinking. I didn't care about life when I felt so goddamn worthless to the one who was supposed to love me most. Then you came around and stole it from me. Yet somehow, it feels like you gave it back instead."

Heart in my throat, I spin to face him completely, trembling in the black water. It just barely covers my chest, yet it feels like I'm as exposed as if I were standing before him.

"I don't see how. I'm broken, and everything I touch bleeds."

Silently, he walks toward me, first his feet, then his legs being swallowed by the abyss. He doesn't even seem to notice how cold the water is. I shudder again as he approaches, though it has nothing to do with the icy temperature and everything to do with the beast coming for me.

He crouches in front of me with a fierce look on his face. I'm tempted to rub my fingers across the harsh lines just to see if I can smooth them out.

Then, he leans in close, his soft lips brushing against my jawline.

"Do you know what attracts a predator to its prey, *amore mio*?"

"What?" I whisper.

"When it's hurt," he murmurs, placing a featherlight kiss on my jaw. "I love it when you're hurt, baby, but only when it's me who inflicts the pain."

A whimper escapes as his teeth graze where his lips once were.

"You will heal, Sawyer. And as long as you are with me, you will never have to cause pain again. But when you are between my teeth, I will make *you* bleed. I will make you hurt instead."

His fingers brush across my hardened nipple, and a gasp rips from my throat.

"That's where you will find the meaning of life. And that's where you will find a life with me worth living."

"Why?" I whisper. "You couldn't even say that you didn't hate me."

"*Non ti odio*, Sawyer," he says roughly. "I wanted to say it was the truth when you asked if I hated you, but I couldn't lie, so I said nothing. And every time I laid eyes on you today, all I could think was that I never really did."

He pulls away enough to catch my watery gaze. "Choose to live, *bella*. Choose me."

I bite my lip, unable to make myself say yes. But how could I possibly give him hope when I have no idea what my future holds?

He told me to stop lying, so I don't. Instead, I lean forward and wrap my arms around his neck, attempting to push him back. But he holds firm and instead wraps his arms around my waist and lifts me up out of the cold water.

I'm not ready to walk away from the whispers of death, but something about the way Enzo holds me is so much more enticing.

He doesn't know it, but in this very moment, I am choosing him.

He lays me down on the sand right at the water's edge, allowing the waves to wash up around our legs, just to retreat again. The tremors in my body have metastasized, and goosebumps have invaded the entire surface of my skin.

Enzo begins to crawl over the top of me, but I stop him and trade places so he is sitting on the sand while I climb onto his lap. I'm too vulnerable, and if I don't have a semblance of control, I'll shatter.

Surprisingly, he doesn't argue and lets me guide his shirt over his head, and then helps me slide his shorts down.

The icy water rolls up to our legs, but he radiates heat, only drawing me deeper into his body.

I'm wrapping my arms around his neck again, holding eye contact with his candescent eyes beneath the moonlight. His face is always set in such a fierce way, but out here, it only heightens his savagery.

I lick my dry lips and whisper, "Slide them to the side."

Amore mio - *My love*
Non ti odio - *I don't hate you*

Understanding my demand, his hands brush across my stomach, causing me to flinch as the icy water rolls up our legs, only heightening the intensity. I'm jittery, but I'm alive, and that's enough right now.

His fingers move to my bottoms, sliding along the edge against my thigh and causing another shiver to cascade down my spine. His finger catches the edge and draws the fabric to the side, baring my pussy to the cold air.

Biting my lip, I reach between us and grab ahold of his cock. A sharp hiss reaches my ears, and that glorious snarl overtakes his face.

He's most beautiful when he's at his most primitive.

He dips his chin, leaning back just enough to give room for spit to stream from his mouth and directly onto the head of his cock. I spread the wetness across his tip.

I don't waste any more time sliding the tip through my wet slit, earning another hiss before I seat myself on him.

Tension fills his muscles like air in a balloon, yet my body seems to go boneless. I can't fit him inside me easily, but I welcome the pain.

"Does it hurt?" he rasps, knowing how fucking abrasive he is.

I shake my head. "Not enough," I bite, forcing myself down until I've taken him completely, shivering from both the feel of him and the water.

My head kicks back, a soft moan slipping from my throat, spreading around us like fog.

His free hand slides up my stomach and cups my breast, squeezing firmly. I begin to rock my hips, angling them, so my clit rubs against his pelvis just right.

"I can make it hurt," Enzo says, a dark promise coloring his deep voice.

"You will," I say, dropping my head to meet his stare. "But only how I want it."

There's a fight on the tip of his tongue, so I roll my hips deeper, and his teeth clamp down on his bottom lip in response, a deep growl building in his chest.

I cover his hand on my breast with my own while I grip the back of his neck with the other, guiding his head toward me without severing our eye contact. His tongue darts out, laving at my hardened nipple before sucking it into his mouth.

My eyes flutter, and I roll my hips with more vigor.

Unable to contain the salacious smile on my face, I lean until my lips brush against his ear.

"Good boy," I whisper.

Immediately, his teeth clamp down on my nipple in response—just the reaction I was hoping for.

"Yes," I inhale sharply, the acute combination of pain and pleasure clashing in a battle of dominance over my body.

Almost uncontrollably, Enzo rips at my bathing suit bottoms, the strings no match for his urgency and easily unraveling. Flinging it to the side, both of his hands go straight to my ass, roughly sliding toward the juncture of my thighs, gripping my flesh harshly and urging my hips faster.

He trades between soothing the sting of his bite on my nipple with his tongue, only to revive the pain with his teeth.

Cries fall from my lips, the pleasure building deep in my stomach addicting. I'm chasing after it, desperate to hold on to this for as long as I can but unable to slow and savor it.

"More," I plea. "More pain."

Releasing my abused peak, he fists my hair tightly and pushes upward until he's on his knees, and I'm balanced on his thighs. I'm forced to plant both hands on the sinking sand behind me, the grains pulled from beneath me as the wave retreats. I'm barely stable enough to keep upright as he begins to power into me.

My mouth falls open on a moan, granting him easy access to let go of my hair and instead hook his finger in my bottom jaw, holding me in place.

My eyes begin to roll when he hits a particular spot inside me. But the moment I do, a sharp crack fills the air, followed by a searing burn across my cheek.

"Eyes on me, Sawyer," he demands hotly.

There's a moment of shock that he slapped me, but my body responds in a carnal way. My back bows and the bliss sharpens. The cry that follows is one born out of pure gratification.

Another wave rushes over my fingers, and I curl them into the sand. The freezing water and the sharp, broken seashells digging into my skin only intensify the moment.

His cock hits deep inside me, and I can feel my pussy flooding around him. Deliberately, I close my eyes, smiling around the digit hooked in my mouth as he fucks me harder.

On cue, he's delivering another harsh slap with his free hand, this time to the side of my breast. I shudder, crowing at the sensation.

Fuck, it feels so good, and I'm tempted to glue my eyes shut just so he never stops. I'm getting so close to exploding, and I begin to meet each of his thrusts, seeking more.

"Tell me the truth, *bella*. Do you think you'll still be smiling when the pain becomes too much?" he murmurs darkly, his tone full of challenge.

Instead of answering, I sink my teeth into his fingers, imparting my own brand of pain and welcoming the consequences, ensuring to grin widely while I do.

He retreats from my mouth and roughly grips my cheeks between his fingers, jerking me into his face.

"If you wanted me to make you smile, all you had to do was ask."

He grabs ahold of my hips and lifts me off him, a protest quickly building on my tongue. For a few seconds, I'm scared he's going to stop. But then I realize how stupid it was to fear such a thing. Enzo will never stop hurting me.

He's forcing me to twist around, seating me back onto his cock, but this time, I have a full view of the black ocean.

There's a seashell cutting into my knee on the sand, but it's yet another pain that I welcome.

"*Sorridi, piccola,*" he orders, hooking his pointer and middle fingers in each side of my cheek and pulling back hard enough to mold my spine to his front.

I gasp, the action beginning in discomfort and morphing into something more agonizing. He stretches them until what feels like every single tooth in my mouth is on display.

And then he restarts his movements, driving into me and using my cheeks as leverage to keep me in place.

Gargled moans are the only thing I'm capable of while Enzo drags his lips across the side of my temple. My eyes are rolling, my pussy pulsing with euphoria as he works me expertly. His proximity alone is intoxicating, but feeling him use my body in such a savage way has me vibrating with desire.

"That's such a pretty smile, *bella,*" he purrs. A tear leaks from my eye, right where his mouth resides. His tongue darts out, catching the droplet.

"What's wrong?" he mocks, pulling tighter until I squeal. "Does it hurt?"

Despite how deeply my face aches, I'm consumed by the quickly building orgasm low in my stomach. My limbs tremble from the threat of it, eager to be devastated by something other than my own self-loathing.

I nod, drool beginning to pool past my lips and trail down my chin. The noises that follow are uncontrollable, their pitch heightening as he brings me closer.

"Clean your hands off in the water when it washes up, then rub your clit for me. I want to watch you come with such a big smile on your face."

Almost mindlessly, I wait for the cold water to roll around my legs so I can rinse the sand from my fingers, then move them between my thighs and rub my clit, slipping from how soaked I've become. But I'm relentless in my pursuit, and soon I'm reaching the precipice.

Sorridi, piccola - *Smile, baby*

"That's it, you love being a good girl for me, don't you, baby?" he drawls. "Just like you love coming all over my cock like a desperate little slut."

I squeeze my eyes shut, feeling another tear slip loose right as the orgasm hits. My hand on my clit freezes as every muscle in my body seizes, unable to move as a storm rolls through it.

I cry out, feeling Enzo wrap an arm around my stomach and bar me against him. I lose all sense of time and space as I'm transported into an entirely different dimension.

A tsunami could sweep us away in this very moment, and I'd be safe from the carnage. I'm no longer wherever I was, I'm only where I should be.

It feels like days pass by the time my consciousness slowly creeps in, grabbing my hand and guiding me back down to earth.

Behind me, Enzo is rolling his hips sensually, working me through the orgasm, his own muscles strained.

My bones are jelly, but my body is instantly hyperaware of his. He's so close to releasing himself, and his speed is picking up again, feeling my comedown.

With what little strength I have left, I wait until he's right on the edge and then tear myself from his grip, catching him by surprise.

I twist, grab him by the throat and practically tackle him to the sandy floor. He falls easily, caught off guard, but my window is minuscule.

His hazel eyes are wide as I position myself between his spread legs, grabbing his drenched cock in my hands and peeking up at him through my lashes.

"You were so close to coming, and I denied you, didn't I?" Anger flashes across his eyes and the corner of my lips curl upward. "Does it hurt, baby?"

He snaps toward me, but I'm faster, wrapping my mouth around the tip of his cock and sucking harshly, tasting myself on him as I do. His fingers plunge through my curls, fisting them tightly, and I plant my hands on his hips, denying him control.

"Fuck, Sawyer, keep testing me. Your smile is only pretty because of those teeth. I'd hate to see them missing."

His threat widens my grin, and I look up at him with wide, innocent eyes.

"I'm a desperate little slut and want to feel you come down my throat."

I'm staring into two pits of golden molten lava as he tightens his hand in my hair, keeping me immobile as he roughly grabs his dick and slides the tip across my lips.

"Good sluts ask nicely," he murmurs, biting his lip when I stick out my tongue, prompting him to slap his cock on it.

I wrap my hand around his wrist and tip my chin back far enough to rasp, "I never said I was good. I said I was desperate."

Then, I'm sucking him back into my mouth, despite his grip on my hair. He groans loudly, growling when I graze my teeth along his sensitive flesh, then use my tongue to lave at the underside of his tip.

I put everything I have into giving him pleasure, drool pooling on his stomach as I suck and lick him with fervor.

It doesn't take long before I have him close to the edge again, his muscles once more locking up. His cock swells in my mouth, and he starts pumping his hips, his head sliding farther down the back of my throat with his thrusts.

"Fuck, just like that, baby. Suck it hard—*fuck,* yes, yes, yes," he chants. His head kicks back; only his strong throat is visible as he erupts.

He shouts, his chin snapping back down to his chest so he can watch me swallow every drop. Mouth parted, and his brows lowered over his eyes, his entire body vibrates from the force, and it feels like I can't drink him down fast enough.

Finally, he forces me away, becoming overstimulated.

"Jesus fucking Christ," he pants, staring at me with wide eyes. I just wipe my mouth clean of the slobber painted all over my chin.

There's an intensity radiating from him, and it's triggering all those typical flight responses. I stand on shaky legs, and his brow furrows with confusion, assumingly sensing my retreat. I stall by grabbing my bathing suit and slipping it back on. All the while, his stare burns through me.

"I'm going to choose to live because I refuse to die for Kevin. But the life I've chosen for myself is something I have to suffer through alone, Enzo."

He just glares, jaw clenched so tightly that the muscle is bursting from his cheek.

Before I lose my nerve, I rush toward the lighthouse, dreading the moment I'm locked in our room with him.

I asked him to hurt me, but it seems I've done a far better job of it.

CHAPTER 23

Enzo

"I**s she ah'ight?**" Sylvester asks from behind me, causing my muscles to tighten impossibly further.

The only response I'm capable of is a grunt.

He mutters something beneath his breath, but it's too low for me to hear, and frankly, I give zero fucking fucks.

I didn't sleep last night after Sawyer left me on the beach. I don't think she did either, but neither of us was willing to break the stilted silence.

I've known her for barely over six weeks, and she's already got me falling at her fucking feet.

Choose me.

She didn't. Instead, she used sex to distract me and then chose a life of suffering over one with me.

"Got any whiskey left?"

Sylvester grunts as he makes his way toward a cabinet.

"You that bent out of shape over a knock to the head? She'll be all right, son."

Every word out of his mouth grates on my nerves, but I keep my mouth glued shut since he's handing over alcohol.

I swallow it in one gulp, holding the cup out while he pours me another three fingers wordlessly. This time, I sip it, appreciating the maple undertone as it burns a path down my throat.

"Lemme tell ya, women like that don't come around often," he remarks conversationally.

"Tell me about it," I mutter. Not every day you meet a girl that lures you between her thighs and then turns around and steals your fucking identity the next day. Nor is it every day the same girl drags you upward of a mile across the ocean to safety.

She's walking lightning. Both beautiful and fucking destructive.

"And I want ya to know, if she decides to stay, I'll make sure she's well taken care of."

He might as well have dumped a bucket of ice-cold water over my head. My spine snaps straight, and I set the glass down before I break it..

"Why would she stay?" I ask slowly, turning to give Sylvester my full attention. He's staring at me with an odd look on his face. It's smoothed out, yet I can see the truth in his eyes. He's excited.

"She clearly has no place outside of here, don't you agree?"

"No," I retort.

He shrugs, not caring if I agree or not.

"Maybe that's 'cause you want to keep 'er. But women like that don't want to be kept."

"Isn't that what you want?" I fire back, arching a brow. "To keep her?"

Something flashes across his eyes, an emotion that's gone before I can place it.

He smiles, revealing blackened teeth.

"Ain't no sense in keepin' something that stays willingly. I don't like possessin' things, not unless I have to."

My brows knit. "I don't think I like what you're implying."

He shrugs again. "That's 'cause you don't like that she might actually choose me over you."

What the fuck?

Fury is building in my chest, but instead of releasing it, I pick up my drink and take another sip, staring at him over the rim of the glass. He's banking on my anger, I can fucking see the anticipation crinkling his eyes. He wants me to snap, so he has the excuse to kick me out.

"Guess we'll see," I murmur, holding his stare as I finish off the drink. "Want me to put in a good word for you while I'm in bed with her tonight?"

His features slacken, and his chin dips as he glares at me with a look so ice-cold that it burns. That's not the type of cold that frosts your insides, it's the type that blackens them.

"Don't be inappropriate, son," he warns. "You should learn some respect. No wonder she runs from you."

I nod my head, a slight grin slipping free. It's not very often I feel the urge to smile. But on those rare occasions when I do, it's because a certain type of madness is being unleashed.

"I know how to catch her," I drawl, then I glance down at his wooden leg. "Can't say it'd take much to get away from you, *stronzo*."

Despite what many would believe, I'm not one to fight. Most aren't stupid enough to push me to that point, and I've never fucking cared enough to get that angry anyway. Yet, at this very moment, I'm imagining the different ways I could make Sylvester squeal like the pig he is.

And as much as I want to, I know better than to risk getting kicked out more than I already have. I need Sawyer somewhere warm and safe; this place is only safe as long as I'm around. I'll be fucking damned if I leave her alone in this lighthouse with a goddamn lonely creep. I know the sick fuck jacks off to the thought of her, and if I ever hear or see it, I'll remove the useless appendage my-goddamn-self.

I push away from the counter and walk past him, glaring down at his much shorter stature as I pass. He keeps quiet, even as I climb the steps.

But I don't miss his muttered words right as I reach the top.

You haven't been able to yet.

Sawyer is dressed in a t-shirt and her bathing suit bottoms when I walk into the room, curled in a tight ball with her back to me.

Careful not to wake her yet, I grab the lighthouse book lying haphazardly on the floor. She reads it every night before going to bed, and every morning when she disappears to her cave, I do the same.

We're both quietly determined to find the beacon. I would guess she doesn't trust Sylvester any more than I do. There's something off about him and this crumbling lighthouse. Too many people have died here, and the common denominator for those tragic events seems to be Sylvester. And I'm less inclined to believe it's simply bad luck.

Now that he's taken an interest in Sawyer, I'm even more determined to get her off this damn island.

Just as I sit on the edge of the bed to read, Sawyer's soft voice pipes up.

"There was a boat yesterday."

My head snaps to her quick enough to break it. "Come again?"

"It was too foggy for them to see us. But ships come by here more often than he implied, and I think if we find the light, we can figure out a way to get their attention next time. At the very least, I'm sure you have people looking for you. Maybe we can see about reaching out to one of them to rescue you."

My brow furrows, and I stare at her while I process what the fuck she just said. She's staring sightlessly at the stone wall, and it feels like looking at the real Sawyer. The one who isn't as bright and chipper as she would like people to believe.

"Me?" I repeat. "You mean *us*?"

Her lips tighten. "I think I might stay here," she says. "I know you asked me to choose you, but choosing you means dragging you into the mess I've created. If I stay, I won't need to steal from anyone anymore. I won't need to keep running."

I'm shaking my head before she even finishes the first sentence.

"Absolutely not," I bark, shooting to my feet. There's a restless energy buzzing in my bones. My fists clench and unclench, a useless attempt to abate the way my body is beginning to vibrate.

She doesn't move. Doesn't look at me. She seems tired in this moment, and I know... I know it has everything to do with me this time.

"You want to keep me because you hate me. I get it," she says quietly. Emotionlessly. "You want to punish me because I remind you of your mother. But please, just give me this. Give me freedom."

"This isn't freedom," I argue. "This is just as much a prison and one that could get you killed."

She shrugs. "So what if it does?"

I glower, my fury growing hotter.

"Don't do that. Don't suddenly give up when—"

"Didn't I already tell you? I'm a coward, and I run. If you care about me at all, Enzo, you will let me stay here. Bringing me back to Port Valen... you're asking me to either go to a real prison or go back to stealing."

I'll take care of you.

The words are on the tip of my tongue, but I can't voice them. We hardly know each other, and we've spent most of our time together fucking, fighting, or just trying to survive. We have little trust in one other, and fuck, she's a goddamn fugitive. I don't see how a future could possibly work between us. Yet, the thought of leaving her behind is enough to send me into a blind rage. The thought of going back to Port Valen alone... without her—it's unfathomable.

"And anyway," she continues before I can respond, feigning a lightness in her tone that I know she doesn't feel. "I think Sylvester wants me to stay."

"Because he's a goddamn *creep*," I snap heatedly.

"He is," she agrees, nodding her head.

And that's it. That's all she has to say.

I shake my head, mind-blown that she isn't scared of him like she should be.

That's when her gaze finally flits to me. She forces a smile—a weak one—in an attempt to placate me.

"Don't worry, I'm used to living with a creep. I know how to handle them."

"That's the problem, *bella*," I say, giving in to my baser instincts and climbing onto the bed next to her. Her eyes round at the corners, but it only makes me want to crawl closer. I lie down next to her, and even though a large part of me is angry with her, there's an even bigger part of me that can't let her go.

"You should have never been put in that position, and you sure as fuck should never have to get used to someone so fucking vile."

She blinks, her eyes glassy. Tipping her chin down, she mutters, "What do you expect me to do? I don't have any other choice."

I close my eyes, and even though I'm giving in to her, it doesn't bother me as much as I thought it would.

"I'm going to protect you, Sawyer," I promise her. Her eyes shoot back to mine, once more widening with surprise.

"I don't agree with how you live your life, but that doesn't mean I don't understand. You're not a fucking coward. You've been fighting your entire life and deserve rest."

Her bottom lip trembles and she captures it between her pretty white teeth. Once more, I'm hit with the craving to taste them. It's not just a want, it's a *need*.

"You can't let them find me," she whispers.

"The only one who will ever find you is me, Sawyer. You can hide from everyone else, but you can't hide from me."

She stares up at me with bewilderment, struggling to accept what I'm saying. I'm struggling to accept it myself, but it feels right. Even when Sawyer did me wrong, nothing about her ever felt that way.

"Why would you help me?"

It's dangerous to touch her, but I'm incapable of stopping myself. I brush a few curled strands from her face, tucking them behind her ear. She shivers beneath my touch, only encouraging the hunger coursing through my system. It's not enough—it never is, but it's all I can give right now.

"Because I feel so much for you, Sawyer."

I allow myself one little taste and lean in until her scent envelops me. She smells of the salty ocean and something sweet. A tiny gasp feathers across my lips, and I know what she's thinking.

Moving my hand to the back of her neck, I grip tight to hold her in place, though she has gone completely still anyway.

"Don't move," I warn her, a shaky exhale her only response.

My mouth brushes against hers, and I dart out my tongue to lick the bow of her upper lip, nearly groaning from the minty taste on her breath.

Moving to the side of her mouth, I place a gentle kiss on the corner and then another farther up her cheek.

"Is it hate?" she croaks, trembling beneath my touch.

"I don't hate you," I say. Another kiss.

"And you deserve to have a life. A real one." *Kiss.*

"Come back with me, *bella*." *Kiss.* This one is salty from the single tear that has slipped from her eye.

"Is that what you really want?" she asks, her voice hoarse. "What will I do then? I have no way to support myself wi—"

"You'll work for me."

She jerks back, staring at me with bugged eyes. "Absolutely not. I will not get in the water with those... those *beasts*."

The laugh bursts from my throat before I can even think to stop it. It causes us both to freeze, but fuck, if I'm breaking the rules tonight, I might as well break all of them.

She lifts up, her fingers smoothing across my lips with wonder.

"Do that again."

"Absolutely not," I say, though the lingering grin refuses to disappear completely. There's a glimmer in her eye, and it's the first time I've seen it since I've met her. If I didn't know any better, I'd say Sawyer is actually happy right now. And the way that collectively makes my chest tighten and want to laugh like a maniac just to see it brighten is concerning to say the fucking least.

"Despite what I did to you on the boat, I have no interest in turning you into shark food."

With the reminder, her hand slips away, and a shadow falls over her face.

"That was really shitty."

"It was," I agree, feeling the regret I swore I'd never feel. "Most would say shittier than you deserved."

She raises her brows. "Would *you* say that?"

After a pause, I admit, "Yes. You didn't deserve that."

Her eyes narrow. "Then say you're sorry."

My gaze falls to her parted mouth, those pink lips puffy and smooth, before returning to her baby blues.

"I'm sorry," I murmur, letting her see how genuine I am. Because I *am* sorry. I assaulted her, and we both know that. I imagine if my mother stuck around, she would've left me then if she knew I treated a woman like that.

She smiles, wide and bright, like the sunshine peeking through storm clouds after a massive storm.

"I don't forgive you," she quips, quickly rolling out of my embrace and taking advantage of my stunned silence. Then, she's backing away and bumping against the round table, leaning against it with her fingers laced. There's a beast inside me that's on the verge of lashing out and trapping her beneath me once more.

"Not until you properly apologize to me," she finishes.

My brows lower, and I straighten, resting on my knees while I silently stare, waiting for her to explain what she means.

"You've been an unbearably raging asshole to me this entire time. Yes, I fucked up, but you're, like... really fucking mean, and you've hurt my feelings more than I care to admit."

I nod slowly. "You're right."

Feeling invigorated, she forges on, "If you want me to stay with you—choose you—then I want you to get on your knees and apologize for how you've been treating me," she tells me, pointing to the floor for extra measure.

I suck my bottom lip between my teeth, trapping the flesh and biting down hard. An insidious feeling is rising in my chest. It's dark and wicked, and it makes me want to fucking smile. I want to grab her by the throat and unleash every one of my darkest desires onto her flesh—with my teeth, my hands, and my cock.

It's also pride, desire, and the unbending need to give her everything she wants.

Because fuck, am I proud of her for making me beg for her forgiveness.

Sawyer deserves better than what I've done to her. We're both broken in our own ways, and instead of seeing that and understanding her, I let my own hurt control me. And all it's done is cause her pain.

I'm still withholding my own forgiveness for what she's done—stealing someone's entire life to do with as they please is not a tiny fuck-up. And there's still a part of me that doesn't trust her yet—that feels like I'm the same fool who took her behind the waterfall, only to be robbed of the most important thing to me. She could've gotten me into some serious trouble if she was careless enough with my identity, which ultimately could've fucked with my research and everything I've worked so fucking hard for.

So, while I'm not entirely ready to give her those things, it doesn't change how I feel about her. It doesn't change that she doesn't deserve my wrath nor my cruelty.

I will always want to cause her pain, but I find no satisfaction in her misery. No, the only thing I want to see when I have her trapped between my teeth is that bright fucking smile.

Silently, I get off the bed and stand at my full height, towering a solid foot above her, her petite stature barely reaching my chest. Her eyes are wide, but the challenge in them is undeniable.

The tension between us crackles, little fireworks detonating around us as I come to a stop before her.

Her blonde curls are wild around her face, falling past her heaving chest. It reminds me of when a wave breaks and forms that perfect curl that surfers strive for. There are so many of them within the strands of her hair, and I want to dive between each one.

She's vibrating from the energy as I slowly approach, but my little thief stands her ground, only tipping her chin up as I near.

When I'm within a foot of her, I drop to my knees, my blood heating when her lips part, an almost inaudible gasp slipping free.

"I'm sorry, *bella*," I start, keeping my voice low and serious while I look up at her, ensnaring her gaze within my own. She stands tall before me, her spine straight and shoulders back. "I've been punishing you for something you didn't do—something beyond stealing an identity. I've been making you hurt because I'm hurt, but you're not the one who broke me. And it was never my right to break you."

She studies me closely, picking apart every detail that makes up my face. My hair has grown, and my beard has thickened, but I wonder if she can see someone different beyond my appearance.

Can she see a man falling in love with a little thief? Can she see that I don't want to but will submit to it anyway? Just as I'm submitting to her now.

"You're not the one who broke me, either," she whispers finally, settling back onto my eyes.

"No, but that didn't stop me from trying."

I reach out and grab her hand, enraptured by how tiny it is compared to my own. How delicate and soft she is on the outside, but on the inside, she's a force to be reckoned with.

She's so goddamn resilient.

She's better than me—stronger than me.

I wanted to take all her broken pieces, and fucking shatter them—turn them into dust so she could never be whole again.

I realize now how foolish it was when I could take those pieces and give them a home amongst my own.

"You *are* good enough, Sawyer. You're nothing like I said you were, and everything I said you weren't. You're strong and brave, and above all else, you're admirable."

Her eyes become glassy, and she looks away, blinking rapidly while crooking her finger beneath her eye. "Can you, like, not make me cry right now, please? I'm trying to look like a badass."

The corner of my lip tips up. She makes me smile, too, but that's something I'd rather show her than tell her.

"Will you forgive me, *bella*?" I ask, my tone hushed.

She refocuses on me, her eyes not any less wet. "No," she declares, but the corners of her mouth curl, and there's a mischievous glint swirling in the depths of her irises.

"I want you to kiss my favorite toe first."

I quirk a brow, and she lifts her left foot and points to her pinkie toe. "Kiss it, Enzo."

I lick my lips, curling my bottom lip between my teeth as I sweep my gaze back up to her. Her mouth parts when she notes the heat in my eyes.

"If worshiping you is what you ask, I'd be happy to spend the rest of my life on my knees," I tell her, my voice dipped so low, it's nearly unrecognizable.

Her throat bobs as she works to swallow while I grab her dainty foot, bringing it to my lips. Gently, I kiss her pinkie toe, feeling her shiver beneath me.

Then, I replace my lips with my teeth, delivering a soft bite and earning a gasp. She will bring me to my knees, and I will bring her pain.

For extra measure, I kiss the other four, too, before straightening my spine and meeting her stare. Her pupils are dilated, and her chest heaves as she drops her foot, attempting to appear collected.

But I can still smell her sweet cunt, and how it weeps for me.

"I don't forgive you yet," she says quietly.

I keep silent, feeling the challenge weaved in her statement. I should've known it wouldn't be so easy, and it only makes me want to dig my knees further into the ground and stay in this place until she allows me to stand.

"Would you like me to crawl to you, *bella*?" I question, gravel lining my throat. "Bow at your feet and find a home beneath you? Or would you like to climb onto my back, where I will serve you and take you to places with a point of your finger?"

"Would you?" she volleys back, lifting off the table and circling me until she's at my back. I keep still, though I can feel her every move, every breath. "Would you cater to my every need, no matter what I ask of you?"

"You will need for nothing, *amore mio. Ti darò tutto.*" I hear her sharp intake of breath, then feel her coming closer, bending at the waist until warmth fans across my ear. My fists curl, clenching tightly to abate the need to grab her by the hair and fling her over my shoulder so I can show her just how well I will cater to her.

"Good boy," she whispers, her voice sultry and teasing.

My bottom lip rolls beneath my teeth again, and I bite hard while my cock thickens. A growl forms deep in my chest, but she knows I won't unleash it. Not until she asks me to.

Ti darò tutto. - *I will give you everything*

Standing, she circles around until she's before me once more, and there's softness around the corners of her eyes. She's at peace, and I hadn't realized how much I needed to see that.

"Does this mean you're going to be nice to me now?" she asks, giving me another mischievous smile.

I feel my lips twitch again, but I manage to refrain. I do plan on giving her everything, just not today.

"I will never be nice to you, *bella ladra*," I swear, raking my eyes over her profile. Her nipples are pebbled beneath her ratty t-shirt, and a flush forms low on her neck, traveling up to her cheeks.

Her thighs are clenched, as if that's going to make her pussy any less wet.

"Didn't the nuns teach you manners?"

"They didn't tolerate disrespect. But I didn't tolerate authority. It took many years for us to find a middle ground with mutual respect."

"Until now," she corrects. "Now I have the authority."

I arch a brow but concede. "You do."

She preens, while my cock begs to be released.

"I still find it odd that nuns raised you," she continues.

I shrug, staying on my knees. She hasn't asked me to stand yet.

"I don't believe in God, but I do believe they were saints for putting up with me."

She sniffs. "Well, I don't either, but if Heaven exists, they've definitely earned their place dealing with you. You're a naturally mean person."

The corner of my mouth twitches again when I see how dilated her eyes are. If I lean in between her thighs, I know I would smell her. I'm at the perfect height to do so.

But she's injured and messing around with her yesterday was already pushing things.

"Naturally," I repeat dryly.

She clears her throat, wiping her hands on her t-shirt. "Well, that apology was very big of you, Enzo," she compliments. "But you can, like, get up now."

It's getting harder to contain my grin. I stand, and she steps back into the table, causing the legs to screech against the wood floor. She looks me up and down, reminded of how much bigger I am than her. She also glimpses how hard I am for her, deepening that pretty flush on her rosy cheeks.

"I'm going to get some water, and then... then I'm going to, like, sleep or something. But tomorrow, I want to look for the beacon."

I dip my chin. "For us both to leave," I push, wanting to hear her agreement out loud.

She rolls her lips, rocking back and forth on her toes.

"For us both," she says finally.

I let my smirk loose just a little when she steps around me, nearly bumping into the table again to get past. She could've gone the other way and had plenty of room. Whether she realizes it or not, she gravitates toward me just as I do her.

I grab her bicep, stopping her. A visceral desire to take her nearly sends me plummeting back down to my knees, and I know that if I succumb to it, she will be standing above me, her cunt resting on my lips.

Feeling her so close, yet unable to fuck her, is like asking a predator to turn its back on their prey, starved and desperate for just a taste.

"Lay down. I'll get the water and some medicine," I order her, my voice raspy with carnal need. I give her another once-over. "Maybe find some pants while I'm gone. I can smell your pussy from here."

Her mouth drops. "You are *so* sleeping on the floor tonight."

For her, I would.

CHAPTER 24

Sawyer

They say you're never supposed to sleep with concussions. That's common knowledge. But I've reached the point where I don't care if it makes me brain dead, I'd rather be knocked out than listen to this.

There's someone—some*thing*—weeping on the third floor, right above us. Enzo said it's the ghost of Sylvester's daughter, Trinity, who hung herself outside our window.

Sylvester said she cried a lot.

And her cries are making me feel physically nauseous. They're muffled, but they sound strange. Almost like's she's trying to scream but can't.

Enzo lays beside me, stiff as a board, as he stares up at the ceiling. We're both on our backs, wide awake and disturbed.

"What do you think is worse? Suffering in life, or suffering in death?" I ask, my voice cracked and uneven.

"Death," he answers quietly. "Then, it's eternal."

I turn to look at him. "Do you believe in an afterlife? You must, right?

Since you were raised by nuns."

He shakes his head. "I believe our souls either move on to somewhere unknown, get stuck, or reincarnate into another body. I never believed in what they did. They hoped God would heal my wounds and guide me in life. Thought I'd eventually become a priest and tell people my story and how I overcame it. But the more I read the Bible, the more lost I became."

I roll to my side to face him and tuck my hands under my head. He sighs, sensing the onslaught of questions, but I'm undeterred.

"What was it like growing up?"

"It's not an interesting story, *bella*."

"It's interesting to me," I argue. "Tell me."

He frowns, making me wonder if Enzo has ever let anyone get close to him. He keeps people at arm's length, too afraid they'll hurt him. And the fact that I *did* hurt him makes me want to stab myself in the eye.

"After *mia madre* left me on the steps, I was taken to the *Istituto Sacro Cuore*, where I was raised and went to school. Every day was prescheduled. I woke up at 7 AM for prayers. Would eat breakfast at 8, then start schooling at 8:30. After, I'd eat dinner and get one hour to say prayers before bed. Just to do it all over again the next day."

There's a thump from above, causing me to jump and sending my heart flying in my throat. Trinity is still crying, and it sounds like she's beginning to grow angry.

"What about your father? He didn't care that she left you?" I ask hesitantly, nervous the question will anger him.

"He died while she was pregnant with me. He was a fisherman. He and his crew got caught up in a severe storm one night. Waves got so high, it's a miracle the boat didn't go under. But there was one that sent six men overboard. There one second, gone the next. *Mio padre* was among those men. It hasn't slipped my notice that I nearly died the same way."

"I'm sorry," I whisper.

"Don't be. I never knew him, but at least he gave me my love for the sea."

I nod slowly. "Did you have any friends in school, at least?"

There's a slight grin. "I did. There were a few others that weren't too keen on the lifestyle."

"You got in a lot of trouble, didn't you?" I gather, imagining a younger version of Enzo sneaking out at night, drinking liquor straight from the bottle, and slipping through the windows of blushing girls.

The last part makes me a little jealous, but I'm not sure if it's because I didn't know him then and he wasn't slipping through *my* window, or if it's because I never got to experience things like that growing up.

Kevin never allowed me to have friends. He never allowed me to live.

"We did," he says. "Not as much as I would've liked, though."

"It sounds mundane."

He hums, a deep, rumbling sound of amusement. "It was, which is exactly why I acted out. Everything is a sin in Catholicism. I was sexually repressed, but considering I refused to conform, I sure as hell wasn't going to allow them to take pleasure from me, too. I attended confessions more times than I could count. I asked for forgiveness, but I never really wanted it."

I snort. "I bet the nuns loved you," I tease.

"They hated me," he says with mirth. "Most of them, anyway."

"Which one raised you? Or did they all?"

"They all played a part, but *suor Caterina* was who raised me primarily."

"Did you have a good relationship with her?"

"She did her best with a child who didn't want to be there and made it very well known. She was nice to me but distant. She wanted me to become something I wasn't—to believe in someone I couldn't understand. I frustrated her, and she... wasn't my mother."

Sadness pulls the corners of my mouth down, imagining a younger version of Enzo. Lost, sad, and angry because he couldn't understand why he was there. Couldn't understand why he wasn't good enough for his mother.

He was never raised in an environment that showed him unconditional love and warmth, so the hole in his chest only deepened.

"You felt like a burden," I surmise.

"I didn't know how to be anything else," he states plainly.

That's a punch to the chest. I bite my lip and reach down, slipping my fingers into his and squeezing tightly. His hand is so much larger than mine, and I wish I could hold it forever.

So badly, I want to show him the warmth and love that he deserved. That he *deserves*.

But I don't want to hurt him more than I already have and give him something I don't know he can keep.

He doesn't squeeze back, but he doesn't reject me, and that's enough.

"Were you ever happy?"

"No," he murmurs. "Not until I moved to Australia. When I learned about great whites, I was instantly enraptured by them—obsessed, even. *Suor Caterina* knew I would never give myself to God, so she gave me what money she could spare, helped me get a visa, and sent me to Australia about a month after my eighteenth birthday. It was the only time I felt like she might have truly cared for me. I got a job working at a bait and tackle shop, put myself through university, and worked my ass off. That... that was when I was happiest. Broke, alone, but in the ocean, doing what I loved."

He finally looks at me, but his expression is on lockdown. It's only now that I notice the crying from above has stopped, replaced by a tense silence. It makes me nervous, yet with Enzo right beside me, I've never felt safer.

"Were you ever happy?" he asks, turning the question onto me.

I twist my lips, contemplating that.

"When I was younger, yeah. Before Kevin changed. We used to have fun playing together. Back then, he was nice to me, and my parents weren't disappointed in me."

"Why were they disappointed?"

"I wasn't him," I say, bitterness leaking into my tone. "Once he started abusing me, I became withdrawn. I was rebellious, while he was the perfect angel. They wanted their sweet little girl back, but they wouldn't listen when I said their sweet little boy was the one who broke me."

I can't see his eyes, but I can feel the anger emanating from him.

"When they died, I was almost glad for it," I admit. "Because at least then, I didn't have to convince them that I wasn't a liar anymore. Funny, that's exactly who I became when I finally got away from him."

"Yet, he still haunts you."

I nod. "Just as your mother haunts you."

A dimple on the side of his cheek appears.

"Then maybe we could show each other how to let go, yeah?"

I bite my lip, a flood of emotion rising up my throat. I'm still terrified, still convinced there's no way Enzo can get me out from Kevin's hold, but I want to let him try, even if it's selfish.

"Yeah," I croak, my voice hoarse with unshed tears.

He faces the ceiling again. "Start by telling me the things that make you happy now."

I smile softly. "Senile Suzy makes me happy. It's an old Volkswagen van I bought when I first came to Port Valen. I left her in *Valen's Bend* campground, and I think she's going to be gone by the time I get back." That hurts a little, so I forge on. "Simon makes me happy, too. He's the one that gave me my tattoo on my thigh. I hardly know him, but he's the first friend I've ever had."

He's quiet for a beat, then he says, "They'll be there waiting for you," he vows. "I'll make sure of it."

The tears are threatening to spill over so I find something else to say before they do.

"Hey, Enzo?"

"Hmm?"

"I'm glad that you found peace. At least until you met me," I say, ending with a sardonic snort.

There's a brief pause before he lets loose the softest chuckle, causing my stomach to somersault.

"You're right. You've brought chaos into my life."

And then, finally, he closes his hand around mine, squeezing back.

"I like it, *bella*."

CHAPTER 25

Sawyer

"Stop elbowing me, you big oaf!" I whisper-shout.

"Then move," he growls. "For a tiny little thing, you take up a lot of fucking room."

"*Moi?*" I ask, aghast, a hand to my chest. "Have you seen the circumference of one of your arms? It's honestly concerning. You probably need to see a doctor for it."

"I'm not the one who needs a doctor. Maybe you should go lie down. You still have a concussion, and it's clearly warping your judgment."

I narrow my eyes, huffing with irritation. "You are impossible," I snap.

Whatever weird little truce Enzo and I came to is up in flames this very second. He's just so... frustrating. Always thinks he's right. A fucking know-it-all, too. And he's always looking at me like he can't tell if he wants to mutate into a shark and eat me or not. And *I* can't tell if that's attractive or not.

Honestly, it's whatever if he does mutate. I think it'd be doing us both a favor at this point.

We're searching for the beacon and have found ourselves in a small closet tucked away on the other side of the hallway. I thought maybe a door might be in here, but I can't see shit around the behemoth of a man taking up the entire space.

"*Move*," I mutter, elbowing him as I look behind a shelf full of... beans. Lots of beans.

"Look, the bean gods blessed you," he mutters snidely.

"Shut up," I snip. I retreat with another harsh exhale. "There's nothing in here anyway."

I go to slide past him, and while that is definitely something I accomplish, I also succeed in rubbing my ass against his dick. His hands fly to my hips, gripping them tightly and holding me hostage.

My breath stalls while my heart rockets up into my throat.

"Careful, *bella*," he warns darkly. "You may not have forgiven me yet, but I have plenty of methods to ask for it."

The only response I'm capable of is an embarrassing wheeze. He squeezes me tighter.

"I can get on my knees again and show you a blessing from a different type of god," he purrs, his accent thickening and only making the words sound more salacious.

That. Is. *Illegal.*

The oxygen has evacuated from my lungs, and I quite literally can't breathe. I wiggle out of his hold, casting a sassy look over my shoulder. Or at least I try to. I'm too distracted by the intense throb between my legs.

"You would sooner give yourself a concussion trying to fuck me in here rather than actually making me come."

His spine straightens, and the look on his face solidifies into cool marble.

Oh, shit.

I dart out of the closet before he can make good on that challenge. I can't let Enzo and his big dick distract me. The energy in this decrepit lighthouse is decaying as quickly as the structure.

Sylvester and Enzo positively hate each other—not that they ever cared for one another to begin with—and when Enzo isn't around, Sylvester talks to me as if I've agreed to stay.

I've only decided to leave last night, but I can't find the words to tell him that. I'm scared of what will happen once I do. So, in true Sawyer Bennett fashion, I keep my mouth shut and let him dream. Even if those dreams are nightmarish.

I know Enzo is aware of Sylvester's growing obsession, but I haven't told him how bad it's gotten. They both have tempers, and I don't want anything jeopardizing our chance to find the beacon and in turn, hopefully, get a one-way ticket off the island.

Ignoring Enzo's heated stare from the closet, I peruse the short hallway. And then I pause, tripping over an idea I hadn't considered before.

"What if the entrance isn't on the second floor?" I wonder aloud. Then, I turn toward Enzo. He gazes at me with a furrowed brow, waiting for me to continue.

"I assumed the entrance would be up here because that's logical, right? You get to the third floor by the second... But what if it's on the bottom floor and leads all the way up?"

He tilts his head, considering that. After a moment, he purses his lips and nods, walking toward me and notching my chin with his knuckle as he passes.

"Good thinking, *bella*," he croons, a devilish glint in his eye. As if answering a mating call, my clit pulses, and arousal gathers between my thighs.

It's that fucking easy.

"Sylvester is downstairs still. We're going to have to wait until he leaves," Enzo continues as if he wasn't two seconds away from staring down the center of my spread legs.

"It's about to storm, and we're supposed to get another tomorrow. How are we going to get him out?" I question, making sure to keep my voice quiet.

He shakes his head. "I haven't figured that out yet. But we're getting to that damn light."

Pinching my lips, I nod and glance at the steps leading downstairs.

"Until then, I need to make nice with him."

He gives me a sour look, as if I just shoved a lemon down his throat. Not very far off from its natural state. Enzo has a bad case of resting bitch face.

"That would only encourage him."

"Yeah, encourage him to trust at least one of us," I argue. "If he believes I might stay with him, he's more likely to give me space. But if he thinks I'm not, he will cling harder."

"I'm not leaving you alo—"

"You are because I asked you to," I cut in. "Believe it or not, I haven't made it this far because I'm incapable, and he isn't the first creepy man I've dealt with."

He studies me closely, an indecipherable emotion in his eye.

"I'll trust you can handle yourself, Sawyer. But the second he takes it too far, or I feel you are in danger in any way, no more. I'm stepping in, and I'll fucking kill the man. There won't be any sneaking around then."

My mouth parts in shock, and my eyes round.

He's serious. Absolutely serious.

With one last heated glance, he warns, "I'll be in the room."

Did it get hot in here? I've begun to sweat, little beads forming along my hairline.

Attempting to shrug it off, I say, "You got it, dude."

And then I take off toward the steps, needing air as much as I need fucking Jesus in my life.

God, this is so fucking uncomfortable.

When I came downstairs and asked Sylvester if he wanted to watch some TV, I was hoping I'd be able to distract myself with a soap opera, considering that's all Sylvester seems to watch.

But the storm outside has already begun to brew, and we don't have any signal. So now we're just sitting on the couch, watching a crackling fire while we both try to carry on a conversation.

He's out of practice, I get it. But I think I'd rather stick my finger down my throat and blow chunks for funsies at this point.

"Did you hear the ghosts again last night?" I ask when another topic fizzles out.

"Meh," he harrumphs, waving a hand. "I've grown used to the noises by now. I sleep like a baby."

"It sounded like something was scratching at the floor above us," I go on. "Like they were trying to claw their way out or something."

His gaze darkens for a moment. Despite how tolerant Sylvester is of the ghosts, he doesn't like speaking of them. Maybe because the spirits that live here are by his own hand.

"Sorry 'bout that," he mutters. "I don't think it'll be too much of a problem for you after 'while."

"You think I'll get used to them?" I wonder.

"Something like that. I think they're just restless. I'll take care of 'em, don't you worry," he assures, patting my knee. I try not to tense under the weight of his calloused palm, but it's nearly impossible. It feels as if slimy bugs are crawling up my spine.

"Relax," he laughs boisterously. "Ya don't need to fear me. I ain't gonna hurt ya."

I force a laugh, but I slide my knee out from beneath his hand anyway.

I may be trying to play nice, but that doesn't mean I'm going to let him touch me. Sylvester is the type to push his luck. He'll keep touching me until I tell him not to, and even then, he'll push a little harder.

Enzo's told him to get his hands off me before, yet, he still persists.

"Why you got a tattoo like that?" he asks, pointing out the two words Simon poked into my skin. *Fuck You.*

I look down, and unwittingly, a smile forms on my face as I brush my fingers across the black ink. I miss him. Probably more than I've ever missed anyone.

I've only met him twice, but he was my first real friend. My *only* friend.

My smile turns upside down. He probably thinks I disappeared on him willingly. And I'm sure he'd understand, but what if I never see him again? What if by the time I make it back, he's disappeared himself?

Simon has said so once; he's a wandering soul. Doesn't stay in one place for long—like me. The thought of never seeing him again is enough to make the backs of my eyes burn.

"My friend did it for me," I answer simply.

He harrumphs, sounding unimpressed. "Well, I'd like to ask you a question," Sylvester starts, shifting uncomfortably. My heart drops, already knowing where this is going.

I clear my throat, my hands fidgeting with shit I didn't give them permission to. They move from my hair to my shirt, then back to my hair again, and somehow land on my bottom lip.

"Sup?" I squeak. I'm so bad at handling awkward situations.

"I wanted to formally invite you to stay here." After a weird pause, he tacks on, "With me."

I think I clear my throat again, but I'm not sure over the sound of my heart beating. I'm not even sure why I'm so damn nervous. All I have to say is *no thanks.* Easy.

"Wow," I breathe. "That's so generous of you."

He nods, like he already knows that.

"The thing is, I think it'd be best if I go back home and, uh, sort my shit out." I end that with a strained chuckle.

He frowns and strokes his bushy beard.

"I don't think that's too smart. Sounds like you got yerself in a bad situation. Best ya stay here." He pats my thigh like the decision has been settled on, then goes to get up.

"Uh, well, thanks for the input, but I'm leaving," I cut in. He pauses, then settles back down. Great. I would've preferred he just accept it and keep it moving.

He sighs, assumingly preparing to share his wisdom that will forever change the trajectory of my life.

"This is a once-in-a-lifetime opportunity to live freely. You won't even have a need for money no more."

My discomfort grows. Honestly, I have no idea why I thought staying here would be a good idea. The thought of it now makes me feel entirely nauseous.

"Yeah, I appreciate that. Totally. But I think I'll be okay." I try to soften the blow with a smile, but there's a darkness emanating from him.

The hairs on the back of my neck rise, and an ominous feeling invades whatever fragile peace Sylvester and I had. Adrenaline slowly releases into my veins, kicking up my heart rate as Sylvester stares at me.

"I'll tell them who you are if you go," he threatens, his tone deeper and severe.

I feel the crease between my brows deepening as I stare at him with bewilderment. My mouth opens, then closes, at a loss of what the hell to say.

"I imagine if the people after you are as powerful as you claim, they'll be very interested to hear about your whereabouts. I suspect you're runnin' from the law and ain't nothin' stopping them from extraditing your arrest."

My vision tunnels until it's reduced to the eye of a needle, a heavy dose of panic mixing with astonishment.

"Why would you do that?"

"I want you to stay here. I could give ya a comfortable life if you'd allow me to."

"By blackmailing me?" I fume, any nervousness forgotten. I'm too angry, and what gave him the impression that I don't bite when backed into a corner?

"Ya know, any other fugitive would be chomping at the bit for an opportunity like this," he snaps, avoiding my question.

"Yeah, like those prisoners you killed?" I mock. "What makes you think I'm a fugitive anyway?"

"Aw, come on, I may be old and a bit behind on the times, but I ain't stupid. You expect me to believe that a young lady like yerself hasn't done illegal things to get by?"

I open my mouth to respond, but he's forging on.

"Prostitutin' yerself, no doubt. Maybe even stealin' from people. Either way, you ain't free of sin. And I bet them cops would be happy to hear about your whereabouts."

For several seconds, the only thing I'm capable of is gaping at him. I knew Sylvester wasn't as friendly as he pretended to be, but I never thought he'd take things this far.

My fight or flight instincts have been activated, and I'm shooting to my feet, even as I try to process the situation. Clearly, he's not going to just let me go. I feel so stupid for not seeing the depths of his loneliness before. Isolation has driven him mad, and he's become desperate.

But while I may be a runner, I'm sure as hell not a fucking doormat. I will always fight back. That's something Kev learned the hard way, and something Sylvester will learn, too.

"You're right. I have done bad things to survive, and I'm definitely not free of sin. So don't be mistaken and think you will be an exception," I snarl.

Sylvester's expression turns thunderous, my only warning before he stands and backhands me across the face, its force sending me crashing to my ass.

He points down at me and growls, "That is the last time you will disrespect me in my own home."

Then, he's charging toward the staircase as quickly as the wooden peg will allow. Reeling, it takes me a second to clear the stars from my vision, fire lancing across my cheek, and blood pooling in my mouth. I've had terrible things happen to me, but even Kev has never hit me like that.

"What are you doing?" I call, panicked as he rushes up the steps.

Scrambling to my feet, I chase after him, making it to the top of the stairs right when he raises his shotgun and points it directly at Enzo, who is halfway down the hallway, a fierce expression on his face.

At some point, he must've grabbed the gun on his way up.

"Get back in yer room, son," Sylvester warns, his tone steady as if trying not to set off a wild bear.

"Not going to happen," Enzo growls, prompting Sylvester to pump the forearm on the gun, a clear threat.

I swear to God, if he shoots, I will kick him in the peg and feel no remorse.

As if disturbed by the commotion, the sound of dragging chains interrupts whatever Sylvester was going to say. His head snaps up, glaring at the ceiling as the restless spirit paces across the floor, its footsteps heavy.

"You've made 'em angry," he spits over his shoulder.

"Me?" I echo, taken aback. "You're the one acting crazy."

"You haven't seen crazy, young lady. Now get in there!" The moment the last word leaves his mouth, the footsteps above freeze, heightening the sound of his voice to a thunderous level.

Get in *where?*

My question is quickly answered when it registers that he's motioning with the gun in the direction of his room.

My eyes widen impossibly further.

"Fuck no," I bark. "I'm *not* staying with you."

Enzo steps toward the unhinged man, but Sylvester notices and thrusts his gun at him.

"Get back! I will blow your goddamn head off."

"Enzo, just go," I bark. His gaze darts to me over Sylvester's shoulder.

Silently, I mouth, "Cave."

He's going to have to trust me to get away. It's what I'm best at.

Enzo clenches his jaw, the muscle threatening to burst. His eyes are turning obsidian, and his stare promises death as he slowly backs toward the room again.

He doesn't remove his gaze until the very last second. Sylvester slams our bedroom door shut and locks it with a key.

Before he can turn the weapon on me, I'm pivoting and sprinting for the stairs.

"Damn it, come back here!"

I speed down them fast enough to nearly send myself pitching forward face-first. Sylvester is storming down the hallway and pounding down the steps behind me, but I'm out of the front entrance before he can reach the last step.

"Get back here!" His shout is cut off by the slamming door. Breathing heavily, adrenaline and panic warring for a space in my bloodstream, I run toward the cave.

It's the only place I can run to.

All I can do is hope he can't find me there.

CHAPTER 26

Enzo

I'm peering through a cloud of red fury as I lift my leg and power it into the door, cracking the wood. I need to get to Sawyer—it's all I can feel, think, *breathe*. Get to Sawyer.

Just as I'm getting ready to kick it through a second time, I hear the tinkle of keys before the lock clicks.

I ready myself as the door swings open, the wrong side of the barrel being pointed in my direction the first thing I see.

Sylvester glares at me from behind the weapon, taking a step back and jerking the gun toward the stairs. "Go."

Fuming and silent, I step out of the room and head toward the steps. The press of metal is lodged into my back as I slowly walk, Sylvester's wooden peg carrying him right behind me.

"Where's Sawyer?" I growl.

"Gone, but don't worry, I'll get 'er back."

"Did you hurt her?" I bite out.

"Ya know, it didn't have'ta go down this way, son," he says, ignoring me.

My fury heightens, and I'm now peering through a black cloud. I'll gladly hand my soul over to the devil if he hurt her.

"I've given you far too much leniency when I shoulda blown yer head off from the start."

"You should've," I agree. That would've been the only thing to save his life.

"And I will once Sawyer comes back. I think if I kill ya prematurely, she'll take herself in that ocean."

Not so sure about that, but I'll let him believe it anyway. Despite what Sawyer thinks, she's a fighter. She's done nothing *but* fight for the better half of her life.

She wouldn't become a meager little slave, resolute to spend the rest of her life trapped somewhere. No, she would do everything in her power to get the fuck out of there, even if it meant getting more blood on her hands.

Fuck, I love her.

The little thief is capable of so much; it'll only be Sylvester's demise if he forces her into that position.

But he won't get the chance to. Instead, I'll be his demise.

Keeping silent, I reach the steps and speed-walk down them, making it hard for Sylvester to catch up. In his attempt to, I hear him stumble forward.

I have literally two seconds, but I'm quite accustomed to outmaneuvering a shark in its own territory. I've no doubt I can handle a man with a log for a leg.

In a blink, I'm pitching myself over the side of the railing, the floor only five or so feet below. He fires off a shot, the heat of the bullet zipping over my shoulder. It hits something in the kitchen while I grab ahold of the long barrel and yank it from his grip.

"Son of a bitch!" he spits, attempting to hold on to it, but I'm too strong for him.

I flip the gun on him, enjoying how he freezes, his face purpling from anger.

"Don't stop on my account. Let's see you finish stumbling your way down."

"I'm going to fu—"

"Not really interested in hearing about your dreams, Sylvester. Hurry up," I snap.

Grunting, he reaches the bottom step, glaring at me from beneath his bushy brows. I glance around, noticing the rug and table have been moved aside. In their place is a cellar, the door wide open. I assume that's where he planned on keeping me in the meantime.

"Don't think you have what it takes to kill a man," Sylvester drawls. He's sweating profusely, the edges of his ball cap stained.

He's wrong. I'd be happy to show him he's not the only one who knows how to take a life. He can have everything he's ever wanted. To forever stay on Raven Isle, even in the afterlife.

As badly as I'm itching to kill him, I care more about what happens to us after than satisfying the need to feel his blood on my hands.

"Get in," I say, motioning toward the cellar with the gun.

"My leg—"

"Is useless, I know. Not my problem. Make me ask again, and I'll shoot off the other, so you have a matching set."

He scowls, aiming another glare my way as he hobbles toward the cellar. Once he's in front of it, I decide to make it easy on him. Lifting my leg, I power it straight into his back, sending him flying down the hole.

He shouts, and whatever way he must have landed isn't too pretty, considering his yelling turns into an outright roar.

Again. Not my problem.

When I look down into it, I find him only about twenty feet down, rolling to lay flat on his back, curses and spittle flying from his lips.

I have no sympathy. Shooting him one last look, I grab the door and slam it shut. There's a simple sliding mechanism to lock it, and while I'd prefer a deadbolt, it's the best I can do for now.

Sylvester never said if Sawyer was hurt, and every molecule in my body is now centered on her.

As I'm making my way to the door, I notice a blanket lying haphazardly on the couch. I snatch it, just in case I need to staunch a wound, or fuck, even for if she's a little cold.

It takes me only a few minutes to get to the cave, every second feeling too long.

"Sawyer!" I yell, stomping through the tunnel.

"Enzo?" she answers, eagerness saturating my name. Just as I reach the opening beneath the glowworms, I see her rushing toward me, her skin awash in blue.

Her face is slack with relief, and her teeth are chattering.

It's freezing in here. With the constant storms, the temperature has dropped significantly.

"You hurt?" I ask, my gaze sweeping across her body while I set down the shotgun. She's still in her shorts and a t-shirt, her arms and legs covered in goosebumps.

But I already have the answer to my question.

I zero in on her swollen eye and bleeding lip. My blood turns glacial.

The muscle in my jaw thrums, and my fists curl as I stalk toward her. She goes to step back, but as quick as a viper, one hand snaps out, grabs the back of her neck, and jerks her face into mine. She stumbles, catching herself on my chest.

Instantly, her hands curl into my shirt, but I can't distinguish if she's trying to push me away or hold on.

My chest pumps heavily, the fury wreaking havoc on my control.

Morirà lentamente. I will claim self-defense when the authorities get here. He put his hands on my girl, and I sure as fuck will no longer allow him the gift of breath.

Morirà lentamente - *He will die slowly*

I lean in close, her body trembling and eyes wide. They're dilated, but it's not with fear this time. There's no mistaking the heat in them.

A small gasp slips free when my lips softly caress the side of her reddened eye.

"Enzo..." she whispers, her words trailing off as I softly press a kiss there.

"Don't worry, baby," I breathe, the ice in my body chilling my words. "I'm going to end him. And I will let you watch."

She shudders, her hands tightening in my shirt. "I hope you do," she rasps, sounding on the verge of coming without me even touching her. However, she gathers herself enough to ask, "Where is he?"

"He had a cellar hiding beneath the dining room table. He's in there now," I explain, remembering to wrap the blanket around her shoulders. She's looking up at me with glimmering eyes, staring at me as if I was the one who saved her.

She's so fucking beautiful.

"That's... interesting. Wasn't expecting that."

"Worked out for us," I mutter, grabbing her hand and pulling her toward the pool.

"We can go back whenever you're ready," I tell her, tugging her until she sits beside me.

"Can we stay here tonight? I know it's not very comfortable, but I just want a night outside of that lighthouse. It's fucking suffocating."

"Whatever you want, *bella*."

Her face twists into a pained expression. "Tomorrow morning, we'll start looking for the beacon again. We have to find it. I don't want to stay here for any longer than we have to."

"I'll get the answer out of him," I swear, wrapping an arm around her and bringing her into my chest.

She snorts, assuming laughing at the awkward angle her head is in. "You've never cuddled a day in your life, have you?"

"No," I clip.

"I can tell. You're tense."

But I'm trying.

"What happened with him?"

This time, she's the one who stiffens. Her discomfort is obvious and only serves to reignite the flames burning in my chest. They never died out, but fuck, if he tried anything with her...

"He asked me to stay. I said no. He threatened to blackmail me, and things went downhill from there."

The muscle in my jaw nearly bursts from how hard I clench it.

"Did he touch you?" I bite out through gritted teeth.

"Aside from him backhanding me? It wasn't anything I couldn't handle."

My fists curl, the image of Sylvester hitting her nearly catastrophic to my control. "The fuck does that even mean?"

"It means Sylvester has always taken it upon himself to lay hands on me, but that doesn't mean I let him."

My upper lip curls into a snarl, and likely sensing the black fury radiating from me, she looks up and rests her cheek on my shoulder. Her hot breath fans across my neck, and I fight the urge to pull her on top of me. I focus on the pool before giving in to my darker instincts.

"What are you thinking?" she asks in a whisper.

"He wants what I have." When she stays silent, I drop my gaze to her. "You, *bella*. He doesn't like the thought of me having you," I say, my voice so deep, I no longer recognize it myself. "Imagine how he would feel if he was made to watch."

"Enzo," she breathes.

This time, I'm unable to look away. My body grows hotter, while my cock stiffens.

Forcing Sylvester to bear something he would deem unbearable... I can't explain the excitement that has adrenaline injecting straight into my heart.

"But then I would really have to kill him," I conclude.

Her brow pinches, and that pink mouth is parted with confusion. Despite her uncertainty, her eyes are blown wide, and little pants are slipping past her tongue.

"Why?" she murmurs. I reach up, thumbing those sweet lips until the sensitive flesh pinches into her teeth.

Who knew a single word could plague me so profoundly?

Mine.

"Because anyone who looks at what's mine will never live to tell about it," I rasp.

"Is that what I am?" she croaks. "Yours?"

"You always have been," I murmur. "Now, it's only a matter of if you stay."

She doesn't say yes, and again, I'm overcome with the need to keep her anyway.

Her tongue darts out, licking the tip of my thumb. All my focus zeroes in on what she's doing, my cock hardening impossibly further.

"*Tu sei mia,*" I growl, hunger clawing at my insides as she draws my thumb between her teeth and clamps down. I hardly feel the pain. I can only feel something dark and primal begging to be unleashed. "What else?" she encourages. "Tell me everything you could never say."

I know what she's asking. Confess to her in a language she doesn't understand. I'm not sure if it's for my benefit or hers. Does she think it's the only way I can profess my feelings, or is it because it's the only way she'll listen without running?

"*È impossibile odiarti quando mi fai sentire così vivo,*" I start, slipping two fingers past her lips and hooking them over her teeth, bringing her closer.

"*Ed è esattamente per questo che voglio odiarti. Prima di incontrare te ero un sonnambulo. Cazzo, non ero pronto a svegliarmi.*"

Tu sei mia - *You're mine*

È impossibile odiarti quando mi fai sentire così vivo - *It's impossible to hate you when you make me feel so alive*

Ed è esattamente per questo che voglio odiarti. Prima di incontrare te ero un sonnambulo. Cazzo, non ero pronto a svegliarmi. - *And that's exactly why I want to hate you. I was sleepwalking until I met you, and I wasn't fucking ready to wake up*

She stares at me as if she understands. Even when I'm speaking another language, she still hears me.

"*Ho sbagliato a dirti che eri debole. Sei così incredibilmente coraggiosa, vorrei che lo vedessi anche tu.*"

Releasing her jaw, I slide my hand beneath her t-shirt, dragging my wet fingers against her soft stomach, eliciting a shiver for an entirely different reason. The fabric lifts as I travel up between her breasts. Growing impatient, she sits up enough to pull the shirt over her head, tossing it to the side and leaning back into me. Next, she removes her jean shorts.

Turning to face me, she crawls on my lap, resting her hands on my shoulders while the blanket falls away.

"Don't stop," she pleads.

"*Ti penso ogni ora, ogni minuto, ogni dannato secondo. Non so che fare.*"

I release the knots around her neck and waist, biting my lip when the material falls away and reveals her pert breasts. I can't resist leaning in and placing a gentle kiss on her rose-pink nipple. She gasps, prompting me to lick it, and I groan from how addicting she tastes.

"*L'oceano era l'unico posto in cui mi sentivo a casa,*" I continue, moving my hands to the knots on either side of her hips. I pluck those, too, raw desire consuming every one of my brain cells when her bottoms drop. I can smell her arousal, and I'm struggling to concentrate on what I'm saying.

Ho sbagliato a dirti che eri debole. Sei così incredibilmente coraggiosa, vorrei che lo vedessi anche tu - *I was wrong to call you weak. You are so incredibly brave. I wish you could see that*

Ti penso ogni ora, ogni minuto, ogni dannato secondo. Non so che fare. - *I think of you every hour, every minute, every goddamn second. I don't know what to do with that*

L'oceano era l'unico posto in cui mi sentivo a casa - *The ocean was the only place I've ever felt at home*

"Era l'unica cosa che mi eccitava e dava pace. Hai rovinato anche questo. Sentirti su di me è meglio di immergersi nell'oceano. Neanche con questa rivelazione so che fare."

Leaning forward, I draw her nipple into my mouth, sucking on it harshly and earning a low, husky moan. I wrap one arm around her, keeping her immobilized, while my other hand teases her entrance, spreading her arousal up to her clit and circling lightly.

"One day," she pants. "I'm going to learn Italian, and I'll know exactly what you said."

I can't explain the visceral emotion that arises in my chest at the thought of her learning my language—immersing herself in my culture. There's no controlling the flashes of Sawyer walking down *Mercato Campo de' Fiori* in Rome, a look of wonder on her face while she visits the *bancarelle* lining the square, smiling at the sellers as they call out to her, attempting to charm her into coming to their stands. She'd marvel over the fruits and vegetables, and gravitate toward the strong aroma of fresh flowers, sticking her button nose in each one. I'd tuck a blue hibiscus into her hair, the color rivaling her eyes.

Un giorno.

She said she'd let me keep her safe, but I don't know what that means for us. I don't know if she'll stay. I'm not sure there will *be* a one day, but I keep that to myself. I have no interest in hurting my own feelings.

Era l'unica cosa che mi eccitava e dava pace. Hai rovinato anche questo. Sentirti su di me è meglio di immergersi nell'oceano. Neanche con questa rivelazione so che fare. *It was the only thing that gave me excitement and peace. You've ruined that for me, too. Being inside you is better than being inside the ocean. I don't know what to do with that, either*

Bancarelle - *A moveable stand where vendors sell their goods*

Un giorno - *One day*

In place of an answer, I sink my middle finger in her wet pussy, my own groan masking her cry.

"*Cazzo, quanto sei bagnata*," I murmur.

"Enzo," she moans, rolling her hips into my hand. I add another finger, curling them as I stretch her, finding that sweet spot and stroking it persistently.

Her cries pitch higher while I use my thumb to rub her clit.

"Please, I need more," she begs, tearing at my shirt. I'm forced to pull away from her to remove it, but the cold air feels good against my heated skin.

She works on my shorts next, and after some maneuvering, she slides them down my legs and mounts me once more.

Just as she prepares to sink down onto my cock, I stop her.

"No need to rush, *bella*," I tell her, and my lips involuntarily pull into a grin when she mewls in outrage.

"You're going to torture me, aren't you?" she pants. "You're supposed to be begging for my forgiveness."

"Can't we beg together, baby?" I rasp darkly.

Her mouth falls open, but I'm standing, lifting her in my arms as I do. She inhales sharply, quickly grabbing onto my neck. As if I'd ever let her fall. Not unless it's for me.

I carry her over to the pool, and with each step, she grows stiffer.

"Enzo," she warns, squirming in my hold and rubbing that sweet, little cunt against my cock. Though I don't think she intended to, I growl anyway, grinding against her. "Enzo," she repeats, hysteria in her tone. "Don't do this to me again. I thought you wanted me to forgive you."

"Shhh, I'm not going to hurt you, *amore mio*. I'm going to replace that memory with something good," I assure her, dropping to my knees and settling her at the edge of the pool.

Cazzo, quanto sei bagnata - *You're so fucking wet*
Bellissima - *Beautiful*

"You wanted me to apologize for what I did to you on the boat, and I said I wouldn't until I was sorry." I brush my lips across her jawline, her body trembling deliciously.

"I'm ready to repent, baby. You tell me to stop, I stop."

She's staring at me with wide, panicked eyes. If Sawyer and I do have a *one day*, then I will make sure she never looks at me like this again. I can't take back what I did, but I will replace it with something good.

"What are you going to do?"

"Adrenaline can be like an aphrodisiac," I explain. "The fear, the possibility of death, makes you feel alive. That's part of the reason why I do what I do."

"Swimming with sharks turns you on?" she questions with doubt, though she's entirely distracted. I twist her rigid body around before she can spot the grin on my face. When she's facing the water, I press my chest to her back, flattening my palm against her stomach and leaning down to whisper in her ear.

"Considering my job isn't remotely sexual, I don't get aroused, no," I say with amusement. "But it does make me feel alive. And this will, too, if you let me show you."

If I had X-ray vision, I'd see two halves of her brain at war with each other. She's scared, but she's also intrigued.

"Will *I* get aroused?" she asks quietly.

"*Si*," I answer. "You will come harder than you ever have before."

She chews on her lip, still contemplating. "That's a big promise to make."

"Then you'd better let me keep it."

After a moment of consideration, her chin dips in the tiniest of increments, and that primal, animalistic part of me breaks free.

"Bend over," I order, pushing her upper back down until her nose is within an inch from the water and her round ass is high in the air.

"*Bellissima*," I praise, brushing my hand across her backside and squeezing firmly.

She's gripping onto the edge of the pool so tightly, her knuckles are bleached white. But I don't give her reassurances. While I want her to feel safe, I also want her to be scared, too.

She *should* be scared.

I lean down, replacing my hand with my mouth and trailing wet kisses down to her dripping pussy. The closer I get, the louder her panting grows.

"Fuck, you smell so good," I groan before diving my tongue inside her tight hole. Sawyer moans loudly, the sound echoing throughout the cave as I begin to eat her cunt with vigor.

"Enzo," she cries, bucking her hips into me. I slide my tongue down to her clit, circling it persistently until her legs are shaking.

"Oh, don't stop!" She widens her stance and arches her back further to give me a better angle.

She'd have to throw herself in the pool to get me away from her. I imagine this hunger I feel for her is no less savage than a starving shark amongst its prey.

Quickly, I turn away from her and lay on my back, positioning my head between her thighs. Then, I lower her hips until she's sitting on my face. Her spine straightens, now riding my mouth with just as much ferocity while I lap up every drop she has to offer.

Her hands cup her breasts, tweaking her hardened nipples while her head kicks back, her cries bleeding into screams. It's the most beautiful sight I've ever seen. Enough to bring me to the edge myself. I grab my cock, squeezing tightly until the pain pushes aside the need.

"Oh my God, Enzo, I'm going to come," she moans. I feel her thighs clenching around my head, and just as she begins to let go, I push her up.

Her head snaps down in shock, a ferocious look on her face. An angry goddess here to take what's rightfully hers, with fire in her eyes, blonde curls surrounding her face like a lion's mane, and a snarl curling her lips.

Christ. She's magnificent and has me on the precipice of exploding like a fucking pubescent little boy.

Before she can curse at me, I'm plunging two fingers inside her and curling them deeply. Her mouth drops, those flames brightening into twin suns as she begins to unravel.

"Now's your time for revenge, *bella ladra*. I've drowned you once. It's your turn to drown me."

Every exhale is a breathless moan, and she pants like she can't get in enough air while I lap at her clit, never removing my eyes from her. I'm putting firm pressure on her G-spot, feeling her arousal beginning to flood past my hand.

"En—oh my—wait," she gasps, her words senseless and garbled. So overcome with pleasure, her hand slaps the top of my head, and I can't tell if I want to laugh or bite her clit.

But then her cunt is tightening around my fingers, and I have to pinch my eyes shut, forcing out thoughts of what it would feel like if she were clenched around my cock instead.

She goes silent for two heartbeats and then erupts. A loud scream pierces the air, and her entire body begins to seize. The moment I retract my fingers, her release is pouring onto me. Quickly, I hook both arms around each thigh and force her back down on my face, opening my mouth wide and drinking from her like a man who's been lost at sea for months.

My name is an echo as she thrashes above me while filling my mouth with her cum, trails of it leaking past my lips.

I'm groaning into her, and I think she's hitting me again, but I'm so far gone in my bliss, so intoxicated by her taste that I hardly notice anything outside of her release sliding down my throat.

It feels like her orgasm drags out longer than normal, and by the time she slumps, I'm vibrating with the need to fuck her.

"Stop, oh my God, I can't take any more!" she begs, attempting to pull away.

I let her go, but only long enough for me to slide out from beneath her and move her back into the previous position. Face above the water and ass in the air.

"Wait, don't put me under yet," she breathes, her heavy exhales disturbing the still water. "Let me—I still can't breathe."

"Baby, you'll never be able to breathe as long as I'm inside you," I retort. I line up my cock with her entrance and slowly push inside her, no longer able to go another second without her wrapped around me.

"Oh, fuck," she bites out, moving to sit up.

"Uh-uh, did I say you could move?" I snap, grabbing the nape of her neck and pushing her back down.

"Too much," she chokes, voice strained as I sink myself deeper in her tight warmth.

"You can take it, *bella*. Let me see your cunt swallow my cock as good as you do with your throat."

Her only response is another garbled moan. I bury myself to the hilt, and my eyes roll from the utter fucking bliss.

"*Cazzo*," I rasp. "That's such a good girl, baby."

I retreat long and slow, dragging my glistening dick from her warmth, enraptured by how fucking soaked she's making me. Then, I drive into her roughly, earning a sharp gasp, followed by my name. It almost sounds like an admonishment, and it brings out a savage grin to my face.

"You can take it," I assure. "Can you feel how tightly your pussy clings to me? Like it never wants to let me go. How deep do you think you can take me before you're begging for me to stop?"

"I—" she gasps, when I angle her ass higher, allowing me a better angle to hit her cervix.

"That—that's my limit," she squeaks.

"Then let me take you to a new limit."

Before she can protest, I fist her curls and push her head underwater.

She thrashes, and I tighten my core to balance myself, so I can reach beneath her and strum her clit.

She jerks against me, and I pull my hips back, only to slam into her again, forming a steady pace while she drowns. Bubbles disturb the surface, but her pussy is tightening around me almost painfully.

Pushing her to this dangerous limit is undeniably erotic. Feeling her fight beneath my hold, unable to stop me from draining the life from her, is addicting.

What she doesn't realize is that I've always held her life in my hands, and she never knew that she was trusting me to guard it.

I pull her head up, and she instinctively inhales deeply—desperately.

"*Brava ragazza.* You're doing so fucking good," I praise, rolling my hips into her. "I'm so proud of you."

She whimpers, mumbling incoherent words. Yet, her hips push back into me, seeking more from me.

Flirting with death is a fucking thrill.

"Deep breath, *bella.*"

She listens while I quicken my pace, making it difficult for her to get a good breath in without huffing out a moan.

"Wait—Enzo," she screams, feeling the narrowing window.

I don't let her finish. I'm forcing her head back down, and a flood of bubbles rises to the surface, presumably from her screaming underwater.

She'll have less oxygen this time, but I want to fuck her while she feels like she's dying.

I circle her clit faster, groaning when her cunt tightens again, her legs quivering as I pick up speed. My cock is thickening, and I'm so close to coming, but I refuse to end this too soon.

Just as I begin to lose myself in her sweet pussy, she begins to fight. She's panicking, but I push it a little longer until she bucks wildly against me. I allow her to come up, another choked gasp of breath.

I don't relent on my pace, her watery screams somewhere between jumbled protests and high-pitched mewls of encouragement.

"Do you forgive me, *piccola*?"

"I can't... Enzo, I don't—"

"Take a deep breath. This time, keep it in," I order. "I'm going to keep you under longer, and I don't care how much you fight me. Your pussy gets so tight when you're on the brink of death."

Her response is a sob, but she does as I say and inhales as deeply as she can.

"Relax, *bella*. I won't let you drown. I want to show you how good it feels to live."

She nods, and her trust only serves to strengthen my obsession with her. The moment her lips clamp shut, I put her back under. I lift one of my knees, planting my foot firmly on the ground for more stability. I'm fucking her hard enough that the sound of our skin slapping and the wet noises her pussy is making are louder than her splashing in the water.

Intense pleasure is building in the base of my spine, and her struggling to breathe is only enhancing it.

I focus on the water, making sure the bubbles are still consistent, but it seems as if she's trying to keep herself from thrashing. Vibrations are racking every single bone in her body one moment, and the next, she goes completely still.

And then, she's exploding. She's tightening around me until my eyes threaten to cross, and I'm lost in the euphoria. I release her head, allowing her to come up, but I'm oblivious to her when she's nearly convulsing around my cock.

piccola - *baby*

"Fuck, *fuck, FUCK*, Sawyer," I chant, crowding over her and sinking my teeth into her shoulder as my own orgasm tears through me. More words slip out, trading between Italian and English. I've no idea what I'm saying, solely that it's the only prayer I've ever believed in.

My vision goes black, and never-ending groans ripple from my throat while I spill inside her, streams of cum filling her pussy until it's pouring out of her.

"Oh my God, oh my God, Enzo," she chokes, voice raspy and hoarse.

The sensation becomes too much, so I rip myself out of her, an animalistic feeling rising in my chest when my release streams down her leg.

Using two fingers, I gather it from her leg and push it back inside her cunt, biting my lip when she chokes on a gasp and turns to look back at me.

"This is mine," I proclaim. Then, I repeat it in Italian. "*Questa è mia.*"

I withdraw my fingers and spread my cum up to her ass, circling the tight entrance before dipping my thumb inside. She sucks in sharply.

"Enzo," she hisses.

I need to know that I've been in every part of her. On every part of her. I gather more of it from her dripping pussy, then trace my name into her skin with it.

"*Now* you can have my name," I murmur. She peeks at me over her shoulder, her cheeks tinted red, eyes dilated, and her pink mouth parted.

I want to keep her. I *will* keep her.

As if hearing me and solidifying it, she licks the salty water off her lip before whispering, "I forgive you now."

A wicked feeling is swirling in my chest. The same feeling I had when her hair was in my fist and my cock buried within her the first time I held her beneath the water.

"Yet, I will never stop asking for it," I tell her. "I will never stop worshiping you."

I cup her again, baring my teeth while the darkness thrashes against my flesh, threatening to tear right through.

"You will be mine until you draw your last breath, Sawyer. And it will be my hand holding you beneath the surface, introducing you to death."

I dip my fingers into her pussy again, then retract them and hook the same two in her bottom teeth, jerking her face toward me. She squeals, stunned as I lean closer until my breath fans across the wet curls matted to her face.

"*Ma solo quando sono pronto a venire con te. Annegheremo insieme, bella ladra.*"

Ma solo quando sono pronto a venire con te. Annegheremo insieme, bella ladra. - *But only when I'm ready to come with you. We will drown together, beautiful thief*

Svegliati - *wake up*

CHAPTER 27

Sawyer

"*Piccola*, wake up."

"Hmm?" I mumble, rolling over only to be greeted with a shooting pain up my back.

Oh my *God*. I may be only twenty-eight, but it feels as if I have aged eighty years overnight. Sleeping on hard rock is terrible for anyone's back, no matter how much of the night you spend sprawled on top of someone else.

"Sawyer, *svegliati*," the voice says more sternly.

"I'm up," I groan, flinching when I roll to my side. I release another long groan. "Fuck me up the nose, dude."

There's a beat of silence, and then, "What?"

My eyes are still closed, but I roll them anyway. He takes everything so literally.

"I'm going to need a serious yoga session," I whine, sitting up and finally cracking open my eyes. Enzo is crouching in front of me, staring at me with a fierce expression on his face.

He never translated what he said last night when marking me everywhere with his cum. But whatever it was, it set off a deep thrill inside me. The type where you're willingly walking into a dangerous situation for the adrenaline rush.

It was... passionate yet unhinged. Like, murder me and stuff me, then try to spoon-feed me beans because he thinks I'm still alive type of unhinged. Some Norman Bates shit. It was a mix of *I want to strangle you* and *I'll never let you go.*

It's how Kev used to look at me, and I recognize precisely what it is. *Obsession.*

Except this time, it sets my insides aflame, and I want to return that look with a smile that says *Never let me go. I'll die with your hands wrapped around my throat.*

Wow. That's fucked up. I need to find a therapist when I get home.

"Sylvester is gone," Enzo says, his brow pinched with concern.

"You went back without me?" I ask, a little angry that he went alone. "Where did he go? How did he get out?"

He shakes his head. "I don't know. The lock on the cellar was unlatched, so I don't know if he slammed up against it until it came out or what. Regardless, we're taking over, finding that fucking beacon, and contacting someone to come get us."

Uneasiness floods my system.

His disappearing doesn't make me feel better. Wherever he is, he's still on this island. Sylvester knows this place far better than we do.

He's not gone. He's *hiding.*

But we can't stay in this cave forever. We have no food or water, and my bladder is taking the opportunity to remind me that I need to pee really bad. And while I could squat in the corner of the cave somewhere, that's not exactly an option for when the beans decide to go through me.

"He probably has a gun," I surmise. Sylvester has several guns, and if Enzo could've predicted the possibility of him escaping, I know those guns would not have been left in the lighthouse overnight.

I feel terrible asking him to stay here instead. Sylvester never would've gotten free otherwise.

Enzo nods. "But so do we. We just need to be careful tonight."

"Okay," I mumble, my face contorting as I stand.

Jesus, my back hurts so bad, but it's my own fault. I did want to sleep here, after all. And I don't regret it. It was refreshing waking up to a different view, even if I did worry that one of the silk strings would drop into my mouth while I was sleeping.

When I straighten, Enzo is staring at me like a crazy person again.

"What?"

"You're in pain," he states bluntly.

I give him a side-eye. "Yeah, and?"

His eyes drop to the floor, like he's considering punching the inanimate rock for daring to throw my back out of place. Ultimately, he grabs the blanket and shotgun, then lifts his eyes and says, "I'll take care of that later. Let's go, baby."

Hesitating for only a moment—mainly because this new version of him still weirds me out—I trudge after him, being careful to keep the pain off my face. He keeps glancing back at me, as if expecting me to keel over and curl up like a dead spider any second—which usually only happens after he fucks me.

As we near the lighthouse, my heart begins to race. The sky is dark gray, the near-constant storms plaguing Raven Isle like it has a personal vendetta against it.

It only makes the lighthouse appear more sinister—the chipped red and white rings around the building darkening the atmosphere of the island. It feels like I'm in one of those horror video games. I'm forced to go into the scary place because that's how I beat the game, but I know something in there will try and kill me. Every step is filled with dread, and it feels as if my heart is being weighed down by the doom headed my way.

Enzo readies the shotgun and quietly opens the front door, the loud creaking of the hinges shattering the silence.

The energy is thick in here—heavy like a weighted blanket. Except this isn't the kind that makes you feel warm and safe, but everything opposite.

"Stay quiet," Enzo whispers. I nod, though he's not looking at me anyway, and shut the door as silently as possible. Which isn't very quiet given the hinges sound like they came from a different century and have never been oiled.

He quickly walks to the kitchen, grabs a huge knife that Sylvester uses to fillet the fish, and then walks back to hand it to me.

"Stay here. I'm going to check every room to make sure he's gone. If you see him, stab him."

I stare down at the knife and begin to shake, nearly stabbing Enzo in my attempt to hand it back. I'd rather take the gun.

"No, thanks," I say, my voice uneven and tight.

His brows lower. "Sawyer, I'm not leaving you unprotected. You need to take it."

"Can't I just go with you? Haven't you seen the horror movies? Separating is *never* a good idea. And I'm in more danger of getting shot if you're not here."

"I'd still like you to hold on to it," he insists, grabbing my wrist and forcing it in my fist. My face twists with discomfort, but I don't argue.

He studies me closely, almost critically, as if trying to figure out a math problem. Eventually, he turns and heads toward the staircase while I follow close behind.

We try to keep our steps light, but the metal is no better than the door and groans beneath our weight as we ascend.

Up here, the air feels denser. For a moment, it feels like I can't take in a deep enough breath. We check the small closet first, then our room, the bathroom, and lastly, Sylvester's room.

He's nowhere to be found. It's deathly quiet in here and nearly impossible to move through this place without making some type of sound. Unless he's standing as still as a statue—he's not here.

I'm not sure if that makes me feel better. While living with Sylvester is far from comfortable, it was still the danger you know and all that. Now the danger is as unknown as his whereabouts.

We know the beacon is still in commission and that he's had access from the day we shipwrecked, so there's still a chance he's here, just not anywhere we can see.

"We need to board up the windows and door so he can't get in," Enzo says quietly. The way he's talking only confirms my own fears. He speaks as if Sylvester might hear us.

"What if we're locking him in with us?" I ask.

The corners of his eyes tighten. "We're going to make sure we have a quick escape route."

Before I can question how, he heads into Sylvester's room and slides open his closet. Then, he begins tearing clothing off the hangers and extra bedsheets from a shelf above.

After our arms are full, he heads back into our bedroom and softly closes the door.

It takes me only a second to catch on when he starts stringing the material together into a rope.

"This is going to be attached to our bed at all times," he explains. "If anything happens, this is our way out."

I frown. "The window is nailed shut."

"No, it's not."

I blink, my brow pinching as I go to investigate. I distinctly remember the nails pinning it down when we arrived.

However, when I check over it now, I find that the nails have been removed.

"When…"

"I started removing them after we got here."

My mouth pops open. This whole time, he's been removing them, and I never noticed. Sylvester must not have, either. It's definitely something he would've spoken up about if he had.

"You sneaky dog," I mutter, grinning at him.

He gives me a pointed look. "I may have given the impression that I was playing by his rules, *bella*, but I will never allow someone to imprison me."

He stalks toward me, and I'm immediately paralyzed by his stare. It's only when he crouches down and starts tying the makeshift rope around the leg of the bed that I realize I'm standing right in front of it.

Heart in my stomach, I take a step back, giving him room to fashion it around the post securely, and then bundle the excess under the bed.

"I've snuck up here a few times to loosen the window. It was stiff at first, but you should be able to get it open no problem," he explains. "Try it just in case."

I don't like this scenario. One where I'm escaping alone. But it's smart to be prepared, so I plant my hands on the window and push up. It takes effort, but it's doable.

"Good," he says before shoving it back down for me. "Let's find something to eat, and then I'll start boarding up the place."

"I can hel—"

"You need to relax," he interrupts.

I blink. "Enzo, it's not the first time I've experienced back pain. I'm not an invalid."

He steps into my space and catches my chin between his fingers. I gasp, and an electric shiver zips down my spine.

"I'm more than aware that you're a capable woman, Sawyer. But that doesn't mean I won't take care of you."

My mouth falls open, but nothing escapes. There isn't a coherent thought in my brain. I'm sure I look no different than a dopey dog. Look into their eyes and see nothing in there.

His stare drops to my parted lips and locks for a few seconds before he focuses on me again.

"*Capito?*"

"Yes," I whisper, understanding what he's asking for.

"Good girl," he murmurs, a note of approval in his tone as he leans in and places a soft kiss on my forehead.

My heart might as well be an overheated baked potato. It's exploding in my chest while my whole body is flushed.

His approval shouldn't make me feel proud, yet it does. With one last loaded look, he nods in the direction of the door and then prowls toward it, the expectation to follow clear.

My oppositional side tells me to keep my feet firmly planted. However, my pathetic need to get another one of those forehead kisses is what ultimately has me following after him.

Sylvester was pretty strict about food portions, which was something Enzo nor I minded considering we're guests and what would normally last him a month was cut into a third. We were just grateful to have food at all.

That meant we were restricted from scouring the cabinets, and it was something we were happy to respect.

Except after rummaging through them, we find that Sylvester has been hoarding a lot more food than he let on. Which I can't really blame him for. If I lived on this island alone and the chances of being forgotten were fairly high, I'd probably do the same.

So, with that in mind, Enzo and I still keep our dinner very light. A single potato and a seasoned chicken breast.

Better than the bajillion Ensure bottles in the cabinet.

We're both confident we can find a working radio somewhere or that the freight ship will come by eventually, but we have to prepare for the possibility that we'll be here for a long time to come.

For all we know, that ship comes by a lot less frequently than Sylvester said. It's better to conserve.

"Lie down," Enzo says, pointing toward the couch. Sighing, I do as he says, not having the energy to argue. This peace between us is exhilarating, and I have no interest in shattering it because he's actually being nice. That would just be stupid.

He gets the little fireplace going while I settle on the couch. Once I'm comfortable, he hands me the shotgun, a grim look on his face.

Staring up at him with wide eyes, I grab the weapon from him hesitantly.

"Sylvester hasn't restocked the wood in the kitchen, so I need to get it from out back. I shouldn't be gone for more than a few minutes. Just keep this close to be safe."

"Okay," I mutter. "Where the hell did he get wood from anyway? This place is practically devoid of plant life."

"He had it imported like everything else. He's got logs for the fire and some two-by-fours. Seems like he keeps it stocked."

I nod, feeling a little burst of relief over that. It's further proof that a ship does come by and confirmation that we *will* get off this island. It's just a matter of when and how long we'll need to live in fear before it happens.

A lot can happen between now and then.

The second Enzo shuts the front door behind him, the stillness grows heavier. I work to swallow, a pit of dread forming in my stomach.

Fuck. This is so creepy.

Just as I reach for the remote, something thumps from above. The muscle in my chest skips over, missing a beat and landing amid a heart attack.

Oh, fuck *this*.

H.D. CARLTON

I stand for no other reason than because it makes me feel less vulnerable. I strain my ears, listening for any more noises.

After thirty seconds, my shoulders relax just as soon as the distinct drag of chains starts up. From how distant it sounds, I'm confident it's coming from the third floor, like it usually does. But it doesn't make me feel any safer.

Adrenaline and terror are circulating throughout my system, mixing until there's a dangerous cocktail in my bloodstream that is just on its knees and begging for me to go into cardiac arrest.

I dance on each foot, groaning softly under my breath for Enzo to hurry. If he doesn't come back within a minute, I'm out of here.

The pacing stops suddenly, and that is one hundred percent scarier than the actual pacing. At least then, I could tell exactly where the spirit was. Now, it could be anywhere.

Whatever it is, it has a tight grip on my lungs. My chest aches from how little oxygen I'm taking in. I'm too scared to breathe correctly. Or rather, my brain is seized by fear, and it is no longer capable of sending signals to the rest of my body.

Shit, all my organs are going to give out by the time the thing even makes itself known, and I think I'm glad for it.

But then, there's a quiet knock from above. It's difficult to hear over the pounding in my ears, but after a few seconds, there's another knock.

It sounds... curious. Like someone knocking on a door to greet their new neighbor with a freshly baked casserole.

For reasons I'll never be able to explain, my feet carry me toward the stairs. I stop before them, and on cue, there's another knock. Louder this time. More direct.

"Hello?" I call.

No one answers, and I feel stupid. But then there's a loud thump as if it's now slamming its fist into the wood. I jump, a startled scream slipping free.

"What's wrong?"

This time, my scream is loud. I whip around to find Enzo standing at the front door, a concerned pinch to his brow.

He rushes toward me, but I quite literally can't move or breathe.

"What happened?" he asks urgently, twisting my body back and forth to check for injury.

I manage to squeak out, "Ghost. Knocking. Scary. Get the water police."

He relaxes, his shoulders dropping. Casting his gaze to the ceiling, his jaw pulses.

"It's okay. It can't hurt you."

"I'm pretty sure that's not true. Have you ever seen *The Conjuring*? Or literally any other paranormal horror movie? They definitely get hurt. People die. Demons are like, serial killers, Enzo."

I sound stupid—I know that—but I'm still struggling to get my brain back into working order, and one thing I am sure of is that whatever it is *can* hurt me. If it's capable of slamming its fist into the floor, I'm confident it can do the same to my face.

"They're not demons, they're spirits," he reminds me.

I shrug. "These spirits were evil people alive. What makes you think they're not evil in death?"

He stares at me.

"Good point," he concedes. "If I need to fight a ghost, I will. Just lay back down for now."

His fists will do precisely zero damage, but since it's a noble thought, I shut my trap and trudge back toward the couch. Enzo digs out some nails from Sylvester's little toolbox he keeps in a closet in the kitchen, then gets to work.

With each two-by-four nailed across the doors and windows, I feel more and more claustrophobic.

This lighthouse is supposed to be safe compared to the cave. Yet, my life feels more in danger than when I was lost at sea.

There's a shark in the water, and just like being in the ocean, we're in *his* territory.

CHAPTER 28

Sawyer

There's a shark latched onto my leg, and I think I'm screaming helplessly when something smacks into the side of my head. In my dream, it's a tennis racket. It's confusing enough to distract me from the beast gnawing on my leg, but the tennis racket is slapping into my cheek again.

Hard enough for the terrifying situation to swirl away and plunge me back into reality.

Something is leaning over me, breathing heavily, and in my discombobulated state, my fists immediately go flying.

"It's me," Enzo hisses, grabbing my wrists before they can connect.

Instantly, I'm overcome with dizzying relief and a touch of disappointment. I'm glad there isn't a shark using my leg for a chew toy, and the person above me isn't Sylvester or a pissed-off spirit. But I'm a little sad I didn't get to hit Enzo. That would've felt nice.

Just as I open my mouth to apologize, I realize that my dream wasn't the only thing keeping Enzo awake.

DOES IT HURT?

The angry knocking is back. And this time, it's on our fucking bedroom door.

It has one two-by-four barred across it, a nail on each end. Enzo left one hammered halfway in so he can easily pry it out and allow us to come and go from the room. But right now, those nails feel as effective as if the wood is being held up by bubble gum.

I freeze, the terror from my nightmare flooding back tenfold. Before, it was only an annoying wave that kept slapping into your face every time you caught a breath. Now, it's a fierce riptide of fear dragging me under and drowning me within it.

"What is that?" I whisper, the words hardly rising above the loud banging.

As if hearing my question, it pauses.

Enzo's tight grip on my arms only confirms that he's still here. Otherwise, his silence would have convinced me that I was alone.

Suddenly, there's another thunderous bang against the door. This time, it sounds like someone either kicked it or rammed their shoulder into it.

Just like earlier when it was pounding on the ceiling, a scream breaks free from my throat. I slap my hand over my mouth, trembling violently as the thing rams into the door again.

"I'm going to open the door," Enzo says quietly.

"No!" I gasp, my hands flying to the collar of his t-shirt. Except he's shirtless, and I only end up digging my nails into his skin.

"We can't just let it keep doing this," he argues through clenched teeth, grabbing my wrists and clutching them tightly.

"What if it's Sylvester?" I reason.

"He'd be shouting or shooting off the gun, and you know it."

"So, then what the hell are you going to do?" I whisper-shout. "Open the door and tell it to quiet down or you'll give it a spanking?"

"I'm going to give *you* a spanking if you keep it up," he snaps.

"You're going to invite it in," I say, ignoring his threat and attempting a different angle. "It wants in, and you're going to just... give it permission."

"It's not a fucking vampire, Sawyer," he growls, obviously frustrated. It's apparent that neither of us has ever had to deal with evil spirits in our lifetime, and we're both severely ill-equipped. It's not like either of us carry around holy water and Bibles. And Sylvester has never given any indication that he's religious and possesses those things, either.

"There's nothing to do but wait it out," I conclude.

BANG!

I jump beneath Enzo's weight, cringing from how fucking awful the noise is. It's the type of sound that makes your ass clench.

There's something outside our door, and it's using all its strength to get in.

That, and it clearly didn't appreciate my idea to ignore it.

"Fuck this goddamn island," Enzo mutters beneath his breath, rolling onto his back. It feels cold without his weight crowding over me, and somehow, I feel more vulnerable. More exposed.

Praying like hell he doesn't reject me, I turn onto my side and lay my head on his chest. He doesn't even hesitate. His arm slips around me, pulling me into his hold.

I have the strangest urge to cry. Instead, I nuzzle my nose against his bare skin, closing my eyes and thanking God that I'm not in this alone.

Something shifts beneath me, disturbing the restless sleep I've gotten lost in. It was a shitty sleep, but it was all I had.

The loud banging lasted deep into the night, and by the time it finally quit, there was a tinge of blue to the sky. We tried our best to sleep through it, but it's safe to say we were both entirely unsuccessful.

I groan and roll onto my back. It's still sore as shit, but laying in an actual bed eased some of the tension.

Enzo sighs from frustration, and I can taste his sour attitude on my tongue. If I'm being honest, mine doesn't taste any sweeter.

We're going to have a *great* day.

He sits up, tossing his legs over the bed, and rolls his neck, letting out a deep sigh. For a moment, he just sits there and breathes. I could slice through the tension with one of those dull plastic knives toddlers get in those kitchen sets.

Then, he stands and trudges over to the wooden board. He grabs the hammer leaning against the wall and makes quick work of prying the nail free. He lets it go, and it slides away, dangling from where it's nailed in on the other end.

He replaces the hammer with the shotgun, tosses a quick glance over his shoulder at me, then whips open the door like there wasn't something trying to break it down all night.

Nothing is on the other side.

It's quiet and cold and it feels almost like a slap in the face. Why does it choose to harass us when sleep is required and then stop when it's time to wake up?

So fucking obnoxiously rude.

I bite my tongue as I stand, the aches in my back screaming. I force myself to stretch, the pain bordering on pleasure and so acute, that I can't help but let out a groan.

Feeling a little dizzy from it, it takes me a moment to focus again to slip on my shorts.

Enzo is staring very intently at me, an angry frown marring his face, then he turns his attention to the opposite side of our door. Furrowing my brow, I approach him to see what the issue is.

I can't tell if he's pissed off at me or the door, but I'm instantly defensive anyway.

Almost immediately, I notice the deep gouges in the wood and how it's splintered from where it must've been ramming its shoulder.

My mouth drops. I don't even remember the clawing. It must've happened when I was delirious from lack of sleep.

"Fucking hell," I murmur, fingering one of the marks.

Enzo is silent, but I can hear the steam shooting from his ears.

"Spirits can't do that," he says.

I shoot him a nasty look. "How would you even know?" I mutter. "Not like you're an expert."

The glare he pins me with could melt fucking Antarctica. But I don't shrink away from him. I'm not sure if it's the severe lack of sleep, the pain throbbing in my entire back, or just that I'm so drained of fear that I don't care if I die today, but I give him the bird and shove past him.

I'm not going to stand there and argue about a ghost defying the laws of physics. I'd rather spend my time gurgling caffeine like I'm a porn star surrounded by five dicks.

Despite the two-by-fours slapped across the windows, morning light peeks through the cracks, washing the bottom floor in deep blue. Dust motes dance in the sunbeams, and I flap my hand at them as if that's going to accomplish anything. I've always been weirded out by the sight of dirt in the air. It's a rude reminder that I'm inhaling some gross shit on a daily basis.

Enzo stomps down the stairs a moment later, and we promptly ignore each other. Even in his annoyance, he whips up a fried egg and piece of toast for each of us, so I concede and pour him a cup of coffee.

In our stilted silence, I notice the steak knife I was using to eat yesterday is now missing. I distinctly remember setting it on the island before I went to bed. Enzo went up before me, so I don't see how he could've moved it.

The notion that a demon stole a knife is more nerve-racking than them scratching a door.

When I tell Enzo about it, he just grunts, though I notice his eyes sharpen and become more alert.

It's not until after we've both eaten and drank our liquid drug that he finally opens his mouth.

"We need to look for the beacon today," he announces.

No shit. What the hell else are we supposed to do? Sit here and come up with a super-secret handshake for kicks?

Okay, so clearly, food and caffeine didn't improve my mood much.

I don't bother responding. Instead, I stand, the chair grinding obnoxiously on the floor and earning myself a severe eye twitch from Enzo.

I'm still convinced the entrance to the beacon is somewhere on the bottom floor. But just like upstairs, there are only so many places the door could be hidden.

I get to work rapping my fist on any open areas on the walls, searching for a hollow point.

"I'm going to keep looking upstairs," he mutters.

"Divide and conquer, sounds great," I comment, knocking on the wall again to double-check that it's solid.

I hope I'm returning the favor and keeping the ghosts up as they did me.

If I don't get to sleep, the dead don't get to, either.

CHAPTER 29

Sawyer

An entire fucking day wasted.

No door to the beacon was found, and I'm ready to pull my goddamn hair out. I spent so much time pounding on walls that it's echoing in my brain, and now my head is pounding just as incessantly.

Mine and Enzo's mood only seemed to worsen as time went on. Apparently, we're still not in a place with each other where we can brood together peacefully.

Last night was a reminder that we don't belong on this fucking island, yet helpless to do anything about it. With the knowledge that Sylvester is somewhere out there and that we're still not any closer to finding the beacon, it's begun to get to both of us—drive us insane.

We've been at each other's throats all day, and while I've been snappy, he's been flat-out angry from the moment we awoke. Though, as time passes, I'm less convinced that he's just having a bad day and wondering if maybe I did do something wrong.

I don't want to go back in the room yet. It's only five in the afternoon, but we decided to call it a day.

I'm standing in the bathroom, fresh out of the shower and feeling on edge. The mirror is fogged, and I refuse to wipe away the condensation. I've never liked looking myself in the eye anyway—I'm too ashamed—but I'm also convinced that the moment I do, there will be a demon standing behind me.

I glance down at the only belongings I possess. Aside from the t-shirt, it's the same clothes I've been forced to wear for over three weeks. I got tired of the musty stench and washed all of Sylvester's shirts and made sure to keep a routine every few days to keep our clothes clean.

He has enough of them that I've been able to rotate them out, but my neon green bathing suit is getting worn out from constant wear.

Now that it's just me and Enzo, I'm tempted to go commando and only wear an oversized t-shirt with nothing underneath.

But then I remember *why* I don't want to go back in the room. Enzo is in there, and for whatever reason, I hate him right now.

Both of us have been assholes today. I can admit that much. This place is driving us stir-crazy, and the longer I stay here, the more I want to stab something. It's unfortunate for Enzo that he tends to be the closest thing to me.

Sighing, I pull on the bathing suit but forgo the shorts and shirt. I'll just grab a new top from Sylvester's closet and deal.

But I'm stopped short at the doorway when I nearly collide with Enzo. He's coming out of the bedroom with the shotgun in his hand—he's been carrying it everywhere—heading downstairs, and he freezes just as I do.

While I stare at him in shock from nearly being run over by an angry six-foot-too-many-inches man, he glares back with a thunderous expression.

Slowly, he rakes his eyes over my half-naked form, then proceeds to curl his upper lip into a snarl. He looks... disgusted, and he might as well have shoved that shotgun into my chest and pulled the trigger.

My mouth parts, hurt and confused, when he resumes his path

toward the stairs.

"Get fucking dressed, Sawyer. That's not what I want to see."

My eyes bug, and I gasp in utter disbelief.

He did *not* just say that to me.

Before I can process how to respond, he's already gone.

That. Fucking. *Asshole!*

Overcome with my freshly bruised ego and fury that he would say something so shitty, I barely remember storming into Sylvester's room and ripping a shirt off a hanger in his closet. There's barely any left, most of them being used for our makeshift rope now.

But before I pull it on, I stop and stand in front of the full-length mirror in his room. It takes a second to realize I can't get a good look at myself because my vision is blurred from burning tears.

I rub at them, forcing them away, and then for what feels like the first time in years, I study my reflection, though I still avoid my eyes. Kev is the last thing I want to see right now.

My roots are starting to come back in again. I've lost a little more weight, but I don't look much different than I did before. What did he see that made him suddenly look at me like he got a whiff of spoiled milk?

Frowning, I finally meet my own stare. I have dark circles underlining my eyes, and I'm definitely wearing my exhaustion, but I can't look that bad.

Right?

Kev is there, shaking his head at me.

When did you get so fragile, pipsqueak? You're so easy to break.

The very thing Enzo had said to me before.

Whatever. Fuck him, fuck Kev, and fuck them both for making me question myself.

Just as I go to storm away, I notice something odd stacked on the floor next to the mirror.

It's a pile of clear plastic bags with a thin, long white hose coiled on top of them.

I blink. I've no idea what the hell their purpose is, but they are so out of place that I can only stare.

Finally, my body moves, pulling the shirt over my head and then approaching the stack of bags like a snake curled on top of them rather than a harmless tube.

There's nothing written on them to indicate what it could be for, but upon closer inspection, I realize they're are sewed shut save for a tiny hole, where I assume the tube is supposed to be inserted.

I flip through the rest to discover that every bag looks the same. They're definitely handmade, and the stitches are a little wonky, but they're all airtight save for the pocket left untouched for the tube.

I shake my head, confounded by what the hell they are, but decide they could be useful for emergencies. If we ever need to vacate the lighthouse, I can fill them with water and use them as makeshift canteens.

I grab the bags and hose and put them in our bedroom, under the bed.

I'm fully prepared to spend the rest of the night in here, but my stomach growls, and I can smell food cooking downstairs.

It wouldn't kill me if I skipped one meal in place of enduring Enzo's presence for even a second, but I realize that it's not very smart. My safety isn't guaranteed, and I will need all the energy I can get. Especially if being kept awake by a spirit throwing a very loud temper tantrum outside the door is going to become a common occurrence.

Sighing, I trudge down the steps, replaying Enzo's nasty words in my head on repeat.

That's not what I want to see.

Sure, we both had an extremely eventful, shitty night and are sleep-deprived, but how could he suddenly switch up on me? After he got down on his fucking knees and asked for my forgiveness for that very thing?

Even when he openly hated me, he never made me feel so... ugly. So undesirable.

If he were Kev, I would kill for him to look at me that way. To be treated like I'm no more desirable than enduring a vasectomy without anesthesia.

Anger renewed, I refuse to look at Enzo and take a seat at the dinner table, glaring at the wood like it's the culprit for the deep ache in my chest.

After a few moments, I see Enzo approach me from my peripheral, and my muscles return to survival mode, tensing as he nears.

"Eat," he orders sharply, nearly tossing the bowl of soup on the table. It slides and knocks against my chest, the burning liquid sloshing onto my skin.

I grimace from the sting and push it away from me, not sure I can eat anymore. My eyes gravitate toward my body, the insecurity rising and singeing my throat.

When I glance back up, he's staring at me with a stoic look on his face, the muscle in his jaw pulsating as he grinds his teeth.

"I'm not hungry," I whisper.

He drops his head, and a flush crawls up my throat when I hear him laugh, the sound lacking humor. Sick with embarrassment, I stand so quickly that the chair tips over. His head snaps up right as I turn to bolt. Tears are welling in my eyes again, and I'm so fucking tired of crying.

I only manage a step before he's lunging across the table and fisting my hair. In one powerful yank, I fly backward, landing painfully on the wooden table with a yelp.

I'm frozen with shock as I try to process what the hell just happened. The only thing I'm capable of is to stare at him with absolute astonishment, my eyes rounded and mouth parted. Even upside down, he looks terrifying.

"Tell me, *bella ladra*, am I so unforgettable that you've failed to remember how deeply my cock has filled you? Or did you hit your head and lose your fucking mind?"

I shake my head, speechless and unable to understand what the fuck that even means.

"Whatever you thought I meant, you're wrong," he says, understanding that his earlier words hurt me.

I blink. "You said—"

"I know what the fuck I said, Sawyer."

"Then why did you say it?" I snap, the anger finally re-emerging.

He leans down, the storm raging in his eyes fiercer than the one that got us in this stupid situation.

"Because it pisses me off that I want you as badly as I do," he growls, his voice deepened with a darkness only found in the depths of the sea.

His hand curls tighter into my hair, and sharp pinpricks pierce against my scalp. I cry out, my back arching and nails clawing at his arm in a desperate attempt to relieve the pain.

Ignoring my struggles, his eyes rake down my body, a volcano erupting in the ocean in his eyes. "I can't stand to look at you. Not because I don't like what I see, Sawyer. It's because I fucking hate how it makes me feel."

He drags me across the table and spins me around until I'm facing him, wringing a gasp from my throat as he forces me into an upright position. I'm reeling and disoriented, so I can only gape at him when he shoves himself between my knees.

I'm trying to make sense of what he's saying, but I'm hypnotized by the lightning in his hazel eyes and the severe expression on his face.

"I don't understand what happened today. You said you wouldn't be cruel anymore."

He reaches behind his back for something and then produces a thin, gold card.

A credit card.

The one I opened in his name. On cue, he flips it around, his full name in my face, nearly mocking me.

"I was taking the sheets off to wash this morning when I found this hiding under the mattress."

My mouth opens, but he's already talking, "You were *hiding* it from me. Why does it feel like another fucking lie, Sawyer?"

"I wasn't keeping it so I could use it, I promise," I swear vehemently. "It was in my back pocket when you brought me onto the boat, and somehow, it didn't slip out from the wreck. I hid it when we first got here, and I just... I haven't gotten rid of it yet."

As the last word leaves my mouth, I cringe, realizing how much that sounded like a weak excuse. He's going to think I'm lying, but for once, I'm telling the complete truth. I don't want to lie to him anymore. I want him to see all my ugly truths and accept me anyway.

"I should've just tossed it in the ocean. I don't know why I didn't," I admit. "But it was never with the intention to use it again."

He tosses the flimsy plastic onto the table next to me and then plants his fists on either side of my hips, getting in my face.

The fire alarm has been switched, and any oxygen I had stored in my lungs has evacuated.

"Why do I believe you?" he asks aloud, though I'm not sure he intended for me to answer.

"I don't *want* to believe you, Sawyer. Because the last time I did, you fucking hurt me."

My lip trembles, guilt and shame crashing through me so profoundly, that it feels as if it's rewriting my DNA. I can feel nothing—*be* nothing—past the damage I've done. Not just to Enzo but to so many innocent people.

"I'm sorry," I rasp, a single tear wiggling loose. He tracks the drop, watching it fall from my chin and onto my bare legs. My shirt has ridden up, and though I'm still wearing my bathing suit beneath, I've never felt barer.

Quickly, I wipe away the evidence from my face.

"You don't get to be the one that cries," he tells me. "You don't get to cry when you're the one who ruined me."

"You're right. I did this to you," I agree, blinking back more tears. I'm not crying for myself. I don't even feel bad for myself anymore.

What I've gone through—what I've done—it's no excuse for how I've chosen to survive. I've placed that on others' shoulders and made strangers responsible for keeping me safe.

I've always known this, but this is the first time I've had to face the destruction that I've caused. It's like a monster took over, and I've been lost to it as it decimated everything around me. And now, the anger has finally receded, and I'm left standing amongst the carnage, having no one to blame but myself.

"I am... *so* sorry," I choke out again, praying he can see the sincerity.

Enzo inspects my face closely, picking apart every micro expression and likely searching for deception.

"I know you are," he murmurs. "But I still don't want to forgive you."

I nod, understanding him, but still hating it anyway. Hating what I've done, but even more determined to never be that person again.

Which means that I need to tell him the complete truth about Kev.

"I understand," I acquiesce, then pause, searching for the right words for my confession. I've no idea how to say it, but before I can figure it out, he's shaking his head as if resigning himself to something.

"But I'm going to. I don't want to be angry with you anymore, Sawyer. I did swear that I wouldn't be cruel, but I realize now that for me to keep my promise, I'm going to have to fucking forgive you. And I'm going to have to trust you. If I'm going to give you everything you deserve, then I have to give you all of me."

He tips his chin down, the look on his face severe. "Can I do that, *bella*? Can I give you all of me?"

"Yes," I vow, the word practically tripping and tumbling out of my mouth. "I won't ever hurt you again. I swear, Enzo."

He's nodding, almost as if he's trying to come to terms with that. Then, he's dropping his head with a sigh for a second before lifting it back to me, something different radiating from the depths of his eyes.

"You're a goddamn siren, and I'm the fool who would gladly drown just to get a taste of you. Starve, for all I care, *bella*, but *I* will be eating tonight, and the only thing I'm hungry for is you."

Surprise muddles my thoughts. I blink at him, ready to ask him to repeat himself just to make sure I heard him right, but when I open my mouth, he's crashing his lips into mine.

He swallows the rest of my words with his tongue and teeth, rendering me silent as he devours my lips. Whether it's from shock or instinct, I open my mouth and allow him in, one hand finding purchase on the table while the other grasps the back of his neck.

My entire body lights up like a city coming out of a blackout, my nerves gridlocked with electrical currents as he claims my lips.

And with each swipe of his tongue, he erases all those ugly feelings built up inside me. He consumes me with such intensity, I don't know how I ever believed he stopped wanting me.

"*Fuck*," he mutters into my mouth before capturing my lips again. His hands grip either side of my face, sliding back into my hair and inhaling me deeper.

It feels like my heart is beating right out of my chest, aching to be free so it can run away with its lover.

I'm out of oxygen and forced to pull away, but he doesn't let me go.

"*Non ancora*," he rasps. "I need more of you."

Then, he's pulling me back in once more, and I forget why I ever wanted to breathe at all. His tongue sensually slides against mine, coercing it into a dance as if they're swaying to a ballad of star-crossed lovers.

Non ancora - *Not yet*

Electricity rolls down my spine, and with each kiss, I feel on the verge of combusting. We're the perfect storm, where he is the thunder, and I am the lightning.

He grabs my hips and roughly jerks me against him, his hard cock seated between my thighs. He swallows a moan, pleasure radiating from where he presses himself into me. Curling my legs around his waist, I roll my hips against his length, seeking more.

If I'm the siren, then he must be Poseidon, an angry god who commands my body like it's the ocean beneath his fingertips.

He thrusts against me so harshly, the table screeches, the legs grinding against the wooden floor. In a matter of seconds, we've become unhinged with need.

By the time he rips himself away, I'm blind with lust. He pushes me flat against the wood while his other hand tears at my bikini bottoms, the strings easily unraveling from the force.

In one movement, he lifts my hips, slings my legs over his shoulders, and crawls onto the table, my upper back sliding against the smooth surface. Another breath scarcely leaves my lips before his mouth descends onto my pussy, stealing the little oxygen I had left.

Once more, I grind against him, eyes rolling as his tongue spears inside me. With a growl, he flattens his tongue and licks up the entirety of my slit, and I lose myself as he licks and sucks, swirling his tongue against my clit before sucking it into his mouth.

"Enzo!" I cry, my hands diving through his hair, though it's still too short to properly grab onto. Instead, I scrape my nails across his scalp, and he growls in response, the vibrations only heightening the pleasure he's drawing out from beneath his tongue.

He feasts on me like a man stranded on an island, deprived of food, and I'm the only thing left to eat.

The orgasm creeps up slowly and then all at once, like the jungle cat pouncing on its prey after stalking it for so long.

Enzo drives two fingers into me and curls them deeply right as I come undone. I'm unable to prepare myself for it, and the bliss is crashing through me before I can take another breath.

Scarcely, I feel a scream tear from my throat, and my vision is consumed by bright starbursts of color and light. It feels like my soul is being ripped from my body, God's hand carrying me into Heaven.

But the ever-persistent devil is fighting for control over my fractured soul, bringing me crashing back to earth and in between his teeth.

It's only when my vision clears that I realize my thighs are soaked, Enzo's face even more so.

"How do you keep making me do that?" I pant. He's not the first man to go down on me and bring me to orgasm, but I feel like fucking Pavlov's dog, and somehow, he's managed to train my pussy to drool for him on command.

"You're a natural, baby. It's just that no one has hit the right buttons," he says, climbing off the table and dragging me with him to the edge.

I'm expecting him to remove his shorts and fuck me, but instead, he grabs my arms and jerks me upright again, a gasp falling from my tongue and feathering across his lips that are only inches from mine.

He flirts with the idea of kissing me, brushing his mouth across mine and making me desperate to taste myself on them. As if sensing that I'm preparing to tackle him, he steps away.

"Drop to your knees, *bella ladra*. I'll give you everything you've been praying for."

Swallowing, I shakily slide off the table and lower myself to the ground, holding his blazing stare while I do. The farther I descend, the hotter his eyes grow.

As if to test him, I tip my chin up.

"Then answer them," I say before opening my mouth, sticking out my tongue, and awaiting his next move.

A smile stretches across his face, revealing both dimples in all their glory.

It's breathtaking but equally terrifying. The smile is nothing short of sinister, but fuck, it's real.

He leans down, brushing the pad of his thumb over my tongue.

"Such a dirty little girl," he croons. "How do you taste so sweet?"

I'm incapable of answering, but he doesn't wait for one.

"Take them off," he orders. Reaching for his waistband, I slide his shorts down and free his cock. I'm not embarrassed by the way my mouth waters at the sight. He possesses something to be worshiped.

He hooks his thumb in my bottom teeth and brings me closer until my mouth is poised at the tip where a drop of pre-cum beads, just waiting to be licked clean.

I try to move forward, but his grip on my teeth keeps me immobile. Dragging my stare up to his, I wait, unable to talk or move.

"Your words have always just been words," he murmurs quietly. "But your silence is honest, and that's where I always find my answers. That's where I hear everything you don't say."

I want to look away, to hide, but I force myself to hold his stare.

"No more words, Sawyer," he commands. "I want you to show me."

Slowly, he drags his thumb out from my mouth, swiping my bottom lip roughly before releasing me completely.

He's testing me, and I'm desperate to give him what he's asking for.

Don't hide, Sawyer.

Don't run.

Just... stay.

So, I do. Without dropping my stare, I lean forward and slip my mouth over the tip of his cock. He hisses, and my eyes flutter from the salty flavor of him on my tongue, but I don't close them. I lick him slowly, intoxicated by his taste and how he feels.

I draw his length in deeper, wetting it so I can easily slide him down my throat. His mouth parts, and his brow furrows as he stares down at me with reverence. And it's now that I realize how much can be said in a single look—how long Enzo has been talking to me—and I've never stopped to listen. But he's been listening to me all along.

Emotion floods my chest, rising up my throat as I hollow my cheeks and swirl my tongue. I suck him harder, swallowing him completely, my lips kissing his pelvis. A shudder works its way through his body and curses spill from his mouth.

I've never had a gag reflex, but it still makes my eyes water from the lack of oxygen. After a few moments, I retreat, a long, slow drag that earns me a few more colorful words. And still, I keep my eyes up.

Can he hear me tell him that he is the first man I could pleasure without feeling sick? Can he hear that with him, inviting a man into my body feels like a choice and not a means to survive? Does he hear me thanking him for making me feel less broken?

He must, because he fists my curls and forces my head back, and yanks me up toward him to capture my lips in a savage kiss. When he pulls back, I reach for his cock again. I wasn't done—I want to keep pleasing him—but he evades me.

"I choose where to make you whole," he growls, helping me to my feet and pushing me back onto the table. He grips the underside of my knees and lifts them until my feet are planted on the edge of the table.

His cock slides along my slit, and I buck my hips uncontrollably, my arms curling around his neck and molding my front into his. My entire body is trembling, and I need him close for reasons I can only say through my silence. I need to feel him.

His hips pull back enough for him to line up with my entrance, and then he pushes in slowly while capturing my bottom lip between his teeth.

I'm shaking, and the urge to cry is burning the back of my throat. My silence is screaming at him now, begging him to see me for who I am and not for what I've done.

His kiss deepens as he buries himself fully inside me, capturing my cry with his tongue. One hand glides through my hair and grips the back of my neck while his other arm circles around my waist, bringing me impossibly closer.

My chin trembles as he begins to slowly pump inside me, long drags out and quick thrusts in. It's driving me wild, and I'm clawing at him to come closer, though it's impossible for him to get any deeper.

It's only when we're out of breath that he releases my lips, resting his forehead against my own as we breathe each other in, trading quiet moans and sharp intakes of breath, as if anything louder will shatter whatever this is.

"Show me, *bella*," he rasps. "Show me where you hurt so I know where to love you most."

Tears well in my eyes, but I force them back, not wanting anything to cloud my vision of him. My brows are pinched as I swallow them down, but I let him watch me fight to stay.

I let him see that he's worth staying for.

"*Mostrami come amarti*," he voices, so deep and alluring that it sends chills down my spine. I don't know what it means, but it sounds beautiful and heartbreaking.

His pace grows rougher, quicker, and his stare blazes brighter. Sweat coats our bodies, and each brush of skin is like kindling in a fire, bringing us closer to combustion.

The bowl of soup crashes to the ground, and one side of the table slips off the carpet, the legs screeching against the wood with each thrust, making it harder and harder to keep quiet.

He feels too good, and his cock is hitting a place inside me that has my eyes rolling. My head drops back, a sob bursting from my throat. I can feel my heart falling victim, and there's nothing I can do to stop it.

Mostrami come amarti - *Show me how to love you*

His teeth scrape against my neck a moment before he bites down on the flesh below my ear. I shudder as he sucks, heightening the euphoria.

I'm so close to shattering. And I'm scared for him to see those jagged pieces and decide they're not worth bleeding for.

"Enzo," I cry, the sound a coalescence of pain and pleasure.

"That's it," he breathes, nipping at my throat again. "That's how I want you to use my name."

He drops his hand from my nape and slides it between our bodies. It takes only a few strokes of his finger over my clit to ignite the fuse.

I detonate, my legs whipping around his hips and squeezing him so tightly, he can barely retreat an inch.

A growl rumbles through his chest, but I can't feel a thing past the string of explosions letting off inside me.

Distantly, I feel him lift me up as he crawls onto the table again, allowing him the angle he needs to continue driving into me.

I cling to him, but he's grabbing my wrists and forcing them above my head. My back arches as wave after wave continues to roll through me.

I can't take any more, but he doesn't relent, strumming my clit until the wave rolls back, just for another orgasm to crash into me.

There's a scream piercing the air, but it's swallowed by Enzo's lips. He moves his hand out from between us and grabs ahold of my hip. And then he's stilling, a savage growl reverberating throughout my throat as he reaches his own decimation.

His grip on my wrists and hip turn bruising, but I hardly notice as he mindlessly slams into me, spilling inside me as he does.

I'm not sure how much time passes before we both go boneless. He manages to catch his weight before he crushes me, but I don't think I'd even mind. I already feel like my soul is only holding on to its vessel purely out of pity.

Just as he goes to sit up, there's a loud groan, followed by a *crack*, and then I'm suddenly weightless.

This time when I scream, it's from fright as the table completely collapses beneath us. It happens too fast for either of us to properly react. The landing knocks the breath from my lungs, while Enzo spits out a curse.

We just stare at each other, wide-eyed and in shock. And then a choked laugh escapes me.

We broke the fucking table. Like... Humpty Dumpty bad. There's no putting it back together.

Enzo's chin drops, and he lets out a slow breath. I'm full-out cackling now, and his shoulders are shaking with mirth. When he lifts his head, the most beautiful smile is spread across his face, and it feels like my heart skids and crashes as hard as this table just did. It lights up his entire face, and his hazel eyes gleam as he stares at me with affection.

"Why did you kiss me?" I wonder aloud, enraptured by how fucking radiant he is when he's happy.

His smile drops, but the intensity in his stare only brightens. He hovers over me, planting his hands on either side of my head and caging me in.

This... this is the only cage I want to be in.

"There's a place in the ocean, so deep, where not a single point of light penetrates through it. And for so long, I've been trapped there, unable to breathe. When I met you, you lifted me out of that darkness, and it was the first time I came up for air. You've become my oxygen, *bella ladra,* and I can no longer breathe without you."

My heart bursts from my chest, and now it feels like *I* can't breathe. I've never wanted someone to love me, but I do now. God, do I want him to love me.

"Beautiful thief," I murmur, recalling what his nickname means. "That's not who I am anymore."

He studies me closely, that affection still present as he leans closer, brushing his nose against mine while a grin pulls his lips up once more.

"You are a thief, baby. You stole my name, and now you've taken my heart, too. Demand anything else from me, and I'll give it to you."

"I don't dese—"

He grabs me by the jowls, roughly pinching my cheeks into my teeth. "Being loved by me will hurt like hell. It's everything you deserve."

Then, he declares passionately, "I love you, and you will love me."

I'm convinced I'm dying, yet it's the happiest I've ever been.

"I do. I do love you," I respond, almost on autopilot. Of course, it comes out jumbled and feels funny, considering my cheeks are still crushed between his fingers, and I have fish lips.

But it's worth it because it pulls another full-forced smile on his face as he releases me. And again, my chest is caving in, and I've forgotten how to breathe.

For whatever reason, he's ready to forgive me. But I haven't earned that yet. Not until he knows everything.

The happiness slips from my face, and when he notices my change in demeanor, his does, too.

"What's wrong, *bella?*"

"I killed him," I whisper.

Enzo jerks back in shock. "What?"

I bite my lip, gathering the little courage I possess.

"I killed Kevin," I say again.

His mouth parts, and it takes him a few beats to catch on to what I'm saying. "You said he was after you."

I shake my head, tears once more burning the backs of my eyes. "The police are after me—his friends. Not because I steal identities or because Kev is trying to find me, but because I killed a cop. I murdered my twin brother."

CHAPTER 30

Sawyer

SIX YEARS AGO

I jump the moment I hear the front door slam. He likes to joke and call out, 'Honey, I'm home!' But today, there's only silence.

It's unnerving, and I'm instantly on high alert. There's a gas leak in my muscles, tension slowly filling them with poison. My stomach churns as footsteps start on the steps, traveling closer and closer.

"Sawyer?" Kevin calls. In a span of seconds, I dissect each syllable and inflection in his tone, searching for a hint of what mood he's in.

"In here," I call, attempting to sound pleasant.

It's summer break from my college classes, and the only thing keeping me away from home—from him—is my job at the library.

But of course, today is my day off, and I'm now considering calling Mrs. Julie and asking to pick up a shift.

I'm sitting on my bed, sifting through a thriller novel. I don't even know *what it's about anymore; I lost track fifty pages ago and I'm on page fifty-four.*

Kev creaks open the door, walking in without waiting for permission. Not that he's ever asked.

He's still in uniform, sans the belt with his gun and Taser. The sight sickens me. He parades as a savior—a protector—but the only thing that uniform represents is my inability to stop him from hurting me.

The energy in the room instantly shifts, plummeting quicker than when a roller coaster crests the top of the hill.

Adrenaline is let off in my bloodstream like a bomb. Sweat forms along my hairline, and my body begins to tremble.

"What are you reading?" he questions, snatching the book from my hands before I can answer. For once, I'm glad for his disrespect because I don't think I could've given him an answer.

He glances at me and tosses the book on the bed, and I watch it fall shut.

Page fifty-four. Don't forget.

"You've been reading all day? Couldn't even clean up the house?" he asks, though it sounds more like an interrogation.

"I did clean," I defend lightly, latching my fingers together to hide my tremors.

"And dinner? Looks to me like you're just sitting on your ass all day while I support us."

"I have my own money, Kev," I grumble. Not much of it, but I do everything I can to pay my own way. Even when I have school, I work part-time to help with bills.

Funny enough, our parents' life insurance was more than enough to pay off the house and car, yet Kev acts like he's scraping pennies to get by. Shouldn't be when he stole my half of the money.

I think he just blows it all on strippers when he's not tormenting me.

"That money should be mine as long as you're living in my house."

"Our house," I correct, keeping my eyes downcast, my heart rate increasing. "We're twins. And I'm three minutes older anyway."

I spare him a glance, noting the fury that flashes across his eyes—a rage so deep, it's something he could only be born with. I was being crafted in my mother's stomach alongside a monster. It's in his very DNA. Sometimes, it scares me that it's in mine, too.

My brother nods more to himself, as if agreeing with his inner demon on something. Can only imagine what about. And that's the saddest part—I can imagine. I've lived every scenario.

"You wear that just for me, pipsqueak?" he questions, pointing to my body. I don't know why I look at what I'm wearing as if I don't already know.

A black baggy t-shirt, loose jeans, and my Maruchan ramen socks.

I spent forty-five minutes carefully choosing these clothes. Just as I do every day. Anything that could be considered suggestive results in unwanted touches, but most times, just existing has the same outcome.

I grab for my book, avoiding eye contact. "I didn't wear them for anyone."

"That's because there's no one else to give you attention, is there?"

Thanks to you.

"That's what you want?" he continues. "Attention?"

"No—"

Kev crawls onto the bed, effectively freezing the words in my throat. My body is as unbendable as a diamond as he crowds over me, a sinister smile on his face.

Disgust and nausea rise in my throat, and a coldness spreads throughout every inch of my being.

He can't do this to me again. He's already invaded my body so profoundly, I have nothing left to give. What else could he possibly want?

A hand brushes across my cheek, but my soul has been transported outside my body. I'm watching from above as he forces me back on the bed.

But I don't bend. I can only stare back with icy rage.

"Lay back, Sawyer. You know fighting doesn't work," he growls.

Tears flood my eyes, and I wonder how he can look in them and not see himself. How can he not when we're both so dead inside?

"Get off of me, you disgusting pig," I hiss, the vibrations throughout my form are heightening until it seems as if an earthquake is devastating it. My brother rears back in shock. *"If you touch me again, I will fucking kill you, Kevin."*

His upper lip pulls over his teeth viciously, and his hands wrap around my throat, squeezing until my oxygen is completely severed.

I'm both staring into his blackened eyes and watching him strangle me from above. I thrash against his hold, my eyes bugged and my complexion purpling.

His own face is red, putting all his strength into crushing my neck between his palms.

My hand pats the bed sightlessly, searching while my life quickly depletes.

I knew it was coming to this. Felt it in my very bones. My mind has been on the precipice of snapping, and with each encounter, he's only pushed me further to the edge.

I started hiding knives around the house, my subconscious understanding how deeply I was unraveling without ever fully acknowledging it.

Finally, my hand closes around the weapon hiding under my pillow, right as my vision begins to snuff out.

Without any direction, I drive the knife into him, feeling rather than seeing it sink into flesh and sinew.

Simultaneously, the constriction around my throat releases while something warm and wet splatters across my face.

My lungs fill with oxygen, the relief almost painfully relieving. But I have no time to appreciate it when a waterfall of red is pouring onto me while Kev convulses above me.

The tip of the knife is plunged deep into the side of his jugular, blood pouring both from the wound and his mouth. His eyes are bulging, and every tooth is bared.

I think I'm sobbing, but my mind is so fractured, I've no idea what my body is doing or feeling.

He's staring directly into my eyes, and I can see the betrayal radiating from *them. You can only betray someone if they trusted you.*

He should've never trusted me.

He slumps, and I have just enough foresight to push him off to the side, his body flopping next to me.

I'm heaving, this time the panic seizing my lungs. My upper half is covered in warm blood, but it feels like thick tar. I need it off me.

Eyes wide, I stumble off the bed, refusing to look back at what I've done, yet feeling the evidence soaking into my pores. I tear off my shirt and wipe myself down as best I can, hands shaking so badly, they're beginning to go numb.

Out of the corner of my eye, I glimpse his still body on my bed, a pool of red growing amongst the sheets.

"Shit, shit, shit," I mutter frantically, practically ripping a new one off a hanger in my closet. I grapple with the fabric, struggling to find the right end to open and shove over my head.

My mind is racing, yet I don't have a single coherent thought. I'm moving on pure instinct alone, and all I know is that I need to run.

Run, Sawyer. Don't look back.

Speeding out of my bedroom and down the steps, I practically trip over my feet in my pursuit to escape. I swivel around, frantically searching for my shoes, whimpering in distress when I can't find them.

Fuck it. There's no time.

I need to run while I still can.

Because once I start, I'll never be able to stop.

CHAPTER 31

Enzo

She's staring at me, waiting for a response, but I'm too stunned to speak. The only thing I can think is *how the fuck am I going to save her?*

Her blue eyes drop, and there she goes, hiding away.

"Look at me," I snap.

She does, her eyes shooting to mine. They're welling with tears, and I know she's expecting me to get angry.

In a way, I *am* angry.

"How long ago?"

"Six years," she whispers. "We were twenty-two. He was fresh out of the academy, but they all loved him instantly. They were devastated when they found out he died." She shrugs awkwardly. "Some of his cop friends were on the news a lot, crying and promising they wouldn't rest until they found me. I always hoped they'd move on somehow, but one of his old friends still emails me every so often."

Blowing out a slow breath, I stand and grab her hands, helping her to her feet. She looks so unsure of herself, and I want to bring her comfort, but I don't have the right words yet.

How do I tell her that I'm only angry because I wanted to see the life drain from his eyes, too? How do I say that I would've loved to see her end his miserable life and then probably fuck her for it after?

Carefully, we make our way off the broken table, ensuring she avoids sharp pieces of glass or wooden splinters. Then, I grab our clothing and help her get dressed, needing to give my hands something to do while I think. When we're done, I grab the shotgun and lead her upstairs to our bedroom.

"Enzo?" she prompts, timid and uncertain.

I run my hand down my face, my mind racing.

"Where did this happen?"

"Nevada in the States."

I sigh. "Australia would turn you into U.S. authorities," he says. "But other countries wouldn't."

She nods slowly. "I was never going to stay in Australia, Enzo. I've been hiding out in different states over the past six years. I finally built up the nerve to use one of the identities to get a passport and leave the U.S., so I got a flight to Indonesia. But someone I knew saw that I was at the airport waiting for a flight, and they were going to out me, so I had to make a split-second decision and change flights. I went with the first one available and ended up in Australia. I've been staying low for now, but I was always going to leave."

I was always going to leave.

And now I don't know if I can let her.

"Look, I know what I did was wrong, but—"

She stops short when my head snaps to hers. Whatever she sees in my expression has her teeth clicking shut.

In the blink of an eye, her face is cradled in my palms, and she stares at me like she isn't sure if she should be scared or not.

"Do you know how envious I am? I only wish I had been there to reward you after. And then, I would've made sure you were never caught for it."

Sawyer shakes her head, confounded. "How are you not upset? I murdered someone. In cold blood."

"Baby, I'm only sorry you spent the last six years regretting it when you could've been rejoicing in it."

I focus on her pink lips. I'm also sorry I waited so long to taste those.

When I drag my focus back on her baby blues, she's just staring at me, puzzled.

"Did you kill me back on that table? Did one of the legs impale me or something? This can't be real."

I grin, and her eyes widen. "Oh my God. I *did* die."

"Do you want me to be angry?"

"No?" she says, but it sounds more like a question. "I guess a normal person's reaction would be shock, a lot of judgment, and then maybe dial 911 on the low-low."

"It's not 911 out here, it's 000. And we've been over this. We can't call them."

She rolls her eyes, stepping out of my hold.

"I just wasn't expecting you to be happy," she admits.

I inspect her closely. There's a hint of relief in her eyes, but she still looks unsure.

"I'm happy he's dead, but that doesn't mean I'm happy about our situation," I correct. "You're in a lot of trouble, and it's going to be difficult to get you out."

Her brow pinches. "Enzo, I don't expect you to save me."

"That's because no one has ever found you worth saving." Her mouth drops, offended, and I take the opportunity to hook her bottom teeth with two fingers and tug her into me. She nearly falls against my chest. "They were wrong, baby. You are worth it."

She digs her little teeth into my digits, and I grin, releasing her.

"I'm capable of saving myself," she tells me, fire in her eyes.

"You are," I agree, brushing my thumb across her cheek affectionately. "You've already proven that when you ended your abuser's life. But you're not alone anymore. Now you have someone to serve you while you seek justice."

She blinks. "This didn't go how I thought it would," she confesses in a hushed tone. She looks scared again; this time, I know it's because she doesn't want to get her hopes up.

Giving in, I softly kiss her lips. "We've known nothing but heartbreak. Maybe we can show each other something different this time, yeah?"

Her lips curl upward, just the slightest bit, then she nods and whispers, "Yeah."

"And we're going to figure this out together. First, we just need to get the fuck off this island."

Again, she nods, her blue eyes shinier than usual.

Satisfied, I release her and head toward the bathroom for a shower when I hear someone moving around downstairs.

Not just their footsteps, but the sound of chains dragging.

"What's that sound?" she whispers.

"Someone is in here. We're not alone anymore."

"Enzo," Sawyer hedges hesitantly. "Don't go down there."

"It's just a ghost, right?" I ask over my shoulder. "It can't hurt me."

She huffs with frustration, quietly slinking up to my side. "And we've been over *this*. If they can hit a solid object, they can hit you—another solid object. I mean, really, Enzo. You need to watch more movies."

"They're fake," I argue.

"But some of them are based on real stories!" she whisper-yells.

"They're grossly exaggerated."

Her little fists are balled, and she's scowling at me. It's pretty cute, but the person—thing—whatever it is, moves something, and it's loud enough to draw my attention away.

"Stay up here," I murmur, ignoring her little mewl of disappointment while I grab the shotgun. Staying light on my feet, I head toward the staircase.

Of course, Sawyer doesn't stay, falling in step behind me. She plasters herself to my back, nearly tripping me as we make our way down, the gun poised in my hands.

I'm tense, and when the bottom floor comes into view, I quickly sweep my gaze across every inch.

There's no one here.

I pause at the bottom step, sensing the stagnant energy in the room.

"Oh, man, this is fucked," Sawyer whines quietly, shifting on her feet and causing the metal beneath us to groan. "Can we go upst—"

"Baby. Shut the fuck up."

"Rude," she mutters, but otherwise, doesn't have any further unnecessary commentary.

Refusing to believe that something can just vanish like that, I scout every inch of the kitchen and living room area. The rug and broken table are over the top of the cellar, so there aren't very many places to hide, and within minutes, I'm forced to accept the fact that whatever was down here, isn't anymore. At least not anywhere I can see.

I'm standing in the living room, glaring at the cold, dead fireplace, when Sawyer creeps in.

She looks around nervously, still on edge that the thing is going to come back.

Good chance it will, and I fucking hope it does. I'd love to see for myself if there really is an invisible spirit walking around, wreaking havoc on the place and our sanity.

"Uhh. You see that?" Sawyer asks, her spine straightening and all hesitance bleeding out in a matter of seconds. I follow her gaze, landing on the two bookshelves up against the wall opposite the couch.

One of them looks shifted. Not to the side, but at an angle.

As if it were a door.

Beelining toward them, I quickly order, "Grab the flashlights in the kitchen."

She hurries off to get them, rejoining my side just as I start to tug at the crooked bookshelf. With little effort, it creaks open, sounding very similar to the noise we heard before we came down here.

Sawyer's gasp is the only thing that can be heard now as we stare into a black abyss. The bookshelf *is* a fucking door, and behind it is a spiraling stone staircase.

"The beacon," she whispers behind me, clicking on the flashlight and moving ahead of me.

"Sawyer, get behind me. You were scared not two seconds ago."

She cuts a glare over her shoulder.

"I'm too excited now. So, *you* get behind *me*. Being a man doesn't make you special. Last time I checked, I'm the murderer, not you."

I raise my brows. "I'll be happy to make it even, *bella*."

She rolls her eyes, muttering *"Men"* derisively as she forges ahead. The corner of my lip curls, and I snatch the extra flashlight from her grip that she forgot to hand over, letting her go ahead.

She's right. She doesn't need me to save her, but that doesn't mean I won't protect her, and it sure as fuck doesn't stop me from aiming the gun over her shoulder in case Sylvester pops out.

We both keep our steps light as we make our way up, spinning around the structure for what feels like forever. When she reaches the top, she pauses for a split second before she squeals with excitement.

"It's the beacon!" she exclaims, though conscious enough to keep it quiet.

I step up into a small spherical area. It's nearly all glass, with a door leading out to a railing that circles around the room. I catch sight of a metal ladder that must lead to the actual light above.

A wide grin spreads across Sawyer's face, and she looks back at me with delight.

A control panel spans across half of the room. And on the far left side of it is a radio.

My first reaction is fury. It's confirmation that Sylvester has been lying to us all along. Keeping us here purposely, imprisoning us.

And though he never said it aloud, I know without a shadow of a doubt that he did it because he's a lonely, fucked-up man and wanted to keep Sawyer here.

"We can get out of here," she breathes, her blue eyes alight with hope and excitement. Even in the dark, it shines brighter than the sleeping beacon.

She rushes to the panel, and just as I take a step toward her, there's a slight shuffling sound from above. I freeze, listening intently while Sawyer presses buttons and tinkers with the radio. Lost in her eagerness, she hadn't heard the noise.

"I think it works!" she squeals, and the low buzz of the radio follows shortly after.

However, I'm too focused on the growing disturbance from above.

"Sawyer," I whisper sharply. She turns to me, her brows pinched with concern. Her mouth opens, readying to say something, but then there's a slow drag across the ceiling.

Chains.

My heart rate kicks up as the drag goes in a circle, as if it's walking around the light.

Whatever was downstairs is now up there, maybe deliberately leaving the bookshelf door open for us to find. Too focused on finally finding the beacon, I hadn't even considered that the... *thing* came up here first.

"Come here, *bella*," I say, holding out my hand for her to grab. The moment it slips into mine, I tug her behind me and reposition the gun.

The chains stop for a brief moment before appearing on the side of the glass where the ladder is. Adrenaline bleeds into my system as a pale, feminine foot appears, and then the other.

Two thick metal bands are clasped around each ankle, a long chain dangling between them.

"Enzo," Sawyer hedges. "Should we shoot it?"

"Thought we couldn't fight ghosts?" I remind her. Though, as it slowly makes its way down the ladder, it's apparent that it's a girl. She's incredibly thin, with a long white dress billowing around her. She reaches the bottom, but her head is tipped down, long tresses of blonde hair covering her face.

"Oh my God. That must be the girl we saw in the ocean," Sawyer breathes.

"This... doesn't make sense," I murmur, thoughts racing while I try to piece together Sylvester's lies.

He had said that the chains were from prisoners he killed years ago, their spirits haunting the lighthouse. He had also said his daughter had killed herself, but if this is her spirit... why is she wearing chains?

My heart drops, and I feel my features slacken.

"Sawyer," I start, watching the girl slowly make her way toward the door, the ring of metal dragging along loudly.

Her head lifts, almost as if hearing me, and my entire being freezes. I barely hear Sawyer's gasp from behind me, both enraptured and disturbed.

She has no mouth. Or rather, where her mouth used to be is a line of thick, black stitches.

"Sawyer," I start again, backing the both of us away as the girl comes closer, her hair blowing almost violently in the wind. "That's not a ghost. She's real."

We watch her round behind us, her eyes straight ahead, and the thick strings in her mouth visible and grotesque.

"What?" Sawyer screeches. "What do you mean she's real? Is that better or worse?"

"I think he lied about the prisoners, which is why we couldn't find a report about it. Sylvester said he had two daughters here, remember? He claimed Trinity hung herself outside our window while Raven and Kacey left. Either she never did, or Kacey never left."

I feel her tremble as she asks, "So, you're saying there aren't any ghosts here? It was just her all along?"

"I think so," I mumble as the blonde girl reaches the door. "That's probably how Sylvester got free from the cellar. She let him out."

"Fuck," Sawyer whispers.

The wind howls as she opens it, tipping her head down again, hiding herself once more. I keep the gun aimed at her, feeling Sawyer move out from behind me as the girl steps inside and closes the door behind her.

For a moment, none of us move or hardly even breathe. And then, she's lifting her chin, and the brutality of what was done to her is glaring. It's enough to curdle my stomach.

The white dress she's wearing is more of a yellow, and there's a rotting stench emanating from her.

But her face... it's so much worse than I initially thought. Thick ropes of black thread loosen across her mouth and up to her cheeks. It appears as if the wound is rotting, the flesh around it blackened and decayed.

She stares at us with pale blue eyes, watery and wide. It takes another moment to realize that she's shaking like a leaf.

Sawyer steps in front of me, and my hand instinctively flies to her wrist. She pauses and looks back at me, mouthing, "It's okay."

I let her go, but I step behind her, refusing to lower my weapon. I've no idea what the girl's motive is. She could be seeking help, or she could have ill intentions.

"My name is Sawyer. Are you one of Sylvester's daughters?"

The girl stares at her for a few beats. It's unnerving, but Sawyer just meets her stare, waiting patiently for an answer. Finally, the girl nods, and it feels like a punch to the chest.

"Is your name Trinity?" I ask quietly.

The girl's eyes snap to mine, and there's still a dark, ominous feeling slithering through my veins. I can't tell if it's because of her or what she represents.

She shakes her head no, so I ask, "Kacey?"

Another pause, and then she's nodding her head again.

Christ.

That means it's entirely possible Trinity did hang herself, and maybe lost in grief or madness, Sylvester never let Kacey leave. So desperate to keep her here that he chained her and kept her locked up. Even sewed her mouth shut, assumingly, so she couldn't make a sound when visitors came by.

Where does she sleep? She's been trapped somewhere the entire time we've been here. It explains why Sylvester locked us in the room and why we hear her in the hallways only at night, when Sylvester must let her roam free. She's been banging on the floor and even at our door, trying to get our attention all along.

Sawyer's hand slides over her mouth, and I know she's realizing these things as I am.

"We're going to get off this island. Do you... want to come with us?" Sawyer asks slowly.

Kacey takes a step toward Sawyer in earnest, and I can't help but grab Sawyer's arm and pull her back into my chest before putting my finger back on the trigger. She pauses, sliding her eyes to mine. I can't read the emotion in them, but there's no question that she's studying me as intently as I'm studying her.

"It's okay," Sawyer assures, drawing my attention to her as she peers over her shoulder at me with a soft smile.

Is it?

Nothing about this situation is okay.

Training my stare on Kacey again, I nod toward the radio on the control panel and tell her, "We need to use that radio to call for help."

Kacey nods, and she steps to the side and away, indicating she's not going to stop us.

"Go ahead, baby," I urge Sawyer. She rushes to the radio and starts messing with the channels, intermittently saying *hello* through the speaker, attempting to get a response. I stand right behind her, ensuring her safety.

Only then do I lower the gun. As much as I want to believe Kacey wouldn't attack us, there's no doubt her mental state is in tatters, and I can't determine where exactly her head is at with us. Sylvester is all she knows—it's entirely possible she will be loyal to him over us, despite what he's done to her.

I keep an eye on her while she studies Sawyer.

"Do you know where Sylvester went?" I ask her while we wait. She cuts her stare to me, and it's almost unnerving how quickly she shifts her eyes.

She shakes her head, glancing at Sawyer again as she continues to fiddle.

"Is there anyone else being kept here?"

Another no.

"Does a ship come here once a month?" I ask, forging ahead.

Kacey nods. He was smart enough not to lie about that. Not with the amount of food and supplies he has, and he doesn't have the space to store a massive stock that will last him years on end.

"Did your mother ever get off the island?" I question bluntly. There's no good way to ask, but I'm curious as to what really happened to Raven, though I have a pretty good fucking guess.

Her gaze drops for a second, the question seeming to sadden her, but she refocuses on me and shakes her head. No.

"He killed her," I conclude, more as a statement than a question.

She nods.

Christ. *Sapevo che lo stronzo stava mentendo.* But I never imagined the truth to be so fucked. The confirmation does little to calm the black fury rising in my chest.

Sapevo che lo stronzo stava mentendo - *I knew the asshole had been lying*

"I'm sorry you went through that. But you won't have to stay here with him anymore now, and we will be happy to help you any way you need."

Though Kacey is unable to speak, her eyes soften.

"Hello? Anyone there? Hello? Three people are being kept hostage on Raven Isle. Please, we need help," Sawyer calls into the radio.

But the buzz of static is her only response. She keeps repeating the same mantra into the radio while Kacey continues to stare.

It goes on like this for a solid minute until there's a loud crack from downstairs. It scares the shit out of Sawyer, a yelp bursting from her throat. Kacey's attention whips to the staircase, her eyes wide with terror.

Then, she drags them to mine, and I know exactly what she's saying without having to hear a sound.

He's back.

CHAPTER 32

Sawyer

My heart is pounding so hard, I'm positive I could lead a boat straight to us.

Enzo looks indecisive, staring at Kacey, then down the stairs. I know what he's battling with—leave me up here with her alone or let me come with him.

"Don't go down there."

He growls with frustration but ultimately looks to me.

"I need you both to stay up here," Enzo says, gripping his shotgun tightly. I'm shaking my head before he can finish.

"No, no, just stay up here until I get ahold of somebody," I plead desperately. The thought of him going down there and possibly getting hurt is enough to make my stomach twist with nausea.

"Baby, this is a tiny space, and it could easily turn into a shoot-out. I won't risk your life. I won't fucking lose you," he argues vehemently, keeping his voice quiet.

"Enz—"

He stalks toward me, halting the protests on my tongue by hooking his fingers in my teeth and bringing me toward him. Then, he switches his hold to the back of my neck, holding me hostage as he captures my lips between his.

It's soul-crushing, the way he kisses me. It feels like love, but even that seems so colorless when my entire being feels vibrant beneath his touch.

My bottom lip trembles and he catches it between his teeth before releasing it with a soft pop, stepping away as he does. My hands are curling into his t-shirt, clinging to him with fright. For so long, I've only ever felt that for myself, and this... this feels so much worse. Whoever created the word *goodbye* never knew loss. There's nothing good about the way he leaves me.

"I've faced predators far more powerful than he will ever be. And now he will face me," he assures me, his voice dropping low, sending shivers down my spine.

I try to nod, but it's choppy.

He absently brushes his thumb over my bottom lip. "I love you," he murmurs, which makes me angry because that sounds more like an omen than a profession of love.

"I love you, too, but can you not say that right now? It's concerning."

That dimple flashes while he removes himself from my desperate grip. "You can take care of yourself?"

I nod. "Yes. I'll be okay."

Appearing unconvinced, he looks at Kacey with a severe frown, as if the dimple never existed.

"I'm going to trust you," he tells her, though it sounds more like a threat. She nods, taking a step back again to assure him she won't come near.

He's still conflicted; however, he gives me one more glance before heading down the stairs.

I'm sick with worry, but I will not stand here and do nothing while he risks his life.

I turn back to the radio, flipping to another station and repeating my call for help, ensuring to keep my voice quiet but clear.

Kacey moves behind me, and an alarm blares in my head the moment she is out of my peripheral vision. I shift toward her, watching her slowly drift toward the steps.

"Stay up here," I tell her. I don't want her to follow Enzo. Something tells me that if she came up behind him unexpectedly, it could be lethal.

There's something off about her. *Obviously,* there's something off about her. She's been trapped in this place for her entire life. Her mouth is fucking sewn shut.

How does she even eat?

Then, it dawns on me. Those handmade plastic sacks with the white tubing in Sylvester's bedroom suddenly make sense. They were feeding bags, which means he must've cut a hole somewhere in her stomach in order to get the nutrients inside her. It also explains why there are so many Ensure bottles in the cabinets.

My stomach twists further, coiling into a tight rope. I feel sick at the thought. I can't even begin to imagine what torture this poor girl has endured.

Kacey twists toward me, and it's still shocking every time I see her mutilated mouth. There's no getting used to the sight of that. It comes straight out of a horror movie and cements the feeling that somehow, I've managed to stumble my way into one.

Guess I can't even be angry. The universe is definitely getting its karma right now, and well, I can't really fucking blame it.

She can't speak, and it doesn't appear that she has any other method to communicate, so after a few uncomfortable seconds, she turns away and just stands at the top of the steps, staring down into the black abyss.

My discomfort grows, alongside my growing worry over Enzo and concern that no one has answered my call yet.

But as the minutes tick by, a new emotion swirls into the already too potent cocktail in my bloodstream. Dread.

Something is wrong, and I feel more and more useless chattering into a radio and getting no response, while Enzo is possibly in danger.

"Maybe we should—" I'm cut off as a loud bang disturbs the otherwise silence. I gasp, dropping the radio speaker and staring down at the stairs with wide eyes. Moments later, a second shot goes off, racketing my heart farther up my throat.

Was that Enzo or Sylvester? There's no telling who's persevering.

"Okay, now we need to go check," I say, my voice uneven and tight.

Kacey slowly turns to me. The energy has shifted, and I'm no longer confident she's on our side.

My lips feel bone dry, and my tongue sticks to the roof of my mouth as she steps toward me.

"Don't do that," I warn her, and she pauses. "I have no intention of hurting you, but I will if you fuck with me."

She cocks her head, and for all I know, she might not even know what that means. There's no doubt she's been extremely sheltered. But rather than confusion, the act almost seems... condescending, like placating a child that is whining because they can't eat cookies before dinner.

Bitch.

She takes another step toward me, and I straighten my spine.

Fuck her for trying to intimidate me. I've fought my entire life just to survive. I'm not going to stop now.

She seems to still, and before I can figure out what her intentions actually are, there's a loud boom, followed by a muffled shout that sounds like *Kacey.*

Her head snaps to the staircase, and then after a few moments, she slowly faces me again. My heart is in my throat, pounding viciously, and my brain can't decide where to focus its attention—on the commotion coming from below and the danger Enzo is likely in, or the girl with a rotted mouth rushing toward me.

I have just enough time to duck out of her way, sending her crashing into the control panel, and race toward the steps.

Fuck this.

I'm not staying up here fighting with a half-dead girl that's clearly not as docile as she seemed to be.

I'm plunged into darkness within seconds of practically tripping down the stairs. I can't hear the chains on her feet chasing after me, but my terror has convinced me of it anyway, and I'm not stopping to verify.

As I get closer to the bottom, my heart rate grows faster. There isn't any noise from beyond the doorway anymore. And I find that far more unsettling than if there were a loud ruckus. At least then, I know Enzo is still alive.

Without hesitation, the moment my foot reaches the bottom, I'm barreling through the door and into the living room.

Sylvester is sitting on the couch with a shotgun in his lap, wooden leg propped up on the coffee table.

I skid to a stop, terror nearly sending me into an early grave. Immediately, I'm whipping my head toward the kitchen, frantically searching the area for Enzo.

He's not here. *Where the fuck did he go?*

"Lookin' for somethin'?" Sylvester drawls lazily.

Heart in my throat, I train my gaze on Sylvester, chest pumping as I try to figure out what the fuck happened in the two minutes we were apart.

"What did you do?" I choke out.

Sylvester's hand rises to his beard and strokes it with mocking contemplation.

"What do you mean?" he questions. "I am simply sitting on *my* couch, in *my* home, and drinking a nice cold beer."

Said beer is sitting on the end table, though the cap is firmly on.

"Where is Enzo?" I push, ignoring his condescension.

Sylvester sighs, as if this whole situation is a huge miscommunication and an inconvenience. As if he didn't attempt to keep me locked away here and grew angry and unhinged when I said no.

As if he didn't lie to us from the very beginning and purposely kept us trapped here.

"I've already contacted someone," I warn. "They know we're here and are being held hostage."

Far from the truth, but it's better than him believing we're completely vulnerable.

Sylvester drops his wooden leg from the coffee table, the thump loud and causing me to flinch. With a grunt, he stands, and instinctively, I take a step back.

A soft breeze of air whispers across the nape of my neck, causing the hairs to stand on end like a petrified cat.

I freeze, and Sylvester grins, a devilish glint in his eyes. He lifts his hand and points behind me.

"She's excited to keep you."

My muscles are stiff with horror, and I refuse to unlock them and turn around.

"I told her you would stay here with her. She's very excited to have a new friend."

I work to swallow, but it feels no easier than swallowing dry sticks.

"Then why did she lead us to the beacon? Why would she help us find a way out?"

His eyes flit over my shoulder, a flash of pure rage in his eyes before it extinguishes. In that tiny increment of time, I see every bit of insanity residing in that empty tomb where his soul is supposed to be.

"Kacey gets lonely sometimes. Doesn't always like being here. She comes around eventually but acts out every now and then."

"Is that why you sewed her mouth shut?" I spit, disgusted with what he did to his own daughter. It sickens me to think what else he might've done to her.

I feel a finger slide across my nape, and I bristle, a slimy feeling trickling through my bloodstream. Her touch moves south, and then begins to swirl in a pattern I can't distinguish. She's drawing something on my back, but I've no idea what. It feels like letters, but I can't be sure in the midst of my panic. I think I feel her trace L-A-R, but my mind is racing too fast to interpret it.

"We all suffer consequences, my dear," he says, walking around the table and coming to stand in front of me. I'm trapped between the two, and I've no idea how the fuck I'm supposed to find Enzo and get us the fuck out of here.

"Was getting a supply drop-off when she started screaming. I had already cut out her tongue the previous time when she tried to call for help, but that doesn't stop someone from making noises of distress, even if it's incoherent. She forced my hand."

Nausea churns in my stomach, the acidity burning a path up my throat.

"You never had to stay here," I remind him, my voice raspy and uneven. "If you were so desperate to not be alone, you could've just left."

"My daughters were born and raised here. I served years upon years manning the beacon. I dedicated my whole life to being here. Why would I just throw that away?"

"Because it drove you insane," I reason. "You don't have to live like this."

He stays silent while his hands clench and unclench. I've no idea what he's thinking, but it doesn't even matter. He's not going to leave, and he's not going to let me go. That much, I'm sure of.

And who I thought might be willing to help is only a broken soul that has been tortured and possibly brainwashed. I know there's one side of her that wants to be free—the same side that left the bookshelf open for us to find and desperately tried to get our attention—but there's another side of her that feels just as hopeless as I do in this very moment, and doesn't want to be alone, either.

"I think I'll be happy here with my two girls," Sylvester says finally. "Your friend is no more anyhow, I've already disposed of him. You have no family, no friends. And from the sounds of it, you've found yerself in a lotta trouble. I'm doing you a favor by keepin' you here."

"What did you do to him?" I bite out through gritted teeth, panic beginning to overwhelm my senses.

There's no blood, is there? My vision is tunneling as I frantically search around for it. He can't be dead. I refuse to believe it.

"He ain't dead yet," Sylvester says. "But he will be."

I shake my head, tears beginning to well in my eyes as the hopelessness deepens.

It's reminiscent of being back in that house with Kev, forced to endure a situation I could see no way out of. My words and cries for help were only being screamed into a void. There was no one to save me—except me. The day I took my life back was the same day it was no longer mine to live. I had to let it slip through my fingers in order to survive.

And for the second time in my life, I'm asking myself yet again—do you want to survive? Or do you want to waste away?

But what is surviving without living, and what is death without pain?

It's an empty, cracked shell where a soul has been born and where that soul will die.

I no longer want to be that shell. I don't want to just survive anymore—I want to *live*. And I won't waste away, spending my days as a hollow being that awaits death like an old dog sitting on a doorstep, waiting for the day someone opens the door and invites him inside to stay.

So, I do the only thing I can think to do. I kick Sylvester right in the dick. A puff of air bursts from his throat, followed by a resounding shout of pain. Assuming Kacey is too stunned to react, I bolt toward the kitchen, screaming Enzo's name and nearly tripping over the rug beneath the broken bits of the dining room table.

He can't be far. I'm positive Sylvester wouldn't have had time to hurt him and hide him outside somewhere, so he must still be in the lighthouse.

"Enzo!" I scream, hoping to God he'll answer. But he doesn't.

Sylvester shouts something at Kacey, but I'm already gunning for the knives in the kitchen. Ripping open the drawer, I quickly grab a knife, slicing my hand on another in the process. The pain hardly registers, especially when a rotten-mouthed girl calmly walks toward me, her chin tipped low and a wicked glare spearing me from beneath her brows.

I hold out the knife, my hand trembling violently. The adrenaline is oversaturating my system, and I'm finding it difficult to concentrate on a definitive plan.

"Enzo!" I scream again. Desperately, I sweep my gaze across the room, confused about where the hell he could be. There's no way Sylvester could overpower Enzo. Which means he had to have taken him by surprise somehow.

Kacey closes in, and I turn my attention back to her.

"Don't come closer, Kacey. I told you we would help you. You don't owe loyalty to the person who has abused and tortured you."

She pauses, staring at me with an emotion I'm too frantic to place.

"Get 'er!" Sylvester shouts, his face purple with pain and fury, while he struggles to get back to his feet with his wooden leg. Curses are spilling from his lips, spit flying and sticking to his beard, but Kacey isn't listening.

"Kacey, please," I beg, voice hoarse. "He's kept you trapped here and hurt you in many ways. He doesn't love you; he just wants to possess you."

Her eyes become glassy, but Sylvester is back on his feet and charging toward her, his wooden peg against the floor echoing with his wrath.

"Useless fuckin'—" he cuts himself off and fists her hair, whipping her behind him and tossing her to the ground. She lands with a thump, but he's already on his warpath toward me.

Admittedly, I freeze for a moment. The terror is a parasite, injecting its venom directly into my bloodstream and paralyzing my muscles.

But the moment his fist cocks back, rage contorting his face, it's like time slows. My body unlocks, and I move on instinct, ducking below his punch and straightening just as he closes in. He grabs my throat, squeezing tightly, but my hand is already pressed firmly into his stomach, blood spurting, and I loosen my grip on the knife handle.

He pauses, eyes widening while he looks down. The entirety of the metal is plunged into his stomach, and the slick, hot feeling of his blood coating my hands has vomit threatening to spew from my mouth.

It feels so familiar. Just like when I had sunk that knife in Kev's throat, red bubbling from the wounds and covering my hand and face in it.

I never wanted to take a life. Yet, here I am, claiming another.

He snarls and grabs ahold of my wrist, squeezing it until it cracks. I cry out, releasing the handle instinctively.

"That was just stupid of ya," he growls, his face twisted with both pain and fury.

Before I can react further, his fist is flying toward me again. This time, I'm too slow to react, and the only thing I recall is a burst of pain, then darkness.

CHAPTER 33

Enzo

My head is splitting into fucking pieces, and something smells putrid. I groan, gritting my teeth as sharp pain pierces behind my eyes.

Mother... *fucker.*

I'm having trouble remembering where the fuck I am, and what the hell happened beyond the throbbing in my skull.

Slowly, fragments filter in. Finding the beacon and then the radio. Kacey appearing, her mouth sewn shut. Sylvester breaking in, and then leaving Sawyer and Kacey upstairs. I remember opening the bookshelf door with my shotgun readied but finding no one. The only difference was the cellar door was open again.

I remember approaching the cellar cautiously and then the creak of the front door right before a shot went off behind me. My recollection is choppy from there, but I recall the bullet hitting the barrel of my gun, forcing it out of my grip. Then Sylvester storming up behind me while I scrambled for the gun again, another shot going off by my hand and destroying the weapon completely. Finally, the butt of his shotgun aiming straight for my face. And then... nothing.

Cazzo.

The rise of fury is enough to force my eyes open and get my body moving. It's nearly pitch black, hot, and it smells dank and like... like something is decomposing.

Glancing up, I can see tiny cracks of light between the floorboards and Sylvester's shadow as he walks through the kitchen slowly, his leg rebounding through the wood, causing dust to fall over me.

There's a string of unintelligible words from what sounds like Sylvester. I've no idea if Sawyer is with him or not, but it's enough to inject another strong dose of adrenaline into my veins.

I pat my hands all around me, feeling fine dirt and what I think is a blanket beneath me. Sitting up further, I continue searching until my hand bumps into something solid. It's cold and hard, and after a minute, I realize it's a shovel. I grab onto it and resume, hoping there's something down here that can provide a light source.

It takes a few more minutes, and coming across several items, I finally find a small gas lantern. It clicks on, barely illuminating more than a couple of inches out.

I'm in a dirt hole with a wooden ladder that leads straight up.

Getting to my feet, I look around, finding myself in a cemetery. There are mounds of dirt spanning across the space, with sticks fashioned into a cross before each one.

Fucking Christ.

It's hard to breathe as I examine just how many people Sylvester has killed. Were they all hostages? They've all clearly fucking died, save for Kacey. Suicide? Or did he kill them when they refused to conform?

Aside from the graves, there's a bucket in the corner with human waste inside, a small cot with a blanket and flat pillow, a knapsack doll, a first aid kit, water bottles, and several empty plastic bags.

Sylvester must've kept Kacey down here at times. Since we've arrived, she could be heard only up in the beacon during the day, presumably because she wouldn't be able to make her presence known as easily and guide us directly to the hatch. Where a fucking cemetery resides.

He knew the ghost stories would lead us to believe that the footsteps from above or in the hall were nothing more than restless spirits.

I shake my head, different scenarios racing through my head on *why* she was in the hallway at night, each one more disturbing than the last. Aside from the restroom, the only other place she had to go was Sylvester's bedroom, and there were many times when that's exactly where she was going and coming from based on the sound of her chains.

I'm going to fucking murder him—slowly. I'd love to start by sewing his goddamn mouth shut just to make him scream. See if he can keep it closed or if he'll rip those stitches wide open from the pain.

Using one hand, I climb up the ladder while holding on to the lantern with the other. As expected, the hatch door is locked, but I can hear the conversation more clearly.

"Stupid little bitch got me good, but yer old man got too much belly for her to hit somethin' vital," he grouses. "Hand me them scissors over there, sweetie."

There's a clatter of metal and another series of grunts and mutters. From the sounds of it, Sawyer injured him somehow, and he's now stitching the wound shut.

That's my girl.

"She ain't gonna be happy at first, ya know, but you weren't either, remember? She'll adjust eventually, and soon enough, our little family will be happy."

A growl forms deep in my chest, and the rage burns hotter from the way he's planning a fucking future with Sawyer. One that consists of her being imprisoned on this island with someone capable of murder and abusing his own daughter. He will hurt her, and most likely take advantage of her body. Those thoughts alone are enough to send me into a tailspin.

Just barely, do I refrain from sending my fist up into the door. It'll accomplish nothing, but even if I did manage to get it open, Sylvester has a gun and can shoot me dead in a heartbeat.

"You know I'm gonna have'ta punish you for what you did," Sylvester continues after a moment. "I only left 'cause my back was hurt, and I needed to get the upper hand. I was forced to camp out in this tiny cave at the opposite end o'the island. They been frequentin' the one with glowworms. And you know my leg ain't no good with climbin' in those caves, but I was gonna take you to see 'em again. Don't think you deserve that anymore, now do ya? I've taken good care of you yer whole life, and you repay me by showin' them the radio."

There's a long pause.

"Come here, Kacey."

I close my eyes, and tremors rack my body from the rage. It doesn't matter if I yell and cause a scene, he's either going to silence me permanently or continue because he knows damn well that I can't do a thing to stop him.

There's an ocean of violence in my bones, but I need to play this smart.

A sharp crack followed by a soft, garbled cry arises, and I silently make my way down the ladder as quickly as possible. There's no fucking way I will let that girl suffer any more abuse. And there's no fucking way I'm staying in this goddamn hole.

I'm taking a massive risk, but my only option is to burn my way out.

I rifle through the first aid kit first, finding a tiny bottle of rubbing alcohol inside, along with alcohol pads. Grabbing the blanket next, I tear off several sections, roll them into tight ropes, and drench them in the liquid. When I'm done, I snatch the gas lantern and pads too, and head toward the ladder. As I quietly climb, perspiration forms along my hairline while the sound of flesh hitting flesh continues.

Once I reach the top, I pause, waiting for a sharp slap to crack open the glass lantern on the ladder, the sound swallowed by an undeserved punishment.

Then, I pause, waiting to ensure that Sylvester didn't hear me. Another loud crack follows up the last hit a moment later, so I quickly unwrap the pads and shove them up between the wooden planks throughout the ceiling. My hope is that he won't notice them until it's too late, distracted by his sick punishment. Luckily, he doesn't, and another *crack* fills the room. Sweating and nearly blind with rage, I stick one of the tattered pieces of the blanket into the open flame.

It ignites in a flash, singeing my fingers as I shove it up between the wooden planks, my eyes burning from the smoke. I repeat the same process with the rest, reaching out past the ladder to spread them out. The flame should catch onto the wet alcohol pads and spread faster.

Then, I scramble back down and tuck myself into a corner, hearing the moment Sylvester either sees or smells the burning cloth.

"Motherfucker!" he bellows, stomping toward the quickly spreading fire. He unlocks the mechanism and throws the cellar door open, proceeding to fire off two shots from his gun, the bullets a loud boom in the small space.

But the fire is still growing, and Sylvester can't afford to let the lighthouse burn down.

If he loses Raven Isle, he loses everything.

Curses spill from his mouth as he returns to frantically working to put out the fire.

I'm flying up the ladder within seconds, finding Sylvester stomping with his boot over the flames, while Kacey watches on, unmoving as she stares at the red glow with wide eyes.

I charge toward Sylvester just as he notices me, knocking him over and landing a single punch into his face, stunning him long enough to rip the gun from his hold and smash the butt of it into his nose.

He's out cold, and I'm already heading toward the stairs.

Sawyer is either on the second floor or up by the beacon, and I don't have the luxury of time to search both.

With Sylvester knocked out, the fire will continue to spread, which could prevent me from getting to her.

I bolt up the steps, down the hallway, and into our shared room. But it's empty.

"Sawyer!" I roar, nearly collapsing when I hear an indiscernible noise coming from Sylvester's room. I skid across the floor as I run back into the hallway, up the steps, and into his bedroom.

She's sitting on the floor by his bed, metal cuffs wrapped around her wrists, a chain dangling between them. The link is trapped around the leg of the bedframe, preventing her from escaping. Dried blood coats her left hand, trails of it leaking down her arm. A piece of duct tape is slapped over her mouth, tears streaming down her beautiful face and brightening her blue eyes to gleaming sapphires.

"That fucker," I spit, grabbing the frame and lifting the entire bed, allowing her to slide the chain out from the leg. She must've been tugging at them, because her tiny wrists are irritated and starting to bleed.

"Baby, you can't be hurting yourself like this," I murmur, helping her up.

She rips off the tape in one go, gritting her teeth and hissing through them from the sharp pain.

"I was worried about you," she admits.

"I'm fine, *bella*. Did he hurt you?'

"I accidentally cut my hand, and I think my wrist might be fractured, but I'm okay otherwise. He just said I needed to stay in timeout and think about what I did."

There's blackness licking at the edges of my vision as I gently grab her arm. After closer inspection, I see a thin cut on her hand, and a faint outline of fingerprints bruising around her wrist, a growl forms deep in my chest.

"Hey, hey," she calls gently, bringing my attention to her. "It's fine. I stabbed him, and this is the result. Totally worth it, if you ask me."

Releasing her, I brush the pad of my thumb across her lip. "You look beautiful painted in his blood. È il colore che preferisco su di te."

The smell of burning wood is drifting toward us, so I quickly spin around and search his nightstand for extra bullets, finding them in the top one amongst a watch, dentures, pictures, and a case of old quarters—typical old man.

"Is that smoke?" Sawyer asks, crinkling her nose as I load the bullets, pocketing extra in my shorts.

"Yeah. He had me in the cellar. I had to get creative to get out."

She wrinkles her nose. "Creative is one way to put it."

"Let's go. We need to get out of here before the fire traps us."

Grabbing her hand, I quietly lead her back down the hallway and toward the stairs.

Thick plumes of black smoke begin to rise, stinging my eyes and burning my lungs.

"I'm going to need you to cover your mouth and take a really deep breath. Hold it in as long as you can and breathe in as little as possible."

Without hesitation, she lifts the collar of her shirt, covering her nose and mouth, and nods at me, signaling that she's ready to go.

I kiss her forehead, purely because I need to touch her, and then raise the shotgun, sucking in a deep breath before slowly making my way down the steps.

The smoke thickens as we descend, but the fire has been put out, which means either Sylvester is awake, or Kacey took care of it. I see a flash of movement cut across the kitchen and run toward the door, the sound of her chains unmistakable.

È il colore che preferisco su di te. - *My favorite color on you*

Another flash darts in my peripheral a second before Sylvester appears, a hammer in his hand and a battle cry on his lips as he goes to strike me.

"Enzo!" Sawyer screeches, grabbing my collar and yanking me back just as Sylvester swings the hammer right where my head had been.

He stumbles in front of me, and I use his momentum to push him all the way down with the barrel of the gun. He crashes into the floor, rolling onto his back with a grunt.

"Fucking *bitch*," he spits on a cough, while I round him and grab the front of his shirt and drag him toward the middle of the kitchen. The cellar is still open, and Kacey isn't visible through the density of the smoke.

The fury I kept simmering beneath the surface is now boiling over the edges. All I can think about is what he did to Sawyer—what he *almost* did to her. Attempting to kidnap her and then tying her up to his bed in hopes he'd keep her here forever. The image of Sawyer with her mouth sewn shut and sad, hollow eyes is charred into my brain as deeply as the burns in the wooden flooring.

I lower myself on top of him, inextinguishable fury polluting my chest and sinking deep into my bones.

His fists fly at me, but he's nothing more than a weak, old man. He trades between sputtering colorful insults and hacking as soot fills his lungs.

Setting the gun down, I grab his wrists, quickly forcing them down and trapping them between my thighs. I squeeze hard as he wiggles beneath me like a worm on a hook, and deliver a succession of punches into his face. I feel the skin over my knuckles tearing and my bones colliding with his over and over.

Through my haze, I vaguely hear an odd, gurgled scream before I'm knocked to the side, and what feels like arms and legs being wrapped around my torso.

I'm disoriented long enough for Sylvester to get on his knees and grab the gun. Right as he lifts it, Sawyer appears behind him, the chain link between her cuffed wrists looping across his throat and pulling tight.

A war cry leaves her throat as she heaves him back with all her strength, a pained expression on her face as they fall backward together. The shotgun falls from his grip and slides a foot away from them.

"Kacey!" I growl, working on getting her off me. I don't want to hurt her. She's conflicted and has been brainwashed for years to protect her father above herself—and in the most brutal of ways. But I won't let her stop me from killing the man who has inflicted pain and torture on innocent people for years. And especially not after touching my girl.

That will never go unpunished.

I manage to remove myself from Kacey's grip and am horrified when I see her mouth is splitting open, the stitches ripping the flesh around her lips away. Blood is trailing down her chin, and broken screams are coming from her throat as her mouth widens, revealing blackened teeth and a severed tongue.

I grab her jaw, attempting to keep her from hurting herself any further.

"You don't have to hurt for him," I tell her vehemently, my stomach turning from the grotesque feel of her rotting flesh and bodily fluids that I don't even want to think about, along with the pungent stench from it. "Not anymore."

She's both fighting for him and against him.

Love is funny that way. It persists even when you've done everything in your power to banish it. It demands its own voice and refuses to be a slave to anyone but its own desires. And despite the power of it, those selfish desires are what make love so weak.

It's accepting the apologies of a cheating lover.

It's returning to a raised hand, over and over, until that hand becomes lethal, and home is in the afterlife.

It's clinging to a mother who never wanted you and hoping she will one day show up on those church steps.

It's grabbing ahold of a hand that belongs to both a father and an abuser, wailing as they slowly slip away.

It's falling in love with a liar, a thief, and praying they never hurt you again.

Kacey shakes her head, a pained, sorrowful cry spearing past her stitches and directly into my chest. Sawyer and Sylvester are still struggling, and as much as Kacey needs comfort, I don't have the fucking time.

Pinning her with one last look—something I pray she interprets as *help us help you*—I turn to the struggling duo. Sawyer is on the floor with Sylvester on top of her, his back to her front, as she attempts to strangle him with the chain.

Both of their faces are cherry red, and exhaustion is etched into the lines of Sawyer's face. Her strength is waning, and Sylvester is beginning to free himself from her hold.

Just as I take a step toward them, Sylvester breaks free and lunges for the gun, grabbing it and pointing it directly at me. But my only focus is Sawyer, and if the fucker wants to stop me from getting to her, he better pull that trigger now.

"No!" Sawyer screeches, jumping on his back and causing the gun to swing. He fires off a shot, the sound booming and hitting the ceiling, causing debris to fall over our heads.

"Sawyer," I snap, and urgency has me rushing toward them. Sylvester bashes his elbow in her face, causing her head to kick back and blood to sprout from her mouth.

My vision goes red, and I feel rather than see something pushing me to the side. I stumble right as another shot goes off, and I wait for the pain to register.

To feel the violent press of a bullet ripping through my body and taking my soul along with it.

Yet, I feel nothing as the scene slowly filters in, and I straighten. Sawyer and Sylvester are staring at me with wide eyes, horror on both of their faces.

But they're not staring at me at all. What they're focused on is beside me. It feels like slow motion as I turn my head, finding Kacey standing where I once was, her chin tilted down. My gaze follows hers, discovering the blood gushing from her chest, pooling on the floor beneath her feet.

"NO!" Sylvester shouts fiercely, the veins in his forehead protruding as he struggles to get up and rush toward Kacey.

I catch her as she falls, softening her impact as her body slumps. Sylvester is crawling toward us, the weapon forgotten on the floor. My head is full of static as I try to process that this poor girl has taken a bullet for me.

"Get away!" I bark. I think he's too shocked to register anything outside of his daughter dying on the floor before him, and from his own doing, no less. So, he stops, his widened eyes staring at her in disbelief.

"Hey, look at me," I murmur, turning her cheek toward me. It takes a few beats before her glazed eyes slide toward me. I clench my teeth, seeing nothing but peace radiating from her.

"*Sei così dolce. Sei un angelo*," I whisper, swiping my thumb across her bloodied cheek as a tear falls from her eye.

"No, no, no, no," Sylvester chants, his voice growing tighter and strained with each repetition.

She stares up at me, and though she can't smile, I see it in her eyes as her small hand cups my jaw. She's dying, yet she's comforting me.

Her gaze focuses on her fingers as they softly brush across my beard, as if entranced by the feel of the coarse hair. Then, her eyes go unfocused, and just like that, she's gone. A life that took years to cultivate into the woman lying in my arms, and only seconds to take it away.

"NO!" he shouts again, banging his fist on the floor. "This is your fault!" he spits at me. Sawyer kneels behind him, tears streaming down her cheeks as she stares at Kacey with sorrow.

Sei così dolce. Sei un angelo - *You are so sweet. You're an angel*

I'm numb as I gently set her on the ground and stand. Grabbing the shotgun from the floor, I walk over to the gas stove and turn one of the nozzles on high, flames emitting from one of the burners.

Then I hold the tip of the barrel in them. Guns are built for heat, so it takes several minutes for the metal to turn a bright, searing red. During that time, I allow Sylvester to suffer from the pain of his loss. I allow him to face what he's done.

Satisfied, I stalk toward the blubbering old caretaker. My thoughts are reduced to white noise, and my body moves on pure instinct as I kick him in the stomach, peering at him with nothing less than revulsion as he flips onto his back. He coughs profusely and attempts to sit up, but I'm pushing him back down with the white-hot barrel in his chest, pulling a pained shout from his throat.

Sawyer crawls toward him, wheezing and coughing, her red, watery eyes pinned to what I'm doing. I move the barrel from his chest to the hollow of his throat, the smell of burnt flesh immediate.

"Do you think I have what it takes to kill a man now?"

Sylvester's eyes bug, and I grit my teeth, snarling as I dig the searing metal into his throat, delighting in his pained wails.

He fists the barrel with both hands, attempting to dislodge it, so I lean heavily against the butt of the shotgun, putting all my weight into it as it slowly but surely begins to sink into his throat. Blood bubbles from beneath it, and his wails turn into gasps, baring his teeth as he continues to struggle.

The barrel sinks further and further until he's convulsing, and I hit his spine. Only then, do I stop and step away, ripping out the gun as I do.

Sylvester chokes on his own blood, seizing as he stares at the ceiling. Is he looking for God between the cracks of the wood, hoping he'll see a glimpse? One tiny look into what he could've had before committing his heinous crimes.

I can assure him, if there is a God, He isn't staring back down at him. I imagine His eyes are turned toward Kacey instead while the Reaper's hands reach for Sylvester, dragging him to a place lonelier than Raven Isle.

Exhausted, I slide my gaze to Sawyer and find her already peering back at me. The whites of her eyes are red, making her blue irises even brighter. And those sad little fucking sapphires are exactly why love is so weak. One look from them, and I'm crumbling.

"Hello? Is anyone there? I repeat, is anyone there?"

The disembodied voice takes a moment to register. It's far away, distorted, and just barely penetrates through my scattered thoughts.

"Hello? We received a transmission calling for help. I repeat, is anyone still there? We're here to help."

CHAPTER 34

Sawyer

Never thought I'd see another dead body.

Let alone two.

I stare at them with utter desolation. Blood is everywhere. All over the floor, splattered across the kitchen counters and walls. All over me. It's... all over me.

Enzo is setting down the weapon and prowling toward me, a savage expression on his face. His brows are pinched, a frown tugs down his lips, and little droplets of blood are scattered across the side of his cheek from when Kacey was shot.

He looks like a valiant king walking off the battlefield, returning to his queen after a hard-fought war.

Is this what it feels like to be treasured?

"Hello? Is anyone still there?"

"We need to answer them," I say. When he reaches me, he crouches and lowers his chin, catching my eyes.

"You know what will happen once we do."

My bottom lip trembles. "The coast guard comes."

"The coast guard comes," he repeats. "And they find a fugitive."

I nod, dropping my gaze. I will have to go to prison for my crime and never see Enzo again. The former feels like when the other shoe finally drops. It's almost a relief as much as it is heartbreaking. And the latter feels like a punch to the gut—hard enough to make me nauseous.

In all my years, I've never allowed myself to grow attached to anyone. It was impossible to when I knew I'd have to run again. Not only did I never want to risk being held down in one place, where I could eventually be caught, but I never wanted to put anyone else in the crossfire of my deception.

By the look on Enzo's face, he looks prepared to grab my web of lies and wrap the strings around himself. But he'd only be creating a noose out of them.

It feels too simple to say that I'm in love with him. Maybe because I've known him for so little time, and we've already gone through hell together. Maybe even because we had a strong connection from the beginning, but it was so visceral and fueled by pain and rage that whatever it has morphed into is beyond a simple, sweet love.

"It's what I deserve," I mumble.

His finger notches my chin, forcing my gaze back up to him.

Enzo grips me by the back of my neck, holding me in place and tipping his chin down until he's staring me deep in the eyes.

"You deserve the worst fucking punishment for what you've done," he growls before slowly swiping his tongue across his bottom lip.

Mesmerized, my own lips part as his heated words burrow deep beneath my skin, setting me aflame.

"No one is capable of making you suffer more than me."

There's a rational part of me that reacts normally to his wicked implication—fear, adrenaline. But a larger part has always ruled my worst decisions, and I can't help but feel thrilled. *Excited.*

"You're not fucking leaving me, Sawyer. You're not going to jail. You're not going anywhere. You want to pay for your crimes? Good. I'm more than happy to make you pay. And if you think for one goddamn second that I'm letting you go, then I look forward to showing you just how trapped you are with me.

"There are many things you deserve, *bella ladra*, but the only prison you will be a captive in is one of my own making. If my love is a prison, so be it."

I can only gape at him, my heart fluttering from his devilish words. They're so wrong, yet so tempting.

"So be it," I rasp.

Whatever fire began from beneath the floorboards has transferred to the depths of his eyes. Heat spreads throughout my bones, and I can only wonder if I've inhaled too much smoke, creating nothing more than a fever dream before I die. Is this my body's way of telling me that I'm no longer amongst the living? My only response would be that I've never felt more alive.

Enzo's lips softly brush against my own, and my eyelashes flutter closed, overcome with the remnants of his devotion.

"The day you stole from me was the best day of my life," he whispers against my lips. "Because then *you* became my life, and I don't want it back. I won't fucking take it."

I'm beginning to tremble, so he captures my bottom lip between his teeth, sensing the rising emotion in my throat. He pulls me into a kiss so powerful, it feels as if the fire did consume me, and I'm melting into the cracks of the wood beneath his palms.

I'm weightless as he gathers me closer, moving his lips over mine savagely.

But it's over too soon, and he tears himself away from the vortex he so unapologetically pulled me into.

I chase after his mouth, but he directs my head down, and I slump against him as his lips press into my forehead.

The distinct voice of someone calling over the radio slices through the lingering tension between us.

"What are we supposed to do?" I ask, my voice still hoarse. "We can go to a different country that won't turn me in to the authorities. But I could never ask that of you. Not with your whole life and career here."

He turns his head to peer over his shoulder at Kacey and Sylvester, and he stays like that for several drawn-out moments. By the time he's turning back to me, there's a spark of determination in his eyes, accompanied by a note of regret.

"We don't have to go anywhere."

"What will we do then?"

"If you want to live free for the rest of your life, then you need to kill Sawyer Bennett."

My mouth parts in surprise. That was the last thing I was expecting him to say.

"Oh, man. Please tell me this isn't a fucked-up way of saying you're going to kill me, too?"

His face drops with exasperation. "No, baby. I'm saying there is a girl here who has no real identity outside of Raven Isle. That could also be you. And Sawyer Bennett was an unfortunate soul who wrecked on this island years ago, only to take her own life."

My brows pinch and I shake my head with bewilderment as I process what unhinged shit is coming out of his mouth. "So, you want me to pretend that I'm Trinity? And then say that a Sawyer Bennett was taken hostage and died?"

He nods slowly.

"You would have to lie, Enzo. For me," I tack on.

The way he stares at me has my stomach fluttering, unleashing winged beasts inside. He looks as if he's a tortured man who has been presented with freedom, and the only way to obtain it is by taking it from me.

"I would lie for you as easily as I would kill for you. If you getting the best of me requires the world getting the worst of me, you will want for nothing in life, *bella ladra.*"

I swallow, but the moisture in my mouth has dissipated. For the first time, I feel like Enzo is exactly who I deserve, and I'm determined to reciprocate that.

"I will do whatever I can to make sure you never have to lie for me again," I vow, my voice hoarse with emotion.

"I know, baby," he says. He glances back at the bodies, then refocuses on me. "Were you ever fingerprinted?"

"No," I confirm, shaking my head. "I was never brought in."

"Good, then they won't be able to identify you. With two dead bodies, they're going to investigate, and we need a story. Rather than telling them who you actually are, tell them you were born and raised on Raven Isle and were trapped here against your will alongside your sister, Kacey. No one knows you were with me that day, so I will say that I shipwrecked and swam here on my own. I found out what Sylvester was doing to you two, and it resulted in a confrontation where he tried to kill me and accidentally shot Kacey instead—that part is true, at least. So, I defended myself and killed him."

"You don't think burning through his throat with a gun won't be a little suspicious? That's not how normal people kill."

He cocks a brow. "First off, there is no such thing as a normal killer. And do I need to remind you of Kacey's face? They will see that, too. I'll tell them the barrel of the gun was laying in the fire and had no bullets, so I was forced to improvise. I think they'll let it go."

"What about me? The real me—not the Trinity me."

"Sylvester has a gravesite in the cellar below. One of them is you."

I rear back in shock. It feels like he reached into my chest and fisted my heart until it's mush. Sylvester's been killing people for God knows how long. They must've been from the freight ships or maybe from those seeking shelter from a storm. And he just... murdered them.

"What if none of the skeletal remains match? What if they're all men or something? Or can be identified by their teeth?"

"Then we hope they assume that Sylvester disposed of the body elsewhere. But you're the real Sawyer, and we can make sure there's evidence that you were here."

Twisting my lips, I contemplate that. My freedom isn't riding on if I can convince them that I was here—only if I can convince them that *I* am not her.

My eyes slide over to Kacey lying on the floor, lifeless and leeching of warmth by the second. It feels grimy to take advantage of her death. To pretend to have suffered alongside her and claim a story that isn't mine.

But it's my only way out if I want to live freely and not have to restart in another country. Away from Enzo.

Maybe it'll be the last shitty thing I'll ever have to do.

Focusing back on Enzo, I slump my shoulders and nod.

"Okay," I agree. "I'll be Trinity. And Sawyer will die with the rest of them."

The freezing ocean water licks at my calves, sending a wave of goosebumps across my skin. The sand is drug out from beneath me as the sea's chilly fingers retreat. The sun will rise within the hour, and it's still cold, but I see it. Gleaming beneath the bright beacon light.

Enzo stands behind me, arms crossed and a frown marring his face as he stares out at the approaching coast guard boat. Twenty-four days on this island, yet it feels like it's been years.

Sadness punches me right in the chest. Kacey should be out here, too. Sitting beside me and waiting for her rescue.

Enzo's already spent the last five minutes arguing with me to get out of the water before I catch a cold. His eye started twitching when I told him I'm very good at dodgeball and promised to duck if I saw a cold coming my way.

I thought it was funny.

I flip the letter in my hand, the sole evidence that Sawyer Bennett lived and died on Raven Isle.

It feels like forever ago when I was sitting on a beach, smoking a cigarette and wishing for death with a man I never learned the name of.

Now here I am, once more sitting on a beach, but no longer wanting anything to do with cigarettes, and behind me is a man I'll never forget.

Despite all that, I still have the same conclusion. Death—cancer—it all tastes like shit.

It takes another ten minutes before the boat reaches us, and the moment it does, I'm reduced to a pile of blubbering emotions. Tears are springing to my eyes, and I'm not sure whether to feel relief or anxiety.

This won't be the first time I've had to pretend to be someone I'm not. But this just might be the last.

CHAPTER 35

Sawyer

"Enzo Vitale?" one of the coast guards questions from the other end of the boat, checking over Enzo's wounds. "There was a massive search party for you, but they didn't look out this way. You're far out from the Australian coast."

I can't hear what Enzo murmurs back, but as usual, he looks positively annoyed.

I turn my attention back to the coast guard treating my wounds just as he finishes putting the splint on my wrist.

"Thanks, Jason," I say.

Enzo found the keys to the cuffs on Sylvester's dead body, but the bright red rings of irritation remain, accompanied by the laceration on my hand.

"We'll get you to a hospital to have it properly treated," he responds.

He already noted the tattoo on my leg, but Enzo and I decided trying to hide it would only seem suspicious. If they don't see it now, they'll most likely see it in the hospital.

We decided to say it was an act of rebellion against Sylvester, and considering it's definitely not professional—it's believable. I've never been gladder that my first tattoo was by a man at a bus stop.

My anxiety took over, so I've kept quiet. Sensing my unease, Jason talked to me the entire time. Told me all about his sick dog back home and how he's recovering from a surgery that removed the cancer from his ear.

"You both will have to go to the station immediately after treatment."

"Okay," I say, injecting as much confidence in my tone as I can muster. That urge to run still lingers, but I push it away. I refuse to cower and hide any longer.

And this will be the last time Enzo and I will ever have to tell a lie in the name of survival.

"Do you have a last name, sweetheart?" the policewoman asks, her brow pinched with concern.

Her accent is strong, but her voice is soothing. She's an older woman with white hair, gentle brown eyes, and soft hands. I don't know why I remember that... It was the only thing I could focus on when she grabbed ahold of my own and said I was safe now.

Safe.

It's something I've never really felt before. Not until Enzo—when it was me and him against Sylvester, and then again when Officer Bancroft held my palms between hers.

It only makes me feel worse that I'm lying to her.

My mouth opens, then closes. I don't actually know the answer to that question.

We're at Port Valen's police station. We spent all of yesterday in the hospital, where my wrist was put in a cast and I was treated for smoke inhalation. Enzo was also treated for the smoke, along with his concussion. He has bruising across his face from when he was hit with the gun, and his back and right shoulder, assumingly from when Sylvester threw him down into the hole.

They allowed us both to stay the night there before sending us off to the station for questioning this morning.

"I'm not sure," I say weakly, blood rising to my cheeks.

Officer Bancroft might assume it's embarrassment, but truly, it's because I'm terrified that I'm fucking this up. None of this sits right in my stomach or my head. Sylvester's daughters deserve to have the recognition for what they endured, and here I am, selfishly erasing one of them for my own benefit.

It makes me sick.

"Okay," she says gently. "Can you tell me a little about what happened when Enzo first arrived?"

I clear my throat, glancing around as if I'm going to find the answer written on the walls. "My... my dad saw him lying out on the beach u-unconscious. He, uhm, he told us to hide, then took the batteries out of the handheld radio and waited for E-Enzo to come in."

The only good thing about being so damn nervous is that growing up sequestered on an island would result in social awkwardness, and I'm bringing it full force. It's only embarrassing because I didn't actually grow up on a tiny island, but at least she doesn't know that.

"Do you know why he took the batteries out?"

I shift uncomfortably, idly scratching my arm just to give my hands something to do.

"When can I see Enzo?" I ask instead. I'm not a trusting person, but the only one Trinity feels safe with is Enzo. She would also be hesitant to talk about her father. He's all she knows.

"You can see him soon, honey. I just need you to answer some questions for me, okay?"

I glance behind my shoulder at the door, mumbling, "Okay," while also wondering if they'd let me leave right now and go find him.

"Can you—"

"He's not in trouble, is he?" I cut in.

"They're just asking him some questions," she assures gently.

It doesn't slip my attention that she didn't answer my question.

"Can you tell me why your father took the batteries out?" she repeats, keeping her tone soft and patient.

She must donate to charities and volunteer at the soup kitchen on weekends—the woman is a saint. I would've lost my patience already.

"D-Dad was worried about him finding me and my sister and didn't want him to have access to the radios in case he did."

"Do you know why he didn't want Enzo to have access?"

I shrug, scratching my arm again. "He likes to have friends."

The officer nods and writes something down in her notepad.

"How many friends has your father had?"

I chew my lip, not wanting to answer that. Trinity might not want to rat out her father, but frankly, I have no idea how many bodies were buried in the cellar.

"You know he can't hurt you anymore, right?" Bancroft asks, tipping her chin down to catch my stare.

"Yeah..." I trail off, shifting in my seat. "He, uh, he didn't let me see them all. I don't... I don't know. I don't know."

"Okay, okay," she placates, sensing my panic. My heart is pounding, and sweat is forming along my hairline, and beads are slowly trailing down my back.

"So, your dad kept you both hidden the entire time Enzo was there, or just Kacey?"

"At first, it was both of us."

When I don't say anything else, she prompts, "And then?"

"Then... then one night, Dad let Kacey and I go into the ocean to get some fresh air and clean up a little. E-Enzo saw me through the window, so the next day, he started questioning who I was. Dad had to let me out the next day and told him he didn't feel comfortable having his daughter around a strange man."

"And Kacey? Did he see Kacey?"

I shake my head, scratching my arm harder. Officer Bancroft reaches across the table and grabs my hand, stopping me. Her hands are *so* soft.

"You're going to hurt yourself, sweetheart."

I remove myself from her grasp, and she lets me go easily.

"Keep going. You're safe now," she reiterates.

Debatable.

Clearing my throat, I forge on, "Kacey was too close to the door and out of sight, I guess. Enzo never mentioned seeing another girl, and there was no way Dad would let Enzo see what he had done to her. He got lucky, I guess..." I trail off.

"Trinity," the officer starts, then pauses, seeming to struggle with her words. "Why was it that Sylvester mutilated Kacey the way he did and not you?"

I look down, discomfort rattling in my bones. "He liked me more," I choke, twisting my face at the implication. "He uh, preferred to... he liked me differently. So, he... punished us differently."

Her face slackens, disgust and fury mingling in her eyes. But she quickly looks down, concealing her reaction toward something horrific and ugly, and fuck, *not* my story.

Officer Bancroft scribbles notes down in her notepad, and it feels like tiny little bugs are nipping at my nerves, growing more aggressive the longer she writes.

Did I say something different than Enzo? Did she find a hole in my story and is writing down how much of a liar I am?

However, she finishes and lifts her head, smiling at me with nothing less than kindness.

"You mentioned there were several bodies buried in the cellar. Do you know who these people were?" she asks. She's back to questions about the people who were found, and my panic once more heightens.

I look down, feeling almost dizzy from how pivotal this single question is. Enzo and I had thought long and hard about doing this after answering that call over the radio—about finally killing Sawyer Bennett. I knew that if I ever wanted to go on living without looking over my shoulder, she had to die.

"Enzo w-wasn't the first to shipwreck on those waters. There were several. And Dad... he didn't let them go. We-we were hidden away from them, so I never got to see them, but... there was one that made herself known."

Bancroft leans forward, listening intently.

Swallowing, I explain, "She wasn't adjusting well, and he thought my presence might help. I guess it did in some way, but I wasn't any less miserable—"

I drag my fingers over my lips, cutting myself off.

"It's okay," Bancroft assures. "You're allowed to say that."

I nod. "Her name was Sawyer. Sawyer Bennett. We were... were friends, I-I think. She told me a lot about her life. But she... she always cried and screamed to be let go. One night, it stopped, and I never saw her again."

Tears fill my eyes, and my bottom lip trembles. While the reason I'm crying is fabricated, it truly feels like I'm killing myself and who I used to be. It's an emotion I'm having trouble putting a name to.

Grief, I suppose.

Maybe relief, too.

I sniff, wringing my hands together to abate my shaking hands.

"Dad wouldn't tell us what happened, but I was heartbroken about losing her, so I went looking through his things to see if I could find why," I croak, my voice raspy with unshed tears. "I... found this."

I shift and reach into my back pocket, pulling out a letter, and handing it over to the officer with a trembling hand.

My heart is beating so hard, I can feel it in my ears. Bancroft's brow furrows as she opens the letter and begins to read it.

LYING WAS NEVER THE WORST OF MY SINS. JUST THE FIRST OF THEM.
THE DAY I TOLD MY PARENTS KEVIN JAMES BENNETT WAS RAPING ME. MY
MOTHER SLAPPED ME IN THE FACE. AND MY FATHER DEMANDED I APOLOGIZE FOR
LYING ABOUT SOMETHING SO SICK.

THEY LOOKED AT ME AS IF I WAS THE ABUSER. HOW DARE I RUIN OUR PERFECT
LITTLE FAMILY WITH THESE DESPICABLE LIES? HOW DARE I ACCUSE MY PERFECT
BROTHER OF SUCH A THING?

I WASN'T LYING THEN. BUT I DID AFTER.

WHEN I STOOD IN FRONT OF MY BROTHER. HEAD BOWED. AND TEARS STREAMING
DOWN MY CHEEKS. AND TOLD HIM THAT I WAS SORRY FOR MY ACCUSATION. MY
PARENTS STOOD ON EITHER SIDE OF HIM. ARMS CROSSED AND FROWNS ON THEIR
FACES. ENSURING THAT I SAID THE WORDS.

THAT WAS A LIE.

AFTER THAT. I GOT GOOD AT TELLING THEM.

EVERY TIME I SAID "I'M FINE". WHEN ASKED WHAT WAS WRONG. WHEN THE
GUIDANCE COUNSELOR AND TEACHERS CALLED MY PARENTS IN. CONCERNED FOR
ME. AND I TOLD THEM MY HOME LIFE WAS GOOD. YET. I WAS FAILING CLASSES.
RETREATING IN ON MYSELF. AND LOSING THE LITTLE FRIENDS I HAD. I CUT MY
HAIR. STARTED WEARING BAGGY CLOTHES. AND STOPPED SMILING.
GONE WAS THE BRIGHT AND SUNNY SAWYER BENNETT. IN HER PLACE WAS A
RAGING LIGHTNING STORM.

AFTER MY PARENTS DIED. KEVIN ONLY GREW WORSE. HE REFUSED ME
INDEPENDENCE. I HAD TO BEG HIM TO GET A JOB AT THE LOCAL LIBRARY. AND
EVEN THEN. I KNEW HE WAS WATCHING ME.

HE FELT SUPERIOR BECAUSE HE WAS GOING TO BE A COP. GOING TO BE A
PROTECTOR.

BUT HE GAINED MORE THAN POWER. HE GAINED POWERFUL FRIENDS.

KILLING HIM WASN'T THE WORST OF MY SINS. JUST THE BLOODIEST.

EVEN NOW. AS I SIT HERE IN THIS DECREPIT LIGHTHOUSE WITH A MAN WHO
DOESN'T WANT TO HURT ME ANY LESS THAN KEVIN DID. I DON'T REGRET THAT
DECISION TO TAKE HIS LIFE. EVEN IF THAT DECISION ULTIMATELY LED ME HERE.
WHAT I DO REGRET IS ALL THE PEOPLE THAT I'VE HURT ON THE WAY.

WHEN I LEFT MY OLD HOUSE. STAINED WITH KEVIN'S BLOOD. I ONLY WORE SOCKS
ON MY FEET. BUT WHAT HURTS IS THAT I SLIPPED THEM INTO OTHER PEOPLE'S
SHOES AND CARRIED MY SINS INTO LIVES THAT HAD NO PLACE BEING THERE.

THAT... THAT I DO REGRET.

I'VE TAKEN ENOUGH LIVES. BUT TONIGHT WILL BE THE LAST.
AND FOR THE FIRST TIME IN MY LIFE. I FEEL AT PEACE WITH THAT.

SAWYER BENNETT

By the time she's done, she's shaking her head, sadness permeating the air. "She killed herself," she states.

I nod, a tear slipping through and trailing down my cheek. I did kill myself, but not in the way she thinks.

"I don't know if her remains are in the cellar, but she was there. She existed."

"How long ago was this?"

I roll my lips. "I-I'm not sure... Time is different there. But I think it was five birthdays ago."

Bancroft nods. "I'll put these into evidence."

My throat dries, and I can't help but stare at the piece of paper and wonder if I just made a huge mistake. They will investigate Sawyer Bennett and my admission of guilt. Eventually, it will lead to my wanted status, and the sighting in the airport from my distant relative. Most likely, it'll be written off because Sawyer Bennett was never there—she died five years ago on Raven Isle.

I'm sure they'll see the picture of me when I was fourteen years old, sitting awkwardly on the couch with a Christmas present in hand. It was broadcasted everywhere after I escaped.

Up until I killed Kev, I had my natural dark brown hair color styled into a boy cut with thick straightened bangs on my face. I was going through a gothic phase then, wearing heavy black makeup and studded chokers. I presented myself that way in the hopes that Kev would find me less appealing, but it never worked, no matter how hard I tried.

It was the only picture they could find of me. My parents weren't big on documenting our happy little family, and once Kev's abuse began, I did everything in my power to avoid being close to them—let alone take pictures with them.

If I'm lucky, they won't be able to see beneath the bad haircut and heavy makeup and discover the girl sitting before them.

For another hour, she continues with her questioning, offering patience and understanding as I trip over my words, grow flustered, and continue to ask to see Enzo.

She asks about how I was raised, if Sylvester offered us schooling—I said he did since she made note that I appeared educated for someone who was so sheltered—about what he did to Kacey and why, and how he would keep us hidden from people when they wrecked, or when he received shipments, and lastly, about the deaths of Sylvester and Kacey. I broke out into tears during that, and while my sadness may have benefited me, it was nothing but genuine. I didn't know Kacey for more than an hour or two, but her story and her death are heartbreaking, and she didn't deserve the hand she was dealt.

In the end, she assures me that I'm not under arrest, but they still will need to ask questions as the investigation unfolds. While walking me out of the interrogation room and to her desk, she speaks to me about options for a place for me to stay until I get an official identity in place.

She's mid-sentence, in the middle of rifling through file folders by her desk, when she stops, her eyes locked onto my thigh.

My stomach twists and my eyes instantly cut to where she's staring.

My tattoo.

I'm still wearing the jean shorts, leaving it entirely on display.

Heart thudding, I fondly finger the wonky black letters, a slight smile on my face. Hopefully, her seeing that I'm not trying to hide it will make her unsuspicious.

"I got in so much trouble for that, but I don't regret it."

Her brow furrows and she comes around to get a closer look.

"The hell is it?"

"I, uhm, I found a sewing needle and got some pen ink and gave myself a tattoo," I explain awkwardly. "I've been angry with my dad for so long, it was one of the few ways I chose to rebel."

I hate that I'm forced to paint over such a special memory with an ugly one, but at least I know the real one. I'll always have Simon to hold on to.

Officer Bancroft chuckles. "I like it. But don't do that again. Could've given yourself a serious infection."

"Okay," I say with a soft smile.

"So, there are a few shelters that will take you in, but—"

"I'd like to stay with Enzo," I cut in.

She tightens her lips, and the look on her face has my nerves reigniting all over again. "Please, he protected me. He *saved* me. I-I don't want him to get in troub—"

"Honey, they're just questioning him right now. I understand that you might feel safe with Enzo and have formed a bond, but why don't we find someplace that might be able to give you around-the-clock care? You're going to experience culture shock and have difficulties acclimating, so it's important that we make sure you're okay."

A shot of adrenaline releases into my bloodstream, and I'm beginning to panic again. It's starting to feel like a constant state of mind.

I don't want to go to a shelter. It feels like, yet again, I'm being forced to give up my freedom.

I shake my head, taking a step back. She sighs softly, noting the distress on my face.

Before either of us can say anything, a door opens from down the hall, and Enzo is stepping out, with a stormy expression on his face.

His eyes immediately find mine, and his shoulders relax an inch. The moment our gazes meet, he beelines for me, cupping my face between his palms the moment I'm within reach. He tips his chin down, searching my face before ensnaring my eyes.

"You okay?"

I nod. "I'm fine," I rasp.

He picks apart my expression for a few more seconds before dropping his hands and focusing on Officer Bancroft.

"She's staying with me."

Exasperation crosses over her face, and honestly, I know she sees mine and Enzo's connection as nothing more than a trauma bond. In some ways, it might be. But she doesn't know that we have so much more than that, and it's not something we'll ever be able to explain.

"We have a shelter that—"

"No," Enzo cuts in, voice stern and final. "I am more than capable of taking care of her."

I bite my lip, trying not to feel good about that but finding it impossible not to.

The officer who interrogated Enzo—Officer Jones—stands beside Bancroft, studying the two of us with a keen eye. He's younger and less impressionable. It makes me nervous, but if he's releasing Enzo, he must not have found anything incriminating.

Yet.

Bancroft sighs again, but she's relenting. She can't force me to stay anywhere—not unless I'm going to jail. Enzo's sharp jaw is set stubbornly, and his eyes are gleaming, daring the officers to argue. There's no denying his fierce protectiveness and that he clearly has no intentions of letting me go.

"You're free to go," Jones says. "But neither of you are allowed to leave the country. I suspect we'll be seeing each other again, Mr. Vitale."

Enzo slides his gaze to Jones, not appearing the least bit concerned. I, on the other hand, am shitting myself.

"And we're under the agreement that her identity will stay hidden from the media?"

"Of course," Jones agrees. "We will protect her."

I hear everything he's not saying.

That doesn't mean we will protect you.

CHAPTER 36

Sawyer

My heart has formed little fists, and they're banging against my rib cage, demanding to be let out.

Enzo is standing ahead of me, a slight impression of a dimple in his cheek as he peers over his shoulder at me. Mirth radiates from his hazel eyes, and I'm tempted to poke them.

"Why the hell is Senile Suzy in your driveway?" I squeak, my tone bordering on hysterical. Right before me is my big, yellow Volkswagen van in all its glory, gleaming beneath the sunlight.

He quirks a brow. "You never said why you chose that name," he deflects.

"She's a goddamn imbecile and moody as fuck. Why is she here?"

"Because this is where she belongs. This is where *you* belong."

I curl my bottom lip between my teeth, tears welling in my eyes.

"How did you find her?" I ask, the words raspy and uneven.

He shrugs casually. "After you fell asleep at the hospital, a nurse let me use her phone, and I called to make sure it was still parked at *Valen's Bend*. It was, so I had my friend, Troy, retrieve it for me and bring it here."

I laugh, because if I don't, I'll cry. The fact that he remembered where I parked it is enough to have my ovaries exploding.

"You didn't have to do that," I choke out.

"Didn't I say it would be waiting for you? Don't ever doubt what I would do for you, Sawyer." He doesn't let me answer, not that I'd have one for him anyway.

Bottom lip trembling, I say, "Is it too late to add you to my list of things that make me happy? Doesn't matter, I'm adding you to it anyway."

A dimple appears in his cheek, and he stares at me as if he already knew that. Nodding toward his house, he murmurs, "Come, *bella*."

I take a single step before my joints lock, my feet glued to the ground and unable to move. When he catches sight of my inability to function, the dimple on his other cheek appears.

"What's funny?" I mutter, my gaze pinned to the house.

"Why are you so nervous to enter our home? Shouldn't it be me?"

"No," I grumble. Sweat is beginning to gather in my pits, and my brain is looping back to him saying *our home* and getting stuck there.

Clearly, I'm still very much ashamed of what I did the last time he brought me here. And what's even more unsettling about this situation is that he wants me to stay.

Because for some godforsaken reason, Enzo decided I was worth loving. I think he hit his head too hard when we shipwrecked and lost his mind, yet I'm too selfish to let him go.

We both lost pieces of ourselves that day. But as time passed while stuck in that lighthouse, we slowly merged our remaining scattered pieces until we made more sense together than we did apart.

There's no doubt Enzo is worth loving, and though it terrifies me, I'm no longer willing to run away from it.

He stops before the front door, turning to me fully, his eyes glinting in the sunlight.

"What?" I snap, though it's missing heat.

A grin slides onto his face, and the hands banging within my chest freeze. My heart and I are paralyzed by that simple action, which is honestly annoying.

"You know I forgive you, right?" he asks.

I sniff. "I don't think you've ever said the words, but yes."

He takes a step toward me, slips two fingers into my mouth, and jerks me into him, effectively arresting the oxygen in my lungs right along with my heart.

"I forgive you, *bella*. And now I'm going to need you to forgive yourself. Can you do that for me, baby?"

I melt. Just that easily.

Unable to speak, I nod, relaxing my shoulders while he releases me.

"Good, now let's go take a hot shower with actual water pressure, and then we're ordering takeout from wherever you want."

Unexpectedly, a sob nearly bursts from my throat. It's so simple—a shower and takeout—but it feels like he's leading me into paradise.

Enzo's hands dive into my hair, lathering the shampoo into the strands while massaging my scalp.

I've missed water pressure. After spending all day at the police station, I thought I'd never get to relax. But now, my bones are liquefying, and I'm on the verge of swirling down the drain with the water.

"If I died right here and now," I start, the last word bleeding into a groan. "I'd actually be upset. You should be proud of yourself. You made me want to live."

H.D. CARLTON

I didn't mean for that to be so heavy, but Enzo shoulders it easily.

"Seems we're even then," he says, his deep voice as smooth as silk.

"If you're up for it, I'd like to show you my lab tomorrow," he continues, grabbing my biceps to pull me back into the spray of water, careful to keep my casted wrist out of it. I tilt my chin up as he rinses out the soap.

"I'd love to," I murmur, groaning again from the feel of his hands in my hair.

"I don't think you ever told me why you love sharks so much."

He releases me, grabs a loofah, and squirts a dollop of body wash onto it. Methodically, he washes every inch of my skin while he speaks.

"I suppose at first it was because I wanted to be like one. They are some of the fiercest creatures in the ocean—at least that we know of. And growing up, I always felt helpless. Like someone else was in the driver's seat, and I had no control over where I was going. They embodied power and freedom. It was everything I strived for.

"As I grew older, it evolved from fascination to near obsession. I can't explain what exactly it is, but they've always just made me happy. The ocean makes me happy."

I bite my lip, turning to him and grabbing the loofah from him. With my good hand, I awkwardly rub it across his chest, uncoordinated with this side.

"Do you ever get worried that they'll hurt you?"

His stare is smoldering as he watches me, and though his dick isn't fully hard, he's not entirely soft, either. But there's an unspoken agreement to just enjoy each other's company tonight. We haven't truly gotten a chance to yet.

"I always get into the water with the understanding that I'm no longer on the top of the food chain. I respect them, and most times, they respect me. But it'd be stupid to think they're not fully capable of ending my life."

There's a twinge in my chest, and I recognize it as anxiety. I would never even think to ask Enzo to stop swimming with them, but I can't deny that him never coming home one day doesn't terrify the shit out of me.

"Well, you better get in the water with the understanding that you have

375

someone to come home to also," I tell him shyly, keeping my eyes focused on my task and avoiding his probing stare.

"Look at me," he murmurs softly, grabbing my wrist. "Don't run."

I bite my lip and peek up at him. There are some growing pains when you've never been in love before. I've lived my life selfishly for the past six years and have run from everything that posed a threat to my survival. It's almost poetic that getting trapped with someone was the catalyst to my redemption.

It's not something I'm used to yet, but I know that one day soon, loving Enzo will come as naturally as the way he loves the ocean. The way he loves *me*.

Energy crackles in the air between us as he pulls me close to him, still conscious of my injured wrist.

"You don't ever have to worry about that. I'll sooner pry open the jaws of a shark if it means I'll be coming home to you."

Too choked up to respond, I reach up on my toes and capture his lips with my own, feeling the energy around us combust. With his tall stature, he has to bend at the waist for me to reach.

I'm swept away by the feel of his mouth moving expertly against mine. Enzo doesn't kiss—he devours, just like the beasts he swims alongside.

His tongue dips into my mouth, curling behind my teeth before stroking against my own. Tingles begin at the tips of my fingers and spread throughout every inch of me until my insides are reduced to static.

I need more of him. Need him so much closer until there's nothing between us but our own desire.

I hook my left arm around his neck, molding his slippery body against mine. I feel every divot and curve against the softened parts of me, and I shudder from the feel of it—of him.

His cock is impossibly hard and thick, sliding against my lower stomach, and just as I'm ready to say fuck the no sex thing, he pulls away.

I mewl in response, too disappointed by the loss of him to be embarrassed.

"We've had a long month, *amore mio*. Let's get some food in your stomach and relax, yeah?"

"I have a really bad joke about putting something else in my stomach, but let's not go there." Just as the words slip from my tongue, my eyes widen. "Wow, I so meant your dick, but that sounded even worse out loud."

He chuckles, the sound deep and delicious, causing a shiver to roll down my spine.

"You don't want babies?" he questions, turning off the water, then handing me a towel. Maybe it's the accent, but something about the way he asked that is criminal.

As if a fire is quite literally licking my ass cheeks, I hightail it out of the stall.

"Hell no," I say, wiping the water off my face before wringing out my hair.

I turn right as he steps out of the shower, droplets cascading across his tanned skin, clinging to the fine dusting of hair on his chest, and getting lost in the divots in his stomach. My mouth dries.

"Okay, *maybe*."

Both dimples are on full display as he stares at me from beneath hooded eyes.

"All it takes is the tip, *bella*."

CHAPTER 37

Enzo

"Selachians? What does that mean?" Sawyer asks, a slight wobble to her tone and anxiety carving lines into her face as she steps on the metal walkway.

She must've noticed the name of my center written across the landing pad. She wasn't ready to get back on to a boat yet, so I got us a ride here on a helicopter instead.

"It's Latin. Sharks are a part of the Selachii family," I explain.

I grab her hand and lead her down the boardwalk, the grated metal ringing beneath our weight. I had glimpsed the shark when we were getting ready to land and wanted to check it out before I showed Sawyer the lab.

"Oh shit," she breathes behind me. "Please tell me there's no head-dunking this time."

I toss a feral grin over my face, and she looks torn between slapping it off and keeping an eye on the shark. "Not this time."

She scoffs while we come to a stop in front of the enclosure. Even distorted from the water, there's no mistaking her size.

"She looks like she's about eighteen feet," I observe, eyeing the shark with a critical eye.

"Are you fucking kidding me right now, asshole?! *Now* you decide to show your goddamn face?" a familiar voice shouts from the elevator.

I look up to find a very pissed-off Troy charging toward us. He's glaring directly at me, likely murdering me in six different ways right now.

"I've missed you, too," I drawl, unbothered by his anger. I haven't had the chance to get a new phone yet, and I've been a little busy getting acclimated to being home again.

When I had called him from the hospital to get Senile Suzy, he about blew out my fucking eardrum with his ranting. It was a small miracle that I was able to shut him up long enough to convince him to get the van.

We only just got home yesterday, and the both of us are still exhausted and need to heal. I hadn't planned on staying here long, but I knew that Troy was losing his mind without me here, and frankly, I was beginning to lose my mind without my job.

"You've been gone near a goddamn month, and I get one phone call to go get a hippie van, and then nothing?"

"My phone is currently at the bottom of the ocean," is my response. "And the van was more important at the time."

Clearly, it's not a suitable excuse for Troy based on the snarl that overtakes his face.

The second he's within arm's reach, I'm preparing for him to cock back his fist and send it flying into my face, but instead, he grabs me by the shirt and tugs me into his embrace.

I sigh and slap his back in greeting, but I'll admit I missed the fucker, too. He'll just never know it.

Troy releases me, then turns to Sawyer. "You came back with a girlfriend, too? Where the actual fuck have you been?"

She gives him a toothy, awkward smile.

"Her name is Sawyer," I supply. She looks to me in shock, a flash of fear in her blue eyes. But she'll never need to worry about him.

He's the only person I've ever trusted, and despite how he loves to run his mouth, he also knows how to keep it shut. And if he doesn't, he also knows I'd kill him.

"I'm Troy," he introduces, holding out his hand to my girl. "Zo's best friend. He'll tell you that I'm not, but he's just being coy."

She grabs ahold of his hand. "He's also just a *stronzo*," she tacks on with a smile, a glimmer in her eye.

My eyes widen briefly, astonishment and something absolutely primal mixing in my bloodstream. I can't tell if I want to spank her or fuck her for insulting me in my language, but I do know that I love her for it.

She meets my burning stare without a concern in the world, a smirk on her pretty lips. I'll correct that later.

A booming laugh bursts from Troy's throat, his head tipped back. It's scarcely enough to pull my attention away from her, my fists and jaw clenched with the desire to take her where we stand.

"Oh, I like her," he chuckles.

Sawyer's mischievous grin widens. "Thanks for rescuing Senile Suzy. I'm not used to driving on the opposite side of the road, so maybe you can teach me," she offers, and by the glint in her eye, I know damn well she's doing it to get under my skin.

It's fucking working.

"Not happening," I growl, pinning her with my glare. "Careful, *bella*. I'm not afraid to murder him, too."

Unfazed, Troy winks at her, silently mouthing, "I'm gonna teach you so hard."

These two together are going to be the death of me.

Snarling, I point at the elevator, already annoyed. "Walk. I'll tell you what happened on the way."

"Damn, Sawyer, you're kind of a badass."

I gave him a quick rundown of the shipwreck, a short explanation of Sylvester, the lighthouse, Kacey, and ultimately, why Sawyer's name and who she really is must be kept under wraps.

I aim a glare in Troy's direction, but he's too busy staring at my girl. I'm seconds from ramming my fist down his throat, but he must sense his impending death and looks away.

On the way down in the elevator, Sawyer's face was plastered to the all-glass windows, watching our descent into the ocean with equal parts fascination and terror.

Even after three years, I'll never get tired of the view. Surrounded by nothing but a vast, blue sea. It's an entire universe below the surface and arguably a greater mystery than the one outside our planet.

The moment we came to a stop inside the center, I took her straight to the small kitchen so she could sit down for a minute. She's already exhausted, and I want to hurry this along so I can get her back into bed.

"I wouldn't say that," she says, brushing off the compliment. She's been sipping on a glass of water while I spoke, listening to the longest days of our lives wrapped up into thirty minutes.

The rest of my research team has gone home for the evening, leaving just the three of us to talk freely.

"I would," Troy retorts confidently.

I would, too.

Uncomfortable with the attention, Sawyer sets down her cup of water and stares up at me.

"I'm ready to see the rest," she declares.

Troy claps his hands, rubbing them together in excitement, with a wide, ecstatic smile on his face.

When I had V.O.R.S. built, I wanted it exposed to the ocean as much as possible. Meaning eighty-five percent of the center is pure glass. Nothing short of a nuclear bomb could destroy this place, but it's easy to feel like you're in a death trap when submerged in something that wields significant power.

I grab Sawyer's hand and lead her out of the kitchen and toward the main room. It's a short walk down a hallway, then we hang a right, coming out into the massive area.

Sawyer gasps, her eyes wide as she slowly walks into what feels like the open ocean.

It's where the team and I conduct our research. Most of the area is filled with desks loaded with monitors and equipment. Part of the job is tracking the sharks, taking measurements, and studying their maturity levels and behaviors.

When we're not out diving, we spend most of our time staring at computer screens.

"Holy mother of shits," she breathes, earning a chuckle from Troy.

Her head swivels back and forth while she twirls on her feet, unable to settle her round eyes on one thing.

A school of bluestripe snappers comes into view to our left, and in seconds, her face is against the glass again, watching the little yellow fish swim by.

"Oh my God, it feels like I could reach out and pet them."

I grin. "That was the idea."

She turns back to me, her eyes rounded with child-like wonder and her pink lips parted.

"What if a megalodon swims by right now? Can it break this shit open?"

I arch a brow. "I'd like to see it try."

Troy shudders. "I wouldn't."

"Do they still exist?" she asks, brimming with excitement.

"It's not impossible," I tell her. "In my opinion, the likelihood is high. Sharks have been around for millions of years. They're adaptable, and I believe they found a new way to survive."

"I want to see one so bad," she says, turning back to stare out the window. "I want to see mermaids, too."

"Some would say they are scarier than the megalodon," I tell her.

"So they are real?" she breathes.

I shrug, smirking when her breath fogs the glass. "Not impossible."

"So fucking cool," she mutters before getting distracted by a clown fish and scrambling over to the other side of the building where it swims.

"It's Nemo!" she screeches excitedly.

Troy looks over at me, and I meet his stare when I feel how deeply it's burning into the side of my face.

He looks amused, but something else also resides in his expression. Something like relief. "Keep her."

As if magnetized, I turn my focus back to Sawyer, where she's following the clownfish around the building.

"I plan on it."

CHAPTER 38

Enzo

Fuck, *I've missed this.*

"You know you'll be walking out of there looking like a sucked-on raisin, right?" Troy calls the second my head pops out from the water.

Except him. Didn't miss him.

I squint at my partner, trying to decide if I want to grab his leg and drag him in here so I can watch him panic, or if I should take my usual route and ignore him.

"And while I'm ecstatic that you finally found someone willing to put their mouth on any part of you, it's not a cute look."

"The fuck are you even saying?" I bark with annoyance. He acts like I'm supposed to know what the fuck a sucked-on raisin is.

"A wet, shriveled raisin. You're going to look like a wet, shriveled raisin. Not cute."

Before I can answer, the water shifts, just enough to draw my attention away from the blabbering idiot. A fin is charging straight toward me, so I steadily sink beneath the water.

The female great white is like a torpedo in the water, swimming at around twenty-five miles per hour.

Adrenaline rushes through my system, my heartbeat pulsing through every atom in my body.

Her mouth opens wide, rows of razor-sharp teeth on display. I kick my legs, angling myself so I'm perpendicular to her. My feet are out past her body and my torso is right in front of her mouth. Just as she reaches me, I grab onto the tip of her nose, using her momentum to vault myself above her, so I'm riding alongside her back.

She thrashes as I grab ahold of her dorsal fin, holding on tight while she glides through the water.

I've agitated her enough, so once she swims by the ladder, I release her and grab ahold of the metal steps, climbing out while she takes off in another direction.

When I pop my head out, I find Officer Bancroft and Officer Jones waiting next to Troy, along with Sawyer standing on their other side, shifting uncomfortably. Their boat is idling at the dock, still running.

Good. Means they won't be out here long.

Sawyer went down to the station to answer more questions, and I've been waiting for them to call me to pick her up. She insisted on going alone, and while I didn't like it, I respected her need to lay her past to rest on her own.

Seems they took the initiative to bring her to me.

"Gotta say, Mr. Vitale, you are an extraordinary man," Officer Jones calls, peering into the water with the typical look I see from people—*couldn't be me.*

"There's nothing extraordinary about humans," I respond. Troy rolls his eyes and mouths *be nice,* which confuses me because I don't know what that means.

Jones chuckles dryly. "I suppose you're right."

I step onto the walkway with a frown, water pouring from my body as I stalk toward the group. I've seen enough of them in the past three weeks, and I'm pretty tired of their faces. Sawyer's eyes briefly round before she quickly looks away, little red dots forming on her cheeks.

A grin tugs at the corners of my lips—something she catches sight of with a quick glance. Then, she's tripping over herself before her gaze solidifies and glues to me, those strawberry lips parting as I approach.

Fuck, I love my little thief.

"Mr. Vitale?" the sudden intrusive voice snaps my attention away, and my smirk instantly drops.

"What?"

Troy sighs with exasperation at my tone.

"I see you're still not interested in therapy," Jones observes, a curl to his lips.

They've tried pushing a therapist on me to deal with murdering someone, but I don't see why, considering I haven't lost sleep over it.

"What gave it away?"

Jones doesn't deign to give me an answer, but he huffs out a dry laugh.

"You might be a good role model for Trinity here," Bancroft cuts in. "She might feel more comfortable going if you do."

I stop before the group, staring at the two officers with a frown. Sawyer has held off on therapy, for now, not wanting to go to someone that was appointed to her. It's hard to seek help when you've been forced to bury everything that gives you nightmares, never being able to tell another soul about it.

"Why are you here?"

Sawyer bites back a smile, shaking her head at me.

"Our investigators have seen substantial evidence of self-defense in this case. We wanted to tell you the good news ourselves that you're no longer a person of interest."

I cross my arms, staring at them for a beat before saying, "I already knew that."

Troy's eyes bug. He's afraid of the police, and disrespecting them is no better than disrespecting the prime minister.

"Did you now?"

I shrug. "It was obvious considering he's been hoarding dead bodies."

"He's very happy to hear that," Sawyer cuts in, shooting me a look.

They don't appear convinced, but I don't really care.

"We gave Trinity some brochures on financial assistance and programs that might help her acclimate to society. I hope you encourage her to find her own independence, Mr. Vitale," Bancroft explains, ending the last sentence with a stern, authoritative tone.

One eyebrow is raised, staring like when a parent is expecting you to go to college instead of living in their basement until they're thirty.

The nuns that raised me are far scarier than her.

Said brochures are in Sawyer's hand, and she's staring at them like she plans on burning them later.

"Trinity is already independent, Officer. I hope you learn to give her more credit," I respond stoically.

She smiles, conceding on that.

"You mentioned wanting to change your name, we can set you up with a lawyer who can help you through that process. From there, you'll be able to sort out an ID as well," Bancroft goes on, turning to Sawyer. "Have you decided what you want your name to be?"

Sawyer's eyes widen as several sets of eyes zero in on her. She wants to keep her name—her real name—but she's been nervous about trying to explain it to the police. Not that she has to explain a damn thing to anyone.

Clearing her throat, she says, "Yeah. I—uh, I know it might sound weird, but I wanted to name myself after Sawyer. My first name, at least. She... she taught me a lot, and I admired her. And she deserved to have a life."

Bancroft might as well have melted in a puddle.

"That's very sweet," she says softly. "It's a beautiful name, too. That poor girl had a very troubling life. So many reports came out about that evil brother of hers. I imagine she did the world a favor."

Sawyer's mouth drops and then snaps shut, confusion written across her face. My own brows jump, surprised that there was more evidence against her brother and that Sawyer never knew about it. I suppose she avoided looking at anything to do with him at all costs.

"Reports?" I parrot.

Bancroft turns to me. "Oh, yeah. Her brother was abusing young girls. Several of them came out after his death."

Sawyer visibly pales, and she's struggling to control her facial expressions.

"All right, let's not gossip," Jones cuts in, shooting his partner a look.

Bancroft faces Sawyer again and rests a hand on her arm in a comforting gesture.

"Let me know if you need help with anything. I'm sure you're in good hands with Mr. Vitale, but I'll be a phone call away if you need me."

Sawyer smiles tightly, and thanks the officers. I watch them leave, then face Troy and Sawyer again. Troy is staring at the latter, who currently looks a little sick.

Troy is the only person that will ever know the truth. He knows I'd wrap him in chum and throw him in the water with a shark if he ever told a soul, and considering I murdered Sylvester, he has no reason not to believe me.

"You okay?" he asks, his brows lowered with concern.

She nods her head rapidly as if she's trying to convince herself.

"Yeah," she croaks. Then she starts shaking her head. "No, actually. Not really."

I brush past Troy, grab her arm, and pull her into me. She's trembling like a leaf.

"Did you know he was abusing other girls?" I ask, dropping my chin to catch her eye. She tucks her head lower, avoiding me.

Pinching her chin between my fingers, I force her gaze to mine.

"No," she whispers, glancing away, her cheeks coloring red.

"Regardless, you did the world a fucking favor," Troy mutters. "Honestly, you shouldn't beat yourself up over it when you saved them from further abuse."

Sawyer nods, but again, it looks like she's trying to convince herself.

"Yeah, it just makes me feel stupid for not seeing that."

Troy shrugs. "How could you have?"

She frowns. "Did I even need to kill who I used to be?"

"Australia would've turned you over to the U.S. If they did, you would've had to go to trial and relive everything, and there's a high probability that you would've been found guilty, despite his abuse," I say. "There is scarcely justice served for abused victims in America. It's better that it's all dead and buried."

"You're right about that," she sighs.

The shark splashes in the water, drawing my attention away.

"I'm going to finish up work here. And then we'll go get your name changed. I already know what I want it to be."

Her blue eyes slide to mine, bewildered.

"You know what *you* want it to be?" she asks sassily.

I grin, and Troy gasps dramatically.

"Yo, did he just smile?"

Ignoring him, I declare, "I'm choosing your last name, *bella*."

CHAPTER 39

Sawyer

ONE MONTH LATER

omething soft presses against the side of my neck, rousing me from a deep sleep. A moment later, that gentle touch turns biting and sharp. I gasp, my eyes snapping open as Enzo sinks his teeth into the flesh beneath my ear.

"Enzo," I groan. "My vagina has literally never been this sore in my entire life."

"You can take it," he mutters, emphasizing his statement with another nip. "You always do."

"You're so rude," I grumble. "So uncaring of my battered, bruised body."

He presses the hard length of his cock into my back, a soft groan slipping past his lips as he does. That small sound is enough to send heat slithering throughout my body, followed by a warm chill down my spine. It's honestly pathetic how attractive he is. The dude could barter world peace or some shit, I swear.

If only he actually gave a fuck about it.

"I would have to disagree, Ms. Vitale."

My heart thuds with the reminder.

Sawyer Vitale.

My first name is the only thing I have left from my old life, and it sounds so delicious every time it rolls off Enzo's tongue. Admittedly, that may be one of the reasons I formed such a strong attachment to it, but considering I've long been running from my name, it feels good to finally be able to use it.

It was Enzo's idea to take his last name. I argued, of course, but he wasn't taking no for an answer. And after his very persuasive techniques, I didn't see the point in fighting it.

It's just a last name...

A name that will forever tie me to Enzo, even if he ever does get sick of my shit.

"Still don't understand why you insisted on me taking your last name. We're not even married."

"Marriage is just a piece of paper. That last name is permanent."

"I mean, *technically,* my last name is also just a piece of paper."

He growls and whips my body to the side, forcing me onto my back as he crowds over me. I laugh at the fierce look on his face. Even through our shared near-death experience, he's not any nicer.

"You're such a brute," I tease, my smile slipping when he slides my—*his*—oversized t-shirt up my stomach, his rough palms gliding against my skin.

I shudder, still not used to how a single touch has me melting like butter.

He leans down close, dragging his lips along the column of my neck.

"*Ti mangerei.*"

"What does that mean?" I whisper.

"It means that I could eat you," he rasps, nipping the side of my neck again. I bite back a gasp, my back beginning to arch involuntarily as shivers roll down my spine, like a sensual brush of a finger from a lover.

A soft moan escapes and my arms wrap around his neck, trapping him on top of me despite how my body protests.

"We have to leave soon," he murmurs, placing a kiss beneath my ear, then another along my jawline.

"Where are we going?" I breathe, my eyes fluttering shut as his mouth slowly travels to mine.

"Out on the boat," he answers, and immediately, my eyes pop right back open, a refusal ready. Taking the opportunity, he dips his tongue in my mouth, capturing my lips between his in a savage kiss.

The fucker uses his mouth like it's a red button to a nuclear bomb. And every time he presses it against mine, it lets off the explosive inside me.

His hand slides through my curls, fisting them tightly as he deepens the kiss, stealing my soul with every swipe of his tongue.

I understand why he never let anyone have a taste of him. They would become addicted, and he'd never be able to free himself from their clutches.

His teeth clamp on my bottom lip, drawing the sensitive flesh into his mouth and sucking. I moan as he releases my lip, only to come back for more, curling his tongue in my mouth and sending electricity down the column of my throat.

By the time he pulls away, I'm bereft of oxygen, and I'm dazed as he resumes kissing the corner of my mouth and traveling down my neck.

"I think we should skip the boat and stay in bed today," I say breathlessly, sliding my hands along his freshly shaved head. It's back to short spikes again, and it feels incredible against my palms.

He draws up, staring down at me with an intensity that has my heart tripping over itself in its pursuit to break free of its cage.

"So we'll go tomorrow then," he states.

"Oh, darn," I drawl. "I have a thing tomorrow. Rain check?"

"*Bella*, I won't ever put us in danger again. Nothing will happen to you."

I twist my lips. I haven't been out on the boat since the wreck, deciding to take my time. There's a fear that karma hasn't finished with me yet, but an even larger part of me won't let me run anymore.

I've found that facing my fears is far more invigorating.

"Fine. But there is one thing I want to do first today. And then you can throw me to the sharks where I will perish via heart attack, okay?"

He shakes his head at my dramatics but backs away.

"Go now. I'll be waiting for you at the harbor at noon."

"Well, I'll be damned! And here I thought I was the elusive one."

The voice brings an instant smile to my face, and before I know it, I'm running to the bus stop. My neon pink flip-flops clacking on the pavement as I rush up to Simon.

I've been checking the bus stop for weeks but haven't seen him. I needed to wait until the situation with the police was sorted first and then gave myself time to heal. I didn't want Simon to see me bruised and broken—I wanted him to see me better than before I shipwrecked on that island.

Before he can get another word out, I'm sitting on the bench and wrapping my arms around his neck, resting my head on his shoulder as I breathe in his salty ocean scent, with a hint of Old Spice.

He chuckles, his entire body vibrating as he pats my hands.

"Well, I missed ya too, young lady."

"Sorry," I say, pulling away. "I just never thought I'd see you again."

"Well, this town ain't that big. Only so many places I can go but down."

I roll my eyes, grinning at him. "You're not going to Hell, Simon."

He snorts. "My ex-wife would tell ya different." He leans back, tipping his nose up to inspect me as if he's staring at me through a magnifying glass.

"What happened to you?"

I scratch my head, debating how much I should divulge.

"I got lost for a little while. But I'm home now," I settle on.

"Uh-huh," he says slowly, his eyes dipping to the brace on my wrist. It's mostly healed now, but it's still a little weak. I'm on the mend, physically and mentally.

Most nights, Enzo and I battle who can wake each other with a brain demon first, but we have someone to reach out to, and though neither of us is fully healed, we're not alone.

"Looks like you're ready for your next tattoo."

I smile wide, showing him all my teeth.

"You fucking bet I am."

He chuckles and pulls out a plastic bag with ink and unopened needles.

"What will you be getting today, on this fine Tuesday morning?"

I hadn't realized what day it is, and it feels a little like déjà vu. Three and a half months ago, I met Simon at this bus stop on a Tuesday and got my first tattoo. I've come full circle, except I'm a completely different person than I was then.

I was sad, broken, and barely surviving.

And now, I'm still a little broken, but it doesn't feel so bad to be alive anymore. And while I'll always have the reminders of what happened to me etched into the inside of my brain, at least I'll be able to look forward now, instead of looking back.

"I want a cactus," I say finally.

He pauses, glancing up at me with raised brows.

"A cactus," he echoes. "Why a cactus?"

I shrug. "They're strong and resilient, and survive under extreme conditions."

My friend juts out his bottom lip, considering that.

"Oh, and they don't harm a fly unless you fuck with them."

That pulls another full-bellied laugh from Simon.

"A cactus," he repeats again with a chuckle, shaking his head almost in wonder.

"That's who I am now—who I choose to be. A cactus."

"Then that's what I'll do," he says. "Where do you want it?"

I unstrap my brace, hold out my arm, and point to my wrist. "Right there, please."

Smiling, Simon grabs my wrist and lays it flat on his thigh. After unwrapping the needle and dipping the tip into his jar of octopus ink, he gets to work, and I watch in comfortable silence as the misunderstood plant slowly forms.

It hurts like hell, but pain always comes before beauty. How else would we appreciate it?

"Done," he announces twenty minutes later, straightening so I can inspect my wrist.

"It's so fucking cute, Simon," I proclaim, smiling at the misshapen cactus on my wrist. "If only you could do this with a cactus needle."

He guffaws. "Don't think there are any cacti 'round here. But you find one, and I'll do ya next time with one."

"You're going to do *what* to her?"

My eyes widen, and I turn to find Enzo storming toward us, a frown marring his face.

"What are you doing here?" I ask, feeling a lot like a child caught with their hand in the cookie jar.

"I was heading to the bait shop and happened to see a little blonde thief sitting at a bus stop."

"Well, hey now—"

"It's okay," I cut Simon off, placing my hand on top of his. "He's a grump, but he's my grump."

Simon glances at me before settling back on Enzo's fierce expression.

I face said grump, and show him my wrist, a bright smile on my face once more, though inside, I'm bartering with Satan not to let this man piss off my only friend.

"Simon gave me another tattoo. It's a cactus."

Enzo's hazel eyes drop to my wrist, and then he's grabbing my arm and bringing it closer. I bite my lip, my body flushing hotter from his tight grip.

I don't know if I'll ever get used to the feel of him, but I don't mind trying.

"Why a cactus?"

I give him the same reasoning I gave Simon, but he doesn't react. He just stares at the plant for another few seconds before releasing my arm.

"That's not sanitary," he states finally.

"It's not," I agree.

He turns his gaze to Simon, and again, he just stares, a frown still on his face. I've no idea what the hell he's thinking, and as usual, I can't tell if he's pissed or not. His normal face and his angry face look the same.

After a moment, Simon sasses, "Well, you gonna sit down for your own or just keep starin' at me like a dead fish?"

Enzo cocks a brow, unimpressed. But to my utter surprise, he sits on the other side of Simon and silently holds out his wrist.

"Make it quick," he grumbles.

My mouth falls open, and now *I'm* the staring dead fish as Simon unwraps a new needle.

"Whatcha gettin'?"

"A shark."

Unbothered by Enzo's short, snappy responses, he leans down and starts working on the tattoo. Hazel eyes are flashing to me, then dropping to my still open mouth.

"You're gonna catch a fly in there," Simon calls out to me, sparing me a glance.

"Uh," is my only response. Enzo just arches a brow again, as if saying

Well? You going to close your mouth or what?

I snap my jaw closed hard enough for my teeth to click.

"You're strange," I tell him finally.

Simon smiles.

"He fits right in, doesn't he?"

Meeting Enzo's stare again, I say, "I suppose he does."

EPILOGUE

Sawyer

TWO YEARS LATER

"Enzo, wait, this is so not safe. We're going to die," I plead, the end of my sentence broken by a moan.

He pulls back his hips only to sink his cock deep inside me, causing my eyes to roll. I force them straight, glaring at the stupid man right as the beast mere *feet* from us whips its tail, sending ocean water spraying into our faces.

Enzo grins and fucks me harder in response, pulling another yelp from my throat.

We've been in the shark cage for the past hour, watching three giant great whites circle around us. All of them have taken a turn biting into the cage, and while I'm slowly getting used to the sight of a shark's mouth right in my face, it doesn't mean my bladder still isn't threatening me in the meantime.

The moment we slipped out of our scuba gear, a relieved smile on my face for not dying today, Enzo proceeded to pick me up and send us both back into the cold ocean water, though still within the confines of the cage.

The top of the metal enclosure is a few feet above surface level, the lid flipped open. If the sharks really wanted to get in, they could probably flop over the top and eat us.

Enzo is confident they won't, but I've seen those fuckers jump in the air to catch a bird. Who's to say one won't jump up and belly flop right on top of us?

"They can feel how fast your heart is racing," he whispers in my ear, hiking my legs farther up his waist. He's got me pinned against the side of the cage facing the boat, but it doesn't feel any safer.

"Enzo, stop it," I whimper, but he doesn't listen. Instead, he slips his hand between our bodies, his deft fingers strumming my clit as he continues to pump inside me.

"Every time I fill you up, they feel it," he tells me, his voice deeper than the ocean we're in the middle of, and rougher than the waves surrounding us.

One of the sharks thrashes in the water again, sending more water over our heads.

"I don't want to do this now," I gasp, shuddering as a fin appears in my peripheral.

He chuckles darkly.

"Are we playing our little game again? You're losing your touch, *mia piccola bugiarda*," he growls before drawing my lobe between his teeth and clamping down.

I gasp, my nails scoring across his tanned shoulders while my back arches. The different sensations from the adrenaline pumping in my veins to between my legs, and what he's doing with his mouth, are sending me into overdrive.

mia piccola bugiarda - *my little liar*

"Your cunt is gripping me so tightly. Do you think I believe a word coming from that sweet mouth? I bet if I pulled out right now, your pussy would cry from the loss."

I shake my head, but he's right. I think I would cry if he stopped now.

"Let me hear you say it, Sawyer. I want to hear how much of a slut you are for my cock, and I want to hear you beg to come around it."

A stuttered, "P-please," rips from my throat, almost without thought. If anyone is the siren, it's him. He bends my will with a simple command, and I'm helpless to resist.

"Please, Enzo," I cry, gritting my teeth as his middle finger rubs my clit firmer.

"Keep going," he encourages, a wicked glint in his eye.

"I'm a s-slut for your cock," I force out, just as a shark pops up from behind him, its teeth on full display as they clamp around the cage and thrash.

A startled squeal follows up my words, but he doesn't relent, utterly unbothered by the agitated sharks.

"Not enough," he clips, keeping his pace steady despite the trembling cage around us.

"Please... please let me come around your cock," I rush out, yelping when the shark bashes against it again.

"Good girl," he praises, grinning wildly. He's fucking unhinged, but God, he feels so good.

"Now, let me hear you say you love me."

"I love you," I breathe hurriedly. "And I love when you make me come."

Both dimples appear while his free hand slides up my throat, squeezing firmly as pleasure invades every cell in my body. With each thrust, his grip tightens until my vision blackens, and I can feel my pulse throughout my skull.

He growls and quickens his pace while another shark bashes into the cage, sending it flying into the boat.

I choke on a scream, my eyes wide as I stare at the man forcing my body into submission. I was wrong. The real predator is already inside the cage, and I'm trapped right between his teeth.

"I told you my love was going to hurt like hell. So tell me, *bella ladra,* does it hurt?"

An unintelligible noise slips past my constricted throat, and I think my nails are sinking deep into his flesh. I can't find it in me to care if I make him bleed while being circled by three starving sharks.

No death will be more agonizing than the orgasm he's forcing me to succumb to.

I squeeze my eyes shut, stars bursting in the backs of my eyelids. The outside world is beginning to fade, and the only thing I can feel is my pussy clenching around him and how he circles my clit with expertise.

My nails move to the hand around my throat, clawing desperately as he takes me higher, while my consciousness begins to slip.

"That's it, baby, fight to let those screams out," he snarls, now rolling his hips, causing my eyes to shoot straight to the back of my head. The tip of his cock hits that damn spot that only he seems to know how to reach, and a full-out sob is desperately trying to get free.

He grinds into me harder, and within seconds, I'm exploding around him. He releases my throat, and all the blood rushing from my head is enough for my world to tilt on its axis, and what used to be the ocean is now outer space.

A scream tears from my throat, and I'm grasping for something solid to hold on to, but I feel lost in the waves as they rip apart everything that makes me whole.

Faintly, I feel Enzo slip an arm beneath one knee and hike it higher as he begins to lose control, chasing his own orgasm.

"Christ, this cunt is too fucking good," he chants through gritted teeth. And then he's letting his own deep moan loose as he releases inside me, filling me to the brim.

A hand slams on the metal bar beside me, and he moves his hips in a staccato, uneven roll.

"Fuck, Sawyer," he growls, but it still sounds far away.

You can't hear a shout in space, can you? There can't be sound when there's no air to speak of.

Slowly, almost reluctantly, I come back down, and when I do, I find Enzo's head resting heavily against mine, and now two sharks are trying to get in the cage, and *Jesus,* I'm dizzy.

"I'm officially a prune, this probably gave me a yeast infection, and those sharks are two seconds away from breaking in," I croak, the low temperature of the water beginning to creep back in. "*Now,* can you let me out?"

Enzo's shoulders bounce as he chuckles, and then he's lifting his chin and placing a soft kiss on my forehead.

"Sure, baby."

He pulls out of me, and I quickly scramble up and over the cage, nearly crawling onto the *Ladra.* Enzo bought this boat the day I said yes to marrying him.

He took me out on the water at sunset, the rays glittering against the surface of the water, and slid the diamond ring on my finger without even asking.

Enzo doesn't do heartfelt speeches, but he did worship me that night while making me scream *yes* until my voice gave out.

Three days later, we eloped, Simon and Troy our witnesses. They're the only family we needed anyway.

I'm still convinced it's bad luck that he named the boat after me. Like tattooing your partner's name on you, it's undoubtedly cursed.

We haven't shipwrecked yet, but if this boat's namesake is to be a thief, then it's only obvious it'll steal a life or two.

Enzo calls me dramatic, but I call it logic.

The second my feet touch the floor of the vessel, I'm tempted to get on my knees and kiss it.

"You're lucky I don't get motion sickness," I mutter, struggling to pull on my bathing suit bottoms due to the waves heavily rocking us from the giant, pissed-off sharks. They were denied a meal, and well, that *is* pretty fucking rude.

Enzo climbs onto the boat behind me, and after slipping his shorts back over his ass, he pushes up the lever to the crane hanging over the boat, drawing the cage up. The whirring mechanical sound is incapable of masking the deep chuckle coming from his chest.

"Is that a challenge, *bella*?"

I narrow my eyes. "If that's a sexual innuendo, then I'm turning you into shark food."

"I'd hate for that to happen," he purrs once the cage is out of the ocean, and only the splashing water can be heard. "You and that sweet pussy would be so lonely without me."

I roll my eyes. "I'll survive, dude. I always do."

"Yeah?" he asks devilishly, his chin twisting over his shoulder. "You and the bean gods going to keep each other company?"

I flip him the bird but instantly chicken out when he turns toward me with a growl and steps in my direction. I'm running away again, a laugh filling the salty air.

This time, I have no intention of getting away.

THE END

GLOSSARY

Bella/Bellissima- Beautiful

Ladra- Thief

Sì- Yes

Cazzo, quanto mi fai godere- Fuck, you feel so good

Ecco la mia piccola ladra- There's my little thief

Cazzo – Fuck

Piccola- Baby

Vieni qui- Come here

Ancora una volta- Just one more

Guardami- Look at me

Andiamo- Let's go

Cammina- Walk

Bravissima- Impressive, well done

Che stronzo- What an asshole/douche

Stronzo- Asshole/douche

Merda- Shit

Amore mio- My love

È davvero bellissima- It is beautiful

Lo uccido- I'm going to kill him

Perché- Why

Che cazzo succede?- What the fuck?

Suor Caterina- Sister Caterina. Literal meaning: nun, used in lieu of Sister.

Vuoi sapere cosa vedo?- You want to know what I see?

Maritozzo- Italian raised dough, sweet filled with whipped cream

Non lo so- I don't know

È una maledetta bugiarda- She's a goddamn liar

Mi sta facendo uscire pazzo, porca miseria- She's driving me insane, dammit

Cazzo, che cazzo hai fatto?- Fuck, what the fuck did you do?

Concentrati- Concentrate

Attenta- Careful

Brava ragazza- Good girl

Non ti odio- I don't hate you

Sorridi, piccola- Smile, baby

Ti darò tutto- I will give you everything

Morirà lentamente- He will die slowly

È impossibile odiarti quando mi fai sentire così vivo- It's impossible to hate you when you make me feel so alive

Ed è esattamente per questo che voglio odiarti. Prima di incontrare te ero un sonnambulo. Cazzo, non ero pronto a svegliarmi- And that's exactly why I want to hate you. I was sleepwalking until I met you, and I wasn't fucking ready to wake up

Ho sbagliato a dirti che eri debole. Sei così incredibilmente coraggiosa, vorrei che lo vedessi anche tu- I was wrong to call you weak. You are so incredibly brave. I wish you could see that

Ti penso ogni ora, ogni minuto, ogni dannato secondo. Non so che fare- I think of you every hour, every minute, every goddamn second. I don't know what to do with that

L'oceano era l'unico posto in cui mi sentivo a casa- The ocean was the only place I've ever felt at home

Era l'unica cosa che mi eccitava e dava pace. Hai rovinato anche questo. Sentirti su di me è meglio di immergersi nell'oceano. Neanche con questa rivelazione so che fare- It was the only thing that gave me excitement and peace. You've ruined that for me, too. Being inside you is better than being inside the ocean. I don't know what to do with that, either

Bancarelle- A moveable stand where vendors sell their goods

Un giorno- One day

Cazzo, quanto sei bagnata- You're so fucking wet

Ma solo quando sono pronto a venire con te. Annegheremo insieme, bella ladra- But only when I'm ready to come with you. We will drown together, beautiful thief

Svegliati- Wake up

Tu sei mia- You're mine

Non ancora- Not yet

Mostrami come amarti- Show me how to love you

Sapevo che lo stronzo stava mentendo- I knew the asshole had been lying

È il colore che preferisco su di te- My favorite color on you

Sei così dolce. Sei un angelo- You are so sweet. You're an angel

Mia piccola bugiarda- My little liar

MORE BOOKS BY THE AUTHOR

ACKNOWLEDGEMENTS

As always, I want to thank my readers first. Thank you from the very bottom of my heart for continuing to read my words and trusting me with your hearts and minds, even though you probably shouldn't. I love you all so much, and words can't describe how grateful I am for each and every one of you.

Secondly, I have to thank one of my biggest support systems, Victor. You're my partner in crime, in life, and let's be honest—in death, too. Thank you for being the glue that keeps me together. I quite literally would've fallen apart without you.

Thank you to my incredible alpha readers, May, Amanda, and Tasha. You three are my rocks. None of my books would be what they are without you and would definitely be straight trash lit on fire. I love you guys so so much.

Thank you to my beta readers, Autumn, Taylor, Keri, Naomi, and Kristie. You guys are the bomb diggity. And special thanks to Veronica for translating all the Italian for me, and Gabby for the Australia education!

Also, can't forget my wonderful PA for keeping my life together and also beta reading for me. I'm so very lucky to have you.

Of course, I will always give a profuse amount of thanks to my editors. Angie, you are my family and I thank you for being someone I can lean on. Thank you for taking care of me, and my book babies, and I love you deeply. And Rumi, I appreciate you times a million, and thank you for doing such an incredible job with my book babies.

Thank you to Cassie for making these babies so pretty on the inside. I love you so much, and I'm so very honored to call you a friend.

Last but not least, thank you to both of my cover designers for the absolutely incredible covers, Emily Wittig and Murphy Rae. You both absolutely killed it with these covers, and I can't thank you enough.

ABOUT THE AUTHOR

H. D. Carlton is an International Bestselling Author. She lives in Ohio with her partner, two dogs, and cat. When she's not bathing in the tears of her readers, she's watching paranormal shows and wishing she was a mermaid. Her favorite characters are of the morally gray variety and believes that everyone should check their sanity at the door before diving into her stories.

LEARN MORE ABOUT H. D. CARLTON ON HDCARLTON.COM. JOIN HER NEWSLETTER TO RECEIVE UPDATES, TEASERS, GIVEAWAYS, AND SPECIAL DEALS HERE.

FACEBOOK
TWITTER
INSTAGRAM
GOODREADS